ARE YOU SURE ABOUT THIS?

Chris Keating asked himself. *If this works, it changes everything. All the dreams of the First Landers, overthrown in an instant. Contact with Earth. Marseguro a colony, not an independent world . . . no more Selkies,* he reminded himself. *No more second-class "landlings," becoming more second-class every year as the Selkies breed like the animals they are. No more men like my father being murdered by the Selkie masters. A chance to return to Earth, where real humans belong . . . a chance to find something better to do with my life than cataloging algae samples and scrubbing growth tanks.*

Chris remembered the Selkies throwing him off the pier just to watch him flounder, just to humiliate him, just to mock him.

He remembered his father, lost at sea.

He remembered his mother, dying in a hospital long cut off from the latest medical advances.

He remembered her words to him, just yesterday morning . . .

"The Selkies murdered him . . . and now they're killing me . . . they'll kill you, too, my boy . . ."

He blinked hard twice. "Not me," he said, and flicked the switch on the Emergency Interstellar Transmitter. . . .

DAW Science Fiction Titles by
EDWARD WILLETT:

MARSEGURO

LOST IN TRANSLATION

MARSEGURO

EDWARD WILLETT

DAW BOOKS, INC.

DONALD A. WOLLHEIM, FOUNDER

375 Hudson Street, New York, NY 10014

ELIZABETH R. WOLLHEIM

SHEILA E. GILBERT

PUBLISHERS

www.dawbooks.com

First Printing, February 2008
1   2   3   4   5   6   7   8   9

For my big brothers, Jim and Dwight: if not for all those science fiction books they brought into the house, I never would have started reading and writing this stuff.

Acknowledgments

This book began with a single sentence, written in September, 2005, as an exercise in Robert J. Sawyer's class in writing science fiction, part of the Writing With Style program at the Banff Centre. Thanks, Rob!

Heartfelt thanks to my editor, Sheila Gilbert, whose insightful comments and questions helped make this a much better book than it would otherwise have been. Any remaining failings are entirely my own.

Finally, special thanks to the staff of Second Cup in the Cornwall Centre, Regina, Saskatchewan, where most of this book was written, fueled by Icepresso Chillers.

Chapter 1

THE MAIN PIER of Hansen's Harbor stank, but that
was only one reason Chris Keating hated it.

He stood in the early spring sun, shivering, glaring
down the three-hundred-meter-long, fifty-meter-wide
stretch of preformed bioplast planks. The pier looked
secure, but Chris knew better. Some of that stink came
from the salt water. Some of it came from the alcohol-
fueled engine of the catamaran-sub *SeaSkimmer*, idling
at the end of the pier. Some of it came from rotting
seaweed. But some of it, Chris knew, came from the
slowly decomposing bioplast itself. To him it always
stank of anaerobic decay, the smell of swamps and stag-
nant ponds. One day—he *knew* it—one of the pier's massive posts would give way, and the whole structure would
collapse, flipping everything and everyone on it into the
deep, cold water of New Botany Bay, where they would
drown like his father drowned, lost at sea, when he
was four.

One day. Maybe even today, while *he* was on the pier.

Chris shivered again. He hadn't expected to come
down to the pier today, and his white shirt and pants
were made of thin cloth designed for comfort in the
warm, humid environs of the genesculpting lab's algae
room, not for keeping out the wind currently whipping
up whitecaps on the bay's blue-green water. But Dr.
Stanless had radioed half an hour ago for someone to
come help unload the samples he'd collected from the

algae fields off Slick Rock, and the only someone who could be spared had been Chris.

He hadn't dared refuse. No one on Marseguro knew his shameful secret except his mother, and she wasn't likely to tell.

He clenched his fists when he thought of her. He'd visited her in the hospital on his way to work that morning. She'd looked so frail, lying in that hospital bed hooked up to the machinery that kept her alive—not at all like the strong woman he remembered from childhood, the woman who had single-handedly raised him after his father's death . . . and single-handedly made sure he knew the truth that lay behind that "accident."

She'd been conscious this morning, an unusual occurrence since the last stroke. She could speak, after a fashion. Most of what she said made little sense, and usually she hardly seemed to know he was in the room, but this morning had been different.

She'd squeezed his hand with astonishing strength for someone at death's door. "Selkies!" she'd hissed, her eyes focused on his face with a feverish intensity he well-remembered but hadn't seen in six months. "They killed your father. They're killing me! They'll kill you, too, if they find out . . . if they know. . . ."

"Shhh!" Chris had shot a look over his shoulder, though he knew he'd been left alone. Still, you could never be *certain* the Selkies weren't listening. . . .

"He hated the sea. They *made* him go on that boat. The Selkies all came back. The landlings all died."

Chris almost reached out and put his hand over her mouth. These were things they only talked about in their own home, never in public, never where someone else might hear.

"They knew . . . they must have found out he Believed . . . he never wanted to be here at all . . . never wanted to be on the *Rivers of Babylon* . . . Hansen kidnapped him . . . the Selkies murdered him . . . and now they're killing me . . ." Her wide eyes suddenly filled with tears. "They'll kill you, too, my little boy . . . my little . . ." Her eyes fluttered closed.

Chris had eased his hand away from her and stood up, shaking. He'd had to take half a dozen deep breaths before he felt calm enough to walk out of the hospital, and it took all his strength not to look over his shoulder to see who might be watching him go.

"It's not just the Selkies," his mother had told him over and over. "Most of the landlings are on their side. A very few of us know the truth. A very few of us cling to the Body Purified. But we can never let on . . . or they'll kill us.

"Like they killed your father."

Chris looked at the alarmingly narrow ribbon of bioplast stretching from the shore into the bay, and the balefully glittering water all around it. *God, I hate this planet.* But he couldn't let on, or the secret Selkie cabal his mother had told him *really* ruled Marseguro would know he had inherited his family's dangerous beliefs, and eliminate him as they had eliminated his father.

Maybe they've already decided to. Maybe this errand is a setup, carefully arranged to provide an opportunity for another "accident". . . .

He shook his head. *Don't be paranoid,* he told himself. If the Selkies wanted to kill him, he'd simply disappear. Hardly anyone would notice. Even fewer would care.

No, the errand was just what it seemed to be. And though he hated his job almost as much as he hated the pier—and the planet—everyone on Marseguro had to work, and if he quit at the genesculpting lab he'd be stuck scaling hulls or filling potholes with a Council make-work crew, doing jobs bots could do better and faster.

Gathering his courage and holding it tight like the teddy bear he'd carried everywhere until his tenth birthday, he set off down the pier.

Halfway to the *SeaSkimmer,* the Selkies swarmed him. They soared out of the bay like dolphins, trailing drops of water that flashed silver in the sun. Their broad, bare webbed feet slapped down on the bioplast with the sound of fish being poured from a net. There were at least a dozen, male and female, all adolescents or young adults, all wearing the water resistance-lessening skinsuits the Selkies favored, vibrant reds and purples and greens and yellows personalized with lightning bolts and starships, Earth dolphins and Marseguroite squigglefish, flames and starscapes and abstract designs that made their owners hard to look at. They surrounded him in a whirlwind of color, and he stopped dead. They laughed and chirped in their own language, one landlings could neither understand nor speak, since they lacked the Selkies' modified vocal apparatus and enhanced hearing.

"What do you want?" Chris could barely squeeze the words out through a throat gone tight with fear. His heart pounded in his chest, a caged animal frantically throwing itself against the bars of its prison. "*What do you want?*"

They ignored him, circling him like Earth sharks were said to circle their prey, chanting—not in Selkie, but in English. He suddenly realized *what* they were chanting: just a silly poem, but one that almost loosened his bowels. "Eeny-meeny-miny-mink, tip a landling in the drink, watch him splash and watch him sink, eeny-meeny-miny-mink." Oversized eyes stared at him, transparent nictitating eyelids sliding sideways across giant green irises.

He knew this "game." He'd known it since childhood. He'd seen Selkies "play" it on other young landlings. He'd always managed to avoid it.

Until now.

The Selkies rushed him, laughing. Strong hands seized him. He felt his feet leave the ground, then he was horizontal, held high above short-cropped hair, pink and violet, green and blue, and shaved pates tattooed to match the skinsuits. They were carrying him, running with him. He screamed, then he was flying through the air, the horizon flipping, the pier suddenly above him . . .

. . . and then he hit the water. Its cold embrace enveloped him. He sank, kicked desperately, managed to get his head into the air, grabbed a precious breath, sank again, and couldn't find the surface. His clothes pulled at him, sucking him down. He floundered, striking out blindly. He couldn't see, couldn't breathe, couldn't think through the heart-stopping terror. *I'm going to die!* his mind shrieked, then shrieked again, a mantra he couldn't stop, running through his head over and over. *I'm going to die! I'm going to die! I'm going to die!*

Something grabbed him. He struck out at it in panic, his body no longer under his control, but the thing was stronger than he was. Against his will it pulled him deeper and deeper into the . . .

. . . then his head broke water and he sucked in a lungful of air, coughing and choking as spray came with it, and he realized he'd been pulled up to the surface, not down into the deeps, and maybe, just maybe, he wouldn't drown after all.

Hands reached for him again, but this time they pulled him up, lifted him out of the water, laid him on the pier. Prostrate, eyes closed, cheek pressed against the reeking wet bioplast, he coughed out the last of the water. Selkies chirped and squealed around him, then a shadow fell across his face and he opened his eyes to see one, a girl, crouching down and looking at him. Her zebra-striped yellow skinsuit, practically painted on, left little of her lithe body to the imagination. She had violet hair and the same green eyes as every other Selkie . . . and she looked familiar. He wasn't sure why. "Are you all right?" she said. "I'm so sorry. We never thought . . ."

Chris closed his eyes, shame and anger choking him in equal measure. He couldn't talk. He wouldn't give them the satisfaction of hearing his voice break. He pushed himself up onto all fours, then stood shakily, ignoring the girl's proffered hand.

"We didn't know," said another Selkie, a boy with a red-and-blue spiral tattooed into his shaved head and wearing a skinsuit covered with iridescent scales. He looked vaguely familiar, too. "We didn't know you couldn't—"

"Chris? Is that you?" A burly, bearded, and bald-headed nonmod pushed his way through the now sheepish-looking crowd of Selkies. Behind Dr. Stanless, Chris glimpsed the rest of the crew of the *SeaSkimmer,* nonmods and Selkies alike, gawking like bystanders at an accident. "Are you all right? What happened?"

Selkie kids at the edge of the crowd began melting away. Three slipped into the bay, barely raising a splash. But the tattooed boy and violet-haired girl stood their ground. "It was just a prank," the boy said. "We were celebrating the end of school. We didn't mean anything by it . . ."

"We didn't know he couldn't swim," the girl said.

"We didn't know *anybody* couldn't swim," the boy said.

Chris felt himself flush. The shame and fury had reached the surface.

Dr. Stanless glared at the Selkies. "It was a stupid prank. It's one thing to pull it on one of your friends, but grabbing a stranger and throwing him into the bay . . ."

"He's not exactly a stranger," the boy said. "We went to landschool together." He glanced at Chris. "Don't you remember? I'm John Duval."

Chris still hadn't spoken. The world seemed preternaturally bright and clear around him, as though the air had turned to diamond. At the sound of John Duval's name, it grew harder and brighter yet.

John Duval. The Selkie boy who had bullied him from the time they were both eight Earth years old until they were thirteen, and Duval had gone off to seaschool. Tripped him in the cafeteria. Pulled down his trunks in the swimming pool, then swam off with them, leaving him naked and shamed in the water, begging someone to bring him a towel while the other kids laughed at him. . . .

He looked at the girl. Emily Wood. He remembered

her, too. Remembered her standing with the other girls pointing and laughing.

How could *they* not know he didn't know how to swim? The teacher had forced him into the pool that day, told him he had to overcome his fear of what had happened to his father. He'd been too little, too scared, not to give in. His mother had always told him if he didn't conform, didn't hide the truth, something bad would happen to him . . . but he'd never forgotten the shame, never forgotten that early proof that Selkies couldn't be trusted. "They're not real humans," his mother had said. "They're monsters." Before that, he'd wondered. After that . . .

He'd never gone back into the pool. And the teacher, once she'd realized what had happened, had never made him.

They knew, he thought. *They knew. It's a warning. I'm being warned. The Selkies . . . the secret cabal . . . they suspect me, suspect I'm like my father . . . they're letting me know what will happen to me if I cross them. . . .*

He shivered as the sea breeze flowed over his wet body. *I'm all alone,* he thought. *Mom was the only one I could talk to, and now . . .*

Something clicked into place inside him, as though a switch had been thrown, and the heat of his anger vanished. Instead, he felt as if he had been doused in water even colder than that of the bay, water that froze into certainty his determination to do something that, until that moment, he had only toyed with on his blackest days.

He didn't say a word to John Duval and Emily Wood. To Dr. Stanless he said, "I hate to ask, sir, but may I have a few days off?"

Dr. Stanless blinked, then frowned. "I understand you're upset, Chris, but it was just a soaking."

"It's not that, sir." Not *precisely.* "It's . . . my mother." Again, partly true.

"Oh." Dr. Stanless knew all about Chris' mother, of course. "Oh, I see. Of course. Take as long as you need."

"A week or two at most," Chris said. "Thank you, sir."

With all the dignity he could muster, letting his gaze slide past the shamefaced Selkies as if they weren't there, he turned his back on the sea and walked inland.

He didn't look back.

Emily watched Chris Keating walk away, and felt her face burn. The prank that had seemed so harmless just an hour before when her waterdance class had streamed out of the Hansen's Harbor Seaschool for the last time now seemed incredibly cruel and stupid. They'd recognized Chris as one of their old landschool classmates, thought he'd get the joke, laugh along with them. . . .

She glanced at John. He stood with his head bowed, biting his lower lip.

"I hope you two are ashamed of yourselves," Dr. Stanless said. "Chris is one of my best lab assistants. A nice quiet kid. He was on his way to help me unload algae samples when you jumped him. Now who's going to help? You two?"

Put like that, they really didn't have a choice, and in fact, Emily thought a few minutes later as she helped pull slimy, stinking buckets of multicolored goo from the hold of the *SeaSkimmer,* she didn't really mind. It was the least she could do to make amends . . .

. . . *although Dr. Stanless isn't really the one you need to make amends to,* she told herself. She shook her head. She could barely remember Chris Keating as a kid; they'd never had much to do with each other. In fact, she couldn't really remember Chris Keating having much to do with anyone. *We should have known he'd react badly. It's our fault, not his. Dr. Stanless is right. It was a stupid thing to do, and it would have been just as stupid even if Chris* did *know how to swim.*

Except how could you live on a planet more than ninety percent water-covered, with fellow citizens genetically modified to breathe both air and water, and *not* know how to swim? She shook her head again. *Well, it takes all kinds of genes to make a genome,* as her mother liked to say.

An hour later they'd loaded the last of the algae tubs onto the rollerbot, and it had trundled off toward the labs. Dr. Stanless, his arms splattered with stinking slime, grinned as he watched the samples roll away. "Some fascinating specimens there," he said. "I can't wait to get at them in the lab." He stretched his arms above his head, yawning hugely, then turned to where Emily and John stood side by side, every bit as splattered and stinking as he was. "A nasty job, but thank you for it." His eyebrows drew together and he gave them each a hard stare. "And I hope you've learned a lesson."

They both nodded. Dr. Stanless held his severe look for a moment, then broke into a grin. "All right. Get out of here. You're probably feeling dry."

"Thank you, Doctor Stanless," Emily said.

"Yeah, thanks," John echoed, and they jumped off the pier together.

With a shiver of relief and pleasure, Emily welcomed the embrace of the water. Muscles landlings didn't even have tightened the passages to her lungs and squeezed her nostrils closed. At the same time, the tight-clamped gill slits on either side of her neck relaxed and opened wide. She wriggled her long, webbed toes and with a flick of her feet dove deeper into the bay. Like all Selkies, she could function perfectly well on land, certainly better than landlings could function in the water, but only for a few hours. When forced to stay on land for extended periods, the Selkies wore special water-filled landsuits that kept their gills and skin wet. Without moisture, tissues modified for life beneath the waves began to dry out. Discomfort would eventually turn to pain . . . and then to lingering, agonizing death. Emily shuddered, and swam a quick figure-eight loop-the-loop to shake the horrible image from her mind.

John swam up beside her, the high-pitched chirps of his underwater laugh tickling her ears. "Feeling frisky?"

he said, though no landling would have heard more than a few clicks.

"Not the way you mean it," Emily retorted. A notorious tailchaser, John Duval had worked his way through most of the seaschool's female population, but hadn't yet managed to land her (so to speak). A quick fling in the foam wasn't what she wanted, or she would have had it by now, from John or any one of a dozen boys. *That's one thing Selkies and landlings have in common,* she thought, flicking her feet in John's face as she turned and swam deeper into the waters of the bay, toward the strings of lights that glowed below, marking the "streets" of the underwater portion of Hansen's Harbor. *All the males can think about is sex.*

Of course, that was partly due to the work of Victor Hansen, the genius genesculptor who had created the Selkie race and shepherded them safely to Marseguro forty years—almost fifty Earth years—ago. He'd wanted them to "be fruitful and multiply," so he'd made sure to build in a healthy interest in sex.

Emily had the same basic genome as every other Selkie and a perfectly healthy interest in sex to go with it, thank you very much—but she had a mind as well as a body, and she'd long ago decided not to take that plunge until she felt mentally and emotionally ready for it. And when she did, it would be with someone for whom it was more than just a splashy game with all the depth of the shallows off Whitesea Point.

For now, she had other things on her mind. She'd finished seaschool. In a month, she would start specialization training. She knew what she wanted to specialize in . . . but she hadn't told her parents yet.

She was pretty sure they wouldn't like it.

John followed her deeper. "I wasn't making a pass."

Emily laughed. "You're *always* making a pass."

"Not this time! I know better. I was just making conversation."

"Sure you were." They'd reached the bottom of the bay. Dome-shaped and cylindrical structures rose from the sandy seafloor on either side, connected by water-filled tubes, heated swimways that freed people from having to wear skinsuits indoors. Emily put a little extra kick into her swimming, but John easily kept up.

"What's your hurry?" he said. "The rest of the class is probably still over at Freddy Fish's. And they've got an hour's head start at drinking. We'll have to hurry to catch up."

Emily sighed, and stopped swimming, holding her position with gentle kicks and arm waves. John stopped next to her and stared, his eyes, so much larger than a landling's, glowing green as they reflected the light of the streetlamp behind her. "I can't come to Freddy's now," she said. "We're late, remember? I have to go have dinner with my parents."

"They'll understand . . ." John began, but Emily shook her head.

"I doubt it. I'm going to tell them my specialization plans."

John's mouth opened in a silent "Oh."

"My mother the eminent practical geneticist and my father the noted underwater construction engineer are unlikely to be thrilled with my decision to pursue a career in the arts," Emily went on. "You know how much trouble I had just convincing them to let me *take* the waterdance class."

"No wonder you were so willing to haul stinking buckets of algae," John said.

"It was probably more fun than what I've got to do next," Emily admitted. But then she grinned. "However, I do have an ally."

John shook his head. "No way. I'm not coming with you to help you do *that*."

"I didn't mean you," Emily said, while mentally adding another line to her secret list of *Reasons John Duval is Never Getting Any From Me*. "Amy has an announcement, too."

"Let me guess. She's decided to marry a landling."

Emily laughed. "Nothing that drastic. But after two

years out of seaschool, she's finally chosen her specialization, too . . . amphibian opera."

"Music?" John stared, and then burst out laughing and flipped head over heels in a swirl of bubbles. "Oh, I almost wish I could be there."

"You can still come if you want to," Emily said sweetly.

"No, no, no." John flicked hands and feet, backing away from her. "No way. I'm off to Freddy's. But I can't wait to hear how it all turns out."

He spun and swam off. Emily watched his wriggling legs and butt fade into the green gloom. *Might be fun . . .* she thought, and then shook her head. *No. There are better Selkie in the sea.*

Anyway, there was no hurry for all of *that.* First things first.

First, she had to face the Selkies whose genomes had blended to make her everything she was today.

That being the case, she thought, you'd think they'd be happier about the outcome.

She jackknifed, kicked, and swam off in a new direction.

Chapter 2

CHRIS KEATING STRODE up through the streets of Hansen's Harbor to the old concrete building that housed his dingy one-bedroom apartment. The building dated from the first wave of construction at the site of what eventually became known as Hansen's Harbor. Flat-roofed, utilitarian, it stood three stories high and housed two other tenants besides Chris. He'd never exchanged more than five words with either of them.

Once inside he stripped off his still-wet pants, shirt, and underwear, rolled them into a sodden ball, and dumped them into the clothesbot for washing, drying, and folding. Next, he took a long, hot shower, only stepping out when he could no longer even imagine he smelled the stink of the pier, the bay, and the Selkies who had attacked him.

He ran a comb through his collar-length sandy brown hair, checked on the still-disappointing growth of his wispy beard, then padded into the bedroom. He liked hiking and until his mother had gone into the hospital this last time had headed inland whenever he had a couple of days off, camping there out of sight and smell of the sea. The last time had been weeks ago, but his pack stood ready, leaning against the closet wall.

He tugged on underwear, then his favorite worn-but-waterproof hiking pants, shirt, and jacket, shoved his feet into his toughest, most comfortable boots, then went into the kitchen and pulled out enough prepackaged camp rations to last him for a week. They were made mostly of algae and seaweed, and tasted like it, but what wasn't made of algae and seaweed on this flooded excuse for a planet? From a cupboard by the door where he kept odds and ends, he pulled out a short crowbar. He stuffed it into his pack.

The last thing he picked up before heading out the door was his multiplayer. He left the stack of music and vidchips on his bedside table. Since his mother's stroke, he'd only been listening to one thing: the ancient, precious chip his grandfather had given his father before shipping him off to the Moon in the hope he'd survive the impending destruction of Earth.

Chris had listened to it before, of course, but its contents had become more meaningful as he faced the dreadful truth that his mother would soon be gone, leaving him completely alone among the monsters of Marseguro. The chip was his lifeline to Earth, to a planet free of Selkies or any other genesculpted abominations.

His grandparents' faith had been weak, he thought, not for the first time. Had it been stronger, his grandfather would have known that the Avatar would successfully Purify the Earth, and that God would repent of Its threatened destruction of the planet. Had his grandfather truly Believed, he would not have secretly paid to have Chris' father, then just eight years old, smuggled to the Moon along with another family and their young daughter . . . and his father would not have been one of the refugees, forced to live on the dry-docked *Rivers of Babylon* by the overtaxed Lunar government, who had failed to get off the ship before Victor Hansen and his followers flung it into space ahead of the oncoming Earth fleet.

Very few of the people trapped aboard were Believers. Of those who were, only one man made the mistake of admitting it. Hansen's followers had thrown the man out of the air lock before the ship crossed the orbit of Mars.

The other Believers had kept quiet, and pretended to be as relieved to be free of the Body Purified as Hansen's followers were. They'd kept on keeping quiet even after they landed on Marseguro. But in the privacy of their homes they'd clung desperately to their beliefs, and so Chris' father, and his mother—the small girl whose family Chris' grandfather had also sent to the Moon, and given the care of his son—had grown up immersed in the truth. Even if they hadn't fallen in love, they would have married, Chris believed. How could either of them have polluted themselves with a moddie-lover?

Chris didn't even know the names of the other original Believers, didn't know if they had clung to their Belief, didn't know if any of the other children of his generation were secretly of the Body. Belief, as his grandfather had demonstrated, could be a fickle thing.

He sometimes hated his grandfather for that reason. *If only he had truly Believed, I would have been born on Earth . . . and everything would have been different.*

Chris locked the door of his apartment behind him and looked up and down the street, empty this time of day: the only buildings on it were clones of the one he'd just exited, and the people that lived there (all landlings like him, of course; Selkies lived in underwater habitats) were either at their low-paying Council-prescribed jobs or asleep because they worked nights.

Nobody to see him leave, then. Just the way he wanted it.

He turned left, then left again down the just-wide-enough-to-pass-through space between his building and the next. A paved alley ran behind both buildings: every night, the sanitation workers—some of whom were probably his sleeping neighbors—drove along it, collecting refuse, most of which they delivered to the microfactories ringing the south side of the bay as feedstock for the fabricators.

On the other side of the alley, rock-strewn ground, barren except for the occasional low purplish-red needle-bush and patches of scraggly blue-green notgrass, rose steeply to a ridge crowned with the open-umbrella-shaped treelike plants dubbed bumbershoots. Following a path up the slope he himself had worn, Chris climbed until he stood beneath one of those plants. There, for the first time, he stopped and looked back.

Hansen's Harbor stretched left and right, curving around the semicircular shore of New Botany Bay, sheltered and surrounded by the ridge he'd climbed. Many of the buildings, especially those farthest from the water, were gray concrete like his own; others sported the violent colors favored by the Selkies. To his left, the microfactories lay haphazardly scattered across the ridge slope like squat black building blocks dropped by some careless giant. Taller structures of glass and black or dark red stone, the homes and offices of well-to-do landlings, rose at the water's edge. The very tallest buildings stood in the water itself, with eight or nine stories above water and another four or five below. To Earth eyes, Chris suspected, the city would have looked half-flooded—but no Earth eyes had ever seen it.

Maybe I can change that. He turned inland. There, ridge after ridge marched toward the horizon, each taller than the next, until the towering, snow-capped mountains no one had ever climbed took over. Massive waves, unimpeded in their sweep around the planet except by this one small continent, crashed against the sheer cliffs on the far side of those peaks, which also broke the backs of the powerful storms that roared across the world ocean. In the relatively calm water and atmosphere in the mountains' lee, Victor Hansen's creations and the nonmodded humans who had accompanied them to Marseguro had carved out a place to live.

If you can call it living.

The trail Chris had made plunged down through native forest to join a larger, paved two-lane road running parallel to the ridge. That highway connected Hansen's Harbor to Marseguro's other eight settlements: tiny Parawing and Roger's Harbor and slightly larger Beachcliff and Outtamyway to the north, and Rock Bottom, Good Beaching and Firstdip, Marseguro's second-largest town, to the south. Only landlings ever used the road; the Selkies preferred traveling by sub or "sputa" (an acronym for Self-Propelled Underwater Towing Apparatus), an unlovely word for a form of travel that terrified Chris just to think about. Some goods rolled along the road in giant transbots, but boats could make the trip just as effectively *and* carry greater quantities of cargo. On those rare occasions when a medical or other emergency necessitated speedy travel, one of the colony's half-dozen aircraft could be called into service.

Chris wished he could call one into service right then, because stuck on his own two feet his destination lay two days away; but since what he had in mind would undoubtedly have gotten him thrown into Hansen's Harbor's tiny Criminal Detention Center, he could hardly file an application for the use of community transportation. Instead, he picked his way down the ridge through the bumbershoots and stickypines and turned left, walking south toward the town of Firstdip, a journey which would take him the rest of the day, if that were where he was going . . . which it wasn't. His real goal was a fork in the road just shy of the Firstdip turnoff, a fork that would take him farther inland.

As he walked, he fished out his multiplayer, unclipped and unfolded the earset, and thumbed the play button.

The male reader's accent sounded strange to Marse-guroite ears, like that of all Earth people in the old vid and audchips Hansen's Hijackers (Chris' private term for the original colonists) had brought with them. But a mere half century wasn't enough time for English—Hansen's language, and thus the language of Marseguro—to drift to the point where it couldn't be understood.

"The Wisdom of the Avatar of God," the voice intoned, "presented for the edification and enlightenment of the Body Purified, that all who are within the Body might know the Truth, and be well-armed against the lies of those who are without. Prologue: The Miracle. Hear the words of the Avatar." The reader paused. "In 2178, through the might of God Itself, the Earth experienced a miracle . . . a miracle I foresaw."

Chris had heard those words more times than he could count, but they never failed to give him goose bumps. Even now he felt his arms and the back of his neck tingling, though he'd begun to sweat in the jacket that had seemed just right when he first stepped outside. He pulled off the jacket and tied it around his waist, rubbed his arms vigorously—but kept listening to the resonant voice.

"The asteroid on a collision course with the planet should have destroyed most of the biosphere. There was no hope of a reprieve. None . . ."

". . . no hope of reprieve. None."

You can say that again, Richard Hansen thought, shifting his weight from one sore hipbone to one slightly less sore on the unforgiving polished oak of the pew. Salvation Day services had just begun, and although bets had been laid, down in the Body Security office, over just how long the reading from *The Wisdom of the Avatar of God* would go on this year, even the most optimistic— who had not been Richard—had predicted the entire first chapter at a minimum. And today Richard had particular reason to want the service to be short.

Of course, he had no say in the matter.

"Those who could—the rich, the politicians, the religious leaders—had already fled the Earth for the Moon, for Mars, for the Belt, for the moons of Jupiter and Saturn, for New Mars and Bon Mot and the other handful of young colonies among the stars. Those who could not—the poor, the working people, the deluded but faithful flocks of the blind and useless pastors and popes, imams and ayatollahs, sages and seers and ministers and monks—waited to die . . ."

The Messenger, a sallow-faced Lesser Deacon with pale blond hair and the most pitiful excuse for a goatee Richard had ever seen, spoke in a singsong, slightly nasal voice, a close approximation of chalk squeaking on a blackboard. Richard had heard of people who claimed to get goose bumps when they heard *The Wisdom of the Avatar of God* read, but he doubted this was quite what they meant.

He tried, as he always did, to imagine what it must have been like, after the scientists proclaimed the planet's death sentence. The World Government, formed at the end of the twenty-first century as the Terror Wars finally stumbled to their bloody conclusion in an orgy of ethnic cleansing, bombings, and poison attacks, had tried to keep the news secret—but no secrets could be kept in those days of instantaneous data transfer and brainwebs.

"Cities burned. Countries crumbled. Hundreds of thousands died," the Messenger said. Stained glass windows behind the pulpit purported to show those events, although the hundreds of thousands were represented by half a dozen figures in a variety of extremely unnatural poses. *Well, you probably can't do much better with stained glass,* Richard thought. It might have been the height of medieval special effects, but it was hardly full-sensory vurt. Not for the first time, he wondered what had been in Avatar Harold the First's background that had made him model the House of the Body—and all the lesser Meeting Halls—after Gothic cathedrals, especially considering he had claimed to hate all established religions equally. *Couldn't he have gone in for padded seats and a concession stand?* Richard thought. *Maybe a vidscreen? If you wanted to distance yourself from religion and were reaching into the past for inspiration anyway, an early twenty-first-century movie house would have been just the ticket, by all historical accounts . . .*

"But one group of people remained steadfast in the face of terror and catastrophe," the Messenger went on. Passion—or something—seemed to have gripped him as he read the words of The Avatar. Unfortunately, it squeezed his voice even higher. "They moved through the chaos, calm and unafraid, giving aid and succor, promising that all was not lost, that the oncoming asteroid need not destroy the Earth." The reader paused.

What *The Wisdom of the Avatar of God* did not spell out, but Richard knew because of his somewhat privileged position within Body Security, was that those early followers of the Avatar had also moved through the corridors of power of the World Government, bribing, assassinating, coercing, convincing, paving the way for the Avatar's rise to power. You had to admire their faith, Richard thought. Everyone else thought the end was near, but *they* believed in a future—a future they intended to control.

"Thus spake the Avatar," the Messenger intoned, the ritual insertion Messengers used when reading from the Great Work whenever they came to a first-person passage, to ensure that listeners understood that what followed were the Avatar's words, not their own. "They were my followers, the Body Purified, the faithful whom I had prepared for the Edge Times for twenty years, for I knew . . . I *knew*, with the certainty that only one who has heard the Whisper of God can know . . . that the asteroid was coming, long before the so-called men of science detected its approach."

As a child, Richard *had* felt a thrill every time he heard *that* passage read. The truth of it could not be denied. The Avatar *had* had advance knowledge of the approach of the Fist of God. Where else could that knowledge have come from but God Itself?

"Those 'scientists' fled, too, those who could. Nothing could stop the asteroid, they said. It was too big, too fast. No power within humanity's grasp could deflect it, or alter Earth's doom." Richard's eyes moved to the next stained glass window, where the asteroid loomed, although the artist, either through scientific ignorance or simply for effect, had surrounded it with blood-red flames that it most certainly had not displayed.

"And they were right. No power within humanity's grasp *could* have stopped it. But what is impossible for humanity is as nothing for God. 'We must show God we repent,' I told my followers, as God had instructed me to tell them. 'We must show God that we will cleanse the planet of the evil that has fouled it, that we will purify humanity, the Body of God. If we do this, God will repent of Its decision to destroy us all. If we do this, humanity will regain its future.'

"Some laughed. Some mocked. Some turned their backs on me and rejected my message. But some remained faithful. And it was they who took the actions that convinced God humanity deserved another chance."

And now they neared the part that Richard had particularly loved as a child, imagining himself as one of the selfless heroes of the Purification . . . and a part he had grown to dread as an adult, since the day he discovered his family's not-so-secret shame. He shifted again on the unforgiving pew.

"It was they who burned the unnatural crops and the evildoers who had defiled Earth's God-given soil with them, they who bombed the genesculpting laboratories, they who slew the genesculptors, and they who hunted down and eradicated the genesculptors' abominable creations, the foul results of their blasphemous defacement of God's Holy Human Genome. Many of those first Holy Warriors of the Body died in battles with inhuman monsters created by scientists blinded by greed and hubris. But the battles were won. Earth was Purified."

Scientists blinded by greed and hubris, Richard thought. *Like Grandfather Victor.* He kept his gaze resolutely ahead, looking at the next stained glass window in the row, showing the burning labs and the battles with gene-modded humans who looked remarkably like the demons of—again—medieval religious iconography. He always felt like everyone in the House was sneaking glances at him when that passage was read. It was no secret—hadn't been since his father's death—that he was the grandson of Victor Hansen, the man who had successfully fled in a starship full of genemodded humans just before the Moon fell to the Avatar's forces.

Richard had never known his mother; his father had told him she had died in childbirth. He did his duty, raising Richard in a stern and rather distant fashion, as though obeying orders rather than because he felt any strong familial connection to the boy.

And then, one day in Richard's thirteenth year, two decades ago now, his father had gone to the roof of a very tall building, taken off all his clothes, and thrown himself naked onto the very hard pavement directly in front of the groundcar carrying the man the Council of the Faithful had just elected and proclaimed the new Avatar, Andrew the First.

He'd left no explanation for his actions: no suicide note, no political rant, no video.

Richard had his own theory: that his father, a minor functionary in the Deaconate of Food Allotment, had been driven into suicidal depression by the way he had been consistently shunted into the nether realms of the Body Purified hierarchy, where his career and his life had stagnated.

It couldn't have been easy on him, losing his wife so soon after their marriage. Richard had never even seen a picture of her, and his father would answer no questions about her, beyond the bare-bones facts of her death; the topic seemed to pain him deeply. In-laws? Cousins? Uncles? Aunts? None that Richard had ever learned about. Just his father and him . . . and now, just him.

On his darkest nights, Richard suspected the Body Purified had eliminated all other relatives of Victor Hansen. Though if so, he had no idea why they would have let his father and him live.

He kept his gaze forward. Maybe people were looking at him, maybe they weren't. He wasn't sure which would be worse.

The Messenger somehow managed to raise his voice even higher, to the point where he sounded like a five-year-old sawing the E string of a toy violin. "The Holy Warriors killed or drove all the moddies from the planet and with them as many of the lesser abominations as they could identify—drunks and drug users, homosexuals and adulterers, pedophiles, and the priests and imams and shamans and sages of all the false religions that have too long held sway over the minds of the ignorant."

At last, the Messenger paused, but only to interject another, "Thus spake the Avatar." Alas, when he continued, his voice remained at the same painful pitch.

"Then one night, just days prior to what the scientists and politicians and religious leaders had told us would be the end of the world, God spoke to me a second time, in a dream. 'You have done well, my servant,' It said. 'I have repented of my decision to destroy your world. But I will still deliver a powerful rebuke. Warn your followers to take shelter. Then, when the rain of fire has passed, emerge and lead the world into a new age.'

"I gave the orders. The Body Purified descended into the shelters I had ordered built beneath our places of worship and training. From deep beneath the surface, we watched the Miracle occur on the vidscreens providing our only link to the surface.

"Within the orbit of the Moon, another asteroid, miraculously unseen until that moment, slammed into the oncoming killer, slapping it out of the way like an annoying fly."

The stained-glass artist had certainly outdone himself depicting *that* amazing occurrence, Richard had to admit. That window rose directly above him to the right, though, and if he did more than glance at it he'd get a crick in his neck. Instead, he dared to look around the House again. Two thousand people, all looking in his direction—but up, at the window. Not looking at him at all.

Not anymore, he thought, fully aware he was being paranoid. But then, he knew that "they" really *were* out to get him, if you defined "them" as the Body Purified hierarchy. He could never be trusted until he had proved his loyalty.

Soon, he thought. *Soon.*

He'd worried the problem so long it had even begun to seep into his dreams. Recently he'd been waking from nightmares in which he was Victor Hansen, desperately loading followers and monstrous creations alike into ships fleeing Earth's imminent destruction. Odd he'd never dreamed of the final flight from the Moon, though . . . perhaps his imagination couldn't extend that far.

Well, if what he'd just discovered panned out, he might be able to put paid to those nightmares forever. Although . . .

He shook his head and tried to refocus his attention on the Lesser Deacon instead of worrying about his own state of mind.

"The asteroid missed the Earth," that worthy continued. "But though God spared us from total destruction, It delivered a stern rebuke, just as It had promised.

"Small pieces of both asteroids streaked into Earth's atmosphere. Some burned up. Some blasted through the ionosphere, and kept going. Some fell into harmless orbits. One, as I fully expected, destroyed *Orbital Orleans,* the space station infamous for its licentiousness and debauchery even among the most godless people of Earth—and crawling with moddies who 'entertained' the patrons of that devil's palace in unspeakable ways.

"That alone was a powerful sign that I and the Body Purified had done the will of God. But the most powerful sign of all was that, though the rocks that made it through the atmosphere destroyed a dozen cities, raised tsunamis that scoured whole islands and coastlands clean of life, and killed tens of millions," (Richard didn't even attempt to crane his neck to see *that* window), "not one—*not one*—of the members of the Body Purified who heeded my call to the shelters died.

"And thus when we emerged we had the supplies, the knowledge, the training, and the inclination" (*and the bribed and cowed government leaders,* Richard thought) "to impose order on chaos, law on lawlessness, and most importantly, godliness on godlessness.

"Thus did the whole world, for the first time in its long, sordid history, fall at last under the sway of God.

"The Day of Destruction proclaimed by the scientists

had become The Day of Salvation, a new beginning for all of humankind.

"Praise God, for It is good, and Its mercy endures for as long as humanity does Its will!"

And then, to Richard's pleased astonishment, the Messenger stopped speaking. He gestured at the girlchoir seated below his elevated pulpit, and a hundred preadolescent children rose and launched into "The Path to God Leads through Destruction," the closing hymn. Richard rose, shaking his head. *Phil wins the pool again,* he thought. *He must be blackmailing the Messenger.*

Not that the service was over yet. The Order of Worship ended with what the Body called the Penitents' Parade and ordinary people called the Parade of Fools.

They came in now, a larger contingent than usual, maybe two hundred in all, escorted by Holy Warriors wearing snow-white dress uniforms highlighted by black piping and looped silver chains. The prisoners wore dark-brown Penitents' Robes, marked with the symbols of their guilt: crosses for the Christians, crescents for the Muslims, Stars of David for the Jews, lotus leaves for the Buddhists, pink ribbons for the homosexuals, old dollar signs for the thieves and interest chargers, and—

Richard blinked. He'd never actually seen anyone wearing the double helix that marked a moddie before. From the reaction of those sitting near him, he guessed they hadn't, either. People craned their necks, trying to get a better look. The robe hid any obvious modification. Of course, it might be something relatively minor and invisible, like enhanced hearing, or extra-sensitive taste buds, something that had shown up in one of the random genome scans Body Security regularly—

Fast as a striking snake, the moddie moved. It ducked behind a Holy Warrior, vaulted the rail separating the stage from the audience, and landed beside the Messenger, still standing at the pulpit. It grabbed his arms and twisted one behind his back until he shrieked like a rabbit in the jaws of a fox. The moddie's hood fell back, revealing a young girl, hair and skin white as the Warriors' uniforms, lips red as blood. Her eyes had the slitted pupils of a cat. She looked wrong, evil, horrible . . .

. . . and yet somehow, to Richard, *familiar.*

She opened her mouth, revealing sharply pointed canines, and screamed, "Free—"

But who or what she wanted freed, no one ever heard. A puff of black, greasy smoke burst from her chest and back. Her voice choked off and she collapsed, the smoke swirling as she fell.

Her body continued to smoke as two Holy Warriors leaped over the railing and dragged her away. The Messenger, now almost as white as the moddie, clutched the pulpit and said, "Behold the . . ." His voice faltered and he had to swallow before beginning again. "Behold those who have been God's Enemies, those whose very existence threatens us all, for God's forbearance on the Day of Salvation was not unconditional, and was not for all time. We must continue in the ways of God, as set forth by Its chosen vessel, the Avatar, or God will unleash Its wrath on us again, and next time there will be no salvation.

"Those such as these—" he pointed to the Penitents standing before the pulpit, and his voice rose to a shriek as fury found its way through the terror that had gripped him a moment before, "—and that!" He pointed after the Holy Warriors departing with the smoking corpse of the moddie, "Deserve death! But the Avatar is merciful and has interceded with God on their behalf. Today these Penitents—those that still live—" he smiled at his own joke, "—begin five years of service to the Body. If they truly repent of their foolishness and embrace the Avatar's Wisdom, they may yet find forgiveness and enjoy the mercy of God. Praise the Avatar!"

"Praise the Avatar," the audience intoned. Not one of the thousands jammed into the House of the Body had made a sound during the drama with the moddie— Richard especially. Most of them had probably seen sudden death before—the Holy Warriors were big believers in summary punishment—and drawing attention to yourself at such a moment could end with *you* being in a Penitent's Robe at the next service.

And Richard, burdened with his family history and also trying to understand how a creature he'd never seen before—had never even imagined—could have seemed so familiar, like an old friend, when he saw it for the first time, had more reason than most to avoid drawing attention to himself.

A dream, he thought. *I must have seen it in a dream . . .*

But if he'd never seen one in real life, how could that be possible?

"Praise God!" the Messenger said.

"Praise God!" the congregation repeated.

"The service is ended," the Messenger said. "Go in Purity and serve the Body."

"We will serve the Body," the audience replied. They watched in silence as the remaining Penitents were led out of the building to the transports waiting to take them to the Body's Penitent-manned mines and farms and factories and lumber camps, then made their own hushed way to the exits.

With everyone else, Richard filed out of the House of the Body (every teenager independently dubbed it "the bawdy house"). He looked up at the single spire that towered above the entrance, pointing the way to God Itself. High above, six Holy Warrior airfighters roared across the city, white contrails slashing the sky like the claws of God Itself. Richard watched them until they were out of sight. As a kid, he'd wanted to be a Holy Warrior, but his father wouldn't let him enter the Junior Jihad program at school . . . and then, by so effectively and publicly removing himself from Richard's life, had ensured Richard could *never* be accepted.

Or so he had thought. But . . .

Shamed and furious after his father's suicide, Richard had promised even then, barely into his teens, that he would clear the family's name within the Body, though of course he had no realistic way of doing so. In fact, as he served out his final few years as an adolescent within

the strict confines of Home and School for Orphaned
Boys No. 381, he had fully expected to be barred from
any service within the Body. It had therefore shocked
him deeply to be summoned, the day before his gradua-
tion, by the Deacon in charge of the school, and informed that he had been selected for service within Body
Security. After four years of training in data analysis and
electronic communications, he had entered Body Security at the lowest possible point, as a data-mining drudge
in the Sub-Deaconate of Planetary Communication
Oversight.

To his own surprise, he had discovered he both enjoyed and excelled at the work. He had a knack for net-
ting and landing important information swimming in the
flood of data that passed through the Planetary Communication Oversight office every day. He'd quickly risen
to the rank of junior analyst, then analyst, and within five
years had become a second-level assistant to Archdeacon
Samuel Cheveldeoff himself . . .

. . . and then he rose no farther, and for three years
watched as others with neither his talent nor his dedica-
tion leapfrogged over him into positions of greater and
greater authority.

And then, late on Richard's thirtieth birthday (which
he celebrated by working late, as he celebrated most
birthdays), Cheveldeoff summoned him to his office.

A summons from Cheveldeoff seldom meant good
news, and something just a bit more solid than rumor
strongly suggested that occasionally those whom Cheveldeoff summoned were never seen again. Heart in his
mouth, Richard took the elevator down to Cheveldeoff's
deeply buried office. No one staffed the receptionist's
desk in the dark-red waiting area, and the double oak
doors stood open, revealing Cheveldeoff at his desk.

Not for the first time, Richard thought Cheveldeoff
looked like an artillery shell. He was bald, broad-
shouldered, thick-necked, and surprisingly short when he
stood up—which he didn't, for Richard. Eyes like polished mahogany glinted beneath bushy eyebrows the

color and texture of steel wool. "Come in," Cheveldeoff said. "Sit down."

Obscurely relieved he hadn't been told to close the door, despite the emptiness of the antechamber outside, Richard followed Cheveldeoff's orders, as did everyone with any sense. "I'm going to explain your predicament to you," Cheveldeoff said, and did, directly, frankly, brutally: Richard, being "the grandson of a traitor and the son of embarrassment," had advanced as far within the hierarchy as he ever would.

Unless . . .

"You have two options, as I see it," Cheveldeoff said. "You can quit the Service of the Body and find an ordinary civilian job. As you are certainly aware, however, we will watch you closely for the rest of your life.

"Or, you can prove that you are to be trusted . . . that you are not tainted by the evil of your grandfather or the weakness of your father. I'll even tell you how you can do it." He leaned forward, hard brown eyes locked on Richard's. "Find the planet to which your grandfather dragged his misbegotten brood of malformed monstrosities. If they're out there, we want them. And if we find them, and you helped us, well . . . then Bob's your uncle, the sky's the limit, you're sitting in the catbird seat, you're God's favorite mortal." He leaned back and smiled, or at least showed his teeth. "Hell, you might even get my job . . . after I retire, of course."

And so Richard Hansen had been handed the quest— the completely hopeless quest, he suspected, but he knew well enough that Cheveldeoff's "two options" had been nothing of the kind—that, should he fulfill it, would redeem him and his family in the eyes of the Body Purified, and by extension, all of unmodified humanity.

He glanced at his watch. And if he didn't hurry, he'd be late delivering his latest report on that quest.

He increased his pace down the broad boulevard leading from the House of the Body to the headquarters of Body Security, at the heart of the City of God (once known as Kansas City, though no one who had lived

there before the Day of Salvation would have recognized
any part of it; the original had been largely pulverized,
then burned, by the nearby impact of one of the larger
chunks of the asteroid, and the remaining ruins had been
scraped away and used as feedstock for microfactories).

For two years, Richard had been reporting to Cheveldeoff at monthly meetings. At the very first one, Cheveldeoff had surprised him by bringing out a chessboard.
"You play, of course," Cheveldeoff said. It hadn't been
a question, and Richard could hardly be surprised that
the Archdeacon of Body Security knew of his predilec-
tion for the game. He hadn't really been surprised to
discover that Cheveldeoff excelled at it, either. Richard,
no slouch himself, always put up a good fight, but hadn't
won once.

He sometimes wondered what would happen if he did.

Two years. Hard to believe. When he'd taken on the
challenge of finding his grandfather's pet moddies, he
hadn't realized just how thoroughly Victor Hansen had
disappeared. He'd assumed the moddies would have
maintained some kind of contact with other colonies settled from Earth, so he had begun his search on New
Scotland, recently Purified and brought under the oversight of the Avatar. But though he had scanned and
searched and combed through current and archived intercepted communications using every tool at the disposal
of the Ministry, he had found nothing to point him to
Grandpa's secret hideout . . .

. . . until yesterday.

He looked up at the cloudless sky and grinned. Today,
he had a surprise for his chess partner.

Samuel Cheveldeoff finished setting up the ancient hand-
carved ebony-and-ivory chess set, and glanced at the
loudly ticking image of a clock on one of the vidwalls,
currently displaying his favorite wallpaper: the interior
of a nineteenth century Italian villa. The images of rich
furnishings and Old Master paintings gave his Spartan

office warmth it generally lacked. Richard Hansen should arrive within minutes.

Cheveldeoff sat back in his chair and glanced at another vidwall, temporarily switched from displaying the villa to showing the rapidly emptying interior of the House of the Body. The automated defense systems in the House had made short work of the moddie who had attacked the Messenger, but Cheveldeoff still felt unhappy about the incident. If the moddie had gone the other way, into the crowd, there would have been casualties, and it looked bad for the Body to lose worshipers on the holiest day of the year. The Avatar . . . he grimaced; no, not the Avatar, but the Avatar's Right Hand . . . would not be pleased.

"Message from the Holy Office," the computer suddenly said, as if on cue. "Your presence is required in the Holy Office at 1900. No rescheduling permitted."

Cheveldeoff clenched his jaw for a moment; then forced himself to relax it. Much as he would have liked to tell the Right Hand what he could do with his meeting, the stakes were too high. The Avatar, felled by a mysterious stroke . . . and though Cheveldeoff suspected the Right Hand suspected *him*, he had had nothing to do with it . . . lay alive but vegetative in his private hospital. The prize Cheveldeoff had been working for all his life was in play—but the Avatar had been struck down too soon. He could not be certain he had enough votes on the Council of the Faithful. His main rival, Ashok Shridhar, Archdeacon of Finance, controlled the purse strings of the Body—and purse strings could easily become puppet strings.

If the Avatar's illness had been brought on by something other than his own penchant for debauchery, it could mean Shridhar *was* confident he had enough votes among the Council members.

Well, Cheveldeoff could not outbribe the Archdeacon of Finance, but he suspected he could outblackmail him.

In the meantime, though the Right Hand officially remained above all such maneuverings for succession, and would serve whomever God in Its wisdom appointed through the deliberations of the Council, in this situation the Right Hand essentially *was* the Avatar, and until the real Avatar died or recovered, Cheveldeoff dared not cross him. The Right Hand could bring his own weight to bear on certain Council members, for he knew everything that had happened in the Avatar's Dwelling, behind the screen of discreet silence even Cheveldeoff had never been able to pierce. Cheveldeoff had heard rumors of some of the activities certain Councillors had enjoyed in the company of the Avatar, but he had no proof. He suspected the Right Hand had pictures, video, and gene samples.

Enough waffling. "Computer, accept meeting request from the Holy Office."

"Meeting accepted," said the computer.

My turn, Cheveldeoff thought. "Computer, request meeting with Grand Deacon Ellers. Topic: the poor performance of the Holy Warriors at today's Salvation Day service in the Central Meeting Hall. Time: tomorrow, 7 a.m." He grinned savagely. "No rescheduling permitted."

"Meeting request sent," the computer said. A pause. "Meeting accepted."

Cheveldeoff nodded to himself. An early morning meeting that forced Ellers to clear his schedule for Cheveldeoff's convenience should powerfully remind the new commander of the Holy Warriors that, since the primary function of the Holy Warriors was to keep the Body secure from enemies both internal and external, the Holy Warriors served Body Security.

Or, to put it another way, they served *him*. Ellers, whom Cheveldeoff knew from his agents on the Grand Deacon's staff would prefer that Shridhar be the next Avatar, needed to be very clear on that point, because Cheveldeoff intended to ensure, by any and all means, that the Holy Warriors *continued* to serve him, in case the coming succession battle moved from the Council chamber into the streets.

The sound of a faraway doorbell rang through the room, and the computer said, "Archdeacon, Richard Hansen to see you. Identity confirmed."

"Computer, all walls to Villa Two," Cheveldeoff said, and the image of the interior of the House of the Body disappeared, replaced by ceiling-high windows framing a sun-drenched view of vineyards and olive trees. "Computer, open door."

A door in the villa apparently opened, and Richard Hansen came in. The ultramodern blood-red vestibule behind him clashed visually with the wood and marble of the wallpaper for a moment, then the door closed.

"Come in, Richard, come in," Cheveldeoff said. "I believe it's your turn to play white."

"Good afternoon, Archdeacon," Richard Hansen said. He crossed the matte-finish black floor and sat down across from Cheveldeoff. Without another word, he moved, pawn to king four, and the game began.

Cheveldeoff played with half his brain. Though a decent enough player, Hansen couldn't really challenge Cheveldeoff, who could have been a Grand Master if he had cared to pursue it. Cheveldeoff enjoyed their games, but not because of the chess. The real reason he brought Hansen in week after week was that the man fascinated him.

As well he should. Richard Hansen had been Samuel Cheveldeoff's pet project for a quarter of a century, ever since Cheveldeoff had taken command of Body Security (at the remarkably young age of thirty) and had first been briefed on the long-term experiments already underway with Victor Hansen's "son" and "grandson."

I wonder if he knows just how much he looks like a young Victor Hansen? Cheveldeoff thought, studying Richard as Richard studied the board. *Probably not.* The Body strictly controlled all information about Victor Hansen, including images. And Peter Hansen, Richard's "father," had certainly not been provided with a stock of images of Victor Hansen to keep around the home.

Even if Richard Hansen were to see a photograph of Victor Hansen at the same age, Cheveldeoff doubted he would put two and two together. After all, many grand-sons looked like their grandfathers. Cheveldeoff's own grandfather had been not that dissimilar from himself.

But Richard Hansen, though he would never know it, was an exact duplicate of Victor Hansen at his age—because Richard Hansen, as only about ten people on the planet knew, was not Victor Hansen's grandson at all.

He was Victor Hansen's clone.

Cheveldeoff moved. "Bishop to Knight Five. Check." Hansen bent to the board, giving Cheveldeoff a few more minutes for reflection.

When that old sinner Victor Hansen had stolen the *Rivers of Babylon* and fled the solar system, he had left behind undercover operatives to cover his tracks. In the chaos and confusion that had followed the Day of Salvation and the ensuing meteor storms, they had had no difficulty clearing the Stellar Survey databases of any trace of any research Hansen might have conducted into possible destinations—and Cheveldeoff, like every head of Body Security before him, had no doubt Hansen had had a specific destination in mind before he fled.

Hansen's followers didn't remain undercover for long. Betrayed for money by someone they had trusted a little too much, interrogated by the Body, they had provided a great deal of information about Hansen and his plans—though not, unfortunately, his ultimate destination.

And one thing they had revealed was that Hansen hadn't been content to leave behind a few loyal follow-ers. He had also left *himself* behind, in the form of five frozen cloned embryos, only awaiting implantation.

Victor Hansen had been long-divorced by the time he fled for Luna. Officially, the split had been vicious, and his wife had become a loyal member of the Body . . . but that, the Hansen loyalists revealed, had all been a ruse. In fact, Hansen's ex-wife had remained fiercely loyal to him, and he had left the clones in her care.

Physically, the clones were all identical to Victor Han-sen. But in their brains . . .

According to Hansen's agents, each of the clones carried within them modified genes that somehow (Cheveldeoff didn't pretend to understand how) would at some unknown point in their lives provide them with unlearned knowledge about Hansen's plans. Hansen's followers said Hansen did not believe the Body's reign would last more than a few years, and he hoped his clones would be able to reconnect his hidden moddie "children" with humanity at some point.

More: just about the last thing Hansen's loyalists had revealed, before they succumbed to the side effects of their questioning, was that Hansen's implanted gene-bombs were expected to do more than just rewrite the clones' memories: they would at least partially rewrite the clones' personalities as well, making them mental as well as physical copies of Victor Hansen.

The man must have thought he was God Itself, Cheveldeoff thought.

Shortly after the interrogations ended, the Body-controlled media reported that Victor Hansen's ex-wife had taken her own life, leaving behind a suicide note that explained she could no longer live with the shame of her former relationship with the evil genesculptor *extraordinaire.*

With her disposed of, the Body had turned its attention to Hansen's clones. Two had been implanted almost at once in surrogate mothers. One had developed abnormalities in the womb and been aborted. The other, however, throve. Given the name Peter Hansen, raised in a Body orphanage and told his mother had died when he was an infant, he had been guided by Cheveldeoff's predecessor into a noncritical job in a minor bureaucracy while the Body waited for the Hansen gene-bomb to explode, at which point he would be interrogated to learn the coordinates of the planet Victor Hansen had fled to. A simple plan, but one that had gone badly awry shortly after Cheveldeoff took over Body Security, when Peter Hansen had decided the best way to celebrate the ascension of a new Avatar was by naked base jumping without a parachute.

Victor Hansen's gene-bomb, it appeared, could have unanticipated side effects.

Cheveldeoff had therefore decided to take a different approach with the third clone, already a teenager, which had been implanted in Peter Hansen's (carefully selected) wife, who had then tragically "died" in childbirth. (In fact, she had died shortly after childbirth, in a sealed room not far from where Peter Hansen already grieved for her—Cheveldeoff's predecessor had not liked loose ends any more than he did.) He directed the clone into Body Security itself.

The geneticists (such as they were; in a society that outlawed genetic modification except within strict guidelines closely supervised by the Body Purified, the best and brightest did not choose genetics as a career) had persuaded him they had a gene therapy that would blunt most of the gene-bomb's personality rewrite. They were *almost* sure it wouldn't interfere with the transfer of "memories" about the destination of the *Rivers of Babylon*.

Cheveldeoff had agreed to the experiment. During an otherwise routine vaccination, Richard Hansen received protection against more than he knew. And then, as Richard approached the age when the gene-bomb should detonate, Cheveldeoff had posed him the very question they hoped the gene-bomb would provide the answer to: "Where did Victor Hansen take his moddies?" And ever since he had kept Richard close at hand and closely watched, waiting to see what would happen.

"So," said Cheveldeoff, several moves into the game he already knew he would win, "how goes the great moddie hunt?"

Richard frowned at the board. *How does he do that?* he wondered. *I'm already struggling. No matter what I do, he's a move—or three!—ahead.*

But Cheveldeoff's question made him smile. "It's going well," he said, looking up from the game, which patently wasn't.

Cheveldeoff's bushy iron-colored eyebrows lifted like caterpillars trying to crawl up onto his shaved skull. "You have news?"

"I do." Richard's smile widened to a grin. "I have a vector."

The Archdeacon sat up straight in his chair, more reaction than Richard had ever seen from him. "Tell me!"

First, Richard moved, advancing a pawn to protect an exposed knight. Cheveldeoff countered without even looking at the board, and Richard suddenly found himself forced to choose between sacrificing a bishop and a rook. Richard studied the board. He didn't like what he saw. "I've concentrated for years on a handful of possible routes the *Rivers of Babylon* might have taken," he said, his hand hesitating over first the bishop, then the rook. "All very logical, all based on the fragmentary records we have of the ship's flight out of the solar system. But last week I decided to take a different tack. I had . . . a hunch. I took a look at some data I'd never bothered with before, because they'd been recorded a quarter of a way around the orbit of Uranus from the last known position of the *Rivers of Babylon.*"

Yeah, call it a hunch, Richard thought. *Whatever you do, don't call it what it was—a sudden flood of complete certainty that if he looked at those long-ignored records, he would find something. Because if you call it that, you'll have to admit you don't know what the hell is going on inside your own head these days.*

He moved the rook. Cheveldeoff took his bishop. Richard studied the board again. The situation had *not* improved. "The records are stored on the far side of the Moon, but they're raw data files downloaded from an old automated deep-space station, ironically one of the ones that first saw the Fist of God approaching. They hadn't been completely ignored—some analyst studied them immediately after Hansen escaped. But the micronuke that destroyed *Sterling Heights* at the moment of departure fried electronics all over the far side, and for several months after a lot of data that came in from deep space was lost or scrambled while equipment was being repaired or replaced. I doubt the analysts of fifty years ago could retrieve anything." He needed the rook more than the bishop, he decided, and pulled it back a rank to safety. "But technology has advanced. My algorithms identified a great deal more data from that deep-space station tucked away in odd corners of the database than those old analysts knew existed." He attempted to threaten Cheveldeoff's king with the rook he'd saved on his last move.

Cheveldeoff blocked the rook with a pawn-protected knight and with the same move opened up a new line of attack from his bishop on Richard's remaining rook. "Go on."

"That space station had picked up something, I could tell that right away, but the signal was almost nonexistent. It took several days of tweaking to filter out the noise burying it, but by yesterday, the computer and I agreed: the space station had recorded—and located in space—the electromagnetic footprint of a Cornwall branespace engine spinning up. The *Rivers of Babylon* must have changed course just before it left the system. Combining the data from the deep-space station with the final observation of the *Rivers of Babylon*'s position within the system gave me . . ." He slid his queen forward, on the theory that the best defense was a strong offense. "Check."

Cheveldeoff blocked with his bishop, without a second's pause. "A vector!"

"A vector." Richard shook his head. The queen move had been an act of desperation. He couldn't sustain the attack. He had to move her back and concentrate on defense again . . . or resign, and he wasn't quite ready to do that. He pulled the piece back toward his side of the board. "It's not enough to tell us where the moddie planet is . . . if it exists . . . but at least it narrows the field of search. All we need now is one unexplained burst of electromagnetic energy, one anomaly reported by some fortune-seeking scout ship . . ."

"And we'll finally be able to Purify the worst abominations the genesculptors ever created," Cheveldeoff said. "And just maybe save the human race from the wrath of God. Excellent news, Richard!" His own queen slashed across the board. "Check. Mate in three."

What? Richard stared at the board. *How did I miss that?* Well, he could see it now readily enough. He reached out and tipped over his king. "Good game, sir."

"I eagerly await the next," Cheveldeoff said, getting to his feet and thus signaling the end of the audience. But he held out his hand, and he'd never done that before. "Good work, Richard," he said as Richard took it. He held it a moment longer than necessary for a handshake, and looked Richard in the eyes. It wasn't a comfortable look; Cheveldeoff's eyes had a way of boring into his head and leaving him with a vague sense of dread, even when he was being congratulated. "If this pans out, the sky's the limit for you." He released Richard's hand. "Now get out of here. Go home. Relax. It's Salvation Day!"

"Yes, sir." With relief (not an unusual emotion when leaving Cheveldeoff's office) and a certain euphoria (which certainly *was*), Richard made his way up from the bowels of Body Security HQ. He emerged onto the front steps and paused to look back along the boulevard, paved with blue tile, lined with white stone sidewalks and white stone buildings, to the needle-sharp spire of the House of the Body pointing the way to the heavens. It pointed the way to God Itself, but now, Richard thought, maybe it also pointed the way to his future . . . a future where the Hansen name was no longer anathema, a future where he could finally get everything he deserved.

He shook his head. *Well, that was pretentious,* he told himself, and headed down the steps toward the undertube station that would take him home. He couldn't help grinning. *But that doesn't mean it's not true.*

Chapter 3

THE FIRST CHAPTER of *The Wisdom of the Avatar of God* ended with "Praise God!" and Chris grinned as he always did, remembering an old Selkie joke about the Avatar that ended with the punch line, "Praise God! That's *not* a request." But today, his grin died quickly. *I shouldn't make fun of the Avatar*, he thought. *Some things are not a laughing matter.* And though there was no one on Marseguro to report him to the Purity Watchers—and no Purity Watchers, either—there might be soon enough.

Best to Purify himself *before* that day arrived.

"Chapter Two," said the reader. "Why the Body Must Be Purified If Humanity Is to Survive." Chris kept walking, and kept listening.

Two hours later, well into Chapter Five, "On the Evils of Historical Religion," he came to a fork in the road. One path was broad and led along the coast to Firstdip, curving out of sight around a hill. The other, though still paved, was narrow and led inland. A small green sign pointed the way: "Landing Valley."

Chris directed his feet along the narrower path. The symbolism, though rooted in a long-banned religion, was not lost on him: if all went well, this straight and narrow way would indeed lead to life, a new life for him and all the other nonmods—"normals," as he now dared think of them—being gradually drowned, symbolically and sometimes literally (in the case of his father) by the Selkies.

He spent the night in a gully beneath a rock overhang that provided shelter from the regular-as-clockwork midnight downpour of the Marseguro interior. Very little of the planet's flora ran to anything tall enough or grand enough to be dubbed a tree, and the species that did—such as the bumbershoots and stickypines—lived only within a kilometer or two of the coast. Nevertheless, even here, certain of the native fernlike bushes grew to almost the height of a smallish man, and enough of those grew thickly enough at the north end of the gully to block the chilly wind that accompanied the rain. With his pocket heater and ultralight sleeping bag, he was comfortable enough.

In the morning, after a quick breakfast of something that was supposed to taste like bacon and eggs but Chris very much doubted really did (because if bacon and eggs had really tasted like that, why would anyone have ever eaten them?) Chris packed up and hit the trail. As the orange rays of the sun cleared the ridges, mist rose from the wet pavement, swirling around him as he walked.

Today he chose to walk in silence. He doubted even an Archdeacon could listen to the Avatar's book every day. It was too rich, like eating bubblesquid *pâté* for breakfast, lunch, and supper. And too infuriating.

The last time he had come this way, he had been one of a company of two-dozen ten-year-olds, Emily Wood and John Duval among them. They had been on the traditional field trip to the Landing Site, and they hadn't been walking. Instead, they'd been riding in big-wheeled electric cars with sealed, humidified interiors designed to keep the Selkies' skin from drying out, never mind how uncomfortable it made the nonmods. "It's only for a short time," the teacher said when he complained. "You'll live."

This morning the air held at least as much humidity as those car interiors had, so much he was almost surprised it didn't trigger his fear of water. Sometimes Chris dreamed about living somewhere dry. The closest thing Marseguro had to a desert was a high plateau in the mountains where it only rained or snowed three or four times a year, but the only way to get there was by air and you had to have a pressing scientific reason to make the trip. Suspecting mold had started growing on your skin didn't count.

After an hour, the road's gentle slope steepened, and it began to wind up the side of the ridge between pink boulders and purplish bushes. Chris walked faster. If he remembered right, once he crested the top . . .

There. Landing Valley, broad and flat as a table: the ideal place to set down a starship.

Very little remained of the *Rivers of Babylon* after all these years. The settlers had stripped the electronics and most of the metal out of her to build Firstdip which, after decades, Chris had always thought, *still* looked like a refugees' shantytown. But the First Landers hadn't been entirely focused on the immediate needs of survival. They'd left one section of the ship undisturbed, as a kind of monument, and it glinted below him in the afternoon sun, a short, stubby cylinder of silvery metal, ten meters wide and a hundred in diameter, set on its side so that it towered over the site: a cross section of the hull taken from the holds, showing the heavy shielding that had protected the Selkie children in their water-filled tanks from radiation through the long trip to the edge of Earth's solar system, through branespace (not that radiation was a problem *there*) and then in from the edges of this system to Marseguro. Years later, a museum and interpretative center had been set up in a low building next to the hull section.

None of that interested Chris. He descended into the valley and strode past both the museum and the hull section without a glance, heading instead for the dark opening in the steep red rock of the far valley wall, maybe three hundred meters farther. He remembered asking the teacher about it during the field trip.

"It's a cave," she'd said. "The First Landers lived in there for a while, even dug out some extra rooms. It's just used for storage now . . . a lot of mothballed equipment. Stuff the First Landers thought might be needed in the future, or if the microfactories failed."

"Like what?"

"Spare parts, survival rations, communications equipment, things like that," she'd said vaguely. "An emergency beacon, I think. Maybe someday we'll want to talk to the rest of humanity again. After the Body Purified is gone. Now hurry up and catch up with the rest of the group. I think there's gelato!"

Chris couldn't remember if he'd had gelato that day, but he'd never forgotten the cave. He'd longed to explore it even then, but of course children weren't allowed in, and nobody ever came here except on school field trips or for significant Landing Day anniversaries—the next would be the fortieth, still half a year away.

They're probably planning something really special, Chris thought. *Well, it will certainly be special if this works out.*

He reached into his pack and pulled out his flashlight and crowbar. He didn't expect much in the way of security, but surely the entrance would at least be locked: and so it was. The mouth of the cave had been closed off with a wall of cement blocks, which held a metal door, painted in peeling blue. A rusty hasp, secured by an equally rusty padlock, held the door closed. The crowbar made quick work of the hasp, and a moment later Chris flicked on the flashlight and stepped out of the just-starting-to-warm-up day into a dank, dark chill.

He had no idea how far into the hillside the cave and its additional rooms reached, or how long he might have to search, but in fact he found the equipment he wanted in the first natural chamber, just inside the cement-block wall, where it could be easily retrieved if needed. The First Landers had only wanted some place out of the rain; they weren't trying to hide anything. Why would they? They believed everyone on the *Rivers of Babylon* was united in purpose, had all thrown in their lot with this do-or-die quest to found a world safe from the Body Purified, a new home for a new, improved breed of human . . . *and their unimproved slaves,* Chris thought. *Us.*

Just the day before, he'd heard once more the Avatar's unanswerable question: "What good are normal humans to superhuman monsters? They'll come to despise us, then enslave us, then eradicate us."

The death of Chris' father was proof enough the Avatar was right. Chris shook his head. "Not me," he growled.

He found the equipment he wanted, clearly marked. No inkling that it should be secured or at least left unlabeled had apparently ever crossed anyone's mind. *Some superhumans,* Chris thought, pushing the white packing crate toward the door. The scraping of plastic on stone echoed back from the cave walls with the sound of a knife on a grindstone. As Chris pulled the crate into the light, the text that he had previously only seen in the circle of illumination from his flashlight became clear: EMERGENCY INTERSTELLAR NULL-BRANE BEACON, and below that, an identification number, and a small panel of instructions. He read them over carefully. Among other things, they told him to make note of the ID number on the case, as he would need it to activate the beacon. He pulled his clunky old datapad from the backpack and stored the number, then turned his attention to getting the beacon out of the cave.

It weighed too much to lift. That meant he'd have to drag it, and that meant he couldn't place it where he really wanted to, one valley over. Not that it was all that likely anyone would stumble over it wherever he put it, given how infrequently people came to Landing Valley, but still . . .

Well, he didn't have any choice. And he could at least hide it a bit.

He tugged and pushed and pulled the crate away from the cave mouth, downslope but off to one side, away from the hull section and the museum, forcing it through a screen of two-meter-tall needlebushes into an open space on the other side. Sucking the back of his badly scratched left hand, he used his right to press the two green buttons on the front of the case. Something clicked and the crate's lid sprang open, revealing the top of a silver cylinder about half a meter in diameter, featuring an alphanumeric keypad and, inside a transparent cover, a green-lit switch.

For the first time, Chris hesitated. *Are you sure about this?* he thought. *If this works, it changes everything. All the dreams of the First Landers, overthrown in an instant. Contact with Earth. Marseguro a colony, not an independent world . . .*

. . . no more Selkies, he reminded himself. *No more second-class "landlings," becoming more second-class every year as the Selkies breed like the animals they are. No more men like my father being murdered by the Selkie masters. A chance to return to Earth, where real humans belong . . . a chance to find something better to do with my life than cataloging algae samples and scrubbing growth tanks.*

He remembered John Duval stealing his trunks, Emily Wood laughing at him, both of them and all their inhuman friends throwing him off the pier just to watch him flounder, just to humiliate him, just to mock him.

He remembered his father, lost at sea.

He remembered his mother, dying in a hospital long cut off from the latest medical advances.

He remembered her words to him, just yesterday morning . . .

"The Selkies murdered him . . . and now they're killing me . . . they'll kill you, too, my little boy . . ."

He blinked hard twice. "Not me," he said again, and flicked the switch.

The transmitter beeped. "Please enter identification number," a male voice said. Chris consulted his datapad, and carefully entered the string of digits and letters. "Thank you," said the voice. "Please step back a minimum of three meters. Transmitter deployment begins in five seconds . . ." (Chris hastily retreated the suggested distance) ". . . four . . . three . . . two . . . one."

The cylinder suddenly got longer, the top rising out of the packing case, which itself sprouted three mechanical spider legs, each of which budded and grew three smaller fingerlike appendages that dug into the ground and gripped. The top of the cylinder, now twice as tall as Chris, split open. A delicate dish-shaped antenna blossomed. The voice spoke again. "This transmitter contains a high-energy battery equivalent in power to a small fission reactor," it said. "This level of energy is necessary to transmit a null-brane pulse of sufficient strength to be detected by any starships within this transmitter's range. Diagnostics indicate that this battery is in good operating condition; however, this transmitter's internal clock indicates that fifty-two Earth years have passed since the last regularly scheduled maintenance of this battery. This increases the possibility of catastrophic battery failure to an estimated one in ten. Such a failure, should it occur, will explosively release energy equivalent in force to two Hiroshima-sized nuclear weapons. Do you wish to proceed with activation?" A panel slid open at the base of the cylinder, revealing a green button and a red button. "Please press the green button, located on the right, if you wish to proceed. Press the red button, located on the left, to cancel."

This time, Chris didn't hesitate. If the battery failed, he'd hardly notice, and at least he would have made a statement they couldn't ignore back in Hansen's Harbor. He strode forward and pressed the green button.

"Activation complete," the transmitter said. "Automated distress signal will be transmitted until battery power is exhausted, in approximately five Earth years. Transmission begins in thirty seconds . . . twenty-nine . . . twenty-eight . . . twenty-seven . . ."

Chris looked up at the sky. He couldn't be sure anyone would pick up the signal, even in five years . . . but at least he had done something. At least he wasn't just a passive victim this time, as he had been on the pier, in the pool, so many other times . . .

. . . like his father had been . . . like his mother . . .

". . . ten . . . nine . . . eight . . . seven . . . six . . . five . . . four . . . three . . . two . . . one . . . transmission begins."

The transmitter did not blow up. In fact, nothing visible happened at all. Chris stared up at the sky for another long moment, then began packing up for the trip home. He'd clean up as many traces of his visit as he could before he left the site—brush away the scrape marks the crate had left in the dirt leading from the cave, do his best to make the padlock look undisturbed. Then it would be back to Hansen's Harbor, back to the algae tanks, back to the bedside of the remnant of his mother, back to being alternately ignored and tormented. Everything would seem just the same to everyone else, but not to him.

The thing he had dreamed of doing for years, he had actually done at last.

Now he would wait, and nurse his secret hope.

The meeting with her parents didn't go at all as Emily had anticipated.

She'd suggested Coriolis for dinner. Since it was a celebration for the end of school, her parents had agreed, even though Coriolis was probably the most expensive restaurant above or below the waves of New Botany Bay. Eating out was one of the activities both Selkies and landlings could enjoy together, since Victor Hansen's modifications had not extended to making Selkies underwater eaters. Who wanted a belly full of seawater? They might be able to breathe underwater, but Selkies were still humans, not dolphins or seals. As well, even though Selkies could communicate underwater, their language, being so new, lacked the richness of English. Conversation in air was both a pleasure and, sometimes, a necessity.

So Coriolis and similar establishments had air. But they also had water. In fact, Coriolis had just about any combination of the two elements anyone could want. There were submerged-seating areas that looked like pictures Emily had seen of swim-up bars on Earth, rooms that were not only nonsubmerged but dehumidified for the comfort of landlings, other rooms that were nonsubmerged but regularly humidified by a fine mist of water vapor (available in a variety of scents from floral to savory), and two-level rooms that allowed Selkies to sit submerged and landlings to sit high and dry.

Emily's parents were waiting for her in a small private submerged-seating room. She swam up into the room from below and surfaced, then ran her fingers through her short violet hair and over her face to clear away the water. "Hi," she said.

"Hi, yourself," said her mother, and Emily instantly knew she was in trouble.

Dr. Carla Christianson-Wood was in her late thirties, local years, which put her in her mid-forties in Earth years. Her hair, much longer than Emily's, remained more blonde than gray, and unlike her daughter and most of the rest of the younger generation, she had never dyed it.

Dr. Christianson-Wood's mother, Dr. Alice Christianson, had been one of the first-generation Selkies on board the *Rivers of Babylon*, and had studied genetics with Victor Hansen himself. Dr. Christianson-Wood, like her mother before her, had focused her research energies on viruses—specifically, the differences between the local equivalent to viruses, which fortunately, as predicted by Victor Hansen's scientific team before the *Rivers of Babylon* landed, were incapable of infecting Earth-evolved life, and the viruses the settlers had brought with them from Earth. "There is some concern that Marseguroite and Earth viruses could exchange genetic information and produce something really nasty that neither we nor Marseguro life would have any immunity to," she'd told Emily once. "We need to know if that's possible and what to do about it if it is." Most of her work was funded by the Planetary Council, Marseguro's elected government, such as it was—with most residents of the planet spread along the coast in widely separated villages, most government was pretty strictly local in nature. However, the Planetary Council did collect taxes to support projects of planetary interest, including an investigation branch that helped local authorities solve crimes, a handful of prisons (almost empty) for people convicted of those crimes, and various research and construction projects.

But somehow, Emily doubted the chill in her mother's voice had anything to do with her research. "Is something wrong?" she asked, but she already knew: her mother had heard about what had happened on the pier.

"What were you thinking?" Dr. Christianson-Wood demanded, confirming Emily's suspicion. "Swarming a nonmod? Dumping him in the bay? Especially one who couldn't swim?"

"We didn't know he couldn't swim," Emily protested, even though she knew it was a pitiful defense. "Every other landling—"

"Nonmod," her mother interjected. "I don't like the term 'landling.' It's disrespectful."

"Every other *nonmod* I've ever met has learned to swim. Why would you live on Marseguro and *not* learn to swim?"

"It's not like he has any choice where he lives," her father said, speaking for the first time. With his bristling beard and bushy eyebrows, Peterson Wood looked a little bit like ancient Earth representations of King Neptune, although he wore a sedate black skinsuit rather than going around bare-chested. One of the leading underwater engineers of the planet, he had helped build Coriolis and the majority of the other buildings constructed within the last twenty years in the waters of New Botany Bay.

"And whether he could swim or not was hardly the point," her mother said. "Throwing someone off the pier is assault, Emily. He could have pressed charges. He still could. And then what would happen to your school career?"

"School career?" said a new voice behind Emily. "Emily, you were going to wait until I got here!"

Oh, no, Emily thought as her two-years-older sister Amy slipped into the water beside her. *I've got to stop her from—*

But it was far too late for that. With her usual knack for saying the wrong thing at the wrong time, Amy said, "Well, if Emily's told you, I guess I'd better tell you, too. I've finally made up my mind. I'm not going into the sciences, either. I'm going to be a singer. Amphibian opera."

Their parents stiffened. "What do you mean, singer?" said their father.

"What do you mean, *either*?" said their mother, gaze slicing from Amy to Emily.

Not the way I intended to break the news, Emily thought. The waiter hadn't even come to take their drink orders yet. "I intended to tell you . . . later," she said, shooting a glance at Amy, who had the decency to look stricken. "I've been thinking about my specialization training and I've . . . I've decided to go into underwater dance." There, it was out.

Her parents stared from one to the other of their daughters, then looked at each other, and then, to her astonishment, burst out laughing. "Opera? Dance?" her mother said. "How long have you two been planning this?"

Amy began to grin. "Well, it was Emily's idea. I thought you'd understand, but she said . . ."

Emily's eyes narrowed. "No, Amy, you don't get it." She glared at her mother. "They think it's a joke."

"But a very good one," her father assured her. "Underwater dancing. Amphibian opera, for God's sake!" He burst out laughing again. "Please."

Amy's grin had faded before it fully formed. "But . . .

we're not joking." She looked at Emily. "At least . . . I'm not."

"I'm not, either," Emily said. "Mom, Dad, I know you want us to go into the sciences. Mom, I know you want a third-generation geneticist in the family. But that's just not what I'm interested in. And Marseguro has come a long way since you chose your specialization. We've been here half a century now. It's time we focused on the arts a little bit more. Dr. Naborikov says that—"

Her parents' laughter had died as she spoke. Now their expressions hardened into anger. "Naborikov," her mother said. "I might have known. 'In the long run, the arts are more important to society than the sciences.'" She mimicked Naborikov's rounded vowels and clipped consonants perfectly. "As if the arts will help us survive on a hostile planet!"

"But that's just it," Emily retorted. "Marseguro *isn't* a hostile planet. After four decades, we *know* that. There are hardly any threats. Some nasty sea predators, but that's about it. You've said yourself there are no native diseases to worry about. Solar radiation? Not a problem. Hurricanes? Rogue waves? The mountains shelter us. Marseguro is a paradise."

"You sound like a Consolidationist," her mother said. She made the word sound like an insult. "We've barely begun to *really* colonize this planet. All our people, non-mods and Selkies, live within a few thousand square kilometers of each other, close to this one continent. The nonmods have barely penetrated the interior, and the Selkies have barely explored beyond the shelf. We may never live in the abyss, but there are shallows that we could make our own, a whole barely submerged continent where we could build underwater habitats—and maybe even anchor floating habitats for nonmods. The Council is already talking of building a prototype float-hab as a test. But if the Consolidationists get their way, this tiny corner of the planet is all we'll ever inhabit."

"I'm not a Consolidationist," Emily said. "But I'm not

an Expansionist either. Those are last generation's labels, Mother. Members of my generation just want freedom to live our lives the way we want. Some of us will go into the sciences. Some of us will help build new habitats. But not all of us." She gestured at Amy. "Not these two of us."

"You're being selfish and shortsighted," her father said, softly but forcefully. She knew that voice: he'd used it when she was a little girl and he was very angry with her but trying not to yell. "You have the brains and the grades to go into the hard sciences, and that means you have a duty to do so. A duty to improve life on this planet and help us spread across its surface. A duty to your ancestors, who fled tyranny to build a new life here. A duty to Victor Hansen, who created our race and led us to safety. Freedom!" Now his voice rose, though he still wasn't shouting—quite. "What kind of freedom will you have if the Holy Warriors find us all nicely bunched together for them to exterminate, amusing ourselves with waterdance and amphibian opera? You know your history. You know the Body Purified is still searching for us. All it takes is one scout to stumble on us, and—"

Emily shook her head, hard. "No, I *don't* know that the Body Purified is still looking for us. It's been fifty years on Earth. The Body Purified probably doesn't even exist anymore." She saw her parents' lips tighten but plunged ahead just the same. "All that crap they said they believed. Nobody could force a whole population to swallow that bunk for fifty years. It's insane."

"I'm going to have to have a word with the head of the Education Committee," her father growled. "They seem to have left Earth history off the curriculum. Fifty years is nothing. Empires based on myth and superstition have enslaved entire populations for *centuries*."

"But not in the scientific era," Emily argued. "The neocaliphatists tried early last century. They couldn't do it."

"But they killed millions in the attempt," her mother said. "And that war went on longer than fifty years.

Maybe the Body Purified is doomed to collapse—I hope so—but that doesn't help us if the Holy Warriors show up in orbit. We can't rest. We have to work, to build, to expand—"

Emily shook her head. "I'm not willing to live my whole life in fear of something that will probably never happen. I want to create, entertain, communicate, move people. I want—"

"You want to be a self-centered, naïve, shortsighted eighteen-year-old," her father said. He looked at Amy. "And twenty-year-old." Amy said nothing, leaving the argument to Emily, as she tended to do when family disagreements broke out. "I understand that. Perfectly natural. But just because I understand it doesn't mean I can condone it.

"And there's another thing, Emily." He leaned forward and shook an accusing finger at her. "Underwater dance is Selkie-only."

"Well, of course it is," she said impatiently. "You can't expect landlings to do it. Even with scuba gear they're about as clumsy as—"

"It's exclusionary," her father said flatly. "It can't be enjoyed by *nonmods*." He emphasized the word. "It's not helping to unify Marseguro society, it's driving a wedge down the middle of it. It's just another example of the kind of mind-set that's creeping into the younger generation of Selkies . . . the same mind-set that led you and your friends to think throwing some poor nonmod off the pier was the height of harmless humor.

"It's a mind-set that will destroy Marseguro if it isn't checked. There are no second-class citizens on Marseguro. We're modified humans, but we're still human, and modified doesn't mean 'better.' That's as bad in its own way as the Body Purified's doctrine that moddies are subhuman at best, nonhuman at worst. Pursuing Selkie-only 'arts' like underwater dancing is counterproductive and antisocial, and I won't have a daughter of mine lending credence to it." He turned his attention to Amy. "And amphibian opera is no better. Nonmods may be

able to appreciate the above-water part of the performance, but not the underwater part. They can't even
hear most of it.

"No. You are both free to pursue your artistic endeav-
ors, of course—your mother and I enjoy and encourage
your creative efforts, you know that—but pursue them
as your sole careers? Out of the question. Our society is
not large enough or well-established enough to allow our
best and brightest to fritter away their talents on frivolities of any kind, much less frivolities that exclude half
our population."

Emily felt her face flush. She'd always blushed easily.
Her father used to call her a Selkie thermometer, teasing
that he could measure her anger or embarrassment by
how high the red wash of blood rose in her face. She
hoped he remembered, because if she were a thermometer, she was sure the top of her head would have burst
by now. "Do you have any idea how pretentious you
sound, Dad?" she said, keeping her voice at a reasonably
normal volume, but only with an effort. "We aren't a
totalitarian state, remember? Society doesn't get a say in
what I do with my life, as long as I don't hurt anybody
else. And just because you're my father doesn't mean
you get a say, either.

"And don't give me that bottomgunk about 'excluding
half our population.' To begin with, last I heard, the
landlings," she emphasized *her* term for the nonmods,
"made up less than a quarter of the population, and
that's falling all the time. So why shouldn't there be some
arts designed for the majority? The landlings are free to
create arts that Selkies can't appreciate—I don't mind a
bit. Why should they care what Selkies are doing out in
the wet where they can barely function anyway?" She
pushed herself away from the table in a welter of foam.
"You're just trying to make me feel guilty, and I'm not
buying into it. I *don't* feel guilty. And I don't think
you're grasping the reality of this conversation, either.
I'm not *asking* your permission to specialize in waterdance. I'm *telling* you that's what I'm doing. Subject

closed. And I'm out of here. Have a nice dinner." She whirled, intending to make a grand exit by plunging straight down through the underwater access, flicking her webbed feet in her parents' faces, but the waiter had chosen that moment to come in through the half-dry access and stood chest-deep in the water right behind her with two floating trays of appetizers her parents must have ordered before she swam in. She stared at him; he stared at her. "Excuse me, miss—" he began.

"Freeze off," she snarled at him. She ducked past him, tipping a tray of unidentifiable tidbits into the water as she did so, and dove out of sight just as her father and mother said, "Now see here!" and "You listen to me!" in a perfect melding of stereotypical parental outrage.

The water cut off their words. She swam toward the glowing globe that marked the exit into the swimways, trailing bubbles, furious with her parents and equally furious with herself for having lost her temper.

"Emily, wait!" someone chirped in Selkie. Almost at the exit, she backwatered and flipped to see Amy undulating toward her. Her sister stopped and floated a few feet away. "I'm sorry," she said. "I didn't mean to surprise them like that. I thought you'd already told them."

You didn't think at all, Emily thought. *You never do.* But that was Amy, and Emily doubted she would ever change. "Not your fault. They would have reacted the same no matter how we broached the subject. They're so . . ." She couldn't find a word in Selkie—or English, either—and finally settled for ". . . . conservative."

"They'll come around?" Amy said, but she added the double click at the end that turned it into a question.

"Sure," Emily said. "We're their only daughters. What are they going to do, disown us?" *They* were *awfully mad,* she thought uneasily. *But they wouldn't really . . .* "The worst thing is that I stormed out before the food came. And I'm starving. I spent an hour hauling algae sample buckets out of the hold of a ship before I came."

Amy blinked. "Why?"

Emily shook her head, a gesture that still meant the

same for Selkies as for landlings. "Never mind. A bunch of my friends are probably still at Freddy Fish's. How about a weedtickler burger?"

Amy nodded. "Sounds good to me."

"Let's go." Emily flipped again and dove through the exit. "We'll talk to Mom and Dad later," she chirped. "After they've cooled down."

They will *cool down,* she thought.

Won't they?

Chapter 4

SAMUEL CHEVELDEOFF ARRIVED in the antechamber of the Holy Office precisely at 1900 hours. It was twice the size of the waiting area for his own office, far more lavishly decorated, with ancient and priceless paintings and sculptures—and empty of staff or supplicants.

No witnesses, Cheveldeoff thought. He didn't think the Right Hand intended to have him arrested, though certainly the Chosen Elite, Holy Warriors loyal only to the Avatar, would have no compunction carrying out such an order. His own loyalists wouldn't stand for it, and at the tricky time of succession, that just might trigger a ruinous civil war that nobody wanted . . . at least, not yet.

No. The Right Hand simply wanted this meeting to be private.

Cheveldeoff planted himself in front of the massive black doors leading into the Holy Office, folded his arms, and waited to be admitted. He half-expected to be held outside for a lengthy period of time, just to emphasize that his otherwise massive authority meant nothing here, but in fact the doors opened less than a minute after he entered the antechamber.

The Right Hand himself greeted him. A slender man with short-cropped gray hair and a neatly trimmed mustache, Karl Rasmusson smiled and held out his hand. "Come in, come in, Sam. Good to see you."

"Karl," Cheveldeoff acknowledged, shaking hands. He

felt off-balance; he'd expected a frosty reception. *What's going on?* It was his job to know the answer to that question, and right now, he didn't.

Rasmusson led him, not to the Avatar's imposing desk in its semicircular, vidscreen-lined niche at the far end of the colonnaded-and-vaulted room, but to a side area with a simple table of polished stone set between two couches covered with buttery black leather. "Drink?" Rasmusson asked, going to the small bar set against the wall.

"Soda and lime," Cheveldeoff said. He wanted his wits sharp.

Rasmusson fixed the drink, poured a glass of white wine for himself, and came back to the table. "I've been wanting to talk to you in private for some time now, Sam," the Right Hand said, handing Cheveldeoff his drink.

Cheveldeoff sipped it. *Here it comes,* he thought.

Rasmusson sat down on the opposite couch, leaned back, and took an appreciative sip of his wine. "I've decided to back you in the upcoming election."

Cheveldeoff had trained himself for decades not to react to sudden surprises like that, so he didn't choke on his soda—quite. He swallowed hard, though, before setting the glass down. Then he leaned forward and locked eyes with Rasmusson. "Why?"

Rasmusson looked away, took another sip of wine, set it on the table, and finally met his gaze again. "Because I do not believe it is God's will that Ashok Shridhar become Avatar at this time."

Cheveldeoff waited to see if Rasmusson would add to that. When he didn't, he repeated, "Why?"

Rasmusson smiled slightly. "I have my reasons. They relate to you only tangentially, however, and therefore I will not share them. In any event, I did not ask you here merely to tell you you have my—entirely unofficial, of course—support. I asked you here to tell you that merely having my support is not enough to guarantee your election."

Cheveldeoff couldn't help it; he blinked. Then he sat back in the couch. "But my count—"

"Your estimate is flawed," the Right Hand said. "Shridhar's influence reaches farther than you know. Six of those who have told you they will support you will actually, come the vote, support Shridhar. I believe I can . . . persuade . . . perhaps two of those to return to your fold, and believe I can turn two currently in Shridhar's camp in your favor without him being aware of it—well, until the vote, of course. But if you will do the math . . ."

Cheveldeoff already had. The Council of the Faithful had twenty-four members. He had been certain of the support of ten of them, and had thought Shridhar had the solid support of nine, leaving five undecided. But according to Rasmusson, he had only four certain votes. The Right Hand promised him another four, putting him only at eight. Shridhar would have eleven. "The undecideds?"

"Are still undecided. But I believe three, possibly four, are leaning toward Shridhar."

Cheveldeoff felt a familiar sensation; cold rage. "What do you want me to do?" he growled.

"I want you to win the election," Rasmusson said. "But to do so, you need a major success, something that will shift Councillors to your side through fear that the people will erupt in the regions they personally supervise if you are not elected. In short, Sam, you need to become a hero—a Julius Caesar, if you will." The Right Hand sipped more wine. "The question is, how."

Cheveldeoff grimaced. It was all very well to tell him to come up with a major success, but if he could do that on demand, he would have done it already, wouldn't he?

Every continent had its hot spot. The Middle East was the worst, of course, but parts of China were almost as bad and even sections of the Rockies were complete no-go zones for Holy Warriors at the moment. "Central America has quieted down," he pointed out. *Mainly because hardly anyone is left alive down there,* he thought, but didn't add. The Right Hand had personally approved that particular pacification program, after all.

"It has," the Right Hand agreed. "But if you'll forgive my saying so, a quiet Central America is unlikely to impress anyone much beyond the few Neo-Incans who still survive down there." He put his now-empty wineglass down and leaned forward, hands folded, elbows on knees. His eyes narrowed. "If we cannot have a security victory—and things do not look any better for such a victory among the colonies, do they . . . ?" He paused.

"No," Cheveldeoff admitted after a moment. The Holy Warriors had so far barely penetrated the New Mars system, where the residents appeared to have built a highly effective space navy and system defense grid, and several ships had been heavily damaged in the attempt. As well, fresh fighting had just broken out thirty light-years in the other direction from Earth on Tuin, which had theoretically been Purified for a decade. "Our space forces are spread thin right now. Even to refocus their energies on one of the remaining colonies on the Unpurified list would take months."

"So I thought," Rasmusson said. "So, if we cannot have a security victory, I believe we need a propaganda victory. I believe we need to 'discover,' try, and execute . . . the clone of Victor Hansen."

Cheveldeoff stiffened. "No!" he said. "We've worked too many years—"

"With nothing to show for it," the Right Hand snapped, his geniality suddenly discarded like the camouflaged cloak Cheveldeoff had always known it to be. "The first clone went mad. This one has done nothing, and most likely will go as mad as his 'father' when Hansen's gene-bomb goes off.

"He'll be worse than useless then, so I say we use him while we still can: grab him, try him, shoot him—openly, publicly, with full-press media coverage—and make sure you get the credit. And with that credit . . . the votes you need to become the third Avatar: Samuel the First."

Cheveldeoff sat very still. He didn't object to having

Hansen arrested if it furthered his own ends . . . but he did object to throwing away years of investment with nothing to show for it. Especially at the very moment that investment might be about to pay a dividend.

He hadn't intended to tell the Right Hand what Hansen had told him just hours earlier. Information was power, and by instinct, he kept as much of it to himself as possible. But now . . .

He cleared his throat. "It's possible . . . just barely possible . . . that I might be able to offer up something rather more grand than a late-blooming clone of Victor Hansen." He had looked down at the thick red carpet while he thought; now he looked up and locked eyes with Rasmusson again. "I may be able to offer you Hansen's Selkies themselves . . . a whole planet of moddies to be Purified."

Rasmusson had worked at least as long as Cheveldeoff to learn to hide his reactions, but three quick blinks betrayed him. "Tell me more."

Cheveldeoff obliged.

Richard Hansen hadn't expected much to change after his meeting with Cheveldeoff. Sure, he had a vector, but one half a century old. All it really meant was that he had doubled the amount of data he had to search through, though at least it was *different* data. . . .

But something did change. The morning after his meeting with Cheveldeoff, he descended to his barely-tall-enough-to-stand-up office in the basement only to find movers stripping everything out of it. For a moment he thought he'd been fired, but then his supervisor explained. "You've been bumped out of here," he said. John Riedl knew all about Hansen's dubious ancestry and had seldom missed an opportunity to belittle his underling for it. Now, it appeared, he didn't dare, which probably explained why his already hollow-cheeked face looked very much like that of someone sucking a lemon. "Cheveldeoff's orders. New office. Three floors up. Follow your stuff." To Richard's astonishment, he offered his hand, and too bemused to do otherwise, Richard took it. "Good luck." Reidl then dropped Richard's hand like wet garbage and disappeared into his office.

Richard took his advice. By late morning he was ensconced in the central office in a suite of rooms, into which his new staff—staff!—members were being installed. By then, at least, he had a better idea of what was going on, though he still couldn't believe it.

Cheveldeoff had left him a private vidmail. "Congratulations," the Archdeacon said in it, and actually smiled. "I have decided your breakthrough warrants full-scale exploration. You and your new staff are to sift through every scrap of data you can find pertaining to the sectors of space lying along the vector you identified. I am confident that if the Selkies are out there, you'll find them. I'll expect weekly reports. Good luck." Then, almost as an afterthought, "Oh, and you are hereby promoted to the rank of Deacon, Third Rank. Your pay will be adjusted accordingly. Again, congratulations."

And that was that. It took a week to get the new staff settled in, assign tasks, begin refining search algorithms; more days before really serious analysis could take place. And then . . .

. . . nothing. Three weeks of nothing, so far. And Cheveldeoff, at their last meeting, had made it very clear to Richard that "nothing" was not an acceptable outcome in exchange for the huge amount of manpower and money Body Security had invested in him. "Time is of the essence," Cheveldeoff said. "To both of us."

Exactly what he meant by that he didn't explain, and Richard certainly wasn't going to ask.

He yawned hugely and stretched. Three o'clock in the morning, and he was the only one in the office. Why hadn't they found anything? How had Grandpa Hansen managed to hide his tracks so thoroughly? *Someone* must have stumbled on them in all these years. . . .

He knew they were out there. He couldn't explain how he knew it, but he had no doubt that the Selkies' planet lay somewhere within the cone of space suggested by the vector. Sometimes it seemed to him that the planet's location was on the tip of his tongue, like someone's name he couldn't quite place . . . but that was nuts. And yet . . .

He rubbed his forehead. He hadn't been sleeping well: more bizarre dreams in which he took the role of Victor Hansen. Just last night he'd spent a large portion of one dream giving a lecture on genesculpting to a large audience in some vaguely tropical location. In the dream he'd known exactly what he'd been talking about. When he'd woken up, what little he could remember of what his dream self had said in the lecture meant nothing to him.

And as if that weren't bad enough, he'd also been having headaches recently. Tonight he had a doozy. *Time to call it quits. I'm not accomplishing anything.*

The computer had just proffered a new star map. Richard leaned forward, intending to close down his workstation . . . but then he stopped. Something, some thought or feeling he couldn't quite grasp, made him peer more closely at the star map. An old Class A star centered it. He looked at the coordinates. No . . . those weren't quite right. . . .

He tapped keys, adjusting the string of numbers. No . . . no . . .

Pain stabbed his head so sharply it frightened him, then quickly subsided. Those numbers . . . looked *right,* in a way he couldn't explain.

This is crazy, he thought. But the star that *now* centered the display had codes beside it that cross-referenced to the databases they'd been searching. The codes indicated that the algorithm only rated the connection as "of potential interest," but it couldn't hurt to look.

"Computer," he said. "Display details of data associated with star at coordinates . . ." He read them off.

The screen changed. He rubbed tired eyes that didn't want to focus, then squinted at the small print. Apparently an automated freighter several light-years from the star in question had picked up a weak signal from its direction. The signal had not triggered any particular action on the freighter's part, since it did not match any current distress codes. In fact, if the freighter hadn't been an ancient piece of crap, still running its original communications equipment, it might not have picked up the signal at all: it arrived as a crude null-brane pulse in a region of the branefield no one had used for communications for a couple of decades. The freighter's computer had flagged the signal as random noise, but logged it nevertheless.

"Computer, download signal, analyze per standard search parameters."

Richard still didn't expect anything. He certainly didn't expect what flashed up on screen almost instantly: PARAMETERS MET. ESTIMATED PROBABILITY 100 PERCENT.

"Parameters met," the computer said redundantly. "Estimated probability 100 percent."

For a long moment, Richard just stared; then he remembered to breathe. His heart raced. *Calm down,* he told himself. *It's not the first hit you've seen, and they've all been false alarms so far.*

Which was true, but he'd never seen, or *expected* to see, a probability estimated at one hundred percent. In fact, the way he'd written the search parameters, he wouldn't have expected to see a rating like that unless—

"Computer, display intercepted message."

It appeared on his screen, and his heart skipped one beat, then another, then raced even faster.

—*unless a transmission came from the Rivers of Babylon herself.*

He opened his mouth to tell the computer to contact Cheveldeoff, then closed it again without speaking. *Double-check,* he thought. *Triple-check. You don't want to wake up the Archdeacon of Body Security only to find out you've been duped by some interstellar con man.*

Not that he thought that likely: you didn't set off something with the transmission power of a ship emergency beacon just for laughs. But he ran the checks anyway. It took him another half hour, and by the time he finished, his heart no longer pounded in his ears, but his excitement soared. Everything matched: the bizarre branefield frequency, the encrypted header attached to the message, even the slightly unfocused quality of the transmission, exactly what the computer predicted a signal generated by fifty-year-old equipment *should* look like.

And it had originated from the very star whose coordinates he had somehow intuited, a star he might never have looked at closely if not for that strange sense of *knowing* he should look there.

I don't believe in ESP. I don't believe in magic. And neither does Cheveldeoff.

He doesn't need to know how I found the star.

"Computer," he said at last. "Contact Archdeacon Cheveldeoff. Priority call."

The opening chords of Beethoven's Fifth Symphony woke Cheveldeoff from a sound sleep. He answered the vidcall prepared to bite off the head of whomever had thought anything short of armed revolution worth waking him at that ungodly hour, but when Richard Hansen told him what he thought he had discovered, Cheveldeoff's sleep inertia vanished. Two hours later, he sat in his office at the same table he and Hansen played chess on every month, *sans* chessboard. Three of the walls displayed the Italian villa interior, but the fourth showed a block of repeating text, accompanied by graphs and lists of numbers providing technical details of the transmission's properties.

Hansen looked rumpled and bleary-eyed: he obviously hadn't been to bed at all. He'd been waiting for Cheveldeoff in the antechamber when Cheveldeoff arrived, and hadn't even sat down before launching into an explanation of what they were looking at. "The signal wasn't strong enough to reach Earth itself," he said, pointing to a series of numbers that meant nothing to Cheveldeoff. "A freighterbot en route from Stableford to Freerock picked it up. It recorded it and logged it, but didn't flag it as anything interesting. When it sent its next data dump to its owners on Freerock, our listening buoy intercepted it."

He's leaving something out, Cheveldeoff thought. *I wonder . . .*

"What made you look at it, then, if it wasn't flagged?"

Hansen looked uncomfortable. "Desperation, I guess. We haven't found anything in any of the obvious places to look, so I just decided to dig a little deeper."

"So it was a hunch."

"I guess you could call it that."

"Interesting," Cheveldeoff said, and meant it. *The gene-bomb's gone off . . . but he hasn't gone mad.*

Not yet, anyway.

"There's no doubt this originated from Hansen's ship?"

Hansen shook his head. "None. I've checked it every possible way, and everything matches."

Cheveldeoff looked at the text of the message, which was less than informative: STARSHIP *RIVERS OF BAB-YLON* REQUESTS ASSISTANCE. THIS BEACON WILL RUN CONTINUOUSLY. STARSHIP *RIVERS OF BABYLON* REQUESTS ASSISTANCE. THIS BEA-CON WILL RUN CONTINUOUSLY. . . . "How long has this beacon been active?"

"That's the strange thing," Hansen admitted. He pointed at another of the analysis fields. "According to the message header, the beacon was activated less than a week ago."

Cheveldeoff lifted an eyebrow. "They've been sitting out there for fifty years and suddenly decided to call for help?"

"Maybe," Hansen said. "Maybe somebody tripped the beacon by accident. After fifty years, they might not even have known what it was. They could be living in primitive conditions. They might not even be technological anymore."

Cheveldeoff nodded. "Hmmm." He read the message

again. "So we know they're out there. But can you pinpoint where?"

"I already have." Cheveldeoff had long ago given
Hansen limited voice access rights to his office computer
so he could display any files he needed Cheveldeoff to
see. Now Hansen raised his voice. "Computer, display
image Hansen Two."

The display changed to a standard star map. A red
circle highlighted a Class M star at its center. "According
to the freighterbot, the transmission originated here."

Cheveldeoff leaned forward. "What do we know about
that system?"

"Nothing," Hansen said. "And that's weird, because
everything around it was surveyed long ago, before the
Purification and the Day of Salvation, in the first few
years of branespace travel. I can tell you, at a minimum,
the number, sizes, and orbits of every planet in every
system within fifty light-years of this one. But there's
no indication this system was ever surveyed."

"Or else the system was surveyed, but somebody tampered with the computer records," Cheveldeoff said. A
surge of excitement raced through him. *My God, he may
actually have found them . . .*

*. . . and I may have just been handed my key to the
Holy Office. I'll be the man who completed the
Purification.*

Beyond what it would do for *him,* Purifying the human
race by destroying abominations like Hansen's moddies
was a sacred duty, part of the constant battle to please
God Itself, so that It did not again turn Its wrath against
humanity. Cheveldeoff believed in that doctrine, of
course—the miracle of Salvation Day left little room for
nonbelief—but as Archdeacon of Body Security he also
had more secular concerns, and it was the prospect of
finally and forcefully demonstrating the futility of rebel-
lion that excited him most, never mind the welcome
boost it would give his own ambitions. He knew full well
that Victor Hansen's thus-far successful hijacking and
flight had inspired and continued to inspire would-be rev-

olutionaries of all stripes. Purifying Hansen's secret planet would be a graphic demonstration that "You can run, but you can't hide," and could well lead to the rolling up of any number of the minor rebellions constantly simmering just beneath the surface of their rigidly controlled society. For every true revolutionary there were others balanced on a knife edge of uncertainty and fear, and the destruction of Hansen's Hijackers might well push them into turning on their compatriots to save their own skins from a suddenly seemingly omnipotent Body Security. "Richard, you're a genius," Cheveldeoff said. "Computer, record message to Grand Deacon Ellers."

"Ready," the computer said.

"Computer, message follows: Grand Deacon, report to my office at 0700 hours with whatever additional staff you need to plan the Purification of a rogue human colony. Message ends. Computer, send."

"Sent," the computer confirmed.

Cheveldeoff smiled at Richard. "If this pans out, Richard, I think we can safely say you've desmirched the escutcheon of your family."

"It will pan out, sir," Hansen said. "I'm sure of it." He cleared his throat. "Sir . . ." He paused. "Sir, request permission to accompany the Holy Warriors on their Purification mission."

Cheveldeoff looked into the projected flames of the Italian villa's fireplace, thinking. Hansen waited silently, watching him. *Well, why not?* Cheveldeoff thought. *If the gene-bomb really has gone off, and the gene therapy keeps him sane, he may have more "hunches" that will serve us well. If Victor Hansen's mad scheme works out fully and he becomes a mental as well as physical copy of Hansen, then he'll be even more valuable as an intelligence asset already in custody and available for interrogation. And if he simply becomes unstable, like his "father" . . . well, what better place to dispose of him quietly than within a combat force in a war zone?*

He looked up. "Permission granted. You will accompany the Holy Warriors as my personal observer."

Hansen's face lit up. "I'd like that, sir!"

So easy, Cheveldeoff thought. *People are so easily manipulated. An implied threat, an occasional treat . . . they're no different from dogs. And as Avatar . . . I'll have my hand on the leash. Earth will be pacified. I'll bring the colonies under control. And after that . . . well, it's a big galaxy. We can and will spread the human race to many more planets.*

God will be mollified. And even if It isn't, It will have lots of planets to choose from if It feels it needs to destroy one to get our attention.

"Good," he said out loud. "When Grand Deacon Ellers arrives, I'll introduce you. And feel free to make any suggestions you may have during the planning sessions, Richard. Your input will be invaluable."

"Yes, sir! And . . . thank you, sir."

"Grand Deacon Ellers will be here in less than three hours, and you look like hell. Go get cleaned up, maybe take a nap, and I'll see you here at 0700."

"Yes, sir. Thank you again."

Cheveldeoff watched him leave, and thought again, *So easy.*

And then he activated his secure comm circuit to the Right Hand, who answered looking as if he'd been up for hours. *Probably a computer-generated image.*

"Yes?" said Rasmusson.

"We've got them," Cheveldeoff said. "Hansen came through." He explained succinctly. "Ellers is coming here at 0700 to begin planning."

Rasmusson (or his CG image) looked thoughtful. "You know that Ellers is secretly supporting Shridhar's bid for the Avatarship."

"I know," Cheveldeoff said. "But he's the Grand Deacon in command. There's no way to *not* involve him. And from my past dealings with him, I don't believe he will sabotage a mission as important as this for political reasons."

"I hope you're right, Archdeacon." The Right Hand nodded. "Well, this is excellent news. Keep me informed."

He moved as if to switch off communications, then paused. "And move quickly, Sam. News of the Avatar's condition is leaking out. Just rumors, so far. We're countering with misinformation about a viral attack that has left him bedridden but still fully functional and in command. But we can't keep a lid on this forever. Eventually . . . within a few weeks, at most . . . we will have to pull the plug and convene the Council of the Faithful.

"Finish your business by then, Sam. Or start making your retirement plans . . . for somewhere far, far off Earth."

The screen went blank.

High stakes, Cheveldeoff thought, then smiled.

He'd always been a gambling man.

Richard left Cheveldeoff's office filled with elation. *At last!* he thought. *At last.* All his life, Victor Hansen's successful escape from the Body had hung around his neck like Jacob Marley's chains. Now he felt like Ebenezer Scrooge on the Christmas morning after the long, haunted night.

Not that anyone legally celebrated Christmas anymore, of course.

His elation persisted through the week of planning that followed, reinforced every time someone asked his opinion. Having the favor of Cheveldeoff, he discovered, made all the difference in the world. Even when they ultimately discounted his suggestions, people listened to them respectfully and explained why they thought they wouldn't work. But a few of his suggestions *were* followed. He'd made a study of his grandfather's abominations, and had already amassed much of the information about the Selkies' abilities that the Grand Deacon needed to know as he outfitted his troops and ship.

"They're not true merpeople," he explained during one session in Ellers' office, as he and the Grand Deacon looked at an image of one of the Selkies. Richard had studied it for years. Maybe that was why it no longer disgusted him as much as it once had. Green eyes without eyelashes, almost twice the size of normal human eyes, peered out beneath naked bony brows and a shaved skull in a face almost albino-white. The nose with its two slitlike nostrils made a barely-noticeable bump in that pale oval, and the ears were no more prominent. The mouth, oddly, appeared completely normal, and it seemed wrong that such an unmistakably human feature should appear in such an inhuman visage. And then there were the gills: three slits on each side of the neck, open in the photo, displaying a pink interior that made Richard think of . . . well, he didn't like to think about what it made him think of.

Alien . . . horrible . . . monstrous. Richard remembered thinking that about the Selkie. But somehow, today, he saw a kind of beauty in the strange face he'd never appreciated before. It wasn't a mutilated human being, after all, but a human-based creature designed—by his grandfather!—to live in an environment alien to normal humans.

An astonishing achievement, when you thought about it. *I wish we didn't have to . . .*

He cut that thought off. He couldn't think that, couldn't let a hint of those kinds of doubts infiltrate his thoughts. The Body did not allow doubt. God did not allow doubt. And while the Purity Watchers might not be able to read his thoughts . . . yet . . . God certainly could.

The Selkies were abominations. Their world had to be Purified. *End of story.*

But that stray thought worried him. Where had it come from?

He continued his mini-lecture. "They can't eat underwater, for example, and they need to drink fresh water just like a normal human. That means that although they may have underwater buildings—if they've got any technology to speak of at all after fifty years—those buildings must have breathable air in them. That means they're most likely to be located in shallow water close to shore, and to have some kind of air intake."

"Which means we can easily find most of them," Ellers said. "Excellent." A trim, gray-haired, square-jawed man, he was the very model of a modern Holy Warrior, like something off of a recruiting poster. He wore a light blue short-sleeved casual uniform. Beneath the skin of the inside of his left forearm, a nanodisplay crawled with ever-changing data. "Anything else?"

"They can function on land, but if they stay out of the water too long their skin and gills dehydrate. I understand that if their gills dry out, the pain is excruciating. Eventually, they die."

Ellers made another note. "Could be useful for interrogation," he said. "What about those big eyes of theirs?"

"Very good underwater vision," Richard said. "But they pay for it on land. They have a third eyelid that improves their vision underwater. On land, they sometimes close it to keep their eyes from drying out. It's transparent, but their vision suffers—they have difficulty seeing things at a distance. They have excellent night vision, at least over the short- to mid-range—much better than ours. On the other hand, a bright, sunny day is quite unpleasant for them; their eyes can't adjust."

"Hearing?" Ellers asked. "They don't seem to have much in the way of ears."

Richard nodded. "My grand—um, Dr. Hansen deliberately atrophied their ears, modifying them so they're more like dolphin ears. They hear much better than normal humans in the water, but worse on land, since their ears don't concentrate sound waves the way normal humans' do. However, they can hear well into what we'd consider the ultrasonic."

"Like dogs."

"Something like that."

"Sense of smell?"

"Probably unchanged. Their noses were modified so their nostrils can be tightly sealed for diving, but smell wasn't considered important for underwater life, so Dr.

Hansen didn't make any other changes when he sculpted the genome."

"What about physical strength?"

"They're very strong. An average Selkie is as a strong as, say, a champion weight lifter. A strong Selkie is more like a gorilla or orangutan. Hand to hand, almost any human will be totally outmatched."

"Intelligence?" said Ellers.

Richard blinked. "They're human," he said. "Normal human distribution of IQs, I presume. I don't have any data on that."

Ellers grunted. "I wouldn't call them human," he said, and Richard felt a chill, remembering his almost admiring thoughts about the Selkies moments before. *What's wrong with me?* But Ellers dropped the subject. "Anything else you can think of that might help us plan?"

Richard had saved the best for last. "I've heard you have some kind of tracker device that's DNA-based," he said carefully. Common knowledge, really, but within the Body Purified, as he knew very well, quite a bit of knowledge was both common and restricted at the same time.

Ellers grunted agreement.

"I have a copy of the Selkie genome."

Ellers head jerked up. "Where did you get *that*?"

"It was in some old personal data files," he said. He hoped Ellers would jump to the logical conclusion that those old personal data files had belonged to Richard's grandfather. In fact, they had belonged to his father, who had hidden them very carefully, deeply encrypted, on his computer. Richard, looking through the family data for anything that might be useful to the coming campaign, had found the file, biometrically sealed, and on a whim had offered the computer some skin cells. To his astonishment, it had accepted his sacrifice and opened all of his father's sealed files to him.

There he had found the Selkie DNA, and a great many more of his grandfather's scientific notes. Tracing back, Richard had discovered that his father had managed to retrieve them from encrypted data stores hidden inside public databases. Exactly how he had known how to access them, Richard didn't understand. From the time stamps, his father had accessed them just days before he had made his fatal leap from the skyscraper.

I should probably hand everything over to Cheveldeoff, he thought uneasily. *In fact, I* know *I should . . .*

But not yet. As Cheveldeoff himself said, knowledge was power. Knowledge you had that nobody else had was the most powerful of all.

That was rationalization, though, and deep down he knew it. The real reason he hadn't given any of the information he had found in his father's records to Cheveldeoff was that, in some strange way, it simply felt like it would be *wrong.* He didn't understand why, but there it was.

"That will be very helpful indeed," Ellers said. "Transmit it to me right away. We're building some special bots that should be able to take full advantage of it."

A few days later, early in the morning, Richard stepped through the door of his nondescript apartment in a nondescript building. He paused in the hallway to make sure the Godseye surveillance camera got a clear shot of him, then headed for the elevator, frowning.

He'd done everything he could to make the mission a success, but he'd almost fatally overstepped his authority at one point during a meeting between Ellers and Cheveldeoff to which he had been invited as Cheveldeoff's soon-to-be observer. Ellers planned to take a single ship, and Richard had wondered out loud if one would be enough. Ellers' response had been withering. "It's a Lebedoff-class multipurpose assault craft. It carries two hundred troopers plus their equipment, three fully armed assault craft and four unarmed cargo/personnel shuttles. It even has an Orbital Bombardment System. The moddies can't have much weaponry, and what they do have must be decades out of date. It's enough."

"They might have been armed by one of the colonies,"

Richard said, even while part of his brain yelled at him to *shut up.*

"Enough," Cheveldeoff growled. "Grand Deacon Ellers is the military commander. You're just a civilian observer. Your opinion has been noted."

Rebuked, Richard hadn't said anything more about it. *But I'd still feel better if we had a couple more ships with us,* he thought. Especially since he suspected the Grand Deacon would have preferred to have a couple more ships, too, but simply didn't have them. "News" accounts were heavily censored and widely thought to only incidentally correspond to the facts, but some of the messages Richard had monitored made him think that the New Martians were having rather more success keeping the main Holy Warrior fleet at bay than the Earth populace realized. As a Security analyst, Richard also knew, though very few other civilians would, that the bulk of Earth's remaining ships were en route to Tuin to deal with the new uprising there. And the system he'd pinpointed as the moddies' likely hiding place lay in a different direction than either of them.

Richard emerged from the elevator into the gray and dingy lobby. The Penitents, whose forced labor supposedly brought them closer to the Truth while benefiting society at the same time, were not the most diligent of workers, even when their overseers liberally applied the electric lash, but through the smeared and flyspecked windows, Richard could see the taxibot waiting in the predawn twilight.

He walked through the sliding doors, his large black suitcase following obediently like a well-trained dog. "Luggage, trunk," he said to it, and it rolled around to the front of the taxi, which obligingly opened its hood and extended a ramp like a black rubber tongue. The luggage rolled up into the trunk and the hood chomped down on it, the "tongue" slipping back inside at the same time. The side door swung up, and Richard climbed into the gray interior and settled on the cracked vinyl. The door closed, the electric motor in the back hummed, and the taxibot rolled away from the apartment building down wet, empty streets of potholed gray asphalt, very different from the sparkling blue tile of the Body Purified's walled city-within-a-city where Richard worked.

Richard could have counted on one hand the number of other vehicles he saw on the way to the spaceport. The City of God, like most large cities on the Purified Earth, had a dusk-to-dawn curfew, so only those with special clearance, like Richard this morning, were allowed out before sunrise. Most of the windows in the run-down office buildings they passed were dark, and there were few residential structures along their route, so the overall effect was of a city where all the people had somehow evaporated.

The illusion shattered as they turned a corner onto a long boulevard lined with walnut trees, and the spaceport came in sight. Brilliant lights struck reflections off the silvered sides of half a dozen ships in launch cradles and lit up the white sides of the support buildings like the midday sun. Richard leaned forward. He'd seen the spaceport all his life, but always from a distance; no one could get within a kilometer of it without good reason, and until today, he'd never had that reason.

Today, though, he'd not only be visiting it, he'd be departing it . . . and departing Earth.

He'd never thought much about the possibility of leaving Earth; had never *dared* think much about it. Not that thinking about it was a crime, but talking about it, writing about it, or encouraging others to think, talk, or write about it *were*, because doing so encouraged people to entertain the possibility that there might be a better life somewhere than life on the Purified Earth, and theologically, that was heretical nonsense. The Body Purified was working toward making Earth perfect, to ensure that God would never again threaten the world with destruction from the heavens. Things therefore had to be better now than they had been yesterday, and would be better still tomorrow. The sole duty of humanity was to make the world into the paradise God Itself intended it to be. Leaving Earth would be abandoning that great calling. For most people, it could never be permitted.

But as of today, Richard was not "most people," and as his taxibot rolled through the main gate of the spaceport and he saw *BPS Sanctification* rising above its loading cradle like a giant beached whale of silver metal, he could think the unthinkable at last:

I wonder what's out there?

He smiled. Well, one thing he knew was out there was the planet where his grandfather's hubristic creations had gone to ground—or water, in their case. *They don't know what's coming.*

Five minutes later the taxibot rolled to a halt by a ramp leading up to the crew entry elevator in the landing cradle. A Holy Warrior stood guard, somehow managing to look both bored and alert at the same time. He glanced at a wrist display on the forearm guard of his navy-blue body armor as Richard climbed out of the taxi and waited for his luggage to join him. Richard glanced up and saw the telltale bump of a Godseye camera housing above the door and knew he'd been scanned, vetted and—he assumed, since he wasn't being arrested—approved to board.

While his taxibot opened its mechanical mouth and extended its rubberized tongue for his luggage to roll down, Richard glanced right. Although one of the landing cradle's huge concrete buttresses blocked his view in that direction, he could hear the rumble of the heavy machinery hauling equipment up the much larger ramp to the giant elevators making trip after trip into the hold of *Sanctification*. The taxibot had brought him past some of that equipment, armored personnel carriers, boxes of ammunition and power packs, aerial bots and folded-wing ultralights, mysterious crates and boxes of uncertain origin and content, several boats, and at least three subs, two small, one fairly large. It all had to be secured for both takeoff and the zero-G conditions that would prevail in much of the ship thereafter. Much of it would be prestowed in the large transport shuttles that would take it to the planet's surface . . . after the assault craft had done their work, of course.

His luggage bumped against his leg as though impatient, and Richard turned his attention back to the crew-entry elevator. He climbed the ramp, luggage following a respectful meter behind. The guard gave him a slight nod, then turned his attention back to the expanse of pavement behind him.

Richard entered the elevator, the door closed behind him, and he began his ascent. *A journey of a hundred light-years begins with a single elevator ride,* he thought, and grinned. *And as long as we're thinking in clichés, "today is the first day of the rest of your life."*

If this mission went well, he expected the rest of his life to be much better than his life so far.

He'd dreamed again the night before that he was Victor Hansen. *Well, watch out, Grandpa,* he thought. *Little Ricky is coming for you.*

The funny thing was, even though he knew the old man must have died long ago, Richard had the distinct feeling Grandpa Hansen would be waiting for him.

Three weeks after the disastrous dinner with her parents (who had not mentioned the evening again, but in that subtle-but-definite "we're not talking about this, but don't believe for a second it's over" way of not talking about it that parents had), Emily saw Chris Keating again for the first time since she'd almost drowned him.

She'd come to the Square to meet her friend Dahlia Schaefer. For weeks, they'd been talking about taking a trip to the Schaefer family's deep-water vacation habitat, but somehow they hadn't managed to buy all the supplies they'd needed. A store not far from the Square offered deep-water equipment, and so they'd agreed to visit it together.

Dahlia was late, not unusual for Dahlia, and Emily was early, not unusual for her; she seemed to be constitutionally unable to show up at the agreed-upon time for any appointment, for fear she'd be (unthinkably!) *late*. With time to kill, she'd ducked into the grandly named though in fact rather dinky Marseguro Planetary Museum for a few minutes.

Its dimly lit halls and brightly lit display cases always took her back to her days in landschool, those first six years when Selkies and landlings studied together. They'd made several field trips here. It hadn't changed: it remained, as it had always been, essentially a shrine to the man who had both created the Selkies and brought them and their landling comrades here—Victor Hansen. In fact, most of the museum's exhibits had been brought to Marseguro in his personal effects. So had about half the contents of the library next door, though all of the First Landers had contributed parts of their digital collections as well. The Old Earth section still dominated the Library, though new work by Marseguroites occupied an ever-growing space. *My generation will fill the place with homegrown music and art and literature,* Emily thought defiantly. *Whatever my parents think about people wasting their time on the arts.*

She wandered aimlessly around the museum. Photographs filled one room, images of Hansen on Earth before the asteroid threat brought the Body to power. Tall, black-haired, handsome, he smiled at the camera with confidence whether standing at a lectern, cutting a ribbon, or shaking hands with the President of United Europe. When he wasn't smiling, it was because the camera had caught him in impassioned speechifying, before the World Assembly, the Council of Scientific Advancement, the guests gathered at the Nobel prize ceremony.

Another room provided more background about Hansen. He'd always loved the water; among his effects had been a ship model, a Yankee Clipper, every piece of rigging impeccably strung in fine thread. Here, too, were the handful of hardcopy books he had brought with him: the Bible ("It's the story of God, isn't it?" she remembered John joking on one school trip to the museum. "Hansen thought it was all about *him*."), *Moby Dick,* a first edition of Darwin's *Origin of Species,* a signed copy of *The Double Helix* . . . and a children's book by Arthur Ransome, an early twentieth-century English author, called *We Didn't Mean to Go to Sea,* which Hansen supposedly included at the last minute as he made his plans to seize (with the approval of the Lunar government) the *Rivers of Babylon,* rebuild it, and get it into space before the Body attacked the Moon. "I loved that book as a kid," he'd said (according to the display text). "And the title appealed to my sense of humor, considering what I hoped to do."

Emily entered the next room. At its center, above a projector set on a pedestal, floated a holographic image of the *Rivers of Babylon* as it had been at launch. If she manipulated the projector's controls, she knew, she could peel the image like an onion, and see how its inner core, normally open to allow zero-G travel the length of the ship, had been bulkheaded and sealed and filled with water for the Selkie families fleeing Earth in Hansen's care. Diagrams and photographs around the room detailed the construction work, carried out under impossible deadlines. The Lunar government, which had sheltered so many refugees from Earth—moddies and nonmods alike—had refused to bow to the threats from the Avatar, firmly ensconced on Earth after the Day of Salvation. The Lunarites had provided the necessary materials and workers and had kept Hansen apprised of the massing of warships in Earth orbit.

Only the chaos on Earth in the aftermath of the Day of Salvation had given Hansen and his work crews enough time to get the *Rivers of Babylon* ready. Most of his followers had been employees in his massive gene-sculpting business empire on Earth; other landlings who had joined them had been refugees, or Luna residents, who chose to throw their lot in with him rather than face life under the Body Purified.

A second ship, unmodified, had taken aboard many other refugees who intended to take their chances in the existing colonies.

Emily paused before the last display in the room, a large photograph of that other ship, *Sterling Heights.* The image, captured by the fleeing *Rivers of Babylon,* showed *Sterling Heights,* twice the size of *Rivers of Babylon,* breaking in two in a blossoming sphere of nuclear fire. An instant later there had been nothing left of it.

She shuddered, and decided she'd seen enough. Besides, Dahlia should have arrived by now . . . not that she minded making her friend wait, for a change.

She exited the museum into the Square. *Still no sign of Dahlia,* she thought, surveying it. A deliberately old-fashioned, white-cobblestoned space ringed by the museum, Government House, Town Hall, a couple of restaurants, a tea shop and the library, the Square's most famous attribute was the statue of Victor Hansen at its center, well-watered by a surrounding ring of fountains. Hansen held a model of the double helix of DNA in one hand and a globe of Marseguro in the other, and if his posture seemed a little off-balance and his face bore only a vague resemblance to the photos of Hansen prominently displayed in the nearby museum, well, the multipurpose microfactories they'd brought along hadn't been programmed for artwork and there hadn't been any great sculptors among the crew or passengers of the *Rivers of Babylon,* either.

But there might be in my generation, Emily thought. And then she looked past the statue and saw Chris Keating coming out of Town Hall.

She'd almost forgotten the incident on the pier, but seeing their victim brought it back and she felt her face turn red. For a moment she considered hiding, but then she stiffened both her spine and her resolve and strode to meet him. He had his eyes on a square of hardcopy and didn't see her until she was almost on top of him. When he did, he stopped dead.

"Hi," she said.

He looked so angry she thought for a second he wouldn't respond. But then, almost as though a switch had flicked inside his head, his expression changed. A little smile even flickered across his face—a secret smile, born of some internal amusement, she thought, not really directed at her. "Hello," he said.

"I wanted . . . I just . . ." She cleared her throat. "I saw you and came over to apologize."

"Really." The odd smile flickered again, but his voice remained cool.

"Yes, I . . . it was a stupid thing to do. As Dr. Stanless made clear to us." She grinned. "But in a way you got us back. We spent the next hour hauling out the algae samples you'd come to help with. What a smell!"

"I've never noticed." Still cool.

"Anyway, I just wanted to, um . . ." *I'm getting nothing here,* she thought. "Well . . . no hard feelings?" She winced a little at her own lameness.

"No feelings at all," Chris Keating replied.

Huh? What an odd way to phrase it . . .

"I'm, uh . . ." She cast around for some way to keep the conversation going, even though she really would have preferred it to end, and something said on the pier came back to her. "I'm sorry to hear your mother's been ill. How is she?"

"She died last week." She wouldn't have thought it possible, but Keating's voice grew even colder, and the strange little smile vanished completely.

"Oh, that's . . . uh . . ." Her voice trailed off. "I'm sorry," she finally said, again. *Sorry in so many ways,* she thought. *Sorry we pushed you in the water, and just about as sorry I came over to apologize for it.*

"So you've said. Several times." Keating gave her approximately the same look she'd use trying to figure out the origin of a slimy glob of floating sea trash. "Is there anything else?"

"No. I'll . . ." She tried a final smile. "I'll see you around?"

"For a while, maybe." Keating strode past her and on down the street.

Now what did *that* mean?

"Emily!" Dahlia's voice rang across the Square, and

she turned to meet her friend, putting Chris Keating out of her mind.

The encounter with one of his Selkie attackers in the Square left Chris shaking with anger and disgust. At first he had rather enjoyed facing Emily Wood again, thinking of how little her apologies would mean when Earth answered his call. But when she dared to mention his mother . . . and then to pretend she actually cared what happened to a landling . . . the hypocrisy infuriated him. The Selkies had no true human feelings. They were nothing but intelligent animals, devolved and degraded from once-human stock. They could manipulate, mock, and mimic true human feelings, but they no more understood it than parrots understood the words they could repeat or monkeys understood the actions they could copy. So said . . . *had* said . . . his mother. More importantly, so said the Avatar.

But shame and guilt mingled with his anger. He'd felt secret relief when told his mother had died at last, and that shamed him, even though she had, in a very real way, died the day of her stroke. But what kind of son felt even an iota of relief at the death of his mother?

And mixed with that shame, the guilt: guilt that he had not triggered the emergency beacon years before, when he had first thought of it and his mother had still been alive. If he had acted then, instead of letting his fear for his personal safety get in the way, the Holy Warriors might have long since come to Marseguro—and brought with them the technology that could have helped his mother recover from her stroke, or even have prevented it altogether.

Now it's too late. He had traveled three blocks at a fast walk since leaving the Square, heading toward the genesculpting lab where he had recently resumed work, but now he stopped and sat down on an empty crate outside a survival supply store, the sort of place that sold deep-sea shelters to Selkies and tents to the few nonmods like himself who liked to travel into the interior. *What if they don't come at all?* It had been more than two weeks since he had triggered the beacon. He knew intellectually it could be months or even years before there would be a response, but knowing that and sustaining the hope he'd had when he first triggered the beacon were two different things. Already he'd begun to worry about what would happen the next time someone visited Landing Valley. Would they discover what he had done? Worse, would they figure out *he* had done it? He didn't think he'd left anything anyone could trace back to him, but there was no such thing as a perfect crime. . . .

He brought himself up short. *What I did was not a crime,* he upbraided himself. *It was my duty to humanity. The Selkies are monstrosities that should never have been created. And they're going to spread across this world like a plague, and someday back out into the universe, if they're not stopped.*

He couldn't believe he was the only normal human who felt the way he did, either, that he was the only second-or third-generation Believer, but he couldn't think of any way to discover others. There were too few nonmods and too many Selkies. Even broaching the subject would almost certainly bring him to the Council's attention and get him arrested. *More likely, it would get me killed,* he thought. The secret, all-Selkie cabal, the one that *really* ran things, didn't have to worry about niceties like a trial. They'd just arrange an accident, like the one that had killed his father.

Well, he didn't intend to be stuck in prison *or* dead when the Holy Warriors arrived and began the Purification Marseguro so richly deserved. He wanted to be free to greet them and then, and only then, reveal himself to be the hero—*hero,* not criminal—who had summoned them.

He heard voices coming along the street and his head jerked up. *Not again!* But there she came, Emily Wood herself, in her landling clothes (*slumming,* he thought), with another Selkie even sleeker and more self-satisfied looking, dressed in one of the barely-there two-strips-of-cloth skinsuits some Selkies had begun to favor, the dark skin of her exposed arms and legs and midriff glistening with moisture-preserving oil, her hair shaved down to peach fuzz and died bright pink. With their vestigial nubs for noses and ears, and their oversized, three-lidded eyes, both "girls" looked so alien to Chris at that moment that the bejeweled navel winking at him from the one girl's naked belly startled him: she looked like something that should have spawned from a drifting egg like a fish. Her body looked human enough, human enough he felt a stirring of desire at seeing it so wantonly displayed, but that stirring died in disgust. He knew plenty of nonmods had had sex with Selkies, who were notoriously over-sexed, courtesy of Victor Hansen, and back in his horny adolescence he might have considered it himself, but now it seemed to him no better than bestiality.

They'll all be Purified, he thought. *The Selkies. The Selkie-lovers. All of them.*

Emily Wood looked up and saw him. The rage and depression that had left him shaking after they spoke in the Square had vanished, replaced by savage, sardonic amusement. He stood, smiled, nodded to her, and went on down the street toward the lab before she could again parrot her empty apologies.

Weeks, months, years: he could wait. His message would be heard, and then she really *would* be sorry.

They all would.

Chapter 5

RICHARD'S CABIN ABOARD *BPS Sanctification* had no windows, and though no doubt the bridge crew could choose from a multiplicity of video feeds showing the ship's exterior, he didn't have access to them on his little vidscreen. In fact, as he quickly discovered, he didn't have access to much of anything, including any part of the ship that wasn't either his cabin, the automated mess hall just down the corridor that he seemed to have entirely to himself, or the recreation room next door to the mess hall that it seemed he also had to himself, if you didn't count the image of the Avatar that appeared every hour on the hour in every holocube in the room to lead whomever happened to be present in the prayer *du jour*.

Despite being alone and apparently unobserved, Richard made a point of being in the rec room at least once every day at a designated prayer time. Just because he *thought* he was unobserved didn't mean he actually *was*. Given his family history, he doubted he'd spent more than a few hours of his entire life unobserved. If he hoped to change that with the success of this mission, it wouldn't do to give anyone any reason to doubt his devotion.

He didn't know what to expect from liftoff, but an automated announcement came on to tell him to strap himself into the chair/acceleration couch thoughtfully provided and to stow all loose items in the nearby drawers. During the launch, he felt very heavy for a few minutes, but not unbearably so. Another announcement urged him to stay strapped in "during spin-up of the habitat ring." For a few minutes he experienced weightlessness and barely managed to keep down his breakfast, but then weight returned, albeit not as much as usual: if he remembered right, the habitat ring spun up to about 0.9 G. Feeling both light and light-headed, he unstrapped when told it was safe to do so.

Some hours later, another announcement told him they had left Earth orbit, though he felt nothing unusual. About two days after that, there came another announcement that they had made the transition to branespace. Effectively, they'd left their own universe . . . and Richard hadn't felt a thing. He lay on the bed, staring at the blank ceiling, and thought that if people knew how boring space travel was, the Body Purified wouldn't have to outlaw talk about it.

Fortunately for his sanity, shortly after that announcement, his vidscreen beeped and lit with an image of Grand Deacon Ellers.

"Mr. Hansen," said the Grand Deacon. "I trust you've enjoyed your journey so far."

"I can't complain," Richard said—the literal truth. "I've been wondering if I'm really on the right ship, though. It seems pretty empty down here."

"I apologize for not speaking to you sooner," Ellers said. "There have been a great many demands on my time. In any event, security protocols are strict: nonmilitary personnel are restricted to isolated quarters during launch and the transition to branespace.

"Now, however, if you'd care to join me, I'd be happy to give you a tour of the ship. I'm sure you'll want to prepare a report for transmission to Archdeacon Cheveldeoff once we're back in normal space."

"I'm sure I will," Richard said.

"Excellent. I'll send an escort."

Twenty minutes later, after being guided through the ship's mazelike interior by a Holy Warrior who seemed to possess a profound aversion to small talk—or talk of any kind—Richard joined the Grand Deacon in a vid-walled briefing room. Three walls were blank, but the forth showed a schematic of an unfamiliar solar system.

"You made it, I see," Ellers said.

"Only with help." Richard nodded at his escort.

"Thank you, Chan. That will be all," Ellers told the silent Holy Warrior, who saluted and left.

"I'm glad I didn't have to find the way on my own," Richard said. "Who designed this ship? Escher?"

"It's a security feature," Ellers said. "Not only is the interior counterintuitive, many of the corridor/room combinations are mutable. Anyone attempting to take this ship by force is going to find it very difficult to reach any of its critical systems."

"I'm glad I didn't try to escape my comfortable little corner of it, then."

"You wouldn't have." Ellers indicated the system map on the vidwall. "I thought you might like to see this. Our branespace probe returned with this information just before we departed."

Richard took a closer look. The system had two Jupiter-plus gas giants in distant orbits, a couple of chunks of rock in close . . . and a fifth planet, third out from the star, right in the middle of what the diagram helpfully labeled the habitable zone.

"Some of this is conjecture—there may still be some undetected planets," Ellers said. "But there's no doubt that *that* planet," he pointed to the third from the star, "is our destination. The beacon whose transmission you uncovered is still yelling its message into space. The probe also detected low-strength radio signals. And," Ellers gave Richard a rare grin, "the probe is quite confident that that world is almost entirely covered in liquid water."

"A perfect Selkie world," Richard said. He thought for a moment how wonderful it would be to be able to breathe underwater and explore a vast world ocean . . .

then shoved the thought down, almost in panic. *They're monsters,* he thought. *Not mythical merpeople.*

"Indeed," said Ellers. "Congratulations. I think there can no longer be any doubt that you have uncovered your grandfather's hideaway."

Richard took a deep breath. He felt huge relief—he'd been confident, but he hadn't been sure—but hard on its heels came a strange surge of . . . sadness? Panic? Anger?

Angst seemed to be the only word to describe it.

And again, he didn't know where it was coming from.

Ellers was still talking. ". . . take you on the grand tour. After that, you'll be free to come and go as you please, at least until we return to Earth." He rose and led the way to the door.

The tour took the better part of two hours. They even ventured up to the ship's core, the central zero-G shaft. The assault craft and transport shuttles were stored at the aft end, but both ends boasted vast air locks. Should something happen to the dock at one end of the ship, the core could be evacuated of air and surviving vehicles could be flown the length of the ship and out the other end. Surrounding the central shaft toward the stern were the vast zero-G holds filled with supplies and weapons. Anything that absolutely required gravity was stored in smaller holds in the habitat ring, the rotating torus where the crew lived and operated. "It has a radius of around ninety meters," Ellers explained, "and rotates at about three revolutions per minute. It's big enough and slow enough that Coriolis forces aren't a problem. It would be difficult to keep troops in fighting trim if we didn't have some kind of artificial gravity on board. The brane-space engineers keep claiming they're on the verge of figuring out how to generate 'real' gravity, but they've been saying that for twenty years now."

Richard discovered he had his own reason for appreciating the habitat ring's artificial gravity: neither he nor his stomach very much enjoyed zero-G. He didn't throw up, quite, but he was very glad to pull himself into the elevator in the core and feel his weight gradually return as it eased its way "down"—really, "out"—into the habitat ring.

The tour complete, Ellers led Richard to the bridge. Here, at last, were exterior views of the ship, but since the featureless void of branespace appeared in vidscreens as pitch-black, they didn't hold much interest. Richard's eyes were drawn instead to interior views that displayed some of the places he'd just been shown, the holds filled with weapons and vehicles, the three assault craft, the training rooms where the Holy Warriors practiced everything from knife fighting to unarmed combat to light-weapons fire. In one large simulator, a half-dozen Holy Warriors put a virtual submarine through its paces. "It's very impressive," Richard said. "I feel sorry for the Selkies . . ." his voice trailed off, and he hastily added ". . . almost."

"I don't," Ellers growled. "They're abominations and they deserve what's coming." He grinned then, or at least showed his teeth. Richard had a momentary and unsettling sense of the skeleton lurking just below the thin layer of skin and tissue that made a living human being. "And what's coming is the Hand of God Itself, made flesh in the Holy Warriors of the Body."

Richard resisted the temptation to say "Oo-Rah," opting instead for, "What's our ETA?"

"Two weeks in branespace, two days in to the planet."

Richard looked back at the vidscreens of the Holy Warriors in training. "I've got a lot of time to kill," he said. "I was wondering . . ."

Two weeks and two days later Richard stood on the bridge again as *BPS Sanctification* entered orbit around the planet where they expected to find the Selkies. Looking at the screens displaying the planet's vast blue curve below them, he rubbed his left shoulder. After two weeks of long daily workouts, his instructor in the form of unarmed combat the Holy Warriors called "angel wrestling" had boosted the level of intensity a notch, and

Richard had the bruises and strained muscles to show it. He'd had more luck with weapons training: much to his surprise, he'd turned out to be an excellent shot with both projectile and laser weapons. And at least now he knew which end to hold, should the need arise, and how to reload both.

He'd also managed to overcome his spacesickness . . . to a degree. He could function in zero-G as long as he didn't perform too many violent maneuvers. Gentle drifting—no problem. Zigzagging and jackknifing back and forth across the central shaft—upchuck city.

Although he had discovered that vomiting could actually be used as a crude—very crude—zero-G propulsion system.

Who knew?

The planet-wide ocean glittered below them, fluffy white clouds dotted across it, each trailing a deep blue drop shadow. It looked beautiful and innocuous, *but "Here There Be Monsters,"* Richard thought. The moment they had exited branespace two days before they had heard the powerful call of the emergency beacon. "STARSHIP *RIVERS OF BABYLON* REQUESTS ASSISTANCE. THIS BEACON WILL RUN CONTINUOUSLY. STARSHIP *RIVERS OF BABYLON* REQUESTS ASSISTANCE. THIS BEACON WILL RUN CONTINUOUSLY . . ."

All the way in they'd also been listening in on the planet's ordinary radio traffic. Accents were strange and references uncertain, but they'd overheard enough mentions of "Victor Hansen" and "Selkies" and "genesculpting" to make it clear to everyone that Richard's claim had been spectacularly upheld. Here at last was the secret hiding place of Victor Hansen's genemodded monsters.

They'd also learned what the residents called their watery home: Marseguro, Spanish and Portuguese for "safe sea."

I don't think so, Grandpa, Richard thought. He'd found himself talking to the long-dead genesculptor more and more in his head, and the weird thing was, it didn't feel like he was talking to himself.

At least the headaches and dreams had subsided during the trip.

Ship sensors had provided more and more detail about Marseguro as they had approached. Water covered all of it except for one largish island or minicontinent and a scattering of smaller ones, some little more than wave-pounded rocks. The ocean was kilometers deep everywhere except for one enormous area of much shallower water, where a continent seemed to be either rising or subsiding.

Human—*near-human,* Richard reminded himself—habitation appeared to be concentrated in a series of towns along the eastern shore of the continent island. (The north and south poles had been designated based on the planet's direction of spin, Earth's "sun-rises-in-the-east" paradigm having been taken as the norm—as indeed, according to Body Purified doctrine, it had to be.)

Twenty-four hours ago, a probe had been sent ahead of *Sanctification* to orbit the planet and collect more detailed readings. That data, now arriving in near real-time, confirmed what they had suspected since entering the system and finding no signs of space travel: civilization on Marseguro appeared focused almost entirely downward, into the ocean. The only artificial satellites ID'd themselves as being part of the complement of *Rivers of Babylon.* Their function seemed limited to providing global positioning information, over-the-horizon communications, and meteorological information. "They knew they might be pursued," Richard had mused out loud to Ellers as they neared the planet. "Why wouldn't they have at least a couple of early-warning sensor platforms?"

"They might have them and we can't see them," Ellers said. "If they were entirely passive, we'd have no way to recognize them as artificial." He shrugged. "But after fifty years, it doesn't matter. Our stealth technologies make us essentially invisible to anything but another Body ship. Whatever ancient sensors they might have hidden around the system couldn't possibly detect us. And even if by some miracle they did see us coming . . . what could they do about it? Fifty years isn't long enough to create the kind of technological and manufacturing capability it takes to build a ship that could challenge *Sanctification*. Their entire complement of microfactories would have to run flat-out for decades even to make a start, and they will have had other priorities. The most they could do if they spotted us would be to run and hide. And since no one is running or hiding . . ."

True enough, Richard thought now. The communications chatter remained mundane, talk of cultural events and sporting competitions and fishing grounds and, of course, what products were needed where, how soon the microfactories could produce them, and how much would be paid for them. It provided no hint that anyone below realized that Victor Hansen's pipe dream of escape from the Body Purified was about to become a nightmare.

Richard glanced at Ellers. The Grand Deacon held his head tilted slightly to the left, listening to the earbud he wore on that side, a tiny device that could also transmit his voice. "Well," Ellers said suddenly, in response to whatever he had heard, "I see no point in delay. Sound General Quarters. Pilots to their assault craft, drop teams to their shuttles. Attack to commence as scheduled, 0945 ship time."

Richard looked at the peaceful ocean passing far below them, then at the day/night terminator approaching. Soon they would swing through the planetary night. On the far side of Marseguro, the town they had learned was called Hansen's Harbor would just be moving into the light, most of its citizens, human and subhuman, still asleep.

They're in for a rude awakening. Grandpa, your dream is over.

He just wished he felt happier about it.

Sanctification swung into darkness.

* * *

"Is that it?" Dahlia asked as Emily tightened the final strap on the last of an inordinate number of bundles in the dolphin sub they'd rented. They were in the dry hold; the last food barrel had gone into the wet hold—which also made an excellent refrigerator—twenty minutes ago.

Emily stepped back and surveyed her handiwork. "I think so," she said. "Nothing to do but say good-bye." She checked the wall chronometer. "We're only an hour later getting away than I'd hoped. Not bad . . . well, not by your standards, anyway."

"Very funny," Dahlia said. "I still don't know why you insisted on leaving in the dark."

"I like the dark," Emily said. "It feels like you're in deep water the minute you undock. It's just more . . . romantic."

"I don't think of you in that way," Dahlia said dryly, and Emily laughed. Dahlia was the most heterosexual girl she knew, as any number of Selkie boys—and, she suspected, more than one landling one—would attest, generally with a blissful smile of reminiscence.

"I guess I'll just have to struggle on somehow," Emily said. "Come on, let's go see if my parents are awake."

They'd docked the sub on the bay side of the Woods' hab. They slipped into the water-filled lower half of the vehicle and swam through the open bottom hatch into the well-lit tunnel leading into the hab proper. Like most shallow-water Selkie habs, it was cylindrical, with the lower half filled with water and the upper half with air. (Deep-sea habitats tended to be spherical, for added structural strength.) Although they could sleep underwater if they had to, most Selkies preferred to sleep dry—albeit in very warm air with a relative humidity of 100 percent. And of course, they had to eat in the air. Socializing with landlings demanded an air-filled space as well, as did waste elimination. *We aren't merpeople, we're amphibipeople,* Emily thought, as she and Dahlia swam up past the wet sleeping, storage, and recreation rooms in the bottom of the hab. They emerged into the large

round pool that was the central feature of the Woods'
main room.

A broad deck furnished with comfortable chairs and
sofas surrounded the pool. A higher, drier level contained the kitchen, the dry recreation room (filled with
non-water-friendly electronics), and the level above, the
top level, contained the bedrooms and bathrooms.

Treading water, Emily and Dahlia looked around the
living room. The only light came from the series of blue-
green panels just below the surface of the water around
the edge of the pool. The wavering illumination reflected
back from the curved metal beams that held up the dome
of the roof and from the thick windows separating those
beams. No light yet filtered down through the cold waters
of New Botany Bay to herald the approach of dawn.
"Still in bed, I guess," Emily said. "I'm surprised. Mom's
usually an early riser."

"What about your dad?" Dahlia asked. She rubbed
her hand over her pink peach-fuzz hair. "Mine would
sleep till the middle of the afternoon every day if he
could get away with it—then stay up until dawn every
morning."

Emily laughed. "Dad would *prefer* to sleep in. But
once Mom is up . . ." She looked up at the top level of
the three tiers rising around them. "Well, I guess we'll
let them sleep . . ."

"Didn't you say good-bye last night?" Dahlia said.
"I did."

"Sort of." In fact, she and her parents still weren't
exactly talking normally. Like a giant weight, the subject
of her choice of specialization crushed all attempts at
normal conversation. Mostly they grunted at each other
or said things like, "Pass the salt." She couldn't help
wondering, as she hesitated in the dark pool in the dark
hab, whether her mother was deliberately putting off getting out of bed until she knew Emily had gone.

No sign of Amy, either, but she'd always been a late
sleeper.

Well. Two weeks away—not just away, but completely

cut off, with no way to communicate without launching an emergency transmitter buoy—ought to give both her and her parents time to think about what they would say to each other the next time they saw each other. Maybe they could manage more than grunts.

"Let's go," Emily said. She flared her gill slits and plunged back beneath the surface of the pool.

The transition from air breathing to water breathing always brought with it a surge of adrenaline, a "Help, I'm drowning!" reflex left over from their landling ancestry. She let the surge of energy carry her down the tube to the minisub. "Hey, wait for me!" Dahlia chirped at her heels.

Ten minutes later, they sat in the dolphin sub's cockpit. It could be operated flooded, but they'd chosen to keep it dry for this trip (except for regular skin-and-gill-moistening sprays of water) to make it easier to talk to each other. Emily had the con in the bay, where there were more subs, buildings, buoys, and boats to avoid. She turned on the bow light with the flick of a switch, hit another switch to disconnect and retract the umbilical, and one more to release the magnetic clamps holding them to the docking tube. The sub shuddered a little, then clanked and rocked as the hatch slid closed and dogged shut. The steering control, a simple wheel, operated like an airplane yoke—push it forward to descend, pull it back to rise. The computer adjusted ballast and buoyancy as required. *Child's play*, Emily thought, but Dahlia, after an unfortunate accident involving an underwater crane, three warning buoys, and a very surprised Selkie construction crew working on the new water-hockey arena, had decided to limit her sub driving to open water.

Emily shoved the throttle lever to one-quarter speed. The sub vibrated a little as the turbines spun up, then the water jets kicked in and they moved smoothly away into the underwater "street," a path reserved for vehicles that was kept clear of buildings and swimmers and delineated by lights at three levels: near the surface, on the bottom, and halfway between. Marseguro's equivalent of plankton formed green halos around the floating light globes. Occasionally a larger creature, one of the many species of what scientists called "flo," for "fish-like-organism," but ordinary people just called fish, appeared briefly in the lights, sweeping through the sphere of illumination, sucking up micro flora and fauna.

They didn't follow the street very long; a kilometer from the Woods' hab the buildings thinned out. Beyond lay only darkness, pierced by their own thin ray of light, a glowing blue-green pole of illumination along which they endlessly slid.

As they entered the uninhabited part of the bay and headed for open water, Emily saw a new light, filtering down from above, through the cockpit's transparent canopy. "Day's breaking," she said.

"Yeah?" Dahlia craned her neck back. "Guess so. Well, it doesn't matter where we're going." She turned back to Emily and grinned. "Stick this thing where the sun don't shine, baby."

Emily laughed. "You've got it." She pushed the steering wheel down, and the faint light of the new day breaking over Hansen's Harbor vanished in the darkness above them.

Chapter 6

CHRIS KEATING WOKE to the gray light of dawn and the sound of thunder.

At least, he thought it was thunder. But as he lay in bed wondering blearily why the weather forecast the day before hadn't mentioned the possibility of a thunderstorm, he realized the "thunder" wasn't stopping. It went on and on, thump and rumble following each other in rapid succession. When a particularly loud bang caused the framed picture of him and his mother that hung over the desk to crash down into the cold remains of the previous night's snapperfish pizza, he sat up straight. When another, even louder boom rattled everything in the room, including his teeth, he staggered up and ran to the balcony, throwing the windows wide.

A blunt-nosed, delta-shaped craft bigger than the biggest surface ship on Marseguro roared overhead toward the harbor, so low he instinctively ducked. Flashes of light rippled along its leading edge, and explosions shook the town. Black smoke billowed up from beyond the buildings blocking his view of the bay. He looked up and down the street. On every balcony people in various stages of *dishabille* stood staring.

His momentary fear gave way to fierce, hot elation. *They've come. They've come!*

But the fear returned when another explosion shook his apartment so violently a large chunk of ceiling plaster dropped onto his recently vacated bed. *They're here, and I could get killed!*

He had to get out of the house. Better still, out of the city. He had faith the Holy Warriors would not target normal humans, but they probably wouldn't be too worried about collateral damage, either, considering the normals were mostly descendants of the traitors who had helped Victor Hansen steal a starship and escape Purification.

His hiking pack lay beside the door, where he had dumped it after he'd returned from his journey to Landing Valley. He couldn't run out naked—though he considered it for a moment as another explosion brought more of the ceiling down—so he took a moment to pull on the clothes he'd taken off and tossed on the floor the night before. Then he headed out, down the stairs in a headlong rush, then between the buildings and up into the hills. He started at a run that quickly changed to a jog and then a brisk, panting walk as the slope steepened.

I can't believe they're here! He'd resigned himself to a wait of months, even years, before his message received a response. But here they were. And such a response . . .

At the top of the hill, he turned to survey what he had wrought.

Black smoke poured up from flame-licked buildings along the water's edge. Half a dozen boats lay on their sides or upside down, hulls holed and smoking. He recognized one as Dr. Stanless' *SeaSkimmer*, and felt a momentary pang of guilt, quickly suppressed. *You can't make an omelet without breaking eggs,* he told himself, quoting the Avatar. Chris had never eaten an omelet or seen a chicken in the feathered flesh (Marseguroite "chicken," like "beef" and "pork"—pretty much everything but seafood—was vatmeat) but he understood the saying's meaning well enough, and now, as he surveyed the destruction he had helped bring about, he embraced it.

The pier where the Selkies had humiliated him had

been reduced to two undamaged sections joined by a long line of half-submerged rubble, awash in the unusually troubled waters of New Botany Bay. In the bay itself, several structures had been hit. One or two had collapsed entirely; others burned enthusiastically, clouds of mingled smoke and steam rising into the clear morning sky, just turning pink as the sun neared the horizon.

For a moment, he thought the attack was over, then three of the black assault craft swept back over the pier, bursting through the pall of smoke that had hidden them from him. Missiles speared down into the city on shafts of fire. Orange flame blossomed. Seconds later the dull rolling WHUMPs of the explosions thudded into Chris' chest.

The assault craft banked, turned, came back for a second pass. This time one of the reaching missiles hit the genesculpting lab where just the day before Chris had been sequencing the new algae samples. Everything he'd worked on for the last two years disappeared in a bloom of red flame, a billow of black smoke, a rain of fragments, and a thump in his chest like a blow from a fist. Chris nodded approvingly. The more he'd listened to the Avatar, the more uncomfortable he'd become with his work in the lab. Genesculpting algae and *E. coli* to produce medicine and food seemed harmless enough, but it was just one short step from that to genesculpting humans and creating monstrosities like the Selkies, wasn't it?

He'd find a new job in the new regime.

The assault craft made one more pass, the wind of their passage swirling the smoke from the burning buildings into miniature sooty tornadoes. This time, dozens of small black objects fell from them, caught themselves, and zipped away across the city like the flying insects Chris knew only from old Earth vids. After that, one assault craft accelerated with a burst of flame and in seconds vanished north up the coast. The other two slowed and settled into the Square where Chris had talked with Emily Wood just a few days before. The blast from their landing jets toppled the statue of Victor Hansen—the sight made Chris grin—and blew the water out of the fountain pool. Both flanks of each of the shuttles slammed down onto the cobblestones. Soldiers in shining dark-blue body armor swarmed out, spreading out across the Square under the cover of constantly swinging weapons turrets on the assault craft.

Chris almost laughed out loud. Of course, they had no way of knowing what he could have told them: there were almost no weapons on Marseguro. Selkies had some powerful spear-and dart-guns used to hunt or fight off some of the larger Marseguroite sea life. He had once heard that the Council kept six ancient automatic rifles—the *Rivers of Babylon*'s entire complement—locked up somewhere, but he'd never heard of anyone firing one. And no one had ever bothered to program a microfactory to manufacture firearms. After all, they were all one big happy family on Marseguro, and the best form of gun control, authorities and residents agreed, was no guns at all, for anyone. Even the Peaceforcers—all twelve of them—didn't have anything except a few stunners (though they could legally gain access to the Council's rifles if necessary), and he didn't see any sign of them attempting to use them on the armored soldiers, which would have been useless and probably swiftly fatal.

Too bad, Chris thought. *It might have been fun to watch.* He'd lost all respect for Peaceforce since his mother had explained to him that it existed solely to keep the oppressed landlings in their place, allowing the Selkies to enjoy and consolidate their undisputed and undeserved place atop the pinnacle of society.

The Holy Warriors had formed a perimeter around the Square. Two strange black vehicles shaped like stubby cylinders, with fins and bumps in odd places, rolled out of the assault craft on multiple wheels. The assault craft promptly lifted off again. One headed toward the harbor and settled there, but intervening buildings and thickening smoke prevented Chris from seeing any details. The other lit its jets and roared south.

He turned his attention back to the Square in time to see a group of soldiers disappear into Government House. One of the wheeled vehicles remained in front while its mate, accompanied by a couple of dozen troops, rolled off down a side street and out of Chris' view. The remaining Holy Warriors appeared to be searching the buildings around the Square. Chris suspected all except Government House and possibly Town Hall were empty this time of morning. Neither would have more than one or two people in it, and probably no one of any importance.

Aside from the symbolic value, why would they want to seize Government House? he thought, then answered his own question: *Planetary Communications. They have a message to get out.*

And I can help them do it.

He'd come up the hill intending to hide out in the interior until things settled down, but now he scrambled to his feet and headed down into the city again, a man with a new mission.

They need someone to help them take firm control. They need a native guide.

He squeezed between two buildings and emerged onto the main road to find that, out of his sight, the streets had filled with people, some running, though from where to where he couldn't guess, some standing in groups shouting at each other, some pushing carts of belongings, some supporting wounded friends or family. A father with a tear-streaked face went by, cradling a little boy in his arms, dead or alive, Chris couldn't tell. For the second time that morning, an unexpected pang of guilt stabbed at Chris' heart. *Couldn't they have been more careful? Why had they hurt normals?*

Eggs, he reminded himself. *Omelets.* And the sooner their liberators established firm control over the city— over the whole planet—the sooner the death and destruction would end.

Well, for normals, anyway.

He hurried on, against the tide of people streaming inland. He had almost reached the Square when someone grabbed his arm from behind.

He yelped and spun to find Dr. Stanless. The geneticist wore only torn and dirty pajama bottoms, and a nasty looking gash on his left shoulder had streaked one side of his body with blood. His right eye blazed at Chris; his left was black and swollen closed. "Chris!" he yelled. "Don't go down there! We've been invaded!"

As if on cue, four soldiers in dark blue body armor burst out of the doorway of the building to their left. Two seized Dr. Stanless, who struggled uselessly in their iron grip. Two seized Chris, who didn't resist at all. "Yes, Dr. Stanless, I know," he said, and smiled. He couldn't resist adding, "I called them." Dr. Stanless' face went slack with shock as the Holy Warriors hauled him away.

The two holding Chris tightened their grip on his arms. He grinned at them. "Didn't you hear what I said?" They exchanged looks. "Well, then, don't you think you'd better take me to whomever is in charge?"

They did, but to his indignation, they weren't gentle about it.

Richard watched the assault from the bridge of *Sanctification*, having been told in no uncertain terms by Grand Deacon Ellers that civilians were neither wanted nor permitted in the assault craft. After it became clear—as it did within minutes—that no organized resistance existed on Marseguro, he began to chafe under that restriction.

Not that he lacked information. The bridge's vidscreens displayed a constantly changing kaleidoscope of carnage, with feeds from cams on the assault craft, the armored personnel carriers, the helmets of the Holy Warriors, hovering reconbots and even the noses of smart missiles all vying for attention. But there were too many images, and too many voices, and vid, no matter how vivid, couldn't substitute for personal experience. Richard desperately wanted to go down on the ground and smell, hear, taste, and feel what was happening for himself. The desire was so strong it was almost a compulsion.

He put it down to his need to see for himself the long-delayed Purification of his grandfather's pet planet—and the long-delayed polishing of his own unfairly tarnished reputation.

He knew that the second wave of ships descending to the planet's surface would be supply shuttles. He'd heard they were a rough way to get through the atmosphere, but he was seriously beginning to wonder how he could talk his way onto one when he discovered he didn't have to.

He didn't pick out the message from Grand Deacon Ellers from the muted cacophony of voices all around. The first he knew of it was when a young man, pink-cheeked, blue-eyed and with the painfully erect bearing of a newly minted Holy Warrior, trotted around the second-level walkway that surrounded the main pit of the circular bridge and saluted. Richard felt his hand twitch in response but managed not to salute back. After weeks on *Sanctification,* he had to keep reminding himself he was a civilian observer, not a Holy Warrior. "Yes?"

"Grand Deacon Ellers' compliments, sir, and he requests your presence on the ground."

At last! Richard thought, but he maintained a studied calm. "Did he say why?"

"No, sir. Just that if you will take the next supply shuttle down, he'll provide an escort to take you to Government House."

"Government House?"

"That's what the moddies and traitors call it," the young man said. "Some kind of tribal headquarters."

"Very well," Richard said. "Thank you."

"You're welcome, sir!" The young man saluted again, obviously having taken to heart the advice given the lowest-ranking members of any military that to be safe one should salute anything on two legs. He trotted back around the bridge to his original post.

Richard stepped to the nearest general information vidscreen and found that the next supply ship, carrying ammunition, food, and medical and communications equipment would launch in half an hour. That gave him just enough time to rush back to his cabin, pull out the bag he had packed the day before in the hope he'd go down to the surface, use the bathroom (it seemed a prudent precaution), and take the lift to the central core. Holy Warriors from the ship's crew stood by at each of the three intraship transporters, platforms that slid along slots placed at equidistant intervals around the cylindrical core. Richard carefully transitioned from the spinning habitat ring to the nonspinning section, and a crewman shoved his bag into a box on the platform and strapped it in place. Richard seized one of the many handholds on the transporter, and they zipped the length of the ship in two minutes. "Thanks," Richard said. The crewman shrugged, handed him his box, and zipped away again.

Richard took a moment to take a couple of deep breaths—the relatively rapid transit of the core had unsettled his stomach a hair—then pulled himself along the soft silvery webbing that covered every wall of the zero-G part of the ship, tugging his luggage behind him. He entered an access tunnel, emerged a moment later in the shuttle launch bay, and flinched: the shuttles were all locked down, of course, but two of them, including the one he wanted, hung overhead from his perspective, fat cargo-carrying cylinders with a much smaller crew compartment at the bow like an olive attached to the tip of a sausage.

Richard knew better than to try to simply jump across the intervening distance: the zero-G training he'd had on board *Sanctification* had brightly and painfully illuminated the difference between mass and weight, and the unforgiving nature of inertia, and he knew he could very easily misjudge the amount of force with which he'd hit the far wall and break an ankle—or his neck. Instead, he continued around the brightly-lit space using the webbing, and finally reached his shuttle with five minutes to spare. The pilot, a man who looked solid enough to have been hewn out of a single—and very large—block of granite, took one look at his passenger, grunted, and pointed him to . . .

"What's that?" Richard said. It looked a bit like a medieval torture device, all black metal, straps, and buckles. There were six in the crew cabin, three on each side of the smallish, white-painted space.

"Is called a rack," the pilot said, apparently confirming Richard's impression. He had a thick Russian accent to go with his bearlike appearance. "I show. Go there." He didn't give Richard an opportunity to do otherwise, manhandling him into position with casual strength. "Straps go here, here—" he pointed to Richard's shoulders, waist, and crotch. "Pull in handles, so—" He demonstrated. U-shaped, padded handles swung away from the wall on hinges and locked in front of Richard's chest. "Helmet . . ." The pilot opened a locker on the other side of the small compartment and took out a dark blue crash helmet with an alarmingly battered look. It had a short bungee cord attached to the back. The pilot jammed the helmet onto Richard's head, almost taking his ears off in the process, clipped the bungee cord onto a metal loop on the wall, and fastened the chinstrap. Then he tapped something on the side of the helmet, and built-in headphones came to life. "You hear?" the pilot said.

Richard nodded.

"You hold on," the pilot said. "Ride rough."

Richard nodded again.

"Ride rough" hardly covered it.

The shuttle's launch cradle first dropped into the launch lock beneath it, then rotated so the top of the shuttle pointed toward the hull. A few moments while the lock cycled—no need to waste air in a nonemergency—three seconds of very gentle acceleration, and they had separated from the ship.

So far, so smooth. But within minutes, they plunged into the atmosphere, which announced its presence with a thin whine that soon grew to an all-encompassing roar. The supply craft bucked, pitched, yawed, did everything but flip end over end, and a couple of times Richard thought it might have done that. Richard's stomach fought to crawl up his throat and hurl itself and its contents into the crew cabin which, in addition to vibrating to the point of blurriness, had reached a temperature that seemed more suited to slow roasting a turkey than keeping its occupants comfortable. "Why . . . so . . . rough . . . ?" Richard called out when the turbulence slacked off just enough he thought he could get out the words without biting his tongue off.

"Some bad design," the pilot said. From his voice, he seemed unaffected by the turbulence, although of course that might have had something to do with the fact he enjoyed the embrace of a padded motion-dampening seat while Richard hung on the wall like a side of beef. "Some bad weather. Some evasive maneuvers."

"But . . . no . . . weapons . . ."

"Seems so," the pilot said. "Don't know for certain. Rather be all shook up and alive than calm and dead. Hold on tighter. Worst about to start."

Richard clenched his jaw, swallowed hard, and prayed he wouldn't embarrass himself by throwing up before they reached the ground.

Alas, as the Avatar liked to say, "All prayers are answered, but sometimes, the answer is 'no.' "

When they were safely on the ground, in a sports field commandeered to serve as a secondary landing site away from the town square for the cargo shuttles, the pilot summoned a cleanerbot to slurp up the widely redistributed remnants of Richard's morning toast, simbacon and near-coffee. He also provided Richard with a clean standard-issue (but insignia-free) light blue Holy Warrior one-piece to wear. Richard retrieved his bag from its locker and rather shamefacedly made his retreat out the tiny personnel hatch and down the five-step ladder to the blessedly solid ground. Bots were already unloading the contents of the fat cargo cylinder.

A fully armed and armored Holy Warrior waited at the bottom of the ladder. "Grand Deacon Ellers is expecting you," he growled. "This way."

As they walked through the streets of the town the Selkies had named after his grandfather, Richard looked around eagerly, finally able to experience it without the mediation of a video camera.

"Primitive" was his first impression. The building styles—lots of brick, with accents of shiny metal and glass and solar panels—reminded him of the seedier parts of the City of God, the ones that predated the Day of Salvation—which made sense, he supposed, since that style had been current when Grandpa Hansen had fled. The buildings didn't look new, though; they looked decades old.

He'd seen newer buildings in the vidfeeds, but they were all down by the water—or partially or completely under it. Or had been, before the Holy Warriors so quickly and efficiently blew them up.

He couldn't see any bomb damage here. He couldn't see any people, either, though the vidfeeds had shown a lot on the streets an hour ago. All hiding somewhere now, he supposed, or in flight, out of Hansen's Harbor. Not that they had anywhere to flee to. The interior was bleak and unappealing and the other towns much smaller. The assault craft had already attacked several of them, to drive home the message that the Holy Warriors controlled the planet. The refugees would probably meet other refugees coming the other way.

He felt sorry for the normal humans, though if they were smart, accepted the Body Purified, and didn't cause trouble, they'd suffer no further harm. But the Selkies . . .

He wanted—*needed*—to see the Selkies. With all the strange, near-treasonous thoughts and feelings that had come into his head in the last few weeks, he needed to know he had done the right thing in pointing the Holy Warriors at this planet.

First, though, he had to find out what the Grand Deacon wanted.

Richard and his escort emerged from a narrow alley into a broad courtyard surrounded by what probably passed for impressive architecture on Marseguro. Nothing stood taller than about four stories, but several of the buildings boasted columns, pediments, and the kind of glittering stucco that had been all the rage in public buildings on Earth at the time of Salvation. (Oddly, though Richard had long laughed at the style when he'd come across it in the City of God, he now thought it looked rather attractive. Context, he supposed.) An assault craft dominated the center of the square—the reason they'd had to land in the sports field—and multiple takeoffs and landings had cracked and blackened the once-white cobblestones. A bronze statue lay on its side in a now-dry fountain in the rubble of its broken pedestal. "Just a second," Richard told his escort. The pedestal still held a bronze plaque, scorched but readable. Richard leaned close. *Dr. Victor Hansen,* he read. *In memory and appreciation of the visionary geneticist who created the Selkie race and preserved it from extermination by the tyrants of Old Earth. Dedicated February 34, Year 34, on the fifth anniversary of Dr. Hansen's death.*

So you lived almost thirty local years after the landing, Richard thought. *Long enough to think you'd really pulled it off, that the Body would never find you.*

Too bad you didn't live a little longer so you could have met your grandson. We would have had a lot to talk about.

Although increasingly he felt as if he *had* met his grandfather. Which was why he kept talking to him directly in his mind. Which was absurd, and possibly slightly deranged.

Several times in the last few weeks he had thought about talking to a Body psychologist, but if he had—

especially since his father had flagrantly demonstrated that mental instability ran in Richard's family—he suspected he would never have been allowed to come on this mission . . . and he couldn't have borne that.

It's just stress, he thought. *That's all.*

"Sir!" said his escort. "The Grand Deacon is *waiting.*" His tone made it clear he did not intend to leave the Grand Deacon in that unaccustomed state merely to satisfy Richard's sightseeing impulses.

"Coming, coming." Richard followed the Holy Warrior into the grandest of the semigrand buildings around the Square, the one with the biggest pillars and the glitteriest stucco, and the words GOVERNMENT HOUSE laser-cut into the Neo-Greek Revival pediment.

Probably as a potent symbol of occupation and defeat rather than for any practical purpose, the big wooden doors at the top of the broad flight of stairs leading up from the courtyard had been blasted into charred flinders. Beyond the wreckage, the lobby looked more like a government building than a palace, with a polished floor—a kind of light-green stone flecked with silvery metallic flakes, in this case—and a long counter on the left-hand side full of wickets-for-standing-in-line-at. Sunlight streamed through multiple skylights in the high ceiling of polished red wood beams, providing plenty of natural illumination for the Holy Warriors now running cables and setting up stands of vidscreen-studded equipment that Richard recognized as belonging to a mobile communications and headquarters module. The Holy Warriors moved with purpose but without unnecessary haste, and mostly without talking, so that Richard could clearly hear the one person who *was* talking, at the top of his lungs, though he couldn't immediately see whomever it was.

The voice was that of a young man, but it had the kind of near-whining, making-excuses tone that Richard associated with a certain kind of much-younger child. "I don't understand! Why won't you let me out? I'm trying to help! I'm on your side! I'm part of the Body. My parents were Believers. I've listened to *The Wisdom of the Avatar.* I can quote—"

"Please don't," said another voice, which Richard recognized as that of Grand Deacon Ellers. "The one thing you could do right now that would really help is to shut up."

"But—"

"That wasn't a request."

"But I—"

"Quiet, or I'll have you gagged!" Richard and his escort rounded one of the vidscreen stands just as the Grand Deacon snapped that, giving Richard his first look at the source of Ellers' annoyance.

It proved to be a short and skinny young man, maybe twenty Earth years old, with light brown hair, a rather scraggly beard and mustache, and blue, childlike eyes that had widened with shock and hurt at the Grand Deacon's sharp tone. Nevertheless, the youth did shut up, pressing his lips together in a scowl that made him look about five, an impression heightened by the temporary holding cell that looked like a playpen imprisoning him.

"Grand Deacon, Mr. Hansen is here," the Holy Warrior escorting Richard said, and snapped a salute.

Ellers sketched a salute in reply. "Dismissed," he said, and turned his attention to Richard as the Holy Warrior turned smartly and lumbered off. Behind the Grand Deacon, Richard saw the prisoner's eyes widen further, then narrow and focus intently on him. "Mr. Hansen, thank you for joining me," the Grand Deacon said.

"My pleasure," Richard said. His eyes on the prisoner, he went on, "I was hoping I'd have the opportunity to see the Purification of Grandfather Victor's vile experiment firsthand."

The prisoner's eyes went wide again. "You're— you're—"

"I thought I told you to be quiet," Grand Deacon Ellers roared, turning on the young man, who wilted under the glare and sat down heavily on the floor of his cell. He pulled his knees up to his chest and wrapped his arms around them, then glared out at the Grand Deacon and Richard, who stepped up beside Ellers.

"Is this who you wanted me to see?" Richard asked.

The Grand Deacon grunted. "He claims he's the one who called us here. Says he activated a distress beacon. Even gave us a beacon ID number." He tapped on his forearm, then held it up, palm toward Richard. "Here it is." he said. Richard saw a string of digits on Ellers' nanodisplay, red beneath his skin like a bloody tattoo. "Look familiar?"

Richard recognized them at once. "Yes. That's definitely the ID of the beacon that led us here."

"So he's telling the truth?"

"I don't know how else he'd know that number."

"Hmmm." Ellers went over to the cell. "Stand up," he said.

The youth got to his feet.

"Tell me your name again."

"Chris Keating." The young man's gaze slid past the Grand Deacon to Richard. "Are you really Victor Hansen's grandson?"

"You're talking to *me*," Ellers snapped. "Why did you betray your planet?"

"My planet is Earth," Chris Keating said, so quickly Richard thought he must either really believe it or had overrehearsed saying it. "I don't belong here. None of us does. We belong inside the Body."

"Even the Selkies?" Ellers growled.

"They're abominations," Keating said, again instantly. "I don't care what happens to them. They're not real humans. Not like the landlings."

"Landlings?"

"Non-Selkies. Nonmods. Us." Chris waved his hand, indicating himself and them. "Normals."

"Do all the . . . landlings . . . feel like you do?"

Chris shook his head. "No. Most of them love the Selkies. But not me! And I'm sure there are others who hate them, too."

"These landlings who love the Selkies. Will they fight us?"

Chris laughed. "With what?" He leaned forward, laughter suddenly swallowed by a look of utter . . . *need,* Richard thought. "Will you take me back to Earth? *I have to go to Earth.*"

"We'll see," Ellers said. "If you cooperate . . ."

"Of course I will! I *called* you here!"

"So you said." Ellers glanced at Richard. "What do you think? Can we let him out?"

Richard blinked, startled at being asked. *What's Ellers playing at?* "Um . . . I think so," he said. "He seems harmless."

"Very well. Slowinsky!" A nearby Holy Warrior put down a spool of cable and saluted.

"Sir?"

"Release the prisoner."

"Yes, sir!"

While Slowinsky busied himself with the jail door, Ellers walked a few steps away and motioned Richard to come with him. "I don't have time to deal with him right now," Ellers said in a low voice. "I'm going to let you take care of him. Grill him for any information you can get—I'm sure Archdeacon Cheveldeoff will want to know everything you can learn. But most importantly, find out if he's telling us the truth. Test him. If you think we can trust him, bring him back to me. We've got our hands full right now, but in a day or so, we're going to be in a position to start hunting down any Selkies that have escaped our initial sweep. We could do with a reliable source of information."

Richard nodded. "I can do that," he said.

"Good." Ellers turned. "Mr. Keating," he said. The youth almost dashed over to him, like a puppy called to play fetch.

"Yes, sir?"

Ellers indicated Richard. "Mr. Hansen, here, is the one who detected the distress call. He is also a direct representative of the Archdeacon of Body Security, and therefore in charge of mission intelligence." Richard smiled inwardly. Only half of that sentence was true. But if Chris thought Richard was the intelligence chief, maybe he'd be more likely to talk. "I want you to take Mr. Hansen around the city. Show him the sights. Tell him whatever you think is important. Answer any questions he may have. Later—perhaps—we'll talk again."

Ellers summoned Slowinsky and another Holy Warrior whose name Richard didn't catch, assigned them to escort Richard and Chris, then turned to Richard. "Mr. Hansen, if you would care to join me for dinner at 1800 local time—your datapad will have been programmed to display that by now; it's in about six hours—you can report back then. I'll leave it to your discretion whether or not Mr. Keating should join us." He turned away. "Dismissed."

Neatly done, Richard thought as Ellers turned his attention back to setting up his headquarters. *He's got this Keating kid and me out of his hair. Any useful information he gets out of either of us is just bonus.*

"Well," said Richard to Chris Keating. "Why don't you give me the grand tour?"

Chapter 7

BEING THROWN IN JAIL had shocked Chris; he
couldn't believe they would do that to the hero who
had handed them Victor Hansen's bolt-hole. But when
the tall, sandy-haired man in a plain blue jumpsuit had
shown up—Victor Hansen's grandson, no less!—and
been introduced as the one in charge of intelligence gathering, Chris had understood. Ellers simply hadn't had the
authority to do anything other than throw him in jail.
He was a military man; Hansen, the civilian, the representative of the Archdeacon of Body Security himself,
must be the real power here. The Avatar himself might
have sent him! And so Chris was more than happy to
show him around Hansen's Harbor—especially with the
reassuring presence of the two Holy Warriors to ensure
that nobody who objected to the Purification of Marseguro put two and two together and decided to mete out
a little vigilante justice to someone they might quite
likely, Chris admitted, see as a traitor.

"Why did you do it?" Hansen suddenly asked as they
walked down a rubble-strewn street. "Why did you betray your planet?"

The question echoed his own thoughts so closely it
made him uneasy—and defensive. "I didn't betray anyone," he said, more hotly than he intended to speak to
the man who might, after all, be the personal representative of the Avatar.

"The Holy Warriors have laid waste to half your city

and must have already killed several hundred Selkies," Hansen said. "Your fellow Marseguroites—Marseguroians?—might disagree."

"You can't betray the Selkies," Chris said. "They're not human. Can you betray an animal?" He kicked half a broken brick out of his way. "And we say Marseguroites."

Hansen shrugged. "If I locked my dog out of my house and refused to feed him, or kicked him every time I saw him, I think most people would think I had betrayed him. Selkies may not be strictly human, but they're more intelligent than dogs. From where I sit, it looks like you betrayed them—although of course I'm glad you did."

"If there were any betrayal, they betrayed us first," Chris snapped. His eyes narrowed as a thought struck him. *This is Victor Hansen's grandson. Why would they trust him? What if the Grand Deacon really is the one in charge, and he's put me with someone he doesn't trust to see if I can be trusted?*

Wheels within wheels. That kind of thinking made his head hurt.

"How did they betray you?" Hansen pressed.

He's in charge of gathering intelligence. He's supposed to ask questions, Chris thought. *He's not trying to annoy me.*

But he was.

"Selkies and landlings are supposed to be absolutely equal," Chris said. "But the Selkies breed like bugglefish and a lot of the landlings are sterile—something to do with radiation levels on the *Rivers of Babylon*. The Selkies' water tanks protected them, supposedly, but I've always wondered if maybe the Selkies are slipping something into the water supply.

"Anyway, there just aren't enough of us, and there are fewer all the time. And there are more and more of the Selkies. They've taken over the schools, taken all the best jobs, taken over the hospitals . . ." *Mom,* he thought, and his heart clenched like a fist in his chest. He wished she could have been alive to see the Selkie city in rubble. *She'd be proud,* he thought. *And so would Dad.*

"But that's not all." Chris fought the urge to lower his voice. *I'll never have to lower my voice again to say what I think about the Selkies.* "They've taken over the government, too. Or maybe they've always secretly run it. Supposedly, the elected Council, half Selkie, half landling, runs everything, but we . . . my parents and I . . . know that there's another Council, a secret cabal, that's really in charge. And it's all Selkie."

Hansen gave him a skeptical glance, eyebrows raised.

"It's true," Chris said. "Everything is set up to make the Selkies happy, and screw the landlings. And anyone who threatens Selkie control, threatens to stir up trouble among the landlings, is snuffed out. Like my father."

"They killed him?"

"The Council—acting on orders from the cabal, of course—ordered him to take a job at sea. The boat sank. The Selkies survived. They managed to save all the landlings, too . . . all but him." Chris' jaw clenched; he had to force himself to relax it. "They murdered him. That's what Mom said, and I believe her. They may have murdered her, too. Probably did. And they almost drowned me, tried to warn me to stay in my place." He grinned, a savage grimace he couldn't have prevented if he'd wanted to. "I guess I showed them."

"I guess you did." Hansen stopped. "I don't think we can carry on this way."

A tangle of steel, masonry, and glass blocked the road. "You're right," Chris said with satisfaction.

Hansen frowned at him. "Then why on Earth—sorry, on Marseguro—did you bring me this way?"

Chris nodded at the wreckage. "This is where I worked," he said. "A genesculpting lab. Most recently, we've been trying to modify native algae to provide more efficient feedstock for the bioreactors that provide air and fresh water to the Selkies' underwater habitats. We've been relying on Earth-native algae we brought with us, but some of the local species are much better producers of oxygen. Dr. Stanless thought—" He cut himself off. "Well, it doesn't matter. The Holy Warriors hit it this morning." He kicked at a lump of masonry. "Good riddance," he snarled. His vehemence surprised him. He hadn't realized how much he had come to hate the mind-numbing work Stanless had put him to. Day after day, he'd observed and noted and cleaned and re-filled, punched buttons and turned dials, and none of it had been of the slightest benefit to landlings like him who never intended to or wanted to visit an underwater habitat. "Working here was my real betrayal," he said to Hansen. "Every day I worked in this lab I betrayed my fellow normal humans. I should have blown the place up myself."

"Is your version of giving me a tour of the city going to consist entirely of you taking me to places central to your personal life?" Hansen said. "Or may I request to see certain specific sights?"

Chris felt himself blush, and hated himself for it. Hansen, and the Grand Deacon before him, made him feel like a stupid little kid. *Maybe I am,* he thought. *Maybe I'm like the kid who tattles to the grown-ups when the other kids do something wrong.*

But you know what? Sometimes tattling is the right thing to do.

He frowned. He wasn't very happy with the simile he'd just come up with, because he'd been *exactly* that sort of kid. It hadn't helped his popularity with the other kids, landling or Selkie.

Out loud, he said, "Of course, Mr. Hansen. I'll show you whatever you want."

Hansen's answer surprised him, not so much for what he wanted to see as the strange vehemence with which he announced it. "Selkies," Hansen said. "Show me the Selkies."

"This way," Chris said, and led Hansen around the ruined laboratory to the road leading down to the pier.

*   *   *

Richard had surprised himself with his intense interest in Chris Keating's reasons for betraying his planet, and as he looked at the ruins of the laboratory where Keating had worked, it crossed his mind that maybe he wanted to understand Keating's betrayal to understand his own. Maybe Keating hadn't betrayed his planet, but hadn't Richard betrayed his grandfather?

Bull, he thought. He spoke directly to Victor Hansen again, as if he had asked the question. *You betrayed me and Dad and every normal human on the planet when you created your pet monsters.*

For the first time, it seemed like Victor Hansen answered, as an inner voice argued with him. *How could I have betrayed you when you weren't even born yet?* And then, *In a way, I am you, and you are me. How could I betray myself?*

I am you? You are me? What the hell does that mean? And why am I arguing with myself?

His emotions, like his thoughts, were confused, guilt and anger all mixed up inside him, fighting like oil and water.

The kid led him down another street—almost choked in places by rubble from collapsed and still-smoldering buildings—and for the first time, Richard got a good look at what the Marseguroites had dubbed New Botany Bay.

It was a mess. The Holy Warriors had concentrated their fire on the waterfront and the amphibian buildings that both rose above and descended below the water. Once-proud towers had been reduced to fanglike teeth of broken masonry and claws of twisted steel. In those buildings still more-or-less intact, the gaping black holes left behind by blown-out windows reminded Richard of a skull's empty eye sockets. Floating debris carpeted the surface of the water—bits of wood, bits of insulation, furniture, clothing . . .

. . . bodies.

Until he saw those dark but unmistakably human— human*oid,* he reminded himself as strongly as he could— forms floating in the turgid, oil-slicked water, he had known intellectually but not viscerally that the Holy Warriors' missiles were destroying more than just buildings. He'd told himself he was okay with that. He'd known from the moment he reported reception of the distress signal that this would be the result.

Hadn't he?

Guilt swelled up in him again, guilt he couldn't understand. *The Selkies are abominations! This planet must be Purified! I'm doing the will of God!* His mind raised its dikes against the welling tide of guilt, but it threatened to overtop them . . . and he couldn't figure out where it came from. It almost seemed separate and apart from him, pouring from some hidden portion of his brain, one that housed a different personality entirely than the one he thought of as himself.

The portion of his brain he'd been addressing, and arguing with, as though it were Victor Hansen.

Am I going mad? he thought. *Like my father?*

Maybe it's a good thing all the buildings are so short . . .

They rounded a corner, only to find the road, which led down to the broken-backed pier that stretched out into the fouled water of the bay like a long brown tongue, completely blocked by smoking, flame-licked wreckage.

Keating looked left, then right. "This way," he said. "This pile of junk must have been the Amphibian Club. Looks like it toppled across the road, so maybe the alley behind it is clearer."

He took a narrow path, just wide enough for one person at a time, between two buildings that seemed to have escaped with nothing worse than broken windows. Richard followed, his so-far-silent pair of bodyguards dogging his heels. He trailed one hand along the rough brickwork to his right. It looked a couple of centuries old, which was impossible, of course. Either the local climate played hell with building materials, or the settlers had wanted to create a false feeling of antiquity to help them forget they were on a brand-new—

He emerged into the alley, and something jumped on his back.

The weight smashed him down onto sharp-edged cobblestones. Strong arms wrapped around his neck. He couldn't breathe. *He's going to break my neck,* he had time to think, the gruesome image flashing into his mind—then he smelled burning meat and whatever had him gave a horrible, gurgling scream and rolled away.

Richard lurched up to his hands and knees, gulped some air, then scrambled to his feet. One of the Holy Warriors—Slowinsky, Richard remembered—stood over a body, laser pistol in hand. The other Holy Warrior had Chris Keating shoved up against the wall of one of the buildings they had just passed between, an armored forearm across his neck. Keating's eyes, wide and frightened, stared at Richard. "What happened?" Richard gasped.

"This *thing* was lurking on the fire-escape balcony," Slowinsky said, indicating the body. "Jumped you when you came into the alley."

"But didn't jump this guy," the other Holy Warrior rumbled. "I think he set you up."

Richard looked up at the fire-escape ladder that zigzagged up the brick side of the four-story building, then down at the "thing."

"A Selkie?" he said.

Slowinsky grunted. "See for yourself."

Richard walked over and knelt down. Oversized green eyes, like something from a cartoon figure, gazed sightlessly back at him, already clouding over. The flat, almost nonexistent nose, the nubs of ears . . . and the gills, triple slits on each side of the neck, relaxed open in death—all just as he had seen in his grandfather's notes, but seeing photos was different from seeing something in the flesh. Photos could have been manipulated, or computer-generated from scratch. But this thing, slumped inelegantly in an alley, shaved skull tattooed with a multi-colored spiral of stars, stinking of burned meat and evacuated bowels, blood leaking from mouth and nose and gill slits, pooling and congealing on the cobblestones, was indisputably real—and moments before had been alive.

From the same wellspring as the guilt, Richard felt pity

and anger rise in equal measure. But he also felt his gorge rising and stood up hastily. He'd thrown up enough for one day. He rubbed his aching neck with his right hand, then went over to the Holy Warrior holding Keating. "Did you set us up?" he demanded.

Keating shook his head and tried to speak, but only managed a squeak. "Let him talk," Richard told the Holy Warrior, who gave Keating a little extra shove with his forearm, then released him. Richard didn't have to look behind him to know that Slowinsky had Keating well covered with the laser pistol.

As Richard had just done, Keating massaged his neck. "No," he said. "Why would I? I activated the beacon to bring you here! Why would I bring you here to kill Selkies and then try to help *them* kill *you*?"

Richard, hurting and knowing how close he had come to death, didn't want to give the boy the benefit of the doubt—but the facts were on his side. Keating had known the beacon ID number, so he must have activated it. *Unless the authorities found it and gave the serial number to this guy so they could get someone into our good graces to . . .*

No, that's crazy. Because that would mean the Marseguroite authorities had known the attack was coming. And if they had, those bodies wouldn't be floating in the bay. They would have evacuated the cities and dispersed the population, and by all the signs, they'd done nothing of the kind.

"He's telling the truth," Richard said. "Let him go." He turned around to look at the dead Selkie again. "But I'd still like to know why he didn't attack *you*."

Chris went over and knelt down beside the dead Selkie for a moment, then lurched up and turned away and did what Richard had managed to avoid, vomiting up the contents of his stomach into the shadows on the far side of the alley. Richard looked up at the sky and swallowed hard.

After a moment, Keating emerged from the shadows,

wiping his mouth and making a wide detour around the Selkie. "That's Peter," he said shakily. "Peter Stamos. He worked in the lab, same shift. He knew me, that's why he didn't jump me. He . . . he probably thought he was rescuing me. From you."

"A friend of yours?" growled Slowinsky, who had never reholstered his weapon.

"No!" The denial came as quickly as . . . well, as quickly as the denial would have come on Earth from someone asked if they harbored doubts about the Avatar's direct connection to God, Richard thought. *Fast learner. He should do well in the Body Purified.* "Just an acquaintance. I don't have any Selkie *friends.*"

"Looks like he didn't know that," Slowinsky said.

"Let's get to the water," Richard said. "When I said I wanted to see Selkies, getting jumped from behind by one wasn't exactly what I had in mind."

Keating nodded eagerly and led the way on down the alley. Richard and the Holy Warriors followed, but this time, he noted, the Holy Warriors followed with weapons drawn. *They screwed up,* he thought. *They forgot that just because there aren't any weapons, that doesn't mean there aren't any threats.* Considering they were supposed to be protecting him, he was glad they'd learned a lesson.

There were no more incidents between the ruined laboratory and the dock; in fact, they didn't see anyone living at all.

They did see several more bodies. Chris Keating, Richard noted, didn't look very closely. *Probably scared he'll see somebody else he knows,* he thought. *He's afraid to face all the consequences of his "heroism."*

The fact he *also* chose to avoid looking at the dead bodies was just . . . sensitivity.

Yeah, that's it.

Finally, as they walked out onto the ruined pier, they saw their first living people.

Half a dozen Holy Warriors stood on the pier, which was made of some unfamiliar material that looked a bit like wood and a bit like plastic. Richard wrinkled his nose. Whatever the stuff was, it stank like rotting seaweed.

Unlike his bodyguards, the Holy Warriors on the pier carried automatic rifles. They guarded a floating cage packed with Selkies.

Richard's knees suddenly felt weak and his heart fluttered as he looked at the massed moddies, males, females and . . .

. . . *children,* one part of his mind supplied.

Offspring, he insisted instead.

It was one thing to see one dead Selkie, it was another to see two dozen living ones. *Beautiful,* a part of his brain breathed, with a sense of pride. *Horrible,* said another. Richard clung to the latter reaction like the . . . offspring . . . in the cage clung to their parents, who petted their heads and hugged them for all the world like humans did. A little female maybe five standard years old looked up as Richard walked to the edge of the pier and looked down into the cage. "Look, Mommy," he heard her say. "He doesn't have a gun. Is he going to let us out?"

The mother turned her green, oversized eyes toward Richard. "Maybe, sweetie," she said, but not as if she really believed it. "Maybe."

Despite himself, Richard felt tears start in his eye. *Damn you, Grandfather!* he thought, turning away. *Damn you for creating these travesties of human flesh.*

They're not travesties. They're beautiful, the strangely traitorous part of his mind replied.

"How goes it?" he said to the nearest Holy Warrior, whom he thought he recognized from the ship. "Sexsmith, isn't it?"

The Holy Warrior nodded. "That's right, sir." He gestured at the cage. "Frankly, not so well. This is all we've managed to round up. All of the others—well, the ones that weren't killed outright, of course—seem to have fled into deeper water."

"They'll have to surface sometime," Richard said.

"They can't eat underwater. Grandfather didn't engineer them that way."

He'd been concentrating so hard on convincing himself the Selkies weren't human that he'd forgotten they could hear and understand him. The Holy Warriors all knew his ancestry; their victims hadn't, until that moment.

"Your *grandfather?*" a voice growled from the water. Richard froze for an instant, then slowly turned and looked down into the cage at an older Selkie male, his close-cropped hair pure silver. "Victor Hansen was your grandfather?"

"I'm not telling you anything," Richard said.

"Your voice and face tell me enough," the Selkie male said. "Listen, everyone," he called. "This new landling is the grandson of Victor Hansen."

After a moment's stunned silence, the Selkies erupted into shouting. "It can't be!" "Then why doesn't he let us go?" "I don't believe it!" "The Creator's grandson would never—"

"Quiet!" shouted Sexsmith. He fired a burst from his automatic rifle over the top of the cage and the hubbub subsided. Sexsmith gave Richard an amused glance. "Looks like your cat's out of the bag, sir."

Maybe this is an opportunity, Richard thought. *An opportunity to show my devotion to the cause.* "That's right," he shouted to the Selkies. "My grandfather was Victor Hansen. But Victor Hansen was a monster, and the father of monsters. I'm here to right the great wrong he did, and make sure abominations like you don't pollute God's creation any further. I serve the Avatar and God Itself, not my twice-damned grandfather!"

Out of the corner of his eye, he saw the little female who had spoken when he first appeared turn and bury her head in her mother's shoulder. Angry at the involuntary pang in his heart, he plunged on recklessly. "Not only that, I'm the one who led the Holy Warriors here . . . with the help of your own Chris Keating, who activated the *Rivers of Babylon* emergency beacon."

That brought a collective gasp, and out of the corner

of his eye, Richard saw Keating cringe. *Actions have consequences, boy,* Richard thought coldly. *Credit where credit is due.*

"Chris! Is he telling the truth?" The call came from a young male Selkie about Keating's age, at the very back of the cage. His bald head featured a red-and-blue spiral tattoo, and the formfitting wetsuit type of garment he wore glittered as though covered with silver scales.

Richard looked at Keating. The young man visibly stiffened his spine and lifted his chin. "Yes, it's true, John Duval," he shouted. "And you of all people should know why I did it."

The young Selkie looked genuinely shocked. "Not . . . not because of that silly game on the pier?"

"Not just because of it . . . but not *not* because of it, either. That was the rock that broke the keel, John."

John Duval's face reddened, making him look even more monstrous. "You betrayed the entire planet . . . led these monsters here . . . helped them kill who knows how many people . . . because you got *wet?*"

"Because you Selkies have lorded it over normal human beings long enough!" Keating yelled. "Because you're a bunch of subhuman monsters who—"

"Damn you!" John screamed.

The open-roofed "cage" extended two meters above the surface of the water. Richard would have bet that no Selkie could possibly make such a leap.

He would have lost.

From the back of the cage, John Duval plunged beneath the water and arrowed toward the front of the cage. The water boiled in his wake, and then he exploded out of it, up and over the front of the cage, landing on the pier in a cascade of salt water. He grabbed the rifle of the nearest Holy Warrior and smashed the butt of the weapon across its owner's face. As the Warrior screamed and fell back in a spray of blood, the Selkie whipped the rifle into firing position, aimed it at Keating, who stood frozen in shock, and pulled the trigger.

Nothing happened.

With a shriek of rage, Duval threw the rifle at Keating, turned, and dove into the bay, clear of the cage.

As he leaped, a single rifle shot rang out, shockingly loud, from just to Richard's left. Then the young Selkie was gone . . . but he left behind a faint red stain in the water.

"Got him," Sexsmith said. "Don't think I killed him, but he's wounded. He can't get far." He turned and shouted down the pier. "Khan! Veldron! Fire up the tracker boat!" As two Holy Warriors ran to comply, lowering themselves over the side of the pier and disappearing from sight, Sexsmith walked over to the Holy Warrior Duval had rifle-whipped. He sat clutching his nose, blood welling between his fingers and dripping on his chest plate. "Why didn't your weapon fire, Murphy?"

"Safety was on, sir," the wounded Holy Warrior said, rather indistinctly.

"Weapons are to be ready to fire at all times, Murphy. One demerit. It would have been two, but I'm too glad to be alive. The medics have taken over the town hospital. Get yourself up there and get your nose patched up. Report back when you can."

"Yes, sir. Thank you sir." Murphy got to his feet and headed up the pier, leaving a splotchy trail of red.

Veldron reappeared over the edge of the pier. "Boat ready, sir!"

"You heard about the DNA trackers?" Sexsmith asked Richard, who nodded. "This is our first chance to try the technology in the wild. We've married it up with a semi-autonomous underwater bot—we call it a 'hunterbot.' Our boy may already be floating belly-up out in the bay somewhere, but if he's only lightly wounded and thinks he can escape, the hunterbot will soon disabuse him of the notion."

Richard looked at Keating, who had found it suddenly expedient to sit down on the pier and put his head between his knees. *I've seen enough on land,* he thought. *And if I go back to the Grand Deacon, he's liable just to send me back up to* Sanctification.

He made up his mind. "I'd like to go out in the boat, see it in action," he said. As Sexsmith's expression turned skeptical, he played his trump card. "I'm sure the Archdeacon will want a complete report on the . . . um, hunterbot. If it works here, I'm sure Body Security will have good use for it on Earth and elsewhere."

Sexsmith hesitated, then shrugged. "All right," he said. "Suit yourself. Veldron!"

"Sir!"

"Mr. Hansen is coming along to observe. Is there a spare survival suit on board? Not that you should need it," Sexsmith said to Richard. "Regulations."

"Yes, sir," Veldron said.

"Good." To Richard, Sexsmith made a grand gesture in the direction of Veldron's head, the only part of him visible above the edge of the pier. "Have fun."

"Thanks." Richard went over to Slowinsky. "Tell the Grand Deacon where I've gone. And deliver Mr. Keating back to him with my compliments."

"The Grand Deacon is expecting you to join him for dinner at 1800," Slowinsky warned.

Richard waved a hand. "That's hours from now. I'm sure we'll be back. And if we aren't, the Grand Deacon will understand that I must fulfill my responsibilities to the Archdeacon first." *Sure* he will, Richard thought, but the worst the Grand Deacon could do would be to send him back to the ship, and Ellers probably intended to do that anyway.

"If you say so, sir," said Slowinsky, his tone implying that he didn't believe a word of it. "Come on, you." He reached down, hauled Chris Keating rather roughly to his feet, and led him away, back up the pier to the mainland, Richard's second erstwhile bodyguard bringing up the rear.

"Sir? We're waiting," Veldron shouted.

"Coming!" Richard jogged over to where Veldron and Khan had disappeared and discovered a metal ladder leading down to a floating dock. A tracker boat floated next to the dock, engine running, puffs of exhaust emerging from the oily water behind its transom as Khan, standing at the wheel in the upper half of the two-level, partially enclosed bridge, kept it in position. About the size of an ordinary Earth speedboat, painted dull gray and bristling with antennae and weapons launchers and dischargers, the boat had an open stern but a decked-over bow. In the center of that deck rode a gray torpedolike cylinder: the hunterbot, Richard presumed.

The boat rocked alarmingly even in the slight swell that made its way into the oil-fouled waters of New Botany Bay, and Richard climbed gingerly aboard it, wondering if he should mention he'd never been on a boat before . . .

. . . except, oddly, he felt as if he *had*.

The moment his feet hit the bottom boards, Khan shoved the throttle forward. The boat eased away from the dock, and Richard sat down hard and abruptly as he felt the boat sway beneath his feet.

They burbled along to the spot where John Duval had hit the water, and Khan backed the propeller, bringing them to a bobbing halt. In the lower half of the bridge, Veldron busied himself at a curved console boasting three vidscreens and a surfeit of blinking lights. "Launching," he called, and pressed a button.

On the bow, something hissed, and a moment later, the hunterbot catapulted into the bay.

"Scanning for blood trace," Veldron said.

Richard wanted to get closer to the console, but the boat's motion made it risky. He elected to stay put and hold on. *If the boat is this unsteady when we're sitting still, what will it be like when we're moving?* he wondered uneasily.

"Got it," Veldron announced. "Hunterbot swimming clear. Homing signal activated . . . have you got it upstairs, Nassar?"

"Got it, J.B.," said Khan. "And . . . we're off!"

Richard braced himself for a surge of power, but the engine barely changed pitch, and as the bow turned toward the middle of the bay, they left the pier behind at something barely more than a walking pace. Richard unbraced himself. "That's it?" he said.

Veldron glanced back at him. "Whaddya want?" he said. "The hunterbot's fast, but the DNA scan takes a second or two every time it's activated, so that's the limiting factor. Don't worry, we'll still catch the fishy bastard. He might be able to outswim us for a while, but he'll have to rest eventually . . . and he's wounded, too. We'll probably have him in a few minutes."

Richard dared to ease his way forward, sliding along the bench that ran just under the gunwale until he could look over Veldron's shoulder. The main screen in the center of his console showed a green line stretching away before the icon representing their boat, spreading and fading the farther it got. "What's that?"

"Possible courses," Veldron said. "The tracker measures the currents to adjust for drift of the DNA it's detecting and extrapolates from that how it should adjust its course. Another reason it's slow." He grinned at Richard. "What, you thought we'd go galloping along like a speedboat and you came along for the thrill?"

"Something like that," Richard said, although actually, considering the way his stomach kept lurching, not-galloping suited him fine.

"Well, we'll pick up speed if we can get a reading from one of the surveillance satellites and don't have to rely on DNA tracking. But that will only work if he's close enough to the surface to produce an infrared trace, or leave a visible wake. I think he'll stay deep."

Richard watched the screen in silence for several minutes. "I can't believe it can pick up such tiny traces of DNA in all that water—and distinguish John Duval's DNA from all the other DNA."

"That's the genius of it," Veldron said. "Some smart guy in the Archdeaconate of Research and Development figured it out just last year. The scanning beam uses— what's wrong?"

Richard had grabbed for support as the boat lurched. It lurched again, and again . . . and kept on lurching.

Veldron laughed. "Oh, the motion. Yeah, we're leaving the bay, moving out into the open ocean. Looks like our boy's headed for deep water. Can't imagine where he thinks he's going. He's still bleeding, too, based on this." Veldron tapped the screen. "Really strong DNA traces. We could track him just from shed skin cells, but it would be slower." He shook his head. "I'm surprised he made it this far. Must not be a very serious wound. But we'll get him."

"In deep water? How?" Richard looked around. "Is there a minisub somewhere on the boat?" He couldn't imagine where.

"We don't even have to get our feet wet—"

As the boat lurched again, a big dollop of spray hurtled over the side and splashed into the bottom of the boat, where it quickly drained into the bilge. Somewhere, a pump started up. Veldron laughed again. "Well, okay, maybe we do. But we don't have to go underwater, doesn't matter how deep our escaped moddie goes. The hunterbot's armed. It'll take care of him for us . . . and any other Selkies it finds."

The boat lurched again, and more spray hurtled in, drenching Richard. "Gah," he said, and wiping salt water out of his eyes. As he did so, he looked up and saw swift-moving gray clouds scudding across the sky that had been mostly blue just moments before. He turned around to look back the way they had come, and his heart jumped in his chest when he discovered a wall of gray mist had swallowed the shore.

"Weather's turning," Khan called down, rather unnecessarily, Richard thought. "We may not be able to stay on station."

"Do the best you can!" Veldron called up. "The boffins want all the data we can provide before they turn the rest of these things loose."

"Turn 'em loose?" Richard said, tearing his eyes away

from the waves that had begun to march past the boat, each bigger than the last. Spray splattered his face constantly now, coming both from the waves they ploughed into and over and from the rising wind, which blew the ridges of water into whitecaps and flung their peaks into the boat. It all seemed oddly familiar . . . from vids, maybe? . . . to his brain, but not to his stomach, which had begun to object . . . strenuously. He swallowed hard and tried to focus on Veldron, who seemed unconcerned.

"The hunterbots are designed to operate autonomously," he shouted above the rising wind. "You can use them to track a particular Selkie like this one," he tapped the screen, "or just let them loose to find any Selkies they can. In that mode, the default one, they just cast around like hound dogs, looking for Selkie DNA—based on that Selkie genome you provided."

Richard nodded.

"When a hunterbot detects some, it tries to track it. And when it finds a Selkie along the trail," Veldron grinned and made a slashing motion across his throat.

The wind howled, and Richard, now soaked to the skin, shivered in the cold blast. "Can't hold on station!" Khan shouted. "We're going to have to cut it loose!"

"Damn," said Veldron. "Okay!" he shouted back. He looked at Richard. "You look like you'll be glad to get back to dry land!"

"N-not at a-all," Richard lied between chattering teeth.

Veldron bent over and opened a locker under his console. He pulled out an orange package. "Put this on," he said. "Survival suit. Regulations say we should all have put one on before we left the pier, but Nassar and I both hate the things."

"W-why now? Are w-we sinking?" Richard said in alarm.

Veldron chuckled. "Takes more than a little squall to sink a boat like this. No, we're not sinking—but this will keep you warm—and dry."

Richard opened the package and began pulling on the

one-piece garment inside. It seemed flimsy as paper, but the moment he had it on it stiffened to something more like soft rubber, and molded itself to his skin. "Might as well go whole hog," Veldron said, and handed him a helmet. Anxious to get the spray out of his face, Richard pulled it on. It sealed itself in place automatically. In seconds, he felt warm and dry and . . .

. . . seasick. He just managed to get his faceplate open and his head over the railing before retching up the mostly liquid contents of his stomach, still essentially empty—he hadn't eaten anything since he'd thrown up in the shuttle.

He hung there with his eyes closed for a moment. He had just opened them and was turning back into the boat when he heard Khan yell, "Shit!", a wordless shout from Veldron, and then the boat leaped up into the air like a dolphin, flinging him up and out. The world spun crazily around him, waves, mist, gray sky. He had a horrifying momentary glimpse of the boat, airborne and upside down, before he plunged into the ocean in an explosion of bubbles and spray.

Chapter 8

THE JOURNEY TO Dahlia's family's vacation habitat passed uneventfully for Emily and Dahlia, as most sub journeys did, since even the largest of Marseguro's nastiest deep-sea predators wasn't big enough to threaten a sub—despite the chilling tales of sea monsters the adventure vidders liked to spin—and even the most violent surface storm couldn't roil the water to the depth to which they were descending. Four hours after they left the bay, the radar profile of the shelter appeared centered, crisp, and clear, in their navigation screens. Half an hour after that, they could see its lights for themselves through the canopy; ten minutes after that, they had docked.

"Shall we take the air tunnel or swim it?" Dahlia asked. The sub had automatically increased its internal air pressure as they descended, so pressurization wasn't an issue, but when Emily saw the outside water temperature, she shivered.

"No, thanks," she said. "Not without a heated skinsuit. I'm a shallow-water girl. Let's take the air tunnel now and we'll go for a swim later."

"Okay." Dahlia flicked a switch on the control panel and the air hatch opened with a slight hiss. Lights came on, revealing a featureless white tube. "After you."

"So formal," Emily said with a grin. She hoisted her personal pack and stepped into the tunnel. It vibrated a little under her feet, which startled her until she remembered that somewhere out of sight bots were moving the supplies they'd brought out of the sub's hold and into the habitat.

The tunnel wasn't very long—five or six meters, maybe—and ended in another hatch, unlocked, of course: by long-standing Marseguro law, no deep-sea habitat *could* be locked, because someone might need it at any moment as an emergency shelter. This hatch led into an air lock—Selkies might be able to breathe underwater, but they still preferred not to have high-pressure water blasting into the air-filled part of their living quarters in the event of a seal failure. Since there was air on both sides of the lock at the moment, though, the inner hatch slid open instantly, revealing the interior.

As Emily had seen from outside—and as she knew anyway—the habitat was a sphere, the upper half full of air, the lower half full of water. Much like in her own home, the central feature of the air-filled section was a round pool. A splash ring about a meter wide surrounded it, and the main dryfloor was a short step up from that. About four meters wide, it was divided into four compartments: a kitchen, a living/dining/rec area (into which the tunnel opened) a sleeping area with four beds in it, and a bathroom, the only room that was fully enclosed.

Emily only had a moment to take in their surroundings before Dahlia shouldered her aside. "Well, don't just stand there," she said. "Let me show you around."

"I think I'm seeing most of it," Emily said wryly. "Not a lot of privacy. Good thing you didn't bring a boyfriend along."

"Oh, there are underwater rooms for *that*," Dahlia said. "Up here is just for sleeping."

Emily laughed and followed her friend into the living room. Dahlia showed her the game and vidscreens and the audio system—all state of the art and very expensive; not for the first time, Emily wondered just how rich her friend's family really was. Despite both her parents having well-paying professional careers, she didn't believe for a second they could afford a private deep-sea getaway. But then, Dahlia's parents owned three of the microfactories that *made* most of this stuff. Maybe her dad got it at cost.

"There's enough food here for a year," Emily said as Dahlia showed her cupboard after well-stocked cupboard in the kitchen.

Dahlia shrugged. "Government regulations. Private habitats have to maintain the same rations as the government shelters. There are supposed to be enough of those to take in most of the population in the event of some kind of catastrophe, but just in case . . ."

"I've never known what kind of catastrophe they think the shelters would be any use in," Emily said. "An earthquake big enough to destroy the shore towns would probably damage the shelters, too. And an asteroid strike would probably just kill us off. You could die right away up top or die slowly down here."

"There's always the Body Purified," Dahlia said in a spectral voice. "They haven't found us in fifty years, but they could show up any day now and start wiping out all us depraved subhuman monsters." She wriggled her fingers at Emily. "Ooooooooooo . . ."

Emily laughed. "Depraved, I'll give you. Or at least perverted."

"My strength is as the strength of ten because my heart is pure," Dahlia said virtuously. "Even if the rest of me isn't." She moved on to the next door. "Now if you'll step this way, I'll show you our extra-fine toilet facilities."

After Dahlia finished showing Emily around, they returned to the kitchen, where they set the cookbot on "Gourmet" and gave it free rein. Dahlia even entered the nutrition override. "A little extra fat and salt won't hurt us just this once."

The resulting concoction, which went by an Old Earth French name that Emily didn't recognize and couldn't pronounce, but which tasted delicious, left them so sated they killed a couple of hours watching a vid. Some very good stuff had recently come out of the fertile minds and computers of Marseguro's small but burgeoning vid community, but tonight's, a tale of a star-crossed love affair between a Selkie and a landling set on a future Marseguro covered with floating habitats and underwater cities, left Emily cold, even though a couple of the actors were friends of hers. Still, it gave them time to digest. When it ended, they finally mustered enough energy to roll off the couches and into the pool (nicely heated, to Emily's relief).

Dahlia led her down into the underwater section of the habitat, which featured a wet-gym and not just one but two romantically lit "recreation chambers." Near the closed bottom hatch she opened a locker containing bright-yellow deep-sea skinsuits, more like the survival suits the landlings wore whenever they ventured out to sea than the usual minimalist Selkie garb. "Government regulations again," Dahlia chirped in Selkie as she pulled one on. Emily pulled on the other. The deep-sea skinsuits included, to her surprise, an oxygenator, full head cover and goggles, and even a small supply of emergency underwater rations in sealed tubes, the kind of thing you could squirt into your mouth and swallow without worrying about taking in too much salt water. "These are the only kind of skinsuits approved for deep-sea excursions," Dahlia went on. "Just in case landlings are in here. That's why they have oxygenators."

Emily nodded. "Do you ever just go for a swim without one of these?"

Dahlia chirped amusement. "Of course. You know how I love skinny-dipping! Especially if I have a boy to skinny-dip with." She laughed. "It's cold, but invigorating."

Emily cocked her head. "The swimming, or the . . ."

"Both! But even I can only stay out for a few minutes down here, and to really see the sights, we need more time."

She slapped a control on the wall, the hatch slid open beneath them, and they slipped out into the Deep.

Emily had to laugh at herself for her unconscious capitalization of the word. Deep? They were still on the continental shelf. The real Deep, the many-kilometers-deep abyss, lay several more kilometers out. Still, they were deeper than she'd ever been before, and as deep as most Selkies ever went, though she knew genesculptors were trying to find ways to further modify the Selkie genome to make them—or future generations, anyway—better able to utilize all of Marseguro: maybe even become true merpeople who would never need to surface at all.

Maybe the government's shelters do make sense, she thought. *We occupy such a small portion of the planet—we've still got all our eggs in one basket, as they used to say about Earth back in prespace days. It wouldn't take much to render Selkies extinct.*

It was the argument of the Expansionists, of course. The Consolidationists would argue that the odds of a species-ending event were so small they should concentrate on creating a society worth preserving before worrying about far-fetched threats.

That reminded her of the argument with her parents, and she impatiently shoved such thoughts out of her mind. *I'm on vacation!*

"This way," Dahlia said, and swam off into the gloom. Light-piping on the skinsuit and her headlamp combined to make her look like some ghostly figure composed entirely of photons. Emily followed.

The seafloor surrounding the habitat proved to be of surpassing beauty, no doubt the reason Dahlia's family had built there in the first place. A natural garden of black volcanic rock alternated with glittering fields of the glassy structures built by the near-microscopic crustaceanlike creatures dubbed "crablets." Many of the rocks sported red, orange, and yellow anemenots. Fish swarmed among their waving tentacles, including the largest pod of bugglefish she'd ever seen, their black-and-white-striped snaky bodies slithering over and over each other like an animated op-art painting.

They returned to the shelter tired and finally hungry again, climbed out of the pool, and shed the deep-sea skinsuits, leaving them by the edge of the water. "We'll need them again tomorrow," Dahlia said, "and it's easier to get into them up here. That's just a glorified storage cabinet down below."

They had another delicious dinner, then turned in while the soft strains of Mozart wafted from the audio system.

An indeterminate time later Emily's eyes flew open at the sound of Dahlia's scream. A dark figure loomed over her bed. "Emily," a voice croaked, and then the figure collapsed across her torso.

"Computer, lights!" Dahlia yelled, as Emily, too terrified to make a sound, scrambled out from under the man's dead weight, staggered to her feet, and pressed her naked back against the wall, staring at the stranger.

Except, when the lights came up, she realized it wasn't a stranger at all: it was John Duval. Her movement had sent him tumbling back onto the floor, where he lay supine, eyes closed, head lolling to one side. His silver-scaled skinsuit had a hole in its left shoulder. Blood trickling from it had already begun to pool on the bedroom's pale blue floor, and a pink trail of mingled water and blood leading back to the central pool gave mute evidence of John's struggle to make it to Emily's bed.

In the middle of the pool floated a sputa, one of the one-person propulsion units used all over Marseguro whenever you needed to get somewhere faster than your own flippers could manage.

Emily dropped to her knees beside John. "John! John, can you hear me?"

"Computer, medical emergency!" Dahlia shouted, and a locker on the bedroom wall beeped and opened. What dropped out of it from vertical to horizontal looked like an old-fashioned four-poster bed—except Emily knew both the "posts" and the "canopy" were stuffed with automated medical scanning, diagnostic, and treatment equipment. "Let's get him into the docbot," said Dahlia. It wasn't easy—he was head-and-shoulders longer than Emily, and Emily was half a head longer than Dahlia—

but adrenaline aided them. As they lugged John across the floor, Emily at his head, Dahlia at his feet, Emily worried about aggravating the still-unseen injury—but on the other hand, he had presumably survived a who-knew-how-long underwater trip with it, so it was probably as aggravated as it was likely to get.

They pulled him onto the bed and started stripping him of his skinsuit. Emily gasped as she got a clear view of his shoulder. "That's—that's got to be a gunshot wound."

Dahlia pulled John's skinsuit down around his ankles; Emily took a quick look at John's nude body, blushed, and then focused her attention on his shoulder until Dahlia—who certainly wasn't seeing anything *she* hadn't seen, and probably handled, often enough—pulled the docbot's body-temperature control sheet over him.

"Don't be silly," Dahlia said. "The only guns on the planet are kept locked up by the Council. What makes you think it's a gunshot wound?"

"It's round," Emily said. She stepped back as the docbot began its diagnostics, activating a full-body scan, extending a robotic arm to take blood, and Emily had only a vague idea what else. "And there's a small entry hole and a bigger, more ragged exit hole. That's the kind of thing they're always pointing out in historical adventure vids."

"You can't believe everything you see in a vid," Dahlia said, but she didn't sound as sure of herself as a moment before.

The room had begun to warm automatically as soon as the shelter realized people were up and moving around, but nevertheless Emily shivered and folded her arms over her breasts. Dahlia slipped away—Emily hardly noticed as she stared at John's face, waiting for the docbot's prognosis—and came back a minute later with a fuzzy pink dressing gown and—Emily did a double take—"Bunny slippers?"

Dahlia shrugged. "They're warm and comfortable—

and comforting. It's hard to believe anything is seriously wrong with the world when you're wearing bunny slippers." She looked at John and bit her lip.

Emily pulled on the dressing gown, grateful for the warmth. But when she slipped her feet into the bunny slippers, they failed to work their promised magic: she was still very much aware, as she looked at John's unconscious form, that something had gone *seriously* wrong with their world. "What could have happened?"

"He probably just thought he'd surprise us," Dahlla said. "And had some sort of accident along the way."

"Surprise us?" Emily said. "Some surprise. He was starting a new job in the mapping corps, remember? He should be on a cat-sub heading out for a three-month voyage. Not bleeding to death down here in the middle of nowhere!" She realized she had raised her voice, and stopped.

"He's not bleeding to death," Dahlia said. "That fancy skinsuit of his has some built-in first aid functions, and it's self-sealing, to boot. It kept the wounds from leaking too much. And this is the latest model of docbot. It can handle a little thing like—"

"Gunshot wound to the left shoulder," the docbot suddenly announced.

"I told you!" Emily said, but she took no pride in being right.

"Blood loss. Shock. Hypothermia. Extreme fatigue. Minor muscle strain." The docbot stopped, and beeped. "Prognosis: good, with proper medical care."

Emily breathed a sigh of relief.

"Docbot, define 'proper medical care,'" Dahlia said.

"This unit will stabilize patient. Patient should then be transported to main hospital, with minimal transit time."

"Looks like our vacation is over," Emily said.

"Before it even really began," Dahlia said. "Well, it can't be helped." She sighed. "I liked being cut off from the world, but . . . guess I'd better send up a transmitter buoy so we can radio ahead and tell Hansen's Harbor we've got an emergency." She went to the edge of the pool, slipped out of her slippers, dropped her dressing gown, and plunged naked into the water.

"Docbot, how long until patient is stabilized?" Emily asked.

"Estimate three point five hours needed to restore body temperature and stabilize pulse and blood pressure," the docbot announced.

Emily looked at the unconscious John and chewed her lip. Finally she said, "Docbot, can patient be woken?"

"Ill-advised," the docbot said. "Necessary stimulant could interfere with stabilization of vital signs. Patient may wake on his own at any time, however. Brain activity is vigorous."

Emily knelt by the bed. She didn't touch John, but she spoke into his ear. "John, are you awake?" Nothing. "John?" she said a little louder, and this time was rewarded by a change in his breathing. Emboldened, she repeated, "John?". Then added, "It's Emily. John, wake up."

John's eyes fluttered, then opened. For a moment, they remained unfocused, gazing blankly up at the lens-studded underside of the docbot's scanner canopy, then suddenly he blinked four or five times in rapid succession and turned his head to look right at her. "Emily?" And then, to her shock, he began to cry, gasping for air between silent sobs, tears streaming from his huge green eyes. He turned his head away from her, obviously fighting to regain emotional control. She stood by helplessly for a moment, then tentatively reached out and touched his red-and-blue tattooed head, petting him as she might have soothed a restive baby. "Shhh," she said. "Shhh. John, it's all right, you're safe now."

"None of us are safe," John choked out. "None of us, Emily."

Dahlia returned at that moment, cinching her dressing gown around her waist. "Buoy's launched," she said. "It'll take a minute or two to reach the surface." She blinked at John. "You're awake!" She grinned.

"Couldn't stay away from me, huh? But what did you do to your—"

"I was shot," John said. "By the Body!"

Emily frowned. "You mean *in* the body? No, in the shoulder—it's a nasty hole, but it's a flesh wound, it—"

"No!" John shouted. The docbot had restrained him at some point, so he could only move his head, but he flung it back and forth so violently Emily feared for his vertebrae. "I was shot by the Body. The Body Purified. It's here. It's invaded. And it's—they're—they're killing us like animals!"

Emily snatched back her hand and surged to her feet as though John had turned into a monster in front of her eyes.

"He's raving," Dahlia said. "I'll prove it." She raised her voice, although of course it really wasn't necessary. "Computer, status of transmission buoy."

"Buoy is on surface and active," the computer said.

"Computer, transmit following to—"

John's head jerked up. "Computer, cancel previous command!" he shouted.

"Command input canceled," said the computer.

"Now what?" Dahlia said.

"If you send a transmission, you'll tell the Body where we are," John cried, the words tumbling out like fish from a net. "They'll hunt us down and kill us, just like they killed . . . so many others . . ." He squeezed his eyes shut. Fresh tears tracked his face.

Dahlia glared at him. "This is going on too long," she said. "It's not funny."

"He's been shot, Dahlia," Emily snapped. "That's a rather extreme step to take for the sake of a practical joke."

"He wants us to stay cut off from civilization so it'll just be him and two girls trapped in this shelter for a couple of weeks," Dahlia said. "John has always wanted his own harem. And I'm not saying he wounded himself on purpose. I'm just saying he's not going to let a little thing like a hole in his arm keep him from fantasizing about threesomes."

Emily knew Dahlia and John had been lovers off and on for years. Presumably, Dahlia knew a lot of things about John that Emily didn't. But Emily had grown up with John, and while she didn't doubt he had a rich sexual life, both in reality and in fantasy, she didn't believe he would play a joke this cruel—or try to maintain it after he'd been injured.

And while she didn't doubt that her reputation for being unattainable would have made her an attractive sexual trophy for someone like John, she also didn't flatter herself to think that John wanted to thrash up some foam with her so much he'd completely change his personality to accomplish it.

"No," Emily said. "Dahlia, I believe him—or at least believe that *he* believes that the Body has invaded."

"You're as crazy as he is, then," Dahlia snapped.

"So you're locked in a shelter with two crazy people," Emily said impatiently. "Safest thing to do is humor us, isn't it? Don't send a transmission. Just listen. See what's being said on the communications channels."

Dahlia rolled her eyes. "All right," she said. "Computer. Scan communications channels and play strongest signal."

There was a long silence. "All communications channels scanned," the computer said. "Only encrypted signals found, at frequencies not normally used by Marseguroite traffic."

"What?" Dahlia glared at the ceiling, even though the AI was actually located somewhere in the wall on the opposite side of the shelter, if Emily remembered right. "Computer, play signal from Hansen's Harbor Public Broadcast Station."

"No signal present at designated frequency," the computer said.

"But . . . oh, stupid thing!" Dahlia looked at Emily. "It's probably just a glitch in our equipment," she said, but she made it sound like a question.

"No glitch," John said. He sounded calmer. Emily gave him a look, and he actually smiled at her. "Pain medication is a wonderful thing," he said. "Dahlia, the tower that housed the Public Broadcast Station is currently a pile of steaming rubble spread along a large chunk of what's left of Pier Two. The antennae cluster crushed two houseboats on its way down and narrowly missed taking out the harbormaster's building—not that it mattered, because the second sweep of the Body's assault craft blew the harbormaster and his building to bloody froth and flinders."

Dahlia stared at him, and suddenly sank down on the floor as though her knees had buckled. "You're serious."

"Serious as death," John said. "Literally."

Emily felt as if a great howling wind had started blowing in the center of her head, a tornado that could suck in her sanity and control and rip it to shreds. "My parents?" she whispered. "Amy?"

"I don't know," John said. "I didn't see them. They weren't in the group of prisoners I ended up with." He took a shuddering breath. "I don't even know what happened to my own family. I was on my way to board the *Magellan* when the attack came. They seemed to be concentrating on the visible structures, so I hope the underwater habs were mostly spared. But when I escaped, they were working on launching a couple of subs. Good thing they didn't have those in the water when I made my run for it. I think they sent a surface boat after me, but a storm blew in. I'm pretty sure it lost me."

"But I don't understand," Dahlia said, sounding young and lost. "How did the Body find us after all these years?"

John looked grim. "You both know Chris Keating."

Emily remembered her unpleasant encounter with him in the Square, when she had tried to apologize. She made a face. "Yes, unfortunately."

Dahlia nodded.

"Apparently he hiked over to Landing Valley and activated one of the *Rivers of Babylon*'s distress beacons."

"What?" Emily couldn't believe it. "He couldn't—he wouldn't—I mean . . ." Her voice trailed off as she remembered some of the things he had said to her. "Oh, God."

"I'll kill him for it, if I get a chance," John said, and made it sound like a promise, not a threat. "I almost had a chance on the pier. They didn't know how far I could leap out of the water. I got clear of the cage and even got my hands on a rifle. But the damned thing wouldn't fire. That's when I escaped. I jumped into the bay."

"And that's when you got shot."

John nodded. "Somebody was awfully quick on the trigger. Nailed me in midair. But I could still swim, and there was a sputa stand just a few meters down. By the time they were searching the area right by the pier, I was already on my way out of the bay." He paused. "There's something else. I don't know if he was telling the truth, or not . . . I don't see how he could be . . . but someone else was on the pier. A civilian." He paused again. "He claimed to be Victor Hansen's grandson. And he said he was the one who picked up the signal from the distress beacon and told the Holy Warriors we were here."

"He's lying!" Dahlia said. "Trying to get under your skin. Victor Hansen's grandson would never betray us."

Emily heard the certainty in Dahlia's voice and really wanted to share it . . . except she remembered how equally certain Dahlia had been, just moments before, that *John* was lying. "It doesn't matter who he was. The question is, what do we do now?"

"John needs a hospital," Dahlia said.

"I doubt we still have one in Hansen's Harbor," John said. His voice seemed weaker than it had a moment before. "I think . . . I'm being . . . sedated . . ." he said, and then his eyes fluttered closed.

"Docbot, did you sedate the patient?" Emily demanded.

"Affirmative," said the machine. "Pulse and respiration showed signs of stress-induced irregularity outside the permissible parameters for proper stabilization of patient for transportation."

Emily turned to Dahlia. "Now what?" she said, trying to keep the despair lurking in the back of her mind from shouldering its way to the foreground. "This may be the safest place for him. It may be the safest place for *all* of us."

"I don't know," Dahlia said. "If we can't take him to shore . . ." She bit her lip. "Docbot," she said. "What is the patient's prognosis if the only medical care he receives is what is available in this habitat?"

"Nontrivial risk of death within twenty-four hours," the docbot said. "Tissue damage too great to be properly treated by this unit. Precise calculation of survival odds impossible."

"Docbot, provide *estimated* odds," Dahlia snapped.

"Best estimation, fifty percent chance of death within twenty-four hours. Risk rises thereafter. Best estimation, odds of long-term survival: no better than thirty percent. Best estimation, odds of survival without permanent disability: negligible."

"That's not good enough," Emily said. "We have to get him more help!" *But if we can't take him to Hansen's Harbor . . .*

Then it hit her. "Jumpoff Station," she breathed. "We'll take him to Jumpoff."

"The research station?" Dahlia said. "How is that any better than here?"

Emily hesitated. Most people thought of Jumpoff as only a small habitat, not much bigger than the one they were in, located on the very edge of the continental shelf, and used as base camp for expeditions into the abyss. But Emily knew better. She wasn't supposed to tell anyone, but she didn't suppose it mattered any more.

"It's a lot bigger than most people realize," she said at last. "It's almost a small town in its own right—the biggest underwater settlement on Marseguro. They do all kinds of research down there."

"Like what?" Dahlia demanded. "And how come I've never heard any of this?"

"It's secret stuff," Emily said. Emily's mother had put in more than a few stints at Jumpoff, and had told Emily about the station, though she'd never talked in detail about what she did there. Emily couldn't even imagine what kind of research needed so much secrecy, but she supposed the Council had its reasons. *Probably worried the Consolidationists would see whatever it is as a waste of money and try to close it down,* she thought. *Located there, it must have some sort of Expansionist agenda behind it.*

"Then how do *you* know about it?"

"My mother's worked there some. But never mind that. The important thing is that because so many people are living there at any given time, it has a full-blown hospital. They'll be able to give John the treatment he needs."

"It's six hours to Jumpoff from here by sub," Dahlia said. "It's only four hours to shore."

"Docbot," Emily said. "Effect of six hours' transit versus four hours' transit time on prognosis of patient, assuming he receives prompt medical attention at the conclusion of that transit."

"Negligible," said the docbot.

Emily looked at Dahlia and spread her hands.

Dahlia frowned, then nodded. "All right," she said. "Then let's get him on the sub. I'll pack some supplies if you'll go fire it up. We'll load the supplies, then take John over last."

"All right," Emily said. She gave the unconscious John a final glance, hesitated, then leaned down and kissed him lightly on the forehead. At the edge of the pool, she doffed the dressing gown and bunny slippers and pulled on one of the deep-sea skinsuits they'd left there the day before. "Computer, open air lock into sub access tunnel," she said. It slid open, and she headed down the air tunnel.

Once inside the dolphin sub, it took Emily only a few

minutes to power up the controls and the engines. She flicked on the exterior lights, which showed the shiny length of tube leading to the sphere of the habitat, anchored to the seabed on three stout legs.

Something flashed in the beam of light between the sub and the habitat.

Fish, Emily thought at first, but something about the shape hadn't looked very fishlike. She activated sonar and the other sensors and got back a strong, sharp, and almost instantaneous return that the computer instantly analyzed as "Small submarine vessel, metal, self-powered by atomic battery."

Emily hit the comm button, hoping Dahlia had the habitat speakers turned up and the umbilical properly connected. "Dahlia, you there?"

No response.

"Dahlia, there's something out here I don't like the looks of. Respond, please."

Nothing.

And then Emily gasped and scrambled up out of the command chair as the strange metallic object stopped circling the habitat, dove straight to the bottom of the sphere . . . and disappeared

"Shit!" Emily hurled herself at the hatch, pounded her fist on it until it opened, and then dashed down the tunnel. The habitat door slid open as she approached and she burst in just in time to see Dahlia dive naked into the water from the other side of the pool. "Dahlia!" Emily screamed. "Dahlia!"

Her friend surfaced. "Don't worry, I'll be there in a second," she said. "I'm just going down to underwater storage to pick up some extra power packs for the—"

"Get out!" Emily screamed. "Get out of the water!"

"What?" Dahlia said. "Why?" And then she looked down, a puzzled expression on her face—and vanished, pulled underwater so fast a whirlpool swirled where she had been.

"Dahlia!" Emily started forward, but had only taken a step when water erupted from the center of the pool as though something had exploded in it—and the pool turned cloudy red.

Dahlia's head broke the surface again, and Emily felt a surge of relief that turned to horror as the head rolled over, revealing ripped flesh and shattered vertebrae. As other body parts bobbed to the surface, Emily screamed, a scream that turned to a choking cry as she vomited, falling to her hands and knees, emptying the green-and-yellow contents of her stomach across the pale blue floor. She hung there, breathing hard, then swallowed and scrambled up. Not looking at the pool and what floated within it, she hurried around the dryfloor to where John still lay in his drug-induced sleep, intending to drag him out of bed and somehow get him to the sub—but she'd just started to pull off his blanket when the lights went out.

For one heart-stopping moment of sheer terror, Emily stood in utter blackness. Then the pale green emergency lighting came on. "Power conduit failure," the computer announced. "Human intervention required to repair. Operating on backup batteries. Eight hours' power at current load."

Had the whatever-it-was that had killed Dahlia actually been smart enough to cut the main power conduit, or had that just been a side effect of its attack?

Either way, it didn't matter. Now she *really* had to get John out of here.

The habitat rang as if it had been struck by a giant mallet. "Computer, what's happening?" Emily screamed.

"Habitat was struck by a second high-pressure pulse."

A second . . . ? Oh. Emily suddenly knew what had torn Dahlia apart. No wonder the power conduit ruptured. *That thing has some kind of . . . of sonic depth charge.*

"Computer, report any damage!"

"Habitat is undamaged," the computer said in the same calm, unconcerned voice it always used—but what it said next filled Emily with horror. "Access tube to currently docked vehicle has failed, however."

"Computer, status of vehicle!" Emily yelped.

"Scanning." A paused. "Vehicle is no longer docked . . . Vehicle now on sea bottom."

Oh, no. "Computer, orientation of vehicle?"

"Inverted. Vehicle computer is no longer communicating . . . Vehicle appears to have lost integrity; numerous pieces of debris detected."

"Shit!" Emily seldom swore, but nothing else seemed to fit the situation. "Shit, shit, shit!"

The computer, not having been directly addressed, said nothing.

Emily looked at John, still unconscious and looking disconcertingly like a corpse in the pale green light. "Docbot," she said. "Patient status."

"Patient is stable and resting comfortably," the docbot responded promptly. "Prognosis has improved."

It has? For the first time, Emily felt a surge of hope. "Docbot, estimated odds of survival without further medical attention." She swallowed, then added, "Assuming power remains constant."

"Best estimate, seventy percent," the docbot said.

She closed her eyes. "Docbot, estimated odds of survival without medical attention once power fails?"

"Negligible," the docbot said. And it didn't put "best estimate" in front of that stark analysis, she noticed.

It'll have to do, Emily thought. *Oh, John.* But at least he had a chance. Unlike . . . Emily looked at the pool. Cleanerbots whirred within it, clearing it of . . . of . . .

Emily shook her head. She couldn't think about it. Not now.

But she knew damn well she'd wake screaming from dreams about it.

The sputa that had pulled John to the habitat still floated in the pool. "Computer," Emily said. "Location of small mobile vehicle that initiated pressure wave."

"Vehicle is again inside habitat," the computer said.

What? "Computer, close bottom sea doors, emergency speed!"

A vibration, an almost audible clang. "Doors closed."

"Computer, location of small mobile vehicle?"

"Unchanged."

Trapped you, you murderous piece of tin, Emily thought. Unless the thing was amphibious and could climb out into the air-filled part of the habitat . . .

If it could, it already would have, she reasoned.

She wanted to destroy it, wanted to destroy it more than anything she'd ever wanted to do before, but she didn't know how. At least she'd rendered it harmless for the time being . . . she hoped.

But she still had to get to Jumpoff Station, and that meant she needed the sputa.

I don't think I'll swim out and get it, Emily thought, as water suddenly surged and swirled for no apparent reason. Fortunately, she didn't have to; as the water bulged again, it pushed the sputa to one side . . . better yet, it pushed it to the same side as the door leading into the access tube air lock. Emily raced around the edge of the pool, being very careful not to slip and fall into the water, and hauled out the device, which looked like a winged torpedo. Nacelles on the ends of the wings held the propulsion jets; the fat part of the torpedo held the power source, a nearly inexhaustible atomic battery, and the pump that pulled water in and forced it out the jets. Two handles, steering planes, fins, and a rudimentary control and sensor panel made up the rest of the device.

Like every other Selkie, Emily had used sputas since the first time her parents had allowed her out of their hab on her own. She'd never handled one out of the water before, and she'd been worried about the weight, but she found she could lift it easily, and she shoved it into the air lock with little difficulty. She paused to issue final commands. "Computer," she said. "Turn off all power-using equipment except for the docbot and the emergency lights nearest to it. . . . and this air lock," she added hastily.

All around the pool indicator lights vanished as the refrigerator, entertainment units, and other electronics shut down.

"Should this unit shut itself down?" the computer inquired.

"No! Uh . . . no. Computer, record voice message."

"Recording.

Emily took a deep breath. "John, a lot has happened since the docbot sedated you. Some sort of bot seems to have followed you here. It's trapped in the pool. It killed . . ." She paused for a long moment before she could get her voice under control enough to continue. "It killed Dahlia and took out main power at the same time. Stay out of the pool, whatever you do, and stay put. I'm taking the sputa to Jumpoff Station to get help. I . . . someone . . . will be back. Computer, end recording."

"Recording ended."

"Computer, monitor docbot patient. If . . . when he regains consciousness, play him that recording."

"Understood."

Emily looked around. Had it just been yesterday she'd arrived here looking forward to a relaxing vacation before she went home and continued struggling with her parents over her choice of career? It seemed more like a lifetime ago.

For Dahlia, it had been the end of a lifetime . . . an all-too-short one.

"Computer, open inner air lock door." The door opened. She slipped into the cramped lock and dragged the sputa in after her. "Computer, close inner air lock door." It slid shut. "Flood air lock and open outer door." Water poured in. Despite the cold, Emily welcomed its clean embrace. Her nostrils snapped closed and her gills opened. She felt her heart change its rhythm, felt the muscles only Selkies had squeeze her lungs, forcing the air up and out of her mouth in an explosion of vomited bubbles, a tickling, pleasurable sensation. Her vision blurred for a moment until the third eyelid slipped over each eye. Then the outer door opened, and she pulled the now weightless sputa out, turned it around, and flicked on its headlight.

What had been just dim shadows against the gradually lightening water above snapped into sharp relief. The air tunnel lay, a twisted, crushed worm, on the ocean floor beneath the habitat, still attached to the largest piece left of the sub; probably its collapse had contributed to dragging the sub down, and the jagged spike of rock Dahlia had told Emily she privately called "Poseidon's Prick" had done the rest of the damage.

Behind her, the habitat rang. *Our little visitor must realize it's trapped,* she thought. *Time to get out of here.*

The habitat rang again . . . and again . . . and again.

At least, I hope *it's trapped!* Suddenly worried the habitat wasn't as secure a prison as she'd thought, Emily activated the sputa's rudimentary computer. "Computer, indicate course to Jumpoff Station," she chirp-clicked in Selkie. The system didn't have any speech capability of its own, but an indicator lit on the circular screen at the center of the control panel. Keep the indicator in the center of the screen, and she'd make it to Jumpoff in . . . six to eight hours, according to the computer.

The habitat rang again, and Emily thought she heard a sound like tearing metal. Saying a prayer for John's safety to whatever deity might be listening—Emily glanced at the priapic rock that had killed the sub; Poseidon, presumably, although he seemed to be thinking about something else—Emily squeezed the throttle on the right handgrip and accelerated away from the habitat into the unknown.

Chapter 9

YOU WOULD THINK, Chris Keating thought as he lay on his thinly padded bed, the only furnishing of note in his cell in the Hansen's Harbor Criminal Detention Center, *that almost having my head blown off on the pier by an enraged Selkie would be enough to convince the Grand Deacon I'm on his side.*

You would think that, but you'd be wrong.

In fact, after Chris had been returned to the Grand Deacon by the dour Holy Warriors who had formerly been Richard Hansen's bodyguards, the story they'd told of John's escape and Hansen's decision to board the boat pursuing him had seemed to increase rather than decrease the Grand Deacon's suspicion. Or maybe the Grand Deacon just didn't want to have to deal with whatever Chris represented, and decided to put him somewhere safe until he was ready.

Whichever, Chris wasn't given a chance to say a word in his defense before being hustled to the small-but-grandly-named Hansen's Harbor Criminal Detention Center. He wasn't the only prisoner; he'd glimpsed other landlings, some of whom he knew, as a Holy Warrior had hurried him down the single central corridor to his cell. He'd half-expected to see Dr. Stanless, but didn't—perhaps he was in the hospital. Or perhaps he was dead, but Chris didn't want to think that. He didn't really care about the Selkies, but despite that whole omelet-egg thing he regretted the landling deaths. He hoped the people he almost thought of as friends weren't among them, even if they were Selkie-lovers.

He'd already passed one night in jail, sleeping well despite everything. After all, he'd had a busy and stressful day, and had been woken early by the arrival of the landing craft.

But now, he found, time dragged, with nothing to read and no one to talk to. He amused himself by imagining what it would be like when Purification was complete and he was formally recognized for his part in its success, but you couldn't kill a whole day that way.

Well, the Grand Deacon would surely want to talk to him again soon.

Time passed. Meals arrived. He used the toilet, and the booth-sized shower stall in one corner. He stared at the ceiling. He stared at the floor. He stared at the walls. And as it started to grow dark again, Chris assured himself the Grand Deacon would surely want to talk to him the *next* day.

But as he settled in for another night on the thin mattress, a plaintive question followed him down to sleep.

But . . . what if he doesn't?

For twenty minutes, despite the noise of the sputa's water jets, Emily could hear/feel the almost constant ring/thump of the habitat as the killerbot tried to break out. At the very limit of her senses, it stopped—and something about the *way* it stopped, some ill-definable quality of the final vibration, made her shut off the sputa and drift, listening.

Nothing.

Maybe the machine killed itself, Emily thought. *All those blasts inside that enclosed space . . . or maybe it just gave up.*

Or maybe, she thought, and wished she hadn't, *it broke out.*

The thing had successfully tracked John for hours—and had been at least an hour behind him when he had arrived at the habitat. It didn't seem to have a problem with a cold trail, and Emily only had a twenty-minute head start.

If it had broken out.

Well, one way to find out for sure would be to float around until it showed up. Emily preferred to be kept guessing. She reactivated the water jets and roared away into the darkness again, still following the blip of light showing her the way to Jumpoff Station.

Her options were, to say the least, limited.

Richard woke to find himself floating facedown and underwater.

The survival suit had lived up to its name. Not only had it automatically closed his faceplate as he hit the water, it had adjusted his buoyancy to keep him well below the surface, far enough down that the storm above could only tug at his limbs with phantom fingers.

Not that he figured all that out when he first woke. It took him a few minutes of panicked flailing and heart-pounding fear and disorientation before the parts of his brain capable of rational thought managed to take over from the parts of his brain convinced he was a) drowning and b) falling. Apparently those more primitive brain parts were unable to grasp the inherent contradiction between those two states.

Once he had his body, pulse, and breathing under control, he turned on his back and looked up at the tossing underside of the waves, not a sight he'd ever expected to see.

The survival suit, a little self-contained submersible, had its own AI and a heads-up display if he remembered right from the training sessions he'd attended on *Sanctification.* "Computer, activate display," he said.

To his delight, a collection of digital readouts appeared, apparently floating in the water a few centimeters outside his faceplate.

The survival suit reported that it was operating normally, that the water temperature was twelve degrees Celsius, and that it was 1754, Hansen's Harbor time.

He'd apparently been unconscious for about half an hour. The computer also informed him that he had incurred a long but shallow gash in his left calf which it had biofoamed shut and pain-deadened, and that it had successfully self-sealed the matching gash in the survival suit's skin. "Blood loss not trivial, but not life-threatening," Richard read. *Well, that's a relief,* he thought. *But it's a good thing I'm not a Selkie. That hunterbot would probably come after me with that much blood in the water.*

Hmmm. I wonder . . .

"Computer, can you track the hunterbot the boat was following?"

Apparently it could; it indicated a direction, but gave no distance.

Is the boat still on its trail? Why didn't Veldron and Khan come back for me?

"Computer," he said. "Locate boat."

The computer instantly indicated that, far from having followed the bot into the indeterminate distance, the boat was precisely 1,957 meters away . . . and, the computer noted helpfully, upside down.

Richard's stomach flipped in sympathy. "Urk," he said. "Computer, locate any other survival suits in vicinity."

The computer informed him there were three survival suits in the vicinity . . . 1,957 meters away, on the boat.

"Computer, any warm-blooded life in the water?"

Nothing.

This is not good, Richard thought. "Computer, any other boats or bots in the vicinity?"

"None detected," the computer said.

He was all alone.

The gray light filtering through the water had faded to almost nothing. Richard wasn't much of a swimmer, and swimming in the survival suit was problematic anyway. But if he remembered correctly . . .

"Computer, provide overview of features of this survival suit."

The computer obligingly listed them, sounding like a

very boring salesperson, and confirmed what Richard had recalled: the backpack held the artificial gill, a filtering unit that created fresh water as needed—Richard took a sip—and a small propulsion unit; just a simple water jet, but it would move him through the water at something better than a walking pace.

"Computer, indicate boat direction and distance."

A blip lit up in his faceplate. "Computer, activate propulsion unit."

The backpack began to vibrate. He surged through the water . . . then rolled . . . corkscrewed . . . flailed . . . jackknifed . . .

It took him several minutes to figure out how to control his direction using his arms and hands and flippered feet as control surfaces. By then night had fallen, and the blip representing the boat had moved to the bottom of Richard's display and started blinking red, which he took to mean the boat was behind him. He activated his helmet lamp, reversed direction, and was rewarded by the blip moving back to the top of his display and turning green.

Traveling the two kilometers to the boat took him more than a quarter of an hour. The oceanic microfauna glowed green and blue and orange in his headlight and flowed past his faceplate like multicolored snowflakes viewed through the windshield of a moving groundcar. They were mesmerizing, to the point that the computer beeped several warnings before he realized the distance to the boat as indicated in his display had shrunk to almost nothing and he must be on the verge of plowing head-on into it.

An instant later, he saw it in his headlamp, upside down, the red-painted keel disappearing out of the water above him, the gray-green superstructure pointing down into the depths.

"Computer, stop propulsion," Richard said. He floated, looking at the boat. *Now what?* He couldn't exactly swim up to it and flip it over.

Unless . . .

"Computer, can you link with the boat's computer? Is it still active?"

"Affirmative and affirmative," the computer said.

"Computer, link with boat's computer."

"Link established. Please refer to this unit as Suit Computer and the unit on the vessel as Boat Computer."

"Uh . . . right." Richard cleared his throat. "Boat Computer, can you hear me?"

"Affirmative." It had, of course, exactly the same dispassionate male voice as the suit computer. Every Body computer Richard had ever talked to used the same voice. You weren't allowed to change it . . . especially to a female voice. That would be enough to get you sentenced to at least a week of penitence.

"Boat Computer, status of boat."

"No significant damage. However, boat is upside down."

Well, I can see that, Richard thought. "Boat Computer, why did the boat capsize?"

"Collision with unknown object," the computer said. "Lack of damage to the hull and analysis of the impact suggests object was large indigenous life form."

What? Richard couldn't help looking around. Nothing swam in the shadowy waters at the very limit of his helmet light . . . but anything at all could be swimming in the black water beyond its reach. *You had to ask, didn't you?* "Boat Computer, do you have self-righting routines in the event of a capsizing?"

"Affirmative."

"Boat Computer, why haven't the self-righting routines been activated?"

"Boat is currently under manual control," the computer said. "Self-righting mechanism has not been activated."

"Boat Computer," Richard said, "deactivate manual control."

"Cannot comply," said the computer.

"Why not?"

No answer. He hadn't properly addressed it. "Boat

Computer, why are you unable to deactivate manual control?"

"Primary control commands must be issued by a certified and rated ship's captain. Your voice pattern does not exist in my approved command identification database."

Great, Richard thought. "Boat Computer, can you tell me how to activate your self-righting mechanism manually?"

"Affirmative."

"Boat Computer, please tell me how to activate your self-righting mechanism."

The computer provided the instructions, which consisted of nothing more complicated than hitting a big red panic button on the main control panel. Presumably you were supposed to hit the button as the boat went over. Something had obviously prevented Veldron from doing so.

"Uh, Boat Computer," Richard said, "how does the self-righting mechanism work?"

"Water is pumped at high speed from starboard ballast tanks to port tanks," the boat said. "At the same time, high pressure water jets are expelled through openings in the starboard gunwale. If necessary, the jets pulse to set up a rocking motion. The self-righting mechanism is successful approximately sixty-nine percent of the time."

"Boat Computer, what happened to the boats in tests where the self-righting mechanism failed?

"Twenty-two percent rolled over completely and remained inverted, usually with significantly more damage. Nine percent broke apart and sank."

Well, I guess I wouldn't be any worse off, Richard thought.

He looked at the side of the boat's hull, then down toward the submerged bridge. "Suit Computer, can you monitor my buoyancy and keep it neutral?"

"Affirmative," said the suit.

"Okay, let's do this, then."

Neither computer, sensibly, replied.

Richard swam down. When he cleared the gunwale

and directed his headlamp into the cockpit, he found out why he'd seen no sign of the ship's crew. Veldron still hung in the straps of his command chair, eyes staring, head at an odd angle. Richard remembered the way the boat had leaped high in the air before it came down, and suspected the impact had broken Veldron's neck. He'd never had a chance to free himself.

Khan he discovered a minute later, as he swam even deeper to the upper bridge level. Either the impact or the flip-over had thrown him into the glass that surrounded the upper bridge on three sides. The glass had shattered, but the opening he had been hurled into had been a little too small for him to pass through completely.

He still hung in the window frame, skin and clothing floating in red strips like gruesome seaweed all around him, face shredded beyond recognition. The blood had long since cleared away, giving him the pale and shriveled look of a laboratory specimen pickled in formaldehyde.

Richard swallowed hard and willed himself not to throw up. It seemed like a really bad idea inside a survival suit.

Then he had to fight the battle all over again when he realized that the lower half of Khan's body blocked most of the control panel . . . including the part with the panic button he needed to reach.

He tried pulling Khan back through the window, but couldn't get enough leverage. He'd move a little the other way, though, and so Richard ended up bracing his feet against the post of the wheel and pushing Khan through the window, its jagged glass teeth shredding the corpse even more, though so little blood remained in it that only a small dark cloud accompanied the effort. By the time Richard had fed the rest of the beefy ex-Holy Warrior through the window frame, he'd forgotten what he was struggling with and was cursing the corpse under his breath like he would a bulky piece of furniture.

At last, Khan's hips were out of the wheelhouse. His

legs followed easily after that, and finally Richard could access the necessary button.

He slapped it. It was almost the last thing he did.

The boat lurched sharply to the side as ballast shifted overhead in the tanks. The side of the wheelhouse that Khan hadn't gone sailing through smashed into Richard's side so hard it knocked the breath from his lungs. He grabbed hold of the wheel, the only thing he could, and struggled for air as water roared from the starboard gunwale in bubbling jets, twisting the boat even farther. It rolled sideways, the jets cut off, it rolled back slightly, and then the jets roared out again, rocking and pushing again and again until, finally, the boat gave a great groan and rolled over completely, dumping Richard hard onto the floor of the wheelhouse. Lights came on, illuminating the deckhouse, the foredeck, and the equipment room below. Khan's mangled body, lifted out of the water as the boat righted itself, slid across the wet bow planking and splashed into the sea. Veldron still sat in his seat below, his head now twisted completely around. Blood mingled with seawater dripped from his nose and mouth onto the deck.

Richard clawed at his faceplate, managed to unseal it, and lifted it up. He took deep, hard breaths of the damp night air. The storm had moved on, and strange stars were beginning to prick the sky between fast-moving galleons of cloud. "Boat Computer," he said. "Can I command you to secure the boat for the night?"

"Affirmative."

"Boat Computer, secure for night."

A red light came on on the port side of the boat, a green light to starboard, and a bright white light at the stern. Something splashed in the water aft: a sea anchor, Richard presumed, to keep the boat's bow facing into the waves.

Richard sat slumped a few minutes longer, then steeled himself and slid down the steps to the main deck. He unsnapped Veldron's body, then hesitated. His first thought had been to drag it down into the hold, but he didn't know how long he'd be out here and his food and other supplies were down there.

Khan had already had an inadvertent sea burial. Veldron might as well join his shipmate.

Not without difficulty, he dragged the corpse to the railing. "May God Itself, the Great Protector and Purifier, welcome you to the Perfect World Beyond, forever free from the fear of God's wrath," he intoned, and dumped the body into the water. Feeling a little giddy, he yelled out in the direction he'd last seen Khan's corpse, "That goes for you, too!"

And then he hauled his own weary-but-still-living body down into the dripping crew cabin—he could hear pumps and fans working hard to dry it—and flung himself on one of the two waterproof mattresses. Despite the survival suit—not that there was any way he was going to take *that* off—he fell asleep in seconds.

Emily wasn't kept guessing long: an hour after the pounding in the habitat ceased, she knew the killerbot had somehow managed to break through the doors and find her trail. The knowledge didn't come through some sixth sense or even through one of the standard five: instead, the minimal display on the sputa lit up as passive sonar (active sonar would have been the equivalent of standing in an empty field shouting "here I am!", so she'd made sure it was turned off) picked up the sound of a high-speed propeller in her wake, the sputa's onboard computer being perfectly capable of compensating for the noise of its own passage through the water.

It took her another thirty minutes of travel to confirm her worst fear: the killerbot swam faster. The closer it got, the better the sputa's computer could estimate its distance, and once it had a satisfactory solution, it began displaying it. Emily watched the digits slowly fall in ten-meter increments, matched that to the rate at which the distance to Jumpoff Station was decreasing, did some careful mental calculation, and swore silently.

The bot would catch her at least an hour before she reached the station.

She didn't know what other weapons it had besides the sonic depth charge, but she had no reason to think that it wouldn't make as quick work of her as it had of poor Dahlia. She needed to find some place to hide that it couldn't reach.

She needed to get out of the water.

"Computer, display chart. Fifty-kilometer radius." The screen display changed. She studied it for a moment. Yes, she'd remembered right. "Computer, display new course to chart coordinates A-36-D-12." The screen lit with an alternate course, one that angled away from her current vector at almost forty-five degrees. But the distance indicated was less than half of that to Jumpoff Station.

Emily hesitated a moment longer. John, if he was still alive, needed help. But he wouldn't get it if she were killed before she reached Jumpoff Station, and she would be if she kept on her present course. As long as she stayed alive, he still had a chance.

And anyway, never mind John's needs: she had her own strong need to stay alive.

She angled off on the new course.

For another hour she swept through the sea, her arms beginning to ache from holding on to the sputa, feeling a great fatigue working its way into her mind and limbs. She watched the readout of the distance to the following bot continue to decrease slightly faster than the readout of the distance to her destination.

It's going to be close, she thought—and then had a shock as a brand-new icon and distance readout suddenly blossomed on the screen.

A boat dead ahead had just started its engines.

Chapter 10

RICHARD GRINNED WITH relief as the engines started on the first try. He hadn't been sure the computer would allow him that much control, but apparently it would. It would also, it had told him when he asked, allow him to set its course. It would *not* allow him to fire weapons, but that didn't worry him—he hadn't even realized the boat *had* weapons.

He turned his attention to the navigation screens for the first time in a while, absentmindedly rubbing his aching calf. The painkiller provided by the survival suit must be wearing off. But the suit's biofoam dressing at least kept the gash sterile and sealed. Nothing to worry about, and they'd soon set it right back on shore.

Which is where he wanted to be, as soon as possible. *I never should have left it in the first place,* he thought. *The Grand Deacon was right to send baby-sitters with me.*

That thought gave him pause, as well as embarrassment. *If I go back without even being able to report where the Selkie fled to, I might as well have myself shuttled up to* Sanctification *and locked in my quarters—and save Ellers the trouble of ordering it done.*

On the other hand, if he managed to return with useful information . . .

He rubbed his calf again. He could put up with the discomfort a little longer. It couldn't hurt to check . . .

"Boat Computer," he said. "Run scan for hunterbot

you were tracking before boat capsized." No doubt it was out of range, but . . .

An icon leaped to life on the screen: less than five kilometers away—and *closing*?

And then two things happened at once. Richard noticed another icon on the display, almost on top of the central blip representing the boat—and the water at the stern erupted, discharging something large and wet into the cockpit.

He yelped and spun, to find a female Selkie with short violet hair, wearing a bright-yellow skinsuit with glowing light-piping along the limbs, hauling into the boat something shaped like a torpedo with wings.

Richard's heart leaped into his throat. He had no weapons, not even a wrench he could turn into an improvised club. *Selkies are enormously strong,* he remembered telling the Grand Deacon. *And fast. Stronger and faster than we are, by far.*

The Selkie spoke, her words accented but understandable. "Who are you? Are you one of the killers from Earth?"

"I . . . I haven't killed anyone," Richard said. "I . . . there was an accident, we hit a . . . a whale, or something . . . and the crew . . . I'm just a passenger." *A passenger who led the killers from Earth right to this planet,* Richard thought, but didn't say.

The Selkie's huge green eyes flicked around the boat, and Richard felt a strange sense of admiration and pride as he took in her alien face.

Pride?

"There's no one else on board?"

"No. Not anymore."

"Then get down from there."

"I—"

So fast he didn't even see where it came from, she drew a knife. Its blade looked like glass, almost transparent in the misty morning light. "Now."

Richard slid down the ladder, and gave the Selkie a

wide berth as she scurried up it in his place. She gave the controls a quick scan, and swore. "The damned thing's practically on top of us!"

The hunterbot, Richard realized. *It's after her. But what happened to John Duval?*

Then he had to hang on for dear life as the Selkie seized the manual controls, which Richard, confirmed landlubber, had hardly dared touch, and shoved the throttle to full. As the boat leaped ahead, the torpedo-shaped device she'd hauled into the boat slid across the deck. Before Richard could react, it smashed into his wounded calf. He yelped, but the Selkie ignored him.

"I hope we're out of—" she began, but never finished. A shock like a giant hammer blow from below struck the boat. The engines stuttered, but kept running, though they now had a vibration that made Richard's bones rattle and the pain in his leg even worse. At least the shock had moved the damned torpedo-thing off his foot. He bent down to check it. The blow had torn open the bio-foam dressing and the survival suit's self-sealing skin. Blood trickled down his ankle to mingle with the water on the deck.

The Selkie came down the ladder. "We're lucky," she said. "It only got in one shot. But it feels like we've lost half a propeller, or warped a shaft, and there may be damage to the engine itself. I don't know how long we can keep running."

"How long *you* can keep running," Richard said. "It's not after *me.*"

The Selkie's mouth tightened. Her face, with its minimal nub of a nose and matching ears, already had a seal-like look. When she compressed her lips and narrowed her eyes like that, she looked totally alien. Richard couldn't look away, but again his emotions confused him. He should be horrified . . . but he found her strangely beautiful, and again he felt that strange surge of pride, almost as though the Selkies were *his* creation. . . .

Am I losing my mind? he wondered, not for the first time. She—*it's*—a monster.

A monster in the boat with him. A monster that held his life in her hands.

"Where are we going?" he demanded. Whatever the cause of his mishmash of emotions, they didn't seem to leave room for fear. "Back to Hansen's Harbor?" He indicated his calf. "I'm injured. I need a doctor."

"I've got a friend that needs one more than you do . . . if he's still alive." The Selkie lunged at Richard, so hard and fast that he gasped. With her face just centimeters from his, she snarled, "And I've got another friend who'll never need a doctor again, because that thing you put in the water blew her into bugglefish bait."

"I didn't—"

"Shut up." She pulled back. "We're not going back to Hansen's Harbor. We're going to a rock that has just one thing going for it: an underwater cave with two entrances. It's very dangerous, very unstable. We're going to lure that thing into the cave, and then we're going to see how it reacts to having a few tons of rock dropped on its back."

The boat shuddered, and the engine coughed. The Selkie glanced astern. A haze of blue smoke hung above their wake. "We'll be lucky if the boat gets us there. We may have to swim the last kilometer or two."

"Swim?" Richard said. "I told you, my leg—"

"The sputa can pull both of us."

"Why not just leave me on the boat? The hunterbot will follow you. I'll just slow you down."

"I may need your help doing what I want to do," the Selkie said. "And I don't trust you. Maybe this boat has weapons I don't know about, and the instant I'm in the water you'll blow me apart like that 'hunterbot' of yours blew apart Dahlia." She shook her head sharply. "No. I want you within reach."

Richard cast around for an argument that might convince her, but they all sounded weak even to him. If he really were a Holy Warrior, one of them would be dead by now, but a couple of week's training on *Sanctification* had hardly prepared him for hand-to-hand combat with . . . *that*. The Selkie might be female, and young, but she was faster and stronger—had been *designed* to be faster and stronger—than he could ever hope to be. And he was injured. He was at her mercy, and knew it.

I hope she shows some, he thought.

But a part of his mind, the same part that found her fierce and beautiful instead of frightening and hideous, wondered how much mercy he deserved from someone whose friends, family, and world he had helped destroy with his betrayal.

Betrayal? I did my duty!

The inner voice said nothing, but Richard's face heated with unaccustomed shame.

Finding the boat had been a stroke of luck, Emily thought. Finding it occupied only by a thoroughly cowed civilian landling instead of an armed Holy Warrior had been another. So it was probably too much to hope that the damaged boat would actually keep running all the way to Sawyer's Point, the cave-ridden, dangerously unstable bit of volcanic detritus she hoped would rid her of what the landling called a hunterbot (but she still thought of as a *killer*bot) once and for all.

Sure enough, they were still a good three kilometers from Sawyer's Point when the engine, which had been running progressively rougher, suddenly sputtered, gave a loud bang, emitted a huge cloud of blue smoke, and died. Moments later almost-invisible flames began licking around the boat's stern; apparently a piece of hot metal had found the alcohol tank. "Better seal your faceplate," Emily told the landling. "We just ran out of boat, and we're about to run out of time."

The landling looked at the growing conflagration—the flames were orange now that they'd found plastic to burn—and sealed his faceplate without comment. As his survival suit stiffened, she gave him a shove that toppled him over the gunwale and into the sea. *No point giving him time to get cold feet,* she thought, picked up the sputa, and leaped in after him.

Only to find him gone. *He couldn't have swum that fast!* Furious with herself, she activated the sputa's navigation screen, and saw the landling at once, heading away from the boat at a right angle to the course she intended to set for Sawyer's Point, and moving at a pace that could only mean one thing. She cursed herself for being an idiot. Why hadn't she noticed his survival suit had built-in propulsion?

Because our survival suits don't.

It wasn't much of an excuse.

Well, she couldn't do anything about it. He'd escaped, and he was right about one thing: the killerbot wouldn't be interested in him. It would come after her. She had to get to Sawyer's Point before it caught her . . . and then hope her scheme actually worked.

She put the landling out of her mind, aimed the sputa toward Sawyer's Point, and squeezed the throttle.

Richard felt proud of himself—terrified, but proud. He'd been hoping for a chance to escape, hoping that maybe the Selkie didn't know about his suit's built-in propulsion, and then she'd handed him that chance on a silver platter by pushing him into the water. Probably she'd hoped to take him off guard and then jump in while he floundered, but he'd been readier than he'd looked, and the moment he'd hit the water he'd activated the water jet.

He'd also felt a twinge in his injured leg. *I must be leaving a blood trail. Good thing I'm not a Selkie or the hunterbot would be after me.*

But now the bot would leave him alone and concentrate on its proper target. *Can she really trap it, even kill it?* He supposed she could; no matter how terrifying the things might be, they weren't indestructible. A few tons of rock dropped on its back ought to squash it flatter than . . .

. . . *than Dad when he jumped off the Meeting Hall.* The metaphor came to him unbidden and unwanted, as thoughts of his father usually did.

He dealt with the family shame his way, and I've dealt with it mine, Richard thought. *He chose to kill himself, and I . . .*

. . . I chose to kill.

He'd denied that to the Selkie, but he couldn't deny it to himself, especially not the newly intrusive part of his mind that seemed intent on upending all his cherished rationalizations. He had pointed the Holy Warriors to Marseguro, and the Holy Warriors had already killed many of the planet's inhabitants, both normals and Selkies. Any Selkies they didn't kill they would confine, and later sterilize. To placate God Itself, to ensure It did not repent of Its sparing of Earth, the Selkies' whole inhuman race must end. Marseguro had to be Purified. He believed that.

Didn't he?

The Selkie are monsters. That alien face . . . those eyes . . .

Beautiful, that strange new voice in his head insisted. *Designed to be beautiful. A masterwork of the genesculpting art . . .*

Which made Purification a hideous mixture of murder and vandalism.

He shook his head. *She'd have killed you in an instant if she'd seen any reason to . . . if she'd known your role in the Purification of her planet.*

Maybe. But in his increasingly confused heart, he couldn't wish her dead.

God forgive me, but I hope she escapes.

He checked the navigation display. It had synchronized with the boat computer while he was on board, and showed him his distance from Sawyer's Point, now receding, his distance from the burning boat, also receding, his distance from the Selkie, receding as she raced toward Sawyer's Point, and his distance from the hunterbot, which had reached the boat's location sometime in the last few minutes. He blinked. Something looked odd. "Computer," he said. "Display hunterbot's course for the last fifteen minutes as a solid line."

The blip representing the bot elongated into a line, straight as an arrow from the edge of the display to the blip of the boat . . . and then, abruptly, curving away from the straight path to Sawyer's Point . . .

. . . curving to follow him instead.

"That's impossible!" Richard said out loud. "Computer, extrapolate your current course and bot's course."

His blip elongated, became a straight line leading off the edge of the display. After five extrapolated minutes, the bot's course matched his precisely, the two lines disappearing into one another.

"Computer, how long until the bot catches me?"

"One hour, two minutes," the computer said.

"Computer, how far to land at current speed, if course is altered as necessary to minimize time?"

"Four hours, thirteen minutes."

Richard swore, but the numbers were implacable. If the bot, impossibly, were following him, then he must also assume that the bot, impossibly, thought he was a Selkie—and would blow him into chum in one hour's time.

He'd started on the boat as a hunter. Now he was in the water as the hunted.

But he wasn't the only possible prey.

"Computer," he snapped. "Display least-time route to Sawyer's Point."

A new line formed, and a blip appeared for him to steer toward. He stuck out his left arm and leg and swung sharply around. With the blip centered, he began racing toward Sawyer's Point, and the blip that was the Selkie girl, almost at the Point already.

"Computer, ETA, Sawyer's Point."

"Fifty-nine minutes."

In his faceplate, the bot's marker altered course again. Its extrapolated course, still displayed, still matched up with his. "Computer, now how long until bot catches me?"

"One hour, four minutes."

He'd arrive at that piece of rock with five minutes to spare.

He hoped the Selkie would welcome his company.

*   *   *

Halfway to Sawyer's Point, Emily realized the killerbot had peeled off to follow the landling. The irony made her bare her teeth in a savage grin. For a moment, she considered abandoning her plan and heading for Jumpoff Station again, but she quickly rejected the idea. If the bot finished off the landling, it would almost certainly come after her again, and if she headed for open water now, she'd be worse off than ever when it caught her.

The wisdom of her decision was brought home shortly thereafter, when she saw that the fleeing landling had reconsidered his actions and was now heading toward her as fast as he had previously been heading away from her.

Moments after that, she surfaced to reconnoiter and saw Sawyer's Point dead ahead.

It rose precipitously from the sea, its base splashed white by the waves pounding themselves to spray against its black volcanic rocks. There could be no landing or climbing on its steep sides, made of rock as sharp-edged and splintery as glass. Even if you could find someplace to ascend, you'd slice off a hand or foot and bleed to death before you'd climbed ten meters.

Both above and beneath the water, Sawyer's Point was riddled with tunnels and caves, some volcanic tubes through which magma had once pulsed, some formed by erosion, some dissolved by seawater from below and rain from above, many formed by the action of the strange rock-eating microbes that some researchers thought were one reason Marseguro had so little dry ground.

Beautiful and dangerous, Sawyer's Point was strictly off-limits to teenaged Selkies and thus much frequented by them. Three young Selkies had died there just a year ago, and ever since then, sensors seeded around the rock had signaled Peaceforce headquarters in Hansen's Harbor whenever anyone ventured too close. Since Peaceforce headquarters was probably now a pile of rubble, Emily doubted anyone was paying any attention to those sensors now.

She'd been one of those teens who had ignored the

restrictions, and she knew Sawyer's Point like the back of her hand—or, at least, she had, five years ago. How many of the tunnels and caverns she remembered remained unchanged she couldn't judge. If the one she was counting on was no longer there, or no longer open, then Sawyer's Point might well prove fatal to her, too.

Of course, it might anyway.

She plunged beneath the waves again, and directed the sputa down, down . . .

There! Thirty meters below the surface, the sputa's headlight picked out a gaping hole, about as wide as she was tall. She could only see it in the wall of black rock because unlike the rock, it reflected nothing. In front of it, the ubiquitous Marseguroite plankton twinkled in her light like stars.

Emily killed the sputa's jets. Then, floating just outside the cave mouth, she pulled her lightband from one of the almost-invisible pockets of her skinsuit and fastened it around her head. The forward half of the circlet lit up automatically. "Computer," she told the sputa, "surface and hold position until retrieved." She released it. Its headlight went out and it rose out of sight to wait for her to reclaim it.

If she ever did.

She reached up and pressed the back of the lightband to deactivate it. She'd need it later, but for now, she would wait in the dark for the landling's approach. With her light out, she'd be able to see his more easily.

Once he arrived, the killerbot wouldn't be far behind.

Richard watched the number indicating the distance to Sawyer's Point and the now-stationary blip of the Selkie count down, and the number indicating the distance between him and the hunterbot count down just slightly more slowly.

The Selkie's blip was almost, but not quite, on top of the blip representing Sawyer's Point. Since his suit could only track the sputa, not her, for all he knew she had left it outside and already entered the rock.

The thought alarmed him. If she had, how would he find the way in? Sawyer's Point rose sheer from the bottom, 200 meters down. The entrance she had taken could be anywhere. He couldn't search a hundredth of that mass of rock in the scant minutes he would have before the bot arrived.

Would the hunterbot's sonic depth charge blow him apart or squash him against the rock like a bug? he wondered sickly.

And then, too soon, he arrived at Sawyer's Point . . . and before he could panic, his display suddenly added a new blip: a warm-blooded life-form at a depth of thirty meters.

He hadn't been that deep before in the survival suit, but he could only assume it was good for it. He angled his hands and arms and aimed down into the darkness, feeling the suit stiffen around him to counteract the increasing pressure.

And suddenly, it wasn't dark. A light shone down there, barely visible at first but growing brighter as he descended . . . and then his own headlight picked up the shadowy form of the Selkie, who wore the light as a band around her head.

He hadn't seen a Selkie underwater before. Her nostrils were clamped so tightly closed he couldn't even see them anymore, making her look almost noseless. Her eyes had a clear membrane across them, and they didn't blink. And her gills . . . they were open, pink and pulsing, the thin membrane of their edges rippling constantly. They looked like horrific, killing wounds, slashes in the side of her neck, but, of course, they weren't killing her at all, they were keeping her alive, helmetless, thirty meters underwater.

Monstrous, he thought automatically, but at the same time . . . *magnificent.* No one but his grandfather had ever succeeded in creating a form of human with so many modifications, one that bred true, one that really *worked,* that didn't suffer from crippling health problems— breathing difficulties, fragile bones, horrific cancers, men-

tal retardation. Victor Hansen's contemporaries had held
him in awe, limited as they were to mere cosmetic
manipulation—humans with tails, humans with cat's eyes.
Victor Hansen had done what they considered impossible.

Not surprisingly, some had doubted his claims at the
time, and in the years since Salvation, some Body theolo-
gians had argued that Hansen's achievements must have
been overstated, that the Selkie race he claimed to have
created must be little more than crippled, deformed
freaks, that God Itself would not allow the Holy Human
Genome to be tampered with to so great a degree.

But the Selkie girl in his headlight didn't look crippled
or deformed. She looked . . . at home. Alive. Vibrant.
Healthy. Bizarre, yes, monstrous, even, but . . .
strangely beautiful.

God forbid, he thought fervently. *Attracted to a Selkie?
The Avatar would put me in an execution sputnik and
have my ashes scattered across three continents.*

No doubt the Selkies had some way to communicate
underwater, but he didn't share it. He expected her to
lead him into the cave behind her, but she didn't move,
and he couldn't interpret the look she gave him. Then
her gaze slid past him to the void beyond.

Of course, he realized. *She's waiting for the hunterbot.
She wants to be sure it follows us.*

Or follows me. He still found it hard to believe he had
become the bot's target, but without a doubt, here it
came, the numbers showing its distance dropping rapidly
now he'd stopped. Five hundred meters . . . four-fifty . . .
four hundred . . . what was the range of its weapon,
anyway? . . . three-fifty . . . three hundred . . . *Why isn't
she moving?* . . . two-fifty . . . *She doesn't have a display!
She can't be expecting that thing to show a light!* . . . two
hundred . . . one-fifty . . .

Finally, she tapped his arm, pointed to the mouth of
the cave, and plunged inside. He started to activate his
propulsion system, thought about the sharp rock lurking
inside the tunnel, thought better of it, and swam after

her, his calf hurting and still, he suspected, leaking blood
into the water.

*The blood the hunterbot is following, even though I'm
not a Selkie!*

Feeling as betrayed by his own body as he had recently
begun to feel betrayed by his mind, he entered the
tunnel.

Emily swam through the tunnel as fast as she could, hoping she hadn't misjudged the killerbot's distance and the
range of its weapon . . . and also hoping its AI wasn't
smart enough to realize just how rotten the rock was in
Sawyer's Point, because she knew full well one sonic
depth charge would bring the tunnel crashing down.

Of course, that was precisely what she was counting
on, but not just yet.

She knew the landling had followed her—what else
could he do?—but she couldn't spare him a thought. If
he kept following her and did exactly what she did, he
just might get out of this alive . . . if either of them did.

She wasn't sure why she cared about that, considering
what his fellow Earthlings were reportedly doing to her
planet, but she'd never killed anyone before, and she
didn't want to start.

The passage narrowed. She arrowed through an opening just big enough to let her pass and emerged into a
giant cavern, a bubble blown in the magma long before.
The upper third contained air, and so she swam up five
meters and burst into the open. As she emerged, rain-
bows erupted from the bubble's lining of volcanic glass,
made iridescent by the action of the rock-eating bacteria,
which left a thin light-refracting slime on every surface.
Spectacularly beautiful and much photographed after it
had been discovered by one of the first-generation Selkies, Hendrix Cavern had also been the first part of Sawyer's Point declared off-limits. Geologists had warned
that the slightest earth tremor or settling of the rock
could shatter its fragile equilibrium and bring tons of
rock crashing down into it, destroying its beauty forever:

a terrible shame in the present and a crime against posterity—and Emily couldn't wait to make it happen.

She swam the cavern's thirty-meter diameter and climbed out onto a ledge. A moment later, the landling emerged. He didn't swim across the cavern: instead he activated his propulsion system and shot across the pool so fast he had to turn sharply at the last minute to avoid smashing headfirst into the rock, and even so banged into it so hard Emily couldn't help but wince in sympathy. He clambered out and unsealed his faceplate. "What is this place?" he said, staring around.

"Hendrix Cavern." She barely glanced at him, keeping her attention on the pool. She pointed behind her, where another tunnel began. "Go through there. It will drop you into water in another five meters. Keep following the tunnel and keep bearing left, and you'll emerge into the open ocean. Don't take any openings to the right or you'll never get out of the rock."

"What are you—?"

"Go!" Emily snapped, and to his credit, the landling didn't ask any more questions, but closed his faceplate and plunged into the tunnel.

Just in time. With a grinding noise, the killerbot burst into Hendrix Cavern.

Emily had hoped the action of the bot breaking through the rock constricting the opening into the pool might be enough to bring the cavern's roof crashing down all by itself, but no such luck. Instead, she saw her pursuer clearly for the first time through the crystal-clear water.

It resembled the pictures she had seen of Earth's giant squid, with a cylindrical body, an arrow-shaped "head" with diving planes on it, and four . . . no, six tentacles writhing and lashing around its stern like snakes tasting the water.

Which, if Emily had figured out how the thing tracked, was exactly what they were doing.

It was what she was counting on . . . although she was also counting on the bot being designed merely to attack things in the water. If it also had the ability to attack things out of the water, she was about to die.

She drew her glassknife from her skinsuit and, with only a moment's hesitation, drew its ultra-sharp blade across the ball of her thumb. Blood followed pain, and she plunged her hand into the pool.

The bot must have instantly picked up the warmth of her hand. She snatched her fingers out of the water just ahead of the tentacle that lashed at her with astonishing speed, barely slower in the water than it would have been in air. Even though she pulled her hand from the water, turned and leaped into the exit tunnel in one motion, she was still half in Hendrix Cavern when the killerbot discharged its sonic weapon.

The water in the cavern leaped up *en masse,* creating a tsunami that hurled her down the tunnel she'd barely entered. She screamed, the sound cut off as the water engulfed her, as her back slammed into the sharp rock and she felt her skinsuit and some portion of her skin tear away. At the same time, she felt a deep, rumbling, grinding vibration all around her, as Sawyer's Point groaned. The water shot her along the tube, and she frantically fended off razor-sharp rock and kicked and pushed as hard as she could to avoid being swept into one of the side tunnels she had warned the landling about. And then, suddenly, she exploded out into the open sea, skinsuit shredded in a dozen places and skin in a half-dozen, bleeding and bruised but, amazingly, still alive.

And the killerbot?

She hovered, gills working extra hard, and looked back at the wall of rock from which she had emerged. No way to be certain it was trapped, no way to be certain it had been destroyed, but she would know soon enough. If it made it out, it would follow her again. If it hadn't emerged by the time she got around to where she had left the sputa, it probably never would.

But how many more of those things are there? she wondered.

The landling would know, but he'd disappeared. She wondered if he'd made it out. If he hadn't, if he'd gone down one of the tunnels that curved, split, and narrowed, and especially if he had been in one of those when that surge of water came, then he was almost certainly entombed in Sawyer's Point, just like the bot.

She flexed her limbs. The lacerations seemed minor and the bleeding already less. She wouldn't bleed to death before she could get to Jumpoff Station, at least. It hurt to swim, but she headed around Sawyer's Point to retrieve the waiting sputa.

She put the landling out of her mind as an unimportant civilian. What she needed now was to get to Jumpoff Station, find out what was going on, and get help for John Duval (*if he's still alive*, she thought grimly). And then . . .

Then we figure out how to drive off these murdering Earth bastards.

She refused to believe that might be impossible.

Somebody will know what to do. Somebody will have a plan.

Somebody has to.

Chapter 11

RICHARD SPED TOWARD Hansen's Harbor, heart pounding, and watched his heads-up display. He had felt Sawyer's Point shrug as he emerged from the tunnel, and had seen a huge boulder race past him toward the bottom, trailing bubbles. But he hadn't hesitated, any more than he had when the Selkie had first thrown him into the ocean. He'd activated the survival suit's propulsion system and set course for Hansen's Harbor again, trusting that the Selkie had taken care of the bot, and that she wouldn't come after him when and if she emerged herself.

Trust, but verify, he thought, the old diplomatic phrase surfacing from somewhere in his subconscious, and kept watching the display.

He didn't see anything for fifteen minutes. The limited sensor capabilities of the survival suit didn't permit him to detect a Selkie in the water on her own from this distance. He wouldn't see her until and unless she hooked up with the sputa again and started it up . . .

. . . and there she is.

A blip separated from the blob that marked Sawyer's Point. He watched it. Would she come after him? The sputa was faster; she could catch him if she tried . . . but she didn't try. She headed off in an entirely different direction, and shortly thereafter faded from the display altogether.

He concentrated on keeping the blip pointing the way

to Hansen's Harbor centered, and trying to reconvince himself of the sanctity of their mission. Nothing had changed. The Selkies were still subhuman abominations, not great works of art, no matter what some traitorous part of his mind might think, and the Body Purified's mission remained clear: such abominations could not be permitted to continue to pollute the Holy Human Genome, for just such pollution had drawn the wrath of God in the form of the giant asteroid fifty years ago, and only the Avatar's unflinching efforts to root out such pollution had earned God's pardon. Failing to destroy the Selkies would be tantamount to taunting God and daring It to destroy the human race after all, and Richard had no doubt that God could do that any time It wished, and quite likely would.

At least, he *thought* he had no doubt.

Didn't he?

That subhuman abomination saved your life, Richard thought. He'd had no way of dealing with the rogue hunterbot. If not for her knowledge of the local geography and her quick thinking, they'd both be feeding plankton by now. And she'd let him go, when she didn't have to, and before that, on the boat, let him live.

An animal wouldn't have hesitated to kill someone so demonstrably a threat. Neither would a subhuman monster. But she had. She'd acted, in fact, like a civilized human being, one who considered killing a last resort . . .

. . . unlike, say, the Holy Warriors.

That was an uncomfortable line of thought. Richard decided to think about something else.

Like, for example, why the hunterbot had altered course to come after *him* when it had sensed his blood in the water, and would other hunterbots do the same—because if there was one thing he was reasonably certain of, it was that there would be more hunterbots in the water at Hansen's Harbor.

All I can do is keep alert, he thought. *I'll be close to land by then. If I head for shore as soon as I detect one . . .*

It wasn't much of a plan. *Most of the hunterbots will be in New Botany Bay itself,* he reassured—or tried to reassure—himself. *I'll come ashore before I enter the bay proper and walk the rest of the way.*

Holding on to that thought, he sped along for another hour through pale-green water stabbed by shafts of ever-shifting sunlight from above. And then, suddenly, all his planning—such as it was—became moot: his display showed him another boat, straight ahead.

And as he watched, a smaller blip separated and raced toward him, the boat following in its wake.

Hunterbot!

He had nowhere to hide, no way to outrun the thing or its follower, no rocks to climb, and no Selkie to lure it to destruction. The best he could do was head for the surface and hope the Holy Warriors on the boat recognized his survival suit and called off the hunterbot before it blew him out of the sea.

He shot up through the water, the suit's water jet giving him enough momentum that he emerged three quarters of the way into the air before falling back with a huge splash like a broaching whale. The waves were modest by ocean standards, but still high enough that, low in the water as he was, heaving green hills cut off all sight of the boat. He couldn't see any sign of the hunterbot, either, but his display showed it getting nearer. His heart pounded as its blip met his blip and he gave an involuntary yelp as he felt a surge in the water beneath his feet . . . and froze as the hunterbot surfaced, wet gleaming metal emerging from the water just two meters away. The bot's tentacles remained tucked tightly to its side, though. It did nothing threatening at all . . . though he still had the feeling he was being watched.

He floated there, staring at it, until the boat suddenly appeared, almost on top of him. It slowed and turned broadside. A moment later, the two men aboard it threw a rope ladder over the side and helped him climb into the cockpit.

He opened his helmet. "Boy, am I glad to see you guys."

"We picked up the distress signal from your suit," the larger of the two Holy Warriors said. "Switched the hunterbot to homing mode instead of Selkie-tracking mode to pinpoint your location for us. But who *are* you?"

"Richard Hansen," Richard said.

The two exchanged glances. "You're Hansen?"

Richard nodded.

"Better call back the bot, Muhammad," the smaller man said. "We're heading back in." The bigger man nodded and went into the control cabin. The smaller man said, "The Grand Deacon has issued standing orders that whoever finds you is to bring you to him at once. I don't think he's very happy with you."

Richard said nothing.

In the boat, with the hunterbot once more aboard, the trip to Hansen's Harbor only took an hour. Richard really wanted to take off the survival suit, but considering he would have been dead if he hadn't been wearing it the last time he was in a boat, decided he could put up with it a bit longer. Once they docked at the pier at Hansen's Harbor, though, he stripped it off with great relish and climbed up the ladder to the pier (not without difficulty; his leg still hurt) once again wearing the unmarked Holy Warrior jumpsuit he'd been given by the cargo shuttle pilot . . . had that only been yesterday?

Unbelievable.

Two armed, armored, and grim-faced Holy Warriors met him and escorted him, limping, back through the town to Government House. Little had changed since yesterday, although the cage that had been full of Selkies floated empty, one side standing wide open. Richard wondered, with an unease that surprised him, what had happened to them. *Surely they weren't executed in cold blood,* he thought. *That was never the plan. They're to be allowed to live, just sterilized and put to work rebuild-*

ing the city in preparation for the arrival of pure human colonists. . . .

Oh, is that all? And that's better, is it?

Again, Richard tried to put such thoughts out of his head. Ideas like that were dangerous, especially when he was about to talk to the Grand Deacon . . . who, in turn, would certainly be reporting to Cheveldeoff. Of course, Richard would be reporting to Cheveldeoff himself, but he had little doubt which report would carry more weight. He might be along as Cheveldeoff's personal observer, but he was also on probation, and he knew it.

Things hadn't changed much since his last visit with the Grand Deacon. Perhaps the sense of barely controlled chaos as people came and went had lessened slightly. Ellers, however, looked much unhappier than he had the day before, and from the way he looked at Richard, Richard suspected a large portion of that unhappiness was directed at him.

Ellers confirmed it. "What the hell did you think you were doing?" he snapped. "You didn't have permission to go out with a tracker boat. You're here to observe, not to take part in operations!"

"I thought it was important to observe the operation of the tracker boats and hunterbots," Richard said, keeping his voice level. "I didn't see how I could do that while remaining on shore."

"You should have requested permission," Ellers said.

"I'm not under your command," Richard snapped back, and instantly regretted it. *What's wrong with you? Are you* trying *to get yourself confined to the ship?*

Maybe he was. Then he wouldn't have to continue to observe the bloody results of his brilliant interstellar detective work.

Ellers' eyes had narrowed. "No," he said. "You're not. But the men you were with were. I've already issued orders to all Holy Warriors that they are not to allow you to accompany them on any operations without my express permission. Have you got a problem with that?"

Richard took a deep breath. "No. And . . ." He found

it surprisingly hard to say. "I apologize, Grand Deacon. I had not thought through the possible consequences of my actions." *On Earth, or here.*

The Grand Deacon said nothing for a moment, his eyes searching Richard's face. "Apology accepted," he said abruptly. "We'll say no more about it."

"Thank you."

"But now tell me: what happened out there?"

Richard explained, as best he could, how he had come to be in the water without a boat and minus two Holy Warriors. When he finished, the Grand Deacon shook his head. "We know there are a lot of underwater habitats out there," he said. "We've found a few in relatively shallow water, but the deep-water ones . . . well, a few hundred meters of salt water makes a very effective sensor shield. It's too bad that Selkie bitch got away. I'd bet a sizable sum she was heading to one."

"I was hardly in a position to follow her," Richard pointed out, while inwardly seething at Ellers' use of the word "bitch" to describe the young woman . . . the *Selkie* . . . who had saved his life . . . *what's wrong with me?* He wondered again. *Why should I care what he calls her?*

Ellers waved a dismissive hand. "I'm not blaming you," he said. "In any event, we're analyzing the computer logs from your survival suit. Maybe there'll be enough data there to at least give us a direction; we can send out a couple of hunterbots along the possible vectors, and maybe we'll get lucky." He frowned. "Although I am also concerned by the rather astonishing fact that a hunterbot, hot on the trail of a well-identified and confirmed Selkie, abandoned that trail to follow you, instead. And you think it was because you were bleeding?"

"I think it must have been," Richard said. The Holy Warriors who had pulled him aboard their boat had resealed and bound the wound, but talking about it made him aware again of that particular, sharper pain mingled with the general aches of his much-abused body.

"I don't like it," Ellers said. "If the hunterbots start

turning on our divers, their usefulness is questionable."
He thought for a minute. "I want you to go to the hospital," he said finally. "I'll radio ahead and explain the
situation. I want the medics to run whatever tests they
can think of, comparing your blood and that of the Selkies. We need to know why that thing attacked you. And
you should get that leg checked out anyway." Ellers gave
him a hard look. "After that, you can continue your
observations for Archdeacon Cheveldeoff. But you *will*
get permission before doing anything like this again, do
I make myself clear?"

Richard resisted the urge to say "Yes, sir." He wasn't
in the military and while he might be at Ellers' mercy,
he certainly wasn't—as he'd pointed out moments
before—at his command. "Crystal clear, Grand Deacon."

"All right, get going. You two," he said to the Holy
Warriors who had stood at attention throughout the exchange, "escort Mr. Hansen to the hospital. Dismissed."

The hospital was only a couple of blocks from Government House. The central part of the city seemed well-
secured; maybe that was why the Holy Warrior on Richard's right, whose name tag read KAVANAGH, felt relaxed enough to chat. "Are you really Victor Hansen's
grandson?" he said as they walked—or in Richard's case,
limped—down the street, feet crunching on broken glass.
Richard could count the number of unbroken windows
he'd seen in Hansen's Harbor on the fingers of one hand.

"I really am," Richard said.

"So . . . look, I know you're not him, and you can't
pick your relatives, but . . . well, why'd he do it?"

"Do what?"

Kavanagh gestured in the direction of New Botany
Bay. "This. Create those monsters." He shook his head.
"They give me the creeps. I feel kind of Unpurified just
looking at them. Like I need a shower and a day's penitence. How could any normal human being create monsters like that?"

Leave it, Richard warned himself, but the newly rebellious part of his mind seized control, and he heard himself say, "They're not monsters."

He became aware of the suddenly more focused attention of the other Holy Warrior, whose name tag read DUNCAN. *Careful,* he thought, and again, *What's wrong with me?*

"How can you say that?" Kavanagh demanded. "Geez, have you seen them? Well, of course you have, I heard you were in the water with one. No nose to speak of, no ears, and those gills . . ." He shook his head. "And they're shameless. Those skinsuits they wear. They might as well go naked. I hear some of the ones they dragged out of the bay *were* naked."

"If they're not human, why do you care whether they're naked or not?" Richard said. *Shut up!* a part of him said frantically.

Kavanagh gave him a puzzled look. "Huh?"

"Never mind."

"So why'd he do it? Your grandfather? Was he, you know . . ." he made a circling gesture around his right ear. ". . . crazy?" He frowned. "Hey, I'd almost forgotten. Your dad was *definitely* crazy, wasn't he? I remember now . . . jumped off a building."

Duncan still watched him like a hawk. Richard's fist clenched. He wanted nothing more than to punch Kavanagh in the nose, but he knew whatever he did or said would be promptly reported back to the Grand Deacon. "No," he said carefully, wresting control away from the strange . . . well, the Body did not believe in demons or demon possession, but "demon" was still the word that came to mind . . . that seemed to have claimed half his brain. "I don't think my grandfather was crazy, even if my dad was. But remember, Victor Hansen created the Selkies before the Avatar's message had been widely disseminated. Humans had gotten away with doing whatever they wanted for decades without giving a thought to the will of God—the true will of God, as proclaimed by the Avatar. Grandfather was . . . misguided. He did not believe that creating a new race of . . ." Richard bit off the next word. He'd been about to say *humans*. ". . . subhumans was evil. He probably didn't think about the ethics and morality of it at all. It was an immoral age."

"But when the first one was born . . ." Kavanagh shook his head. "When he saw what it looked like, why didn't he just strangle it at birth and burn his research?"

What kind of monstrous father would strangle his child at birth, no matter what it looked like? Richard thought, but managed not to say. "I can't speak for my grandfather," he said instead. "It's not my place to defend him."

But for the first time in his life, he'd found that he wanted to, and that troubled him as they walked through the sliding doors into the reception area of the hospital.

Grand Deacon Ellers had clearly been true to his word. A Holy Warrior medic awaited them just inside. "You can go," he told the Holy Warriors, who nodded and left, Duncan giving Richard one last suspicious look before exiting.

The medic jerked his head toward the hallway that led off the deserted reception area. Richard followed him. "Pretty primitive conditions here," the medic said conversationally as they walked. "They don't seem to have advanced much since pre-Salvation days."

Richard looked around. He couldn't tell; to him it looked a lot like any other hospital he'd ever been in: the same white-and-blue corridors, the same beds, the same cryptic signs. But the beds were empty and the rooms they passed, offices and labs and patients' rooms alike, had a disordered look as though people had fled them in a hurry. "Where are the patients and doctors?"

"Still here," the medic said. "We just moved them all into a single wing, so we could secure it better. They're all normal humans, so it's no problem."

"There aren't any Selkies here?"

"No, they had their own hospital down in the harbor," the medic said indifferently. "One of those half-submerged buildings. Three times the size of this dinky place. Took a couple of direct hits. We don't have to worry about it." Two Holy Warriors stood guard at a fire door up ahead; the medic nodded to them and they let him and Richard pass without challenge.

Beyond the fire door, the hospital seemed more normal. People in blue, green, and white coats moved from room to room and an orderly pushed someone on a stretcher through swinging doors, but Richard didn't get a good look at any of them: the medic gestured to a door immediately to their right. "In here."

Richard followed him in, but in his mind, he couldn't help picturing that other hospital, the one in New Botany Bay. Early morning, nurses doing their rounds, patients sleeping . . . Selkie patients, but still . . .

And then . . . explosions, fire, screaming, smoke, crushing darkness, pain, death. Death. And more death. And those who survived . . .

. . . no rescue. No relief. A slow death instead of a quick death, in a place that should have been a place of shelter, a place of succor and relief from pain.

They were just Selkies, he thought fiercely. *They're not human!*

But again, he thought of the Selkie woman who had let him go and saved his life.

Dogs aren't human, either, he argued with himself. *But I wouldn't bomb a veterinary hospital.*

It's war. Things like that happen in war.

If this is war, why is only one side shooting?

The medic first took a look at Richard's leg. "Looks like the guys on the boat did a good job," he said. "It should heal fine. Come back in a couple of days and we'll check it again."

Then he stabbed a needle into the crook of Richard's elbow to draw blood. "It will take a few minutes to run the various tests. I could use this stuff," the tech gestured at the racks of diagnostic equipment that lined the walls, "but it's all museum pieces. I'll just run down to our own portable lab. You can wait here, if you like."

"Can I look around the hospital instead?" Richard said. The tech looked startled. "Sure, if you want to. Both floors in this wing are guarded, and anyway, the staff and patients haven't given us any trouble." He shook his head. "I don't understand them, though. Here we've liberated them from the rule of mutants and they look at us like we're the bad guys. Stockholm syndrome gets pretty bad after a few decades, I guess. Well, I'll meet you back here in fifteen minutes." He went out.

For a moment, Richard stayed put. He wasn't sure why he'd asked to see the rest of the hospital. The strange confusion that seemed to have gripped him was unlikely to be eased by whatever he might see. *I'm an observer, damn it,* he told himself. *It's my job to look around. I don't have to make any policy decisions, anyway, thank God. I just have to tell Cheveldeoff what I've seen.*

He got down off the examining table and headed out the door.

Again, he was struck by how little difference there was between this hospital and those he'd visited on Earth. It even smelled the same, of strong disinfectant, mostly, occasionally mingled with the less pleasant smells associated with the very old and the very sick. He passed doctors and nurses who looked pale and worried and gave him a wide berth—the locals, he guessed. The patients watched him from their beds with eyes variously wide with curiosity, narrowed with anger, or clouded with pain or drugs. No one spoke to him except for the Holy Warriors guarding each floor. "Quiet place," one said. "Guess they haven't warmed up to us yet."

"Have you talked to anyone?" Richard asked.

"Most of them won't talk," the Warrior said. "Not to us. Except for one." He pointed down the hall. "Second door on the right. He's had a few things to say." He laughed. "Crusty old coot. Haven't heard language like that since basic training."

"Thanks." Richard headed down the hall toward the indicated door.

"He'll blister your ears!" the Holy Warrior called after him, and laughed again.

The "old coot" certainly looked old. He lay with his

eyes closed, so painfully thin that he barely raised a bump in the blue blanket covering him, except for the twin hills formed by his feet. His skin had the white, papery appearance of someone who hadn't left his bed for a very long time, and was unlikely to leave it ever again. A handful of silver hairs stuck up at apparently random intervals from his brown-mottled pate. An IV fed something into his scrawny left arm, lying exposed on top of the blanket, and a metabolic monitor beeped, clicked, and flashed. Several of the indicators showed yellow warning lights.

Richard hesitated in the doorway, not wanting to wake the old man, but just as he'd made up his mind to leave, the man's eyes opened. They were a startling bright blue. "What do you want?" he growled. "Bastard."

Richard stepped closer. "No need to call me names," he said.

"Can't pull a gun and shoot you. What have I got but names?" The old man's face contorted. "I'd spit in your face if I had enough spit," he growled. "But my throat's too dry."

A carafe of water and two glasses stood on a table by the bed. Richard filled one of the glasses and held it to the man's lips. He hesitated, then accepted the drink. But he took only two swallows before a fit of coughing seized him. Richard pulled back the glass. "Damn it," the old man wheezed when he'd managed to gain control of his breathing again, "that actor lied."

"What actor?"

"The one that said dying is easy, comedy is hard. Dying is damn hard, too." The old man squinted at Richard. "You're not a doctor. And you're not one of those motherless Holy Warriors, either, unless you're out of uniform. So who the hell are you, and why are you bothering an old man on his deathbed? Haven't you got some nice Selkie babies to kill?"

"My name is Richard Hansen," Richard said quietly. "No, I'm not a doctor or a Holy Warrior. I'm just an observer."

"Hansen? Well, that's a kick." The old man wheezed a laugh. "A Hansen in Hansen's Harbor who's not related to Victor Hansen. Never thought I'd see the day." He snorted. "Wish I hadn't, considering it's the end of the world."

"Actually, I am related to Victor Hansen," Hansen said. He hesitated. *Is this really a good idea?* he wondered, then, *Well, what harm can it do. He's hardly going to climb out of bed and attack me. He already would have, if he could.* "I'm his grandson."

"His—" The old man squinted. "Damn these old eyes," he said. "I can't . . . come closer."

Stepping a little closer, but not too close, Richard leaned down toward the old man, who turned his head to get a better view. His eyes widened.

"Shit," he said. "It's true. You look just like him, like a younger him. Like he looked when I first saw him."

Richard gasped as though someone had thrown ice water in his face. "You . . . you knew my grandfather?"

"Hell, yeah. I mean, I was just a kid . . . but of course I knew him. There weren't that many of us basics—that's what we called ourselves then—on the ship. We all knew each other, kids and grown-ups alike." That had obviously been a long speech for him. He had to stop and catch his breath, and for a moment he lay with his eyes closed, chest heaving. Richard wanted to shake him, but all he could do was wait. Finally, the old man opened his eyes again. "I'm the last one," he said. "Last one of the First Landers. Landlings live longer than Selkies, so there's none of *them* left. And even the kids that were littler than me when we landed are gone now. I've outlived 'em all. Wish I hadn't." He took a few more labored breaths. "Saw the beginning of Marseguro. Never thought I'd see the end." His voice roughened with emotion, emotion that also seemed to give him a burst of energy. "And never thought the grandson of Victor Hansen would be part of ending it."

"What . . . what can you tell me about him?" Richard

said. "What happened on the ship? What was he like? How . . . how did he find this place? What—"

The old man laughed, a harsh, pain-filled sound. "Why should I answer your questions, you fucking traitorous genocidal asshole? You want to know about your grandfather? Here's all you need to know: he was a better man than you or that cocksucker you call an Avatar will ever be, and if he were here, he'd tell you the same thing I'm telling you: go to hell. I'll be along to join you soon enough, and then I'll kick your ass for all eternity . . ." He began coughing again, and this time he didn't stop. Several of the metabolic monitor's readings slipped into the red and an alarm began whooping. As doctors and nurses ran in, Richard backed out. "What have you done?" one of the doctors snarled at him as he went past. "You've finished killing the Selkies, now it's our turn?"

"I didn't . . ." Richard began, but no one was listening to him.

He watched the doctors and nurses work for a moment, then turn and walked away, deliberately taking a route that didn't lead him past the Holy Warrior who had pointed him to the old man. Avoiding everyone, he made his way back to the lab where the medtech had taken his blood. Shaken, he'd barely sat down on the examining table when the door opened. The medtech entered carrying a datapad. He gave Richard an odd look. "Are you all right?"

"Sure," Richard said. "I'm fine." But he wasn't, and he knew it. From the moment he'd landed on this planet, the foundation he'd built his life on had been slowly eroding. He felt like his very soul stood on shifting sands instead of solid rock.

And then the medtech gave his tottering belief system a good, solid shove.

"Well, I know why the hunterbot came after you," he said. "It's the strangest thing, and I can't explain it. I mean, it's obviously nonsense, but . . ."

"Just tell me," Richard said.

The medtech held out the datapad. Richard took it and glanced at it, but the strings of numbers and letters it displayed meant nothing to him. "Selkies have a great many difference in their genome from normal humans, but just to make it simple, we picked one particular extended sequence of DNA that every Selkie has. It doesn't seem to code for anything—it's what we call 'junk DNA'—but we've never seen it in normal humans. Until now." He came to Richard's side and pointed at something on the datapad. It still didn't mean anything to Richard. "You've got that same sequence, Mr. Hansen. Based on your blood, you're a Selkie."

If Richard hadn't been sitting, he almost certainly would have fallen. Because suddenly, a great many things made sense—and the sense they made hit him with the force of a whole world turning upside down.

Chapter 12

THE REST OF EMILY'S journey to Jumpoff Station
passed uneventfully, compared to the first part: no
boats, no strange landlings, no multitentacled killerbots
tracking her down to blow her into pink froth . . .

She shook her head. *Dahlia. Maybe John, too . . .*

My parents . . .

How many are dead?

They'll know at Jumpoff.

Wishing she could somehow make the sputa go faster,
she pressed on.

The station first appeared on her navigation screen,
but just a few minutes later, she also saw its lights, and
felt relieved. Until that moment, she hadn't wanted to
admit her greatest fear: that the attackers had already
destroyed the station and everyone in it.

She was even more relieved to detect two other sputas
heading out from the station to intercept her. Their head-
lights blinded her to everything else as they approached,
but when one swung in front of her, she glimpsed the
helmetless operator. *Selkie,* she thought. *The station* must
still be intact, and still in our hands.

But the greatest relief of all came when she swam up
into one of the entry pools—Jumpoff Station consisted
of a dozen habitats the size of Dahlia's family's, all linked
together and surrounding a truly enormous sphere bigger
than anything in New Botany Bay—and saw who was

waiting for her. "Mother! Amy!" And then, without any warning at all, she burst into tears.

An hour later, with a sub already on its way to the habitat where she had left poor John, she sat on a bed in the hospital habitat, sipping blueblad tea and wrapped in a warming cloak. Amy sat beside her, her arm around her back, which would have been uncomfortable except that her multiple scrapes and cuts had just been cleaned, desensitized, and spray-sealed by the doctor who had just left the room. As it was, she welcomed the addition of Amy's body heat to that of her cloak. Selkies rarely suffered from hypothermia, but she'd almost managed it. She suspected it had more to do with shock than the temperature of the water.

Her mother had just delivered a different kind of shock, telling her in short, bald sentences what the Body Purified had done to Marseguro and its people—so far.

Casualties had been horrendous, she had said. Nobody knew how horrendous, because they didn't dare radio for fear of giving away their location. But they had heard the other towns talking before they, too, fell silent. "We think a lot of Selkies have made it to the emergency deep-sea habitats, or are en route to them," Emily's mother said.

Dr. Christianson-Wood looked tired, and somehow older than Emily had ever seen her look, even though Selkie faces didn't wrinkle as landlings' did when they aged. "We don't expect to see very many of them here, though, because we're so far offshore and most Selkies think this is just a tiny research hab."

"Dad . . . ?" Emily said in a small voice, dreading the answer. Amy squeezed her hand.

Her mother shook her head. "I just don't know. I . . ." Her voice broke, and she blinked and looked away before continuing. "It's only luck that I'm here . . . and even luckier that Amy is."

Emily looked at her sister. "What *are* you doing here?"

"I felt bad about . . . that argument we had," Amy said. "I knew Mom was planning to come out here, and I thought, maybe if I went with her, we could talk, I could make her see . . . it was just a spur-of-the-moment decision."

"We left in the middle of the night," her mother said.

"But you didn't tell me!" Emily said. "I thought you were still asleep."

"I didn't tell you because . . . we weren't really talking. I didn't even tell you we were going. I was . . . still upset with you. I left your father sleeping. I didn't even wake him." Her voice broke. She pressed her lips together and took a deep breath before adding, in a voice as cold and bleak as the bottom of the Deep, "I didn't even say good-bye to him." She fell silent, looking down at her hands. She fingered the ring on her finger. "I'll hope for the best until hope is gone."

"I didn't really make up my mind to go with her until just before I went to bed," Amy said. "I surprised her by getting up when she did. We found out about the attack when we reached Jumpoff." She squeezed Emily's hand again. "I didn't say good-bye to Dad, either. I haven't even really talked to him since . . ."

"Me, either," Emily said. "Oh, Amy." She hugged her sister close to her, and a moment later, their mother joined them, her arms around them as they had been so many times while they were growing up, but this time, Emily sensed, as much to take comfort from them as to give it.

They clung together for an indeterminate time, until at last Dr. Christianson-Wood pulled away, wiping her eyes. Emily wiped her own. She'd been focused on survival, then on getting help for John. Now, for the first time, she could think about the larger picture, and it terrified her. "What are we going to do, Mama?" she almost whispered. "They've destroyed our cities and towns . . . they've killed . . . God, they may have killed hundreds of us. Thousands. We have no weapons, no way to fight back. What are we going to do? Are we going to . . ." She paused, almost afraid to finish her question. "Are we going to surrender?"

Her mother had looked small and defeated as she stepped back from her daughters, but now she looked up, eyes flashing in the cold medical light, and her back stiffened. "We will not," she said. "And we *do* have weapons. We can—and *will*—fight back."

Emily blinked all three eyelids. "We do? We will?"

Amy seemed as startled as she felt. "What are you talking about, Mama?"

Dr. Christianson-Wood looked at her daughters as though taking their measure. "Have you ever wondered why this station exists, girls?" she said softly. "Or what we do here?"

"Research," Emily said. "Deep-sea research."

"It's on the edge of the abyss," Amy said.

"It is," her mother agreed. "In more ways than one." She hesitated. "Emily, Amy, what I'm about to tell you has always been secret. Even most of the people who work here don't know about it.

"Yes, most of the research conducted here is what you'd expect: we launch probe-subs into the Deep, we map the ocean bottom, we experiment with technology that might allow Selkies, even landlings, to someday colonize every part of this planet. But there's a habitat, the only one not directly linked to the main complex, that is off-limits to everyone except a small group of people, mostly geneticists, a few medical doctors."

She started pacing. "Victor Hansen never believed Marseguro would remain hidden from Earth forever. He hoped that by the time the rest of humanity found us, the Body Purified would be just a historical curiosity, a brief fling with unreason in a time of threatened destruction. But he didn't rely only on hope. He launched a research program designed to protect Marseguro.

"For the last ten years, I've been the head of the program. And a little over a year ago, my research into Marseguroite viruses allowed us to bring the program to a successful conclusion." She stopped pacing and faced Emily and Amy squarely. "As Victor Hansen wanted, we've created a biological weapon, a weapon that strikes fast, and hard, and is almost impossible to defend against. A year ago, we deployed it. And now we're ready to use it . . . against the Holy Warriors."

Emily stared at her. She couldn't have heard right. "But . . . biological weapons were banned long before the asteroid threatened Earth. Victor Hansen himself helped negotiate the worldwide treaty! After the War . . ."

Beside her, Amy nodded vigorously. "They even scrubbed all the information about bioweapons research out of the computer networks. We learned about it in school."

"Yes, they were banned and rooted out on Earth, where there were multiple nations, nongovernmental organizations, and shadowy terrorist groups, any of which could have launched a plague that would have devastated the Earth as surely as the asteroid eventually threatened to do," her mother said. "But our situation is somewhat different, don't you agree? We have always had only one possible, well-defined enemy, the one that already tried to destroy us: the Body Purified. We would never use the weapon against anyone from Marseguro. It is a weapon with only one target. And now that target has presented itself, and beyond any doubt has given us *casus belli.*"

"But . . . one reason biological weapons were banned is because they affect *everyone,*" Emily said. "You can't limit their effect."

"On *Earth,* they couldn't limit their effects, because all humans are the same," her mother said. "*On Earth.* But not here. Here there are two kinds of humans. Selkies, and . . . and the others."

Emily felt cold again despite the warming cloak she wore. "You've made a biological weapon that only affects *landlings*?" she whispered.

"But . . . you can't . . . you'll kill all the non-Selkie Marseguroites!" Amy protested.

"No!" Her mother made a violent chopping gesture. "No," she said more softly. "If we did that, we truly would be the subhuman monsters the Avatar calls us. No, Emily, Amy, we won't do that. Before we made the decision to deploy the weapon, we created a vaccine—a hypervaccine, really, one that provides immunity within minutes of its injection, thanks to some cleverly designed nanobots. Those who receive it will live. Those who do not will die. Horribly."

"But how will you get the vaccine to our landlings?" Emily said. "Without warning the Holy Warriors?"

"Selkies have volunteered to go into every community and secretly vaccinate as many landlings as they can find—and give them their own doses of vaccine so they can then vaccinate everyone *they* can find."

"But . . ." Emily shook her head. She couldn't believe what she was hearing. "You can't possibly get them all. What happens to the landlings that are missed?"

Dr. Christianson-Wood turned even paler, but her voice remained steady. "They will die," she said. "And we will grieve for them. But civilian casualties are an inevitable result of war. If you are unwilling to risk them, you cannot win: and if we do not win this war, Marseguro will cease to exist, and so will the Selkies." She suddenly turned toward a vidscreen on the wall of the examining room. "I wasn't going to show either of you this—I wanted to protect you—but I must. I *can't* protect you from what we are about to do—and therefore I should not protect you from what has been done to us. So watch, and then judge." She raised her voice. "Computer, display vidrecord Alpha Three Nine Gamma, vidscreen nearest my present location. Start playback in ten seconds." She turned back to Emily as the screen behind her lit. "This is video from one of the assault craft that conducted the initial attack on Hansen's Harbor. We intercepted it before we decided the risk was too great and pulled down our floating arrays."

The playback began, and Emily watched in horror as the Body Purified destroyed her world.

Buildings she had known all her life vanished in orange blossoms of flame, then collapsed into smoking or steaming rubble. She heard Amy gasp as the above-water tower of the school where she had planned to study dance and Amy to study opera split like a gutted fish at the impact of a missile, half of it sliding into the water, the other half left shattered, twisted, and burning. And though few people were about at that time of the morning, she caught glimpses of bodies flung through the air to lie crumpled and still . . . and bodies floating in the now black-and-greasy water of New Botany Bay.

But not all were floating. Selkies began appearing on the surface, swimming up to see what was happening, some naked from their beds . . . and as she watched, the image tilted and turned. Lines of white fire traced the paths of bullets as they ripped into the bay and the Selkies swimming there, tearing apart flesh and bone, adding spreading washes of red to the already fouled water. Amy cried out and covered her eyes.

Emily closed her own eyes. "Shut it off," she begged her mother. "Shut it off."

"Computer, end vid playback," Dr. Christianson-Wood said, but Emily kept her eyes closed.

"We must strike back, Emily," her mother said softly into her personal darkness. "We must strike back, or be utterly destroyed."

Emily could still see the terrible images. She suspected she always would. She opened her eyes and looked at her mother's drawn face. "Yes," she said. "Yes. I understand." And as she said it, something woke inside her, something hot and wild and angry. *I had one in my hands,* she thought. *I had one of those Earth bastards in my hands, and I let him get away. I* helped *him get away.*

I won't make that mistake again.

"And I want to help." She kept her eyes locked on her mother's. "I want to be one of the ones to help distribute the vaccine."

"Emily . . ." Amy said beside her, sounding horrified. Her mother opened her mouth, almost certainly to say,

"No," but something in Emily's expression must have stopped her. Slowly, she nodded.

"Fair enough."

"Mom!" Amy said. Her arm tightened around Emily's shoulders.

Emily shrugged it off and turned on her, though she knew the anger rising in her didn't really have anything to do with Amy's protectiveness. "We can't just sit here, Amy! You saw what they did. We have to help."

"There are other ways," Amy said. "They need people here, too. We're expecting refugees. There may be wounded. I've volunteered to—"

"And that's fine," Emily said. "For you. But not for me." Her throat tightened. "My God, Amy, they've probably killed Dad. They certainly killed Dahlia. They may have killed John. Who knows how many more of our friends are dead?" She looked at her mom. "Have we heard anything from Uncle Dwight in Firstdip?" Dwight was Dr. Christianson-Wood's brother. Emily's mother shook her head. "Or Uncle Phillip?" Phillip was Emily's father's brother. "He was out at sea somewhere, wasn't he?"

"Nothing," Dr. Christianson-Wood said.

Emily looked at Amy's tear-streaked face. "They may have killed our whole family. We may be all that's left. Doesn't that make you want to strike back?"

"Yes, but . . ." Amy held out her hands to Emily. "I don't want to lose you, too."

Emily took the proffered hands, hands that she remembered lifting her up when she was little, helping her to her feet after she'd taken a tumble, pulling her out of the water after they'd swum home together from school, hugging her on her birthday. Amy had always looked out for her, protected her little sister as best she could. "I'm not a little girl anymore, Amy," she said. "And neither are you. You can't protect me anymore."

"You may not be a little girl, but you're still my little sister," Amy said. "Emily, if you have to do this . . .

please, please be careful." She squeezed Emily's hands; Emily squeezed back, hard.

"I will." But she knew it was a promise she couldn't really keep.

Dr. Christianson-Wood took a deep, ragged breath. "I'm proud of both of you," she said. "Emily, you know I don't want you to go, either. But if you must . . . I won't stop you. It's not a time for any of us to worry about our own safety." She touched a control; the door slid open. "You'd better come with me. We don't have much time."

They left Amy still sitting on the bed in the examining room, head bowed, holding Emily's warming cloak in her lap.

Emily's mother led her through air tunnels to her main lab in one of the smaller and more nondescript habitats, talking as they went.

Nobody knew when Victor Hansen had conceived of the last-ditch defense of Marseguro, she said. During his lifetime, he had done nothing to implement it. The very real threat of everyone starving to death in those early years had overshadowed the much more remote threat of being found by Earth's Holy Warriors, especially since Hansen had known Earth had its own recovery to look after in the aftermath of the Day of Salvation and the brief but violent Moon War. (Before they were destroyed by the same fleet the *Rivers of Babylon* had barely eluded, Luna's mass-drivers had landed a couple of wallops on Earth as hard or harder than those delivered by the pieces of asteroid that had not been deflected.)

But before he died at an improbably (as he himself said at his ninetieth Earth-year birthday celebration) ripe old age, Victor Hansen had left detailed instructions for the Council. Not all were followed—despite the reverence the Selkies held for Dr. Hansen, they knew well enough that while he might be their Creator, he certainly wasn't God—but his suggestion that they secretly research a doomsday weapon to counter some possible future attack from Earth had been.

"In every town, there are hidden germbombs." They'd reached the lab, and Emily's mother had called up a display of Hansen's Harbor on her biggest vidscreen. She pointed to the Square. "In Hansen's Harbor, there are several small ones, and one really big one—right here, under the pavement, not far from where the statue of Victor Hansen stood. Remember all that work on the fountain last year? That was the cover for installing the biggest bomb." She smiled grimly. "It seemed appropriate.

"When we send the signal, those bombs will explode. They're powerful enough to kill anyone nearby and destroy any vehicles that might be above them—but the explosion is only a way to make sure that the real destructive contents, our nasty little bugs, are spread far and wide.

"The thing multiplies unbelievably fast. It's highly infectious. It can be passed from one human to another with the most casual of contact: a touch, a sneeze, sharing an item of clothing. Not only that, it has a symbiotic rather than destructive relationship with many widespread Marseguro bacteria: that is, it can use their genetic machinery to reproduce itself without necessarily killing the host. That means that on Marseguro—or on the Holy Warrior ship, which I suspect has been thoroughly colonized by those otherwise harmless bacteria, whether the Holy Warriors realize it or not—it doesn't need to pass from human to human. It can reproduce on its own—not as fast, but fast enough. So simply quarantining those who are sick isn't enough to stop the spread of infection. It will colonize and contaminate air, water, and soil. And it will kill any nonmodified human it infects within a day."

"How?" Emily said. *Horribly, I hope.*

She needn't have worried. "It's a fast-acting hemorrhagic fever," her mother said. "A kind of super-Ebola. The first symptoms—if our computer simulations are correct, since we obviously haven't tested it in an actual human being—will appear within minutes of infection. A tickle in the throat, maybe a bit of soreness. A nosebleed. Within hours, a debilitating headache, followed by extreme lethargy, internal hemorrhaging . . . death."

"Is there a treatment?"

"None we've been able to devise," her mother said. "Except for the hypervaccine, and it has to be taken either before exposure or within six hours of exposure to be effective. It should be completely effective if taken before exposure, and about sixty-five to seventy percent effective after exposure, with its effectiveness dropping off as the time from exposure increases . . . as you'd expect."

"So the volunteers' task is to get the vaccine to as many of 'our' landlings as possible before the bombs are detonated."

"Yes. Without being killed, preferably." Emily's mother tried to smile, but couldn't quite make it convincing. "Please, without getting killed, Emily. Your father . . . your uncles . . . may be . . . I don't . . ." Her lower lip trembled and she pressed her mouth tight.

"I don't intend to get killed," Emily said. "They've already tried once, remember. If their super-duper underwater killerbot couldn't kill me, I don't see an ordinary stupid landling managing it."

As if the one has anything to do with the other, Emily thought, but she'd watched enough adventure vids to know how the dialogue was supposed to go in these situations. *You say what you have to in order to keep going. Otherwise, you might as well curl up and die.*

Her mother's left eyebrow raised; she knew all the clichés, too. "All right, then. Have you thought about where you want to go?"

Emily nodded. "There's only one place, isn't there? One place I know better than anywhere else." She pointed at the screen. "Hansen's Harbor."

Grand Deacon Ellers stared at the report from the medtech while Richard, once more back at Government House, stood silently by. "What does this mean?" Ellers growled.

"It doesn't mean anything," Richard lied. "It's just some fluke. You know I'm not Selkie."

Ellers gave him a look that matched his growl. "I can see that. But I don't understand how this could happen."

The medtech hadn't come back to Government House himself; instead, he'd called in an expert. The expedition included a geneticist of the Body-approved variety, a Dr. Jan Aylmer. A tiny woman with steel-gray hair, she had arrived just moments before and now peered nearsightedly at her datapad. Getting no satisfaction from Richard, the Grand Deacon turned to her. "Well?"

"I see two possibilities," Dr. Aylmer said. Her voice, so deep it could almost be called sultry, belied her tiny size. "One, this is merely coincidence. The number of base pairs involved, however, makes that extremely unlikely.

"Two, and I think this more likely: Victor Hansen used his own genetic material to create the Selkies."

Richard, who had come to the same conclusion the moment he heard the news, felt a chill that had nothing to do with the air temperature.

Ellers looked skeptical. "If he had, surely that stretch of DNA would not have survived in every Selkie, through—what, three generations now?"

"Not unless he *designed* it to survive. It's 'junk' DNA—DNA that does not, so far as we know, code for any proteins." She tapped the screen. "I think it's Dr. Victor Hansen's . . . well, call it a signature . . . and I think it originated in his own DNA."

"Then why does *he* have it?" Ellers indicated Richard. "If Victor Hansen had to carefully design the Selkies to ensure that that piece of DNA remained untouched from generation to generation, how did it end up in *him*? He may be Hansen's grandson, but that still means only a quarter of his genes are Hansen's."

"Perhaps the answer lies in Hansen's own genome,"

Dr. Aylmer said. "We do have a copy of it on record up on *Sanctification*, since he lived at the time when everyone's genome was sequenced and stored, by law, for medical and evidentiary purposes." She touched the screen of her datapad. "I think they've got the airnet up and . . . yes, here we go. Computer, ID me."

"Dr. Jan Aylmer, chief geneticist, Blessed Avatar Hospital, currently assigned to Extraterrestrial Purification Force, Holy Warriors."

"Computer, access and upload to this unit the genome on record for Dr. Victor Edmund Hansen."

A pause. "Done," said the computer.

"Computer, switch voice control to local access node."

"Done," said the computer, but this time the voice came from the display showing Richard's genome.

"Computer," Dr. Aylmer said, "compare genomes of Victor Edmund Hansen and Richard Arthur Hansen."

Another pause.

"Genomes are identical," the computer said.

"What?" the explosive syllable came from the Grand Deacon. Richard couldn't speak; the chill he'd felt had become cryogenic, freezing him solid.

"Computer, recheck and confirm," Dr. Aylmer snapped.

"Genomes are identical," the computer repeated.

Dr. Aylmer turned and stared at Richard as though he'd turned into a poisonous snake in front of her eyes. "Clone," she said. "He's a clone." She pointed a finger at him. "Anathema!"

Richard still couldn't speak. He'd guessed, when the medtech told him what he'd discovered, that the Selkies were his kin, almost literally cousins, children of the children of his grandfather. That had been troubling enough, but this?

This couldn't be happening. A clone? How? Why? It didn't make any sense.

But genomes don't lie, he thought. The results were right there for him to see. And they spelled the end of any hope he had of rising in the Body, of shaking off the taint of carrying Victor Hansen's genes. They spelled the end of everything.

He wasn't just related to Victor Hansen; in some ways, he *was* Victor Hansen, the most vilified man in the short history of the Body Purified.

No, it's worse than that. To the Body, a clone is no better than a moddie. To the Body, I'm not even human . . . I'm no more human than the Selkies. Maybe less.

He didn't realize he'd been backing up until he bumped into the wall. Grand Deacon Ellers' shocked stare transformed into a glare of fury. "Arrest this . . . thing," he said to the two Holy Warriors who stood at attention at the door.

"Grand Deacon—" Richard began to protest.

"Silence, or be silenced," the Grand Deacon said. The faces of the Holy Warriors headed his way might have been cast in steel; Richard had no doubt they would be glad to do the silencing. "Two good Holy Warriors are dead because of you, *clone*," the Grand Deacon snarled. "Trained, seasoned men, and yet they're dead and you, somehow, are alive. No wonder the Selkie bitch let you go—you're one of their inhuman kind. Hell, you're a clone of their God. You bear the mark of the beast in your very DNA."

But I led you here, Richard wanted to cry out. *You'd never have known this planet existed if I hadn't been searching for any clue.*

Except somehow he'd known where to look. And somehow he'd known other things since then. And thought other things. Things that made no sense, things that didn't come from *his* experiences, from the things *he'd* learned.

Clones are just identical twins. They don't contain the memories and personalities of the original person!

But that same strange part of his brain that had been bubbling up odd thoughts and emotions for weeks seemed . . . unsurprised.

God! Richard thought, as sudden realization almost

choked him with panic. *Grandfather Hansen is inside my head!*

The Holy Warriors seized his arms and held him tight. The Grand Deacon suddenly strode over to him, and Richard flinched, fully expecting a blow. "So why did you really lead us here?" Ellers demanded. "Did you know we were about to find this planet anyway, and you thought this way you'd at least have a chance to warn them? What did you tell that Selkie bitch? She was your contact, wasn't she?"

Richard could only shake his head.

"Speak!" Ellers ordered.

"I didn't know I was a . . ." Richard swallowed; he could barely say it himself. ". . . a clone until this moment, I swear, Grand Deacon. Everything I have done I have done in good faith. Everything has happened just the way I said!"

. . . except for the little matter of tips coming from the ghost of my grandfather . . .

He'd thought he might be going mad. Now he was almost certain of it.

And if *he* were a clone . . .

Father, Richard thought. *Father must have been a clone, too. I'm not really his son at all. And he* did *go mad . . . did he hear these voices, feel these feelings? Is that what—literally—drove him over the edge?*

"Lies," the Grand Deacon said. "You're a clone of Victor Hansen. How can you possibly expect me to believe anything you say?" He gestured to the Holy Warriors. "Take him to the prison. The Interrogation Team can have him when they return from Firstdip."

Once again Richard found himself escorted by two Holy Warriors; but this time they weren't there to protect him but to guard him, and this time they didn't walk in front and behind, but half-dragged him, each holding an arm in a painful, iron-hard grip.

Despite their roughness, his legs felt so wobbly he was almost grateful for their support.

The Hansen's Harbor Criminal Detention Center, untouched by the Holy Warriors' aerial attack, stood in an empty cobblestoned courtyard several blocks from Government House, on the inland edge of Hansen's Harbor. A long, low building, it contained just a dozen cells and had a single entrance at one end, where two very bored-looking Holy Warriors stood watch in a guardroom. Inside, the cells opened, six on each side, off a central corridor. Whoever had laid out the cells must have gotten his ideas of jails from old vids, because the cells were made of concrete blocks and their doors were open steel bars. Harsh halogen lights lit the hall and the contents of each cell: a fold-down bed/bench, a toilet, a sink, and a shower stall.

Only two cells contained inmates, Richard saw as his guards dragged him down the hall to the cell farthest from the guardroom. In one a fat, balding man slept, or at least lay, with his back to the corridor. The other inmate, though, leaped to his feet and watched with wide eyes as Richard passed.

It was Chris Keating.

The door clanged shut and the Holy Warriors clomped out. Richard heard the door into the guardroom slam shut.

"Richard Hansen?" he heard Keating's voice. "Can you hear me?"

Richard ignored him. He sat on the barely-padded bed/bench beneath the tiny window, and put his head in his hands.

"Damn you, Victor Hansen," he whispered. "I've spent my whole life trying to escape you and what you did, and now I find out I *am* you."

Why had Victor done it? Why leave clones of himself behind on a planet taken over by a religion that considered them monsters?

And from that strange repository of memory and emotion Victor Hansen had apparently *also* managed to leave behind in his clones, Richard dredged up an answer. It didn't feel like a guess, or something he had reasoned out: he just *knew,* the same way he knew his name or . . . former . . . address.

Grandfather didn't believe the Body would remain in power long, Richard thought. *And he didn't want the Selkies to be cut off from the rest of humanity forever. He left his clones in someone else's care* . . . Richard half-remembered a name, had it on the tip of his tongue . . . but he couldn't bring it forward, and lost it again.

Something must have gone wrong, and only one thing *could* have gone wrong. The Body. Somehow, the Body had learned of the clones' existence. The Body must have had them . . . decanted. At least in Richard's case, and probably in his father's.

Richard's father had told him his mother died in childbirth. He'd rarely said much else about her, except that he had loved her very much, and it had seemed like a miracle when they met, that such a beautiful woman would take such an intense interest in an ordinary Body functionary like him.

I'll bet it was a miracle, Richard thought. *A miracle of the Avatar. The Body arranged that marriage. The Body implanted me in her. And the Body made sure she died in childbirth, so the secret would remain safe.*

The Body raised me, and probably Father, for one reason: so that we could help lead them to Victor Hansen's Selkies. They must have known not only that we were clones, but that somehow . . . how, Richard could only dimly imagine . . . *Victor managed to implant a portion of his memories and personality in us, as well.*

Hansen's little experiment killed my father, Richard thought. *Except he wasn't really my father at all, was he? He was my* . . . *elder twin brother.*

From the point of view of the Body, Richard's father had been a failed experiment. Richard, though . . .

Richard thought of the Selkie bodies floating in the harbor, the greasy black smoke pouring up from the shattered buildings, the little Selkie girl in the arms of her mother, in a cage . . .

I've been a tremendous success.

For the first time in his life, Richard wished *he* had a building to throw himself off of.

The Grand Deacon is right, he thought blackly. *I am a subhuman monster . . . but not because I'm a clone.*

Because of what I've done.

"Richard Hansen! Richard Hansen!" Chris Keating kept calling from the other cell, but Richard, sunk in shame and bitter regret, berated by both his own conscience and the lurking ghost of his grandfather, barely heard him.

For ten minutes Chris Keating called Richard Hansen's name, but finally gave up and sat back down on his bed. *Why is* he *a prisoner? What's going on?*

The last time Chris had seen him, Hansen had been getting on the boat with the two Holy Warriors, about to set off in pursuit of John Duval. Now Hansen was here, and obviously no longer in the good graces of the Grand Deacon. *Did something happen on the boat? Or is he simply being disciplined for getting in the boat without permission?*

But he's an observer for Archdeacon Cheveldeoff. And the Grand Deacon said he's in charge of intelligence gathering. Why should he have *to ask permission?*

Too many questions, no answers, and none likely to be forthcoming. Chris didn't even understand why *he* remained in prison. Most of the other landlings he had seen in the cells had been kept and questioned for a few hours, then released. But not him, even after all he had done to bring about the Purification of Marseguro.

In a way it comforted him to see someone else imprisoned for no reason he could imagine. *The Grand Deacon is just being firm,* he thought. *This is an ungodly planet. Its Purification must not be impeded. He's not certain of me and has no time to make certain of me, so he's just put me here for the time being, for safekeeping. Maybe even for my own protection. Hansen told those Selkies what I did. If word got around . . .*

He shivered. Maybe prison wasn't such a bad place to be after all. *When things have settled down, Ellers will send for me, and then I can show him just how helpful I can be . . . and earn a ticket to Old Earth.*

Once he had the ear of the Grand Deacon, he could find out what Hansen had done.

For now, he could only do what he'd been doing for two days.

He waited.

Chapter 13

THE PROPHYLACTIC PATROL, as someone had dubbed them, set out from Jumpoff Station over the space of two hours as darkness fell far above on the second day of the invasion. There were thirty-six Selkies in all, twenty men and sixteen women, all wearing special black landsuits, the Selkie equivalent of the survival suit worn by the landling Emily now so much regretted allowing to escape.

The landsuits kept them both wet and cool. Wearing them, they could stay on land indefinitely. Better yet, the landsuits would also make it harder for infrared-based sensors or night-vision equipment to distinguish them from the background as they moved through the landling towns.

Each landsuit had also been equipped with two forearm dart-guns, loaded with four compressed-air-powered darts apiece. The guns were normally used to ward off hungry ocean predators. No one knew how effective the weapons would be on land, but they were the closest things to firearms available.

"We have one thing going for us: the invasion force is small," Emily's mother had told the assembled group as they suited up, Amy and other friends and family members of the volunteers looking on. Amy looked pale and worried, Emily thought. She suspected she did, too.

Her mother continued. "Survivors report no more than

a dozen Holy Warriors in each small town, with maybe ten times that many in Hansen's Harbor, plus at least that many more supporting personnel.

"The Warriors are heavily armed, of course, and armored. Attacking them with improvised weapons or trying to overpower them would be suicide: the kill rate would be two or three hundred to one in their favor— or worse. Nevertheless, they are very few and even a small fishing port is a big place. If you keep your wits about you and keep your eyes open, you've got a good chance of going undetected."

"What if the landlings refuse the vaccinations?" a young man about Emily's age asked.

Emily shook her head. She already knew the answer.

"Then they will die," Emily's mother said. "That is their choice. Any other questions?"

"When will the detonation occur?"

Emily's mother looked at a man who stood behind her, one of the few bearded Selkies Emily had ever seen: Anton Scale, vice-chair of the Council. He nodded to her, assenting to whatever she was about to say.

Dr. Christianson-Wood turned back to the assembled Selkies. "The signal has already been sent," she said.

A shocked murmur ran through the group. She raised her hand. "I don't mean the germbombs have already detonated. I mean we've started a countdown." She glanced at a chronometer above the door of the main recreation hall where they were gathered, their somber black landsuits a sharp contrast to the brightly lit vidgames and vurtbooths lining the walls and the lights cycling through rainbow colors in the central pool that led to the underwater rec hall directly beneath. The design reminded Emily of the habitat belonging to Dahlia's family, and her heart clenched with sorrow and anger at the thought.

She still hadn't heard any news about John Duval.

"Detonation is at 0800 tomorrow," Dr. Christianson-Wood said. "Dawn, to ensure as much confusion as possible. You should all reach your targets by 2200 tonight. You'll have about twelve hours to vaccinate as many landlings as possible."

"What if there's a problem?" an older woman, probably in her mid-thirties, said from the middle of the front row. "What if we can't reach very many landlings? Will you delay the detonation?"

Emily's mother opened her mouth to reply, but Anton Scale stepped forward and held up a hand to forestall her. "This is a doomsday weapon," he said. "It always has been. 'Fire and forget.' Nothing *can* stop the detonation now. If this station is attacked and destroyed, if they run more bombing runs and level every town on the planet, they will still all be dead two days from now . . . and the Selkies that remain will begin to rebuild. They may intend to kill or enslave us all, but they can't do it in the time remaining to them."

There were no more questions. Emily glanced around the room. One or two Selkies met her eyes, than looked away. Many others stared at the floor, absorbing what they'd been told, or possibly praying, though from what Emily had seen, Hansen's Harbor's sacred buildings, Selkie and landling alike, had suffered the same fate as the secular ones. *They were probably specially targeted*, she thought. *No religion but the Body Purified can be permitted. They've driven Christians, Jews, Buddhists, Muslims, Animists, Wiccans, and every other flavor of unsanctioned belief to extinction or underground on Earth. They'd hardly spare them here.*

She looked up at Scale, who was talking in a low voice to Emily's mother. *He understands,* she thought. *There can be no negotiating with the Body. They don't want anything from us but our deaths. We're not human. We're a work of evil, and we must be eliminated.*

Which means we have to eliminate them first. Whatever the cost.

Finally, Emily looked at Amy. Their eyes met for a long moment; then Amy raised a hand in silent farewell, lowered her gaze, and slipped out of the room.

A moment later, the black-suited Selkies began slipping into the water.

They would travel in pairs, one pair each to the smallest communities of Parawing, Roger's Harbor, Rock Bottom and Good Beaching, two pairs each to the slightly larger towns of Beachcliff and Outtamyway, three pairs to Firstdip, and the remaining seven pairs to Hansen's Harbor.

Fred Notting, an engineer who had done occasional work with Emily's father, commanded the Hansen's Harbor group. He'd been working on a new habitat at Jumpoff Station at the time of the attack. He'd paired Emily with Domini Asolo, a young man in his late twenties whom she knew vaguely—he had been one of her mother's graduate students when she was still a little girl. As they waited for their call to set off—the Hansen's Harbor group would depart second to last—Emily's mother swam over. "Come talk," she chirped. "Domini, if you'll excuse us?"

He nodded, and Emily swam off a little way with her mother. The lights from Jumpoff Station provided plenty of illumination this close to the giant spheres, but not far away the darkness waited.

"The rescue team returned from the Schaefer habitat," her mother said.

"John?"

"Alive."

Emily felt a huge rush of relief. She hadn't realized how guilty she'd felt about leaving him in the failing habitat. "Oh, that's good news!" *About time we had some!*

"It could be better," Emily's mother said. "He's still unconscious, and they're worried about permanent disability."

Emily nodded, but she still felt relieved. John's chances were certainly much better at Jumpoff Station with proper medical attention than they had been in the clutches of a power-starved docbot.

"Your turn," Emily's mother said, gesturing at the

Hansen's Harbor group. "Take care. I love you. And if you see your father . . ."

Emily nodded, gave her mother a quick embrace, and swam back to Domini.

The sputa journey to Hansen's Harbor was long, dark, and utterly uneventful. They detected no craft of any kind, sub or surface, and none of the murderous bots. In discussions beforehand they had decided that the killerbots would almost certainly be roaming New Botany Bay itself, so they had decided to land along an uninhabited section of the coastline south of the city, at a place where Marseguro's single road, which strung the towns and villages together like pearls, lay well inland and out of sight within thick brush.

Once on shore they programmed their sputas to return to deep water and sink themselves until called for. Then, at ten-minute intervals, they slipped off in pairs toward the town.

Emily and Domini were third in the lineup. "Good luck," Fred Notting said when the time came. They nodded and set off, staying close to the water, the previous pair having gone inland.

High clouds obscured the stars, so that the only light came from the faint glow of Hansen's Harbor itself, still a good six or seven kilometers away and on the other side of the outthrust ridge of land that formed one of the jaws of the mouth of New Botany Bay, whose circular shape suggested it had been formed by either an asteroid impact or a volcanic explosion. But Selkie vision needed no more light: they made good time, and within an hour had climbed the ridge to look down into the town.

The normal grid of street and building lights had gaping black holes, in some of which still glowed the duller, redder light of fire. Smoke blurred those lights that remained. The brightest light came from the Square. Emily could see a cargo shuttle there, and distant figures in shining blue-black armor moving around.

In their planning, they had divided the landling part

of town into seven areas of roughly equal size. Each pair of Selkies would scour one of those sections street by street, vaccinating any landlings they found and giving those who could use them their own supply of one-dose hypos.

Emily and Domini's assigned area encompassed some of the oldest buildings in the city, recently turned into apartments, some craft shops and warehouses where they didn't expect to find anyone, and a few old government buildings, including the Hansen's Harbor Criminal Detention Center. The prison had been empty at the time of the attack, as it usually was on low-crime Marseguro, but they'd agreed they needed to check it in case the Holy Warriors had decided to use it as a holding pen for recalcitrant landlings.

They reached the first of the apartment buildings, coming up on its dark bulk from the inland side. Domini slipped down the gap between it and the next building, checked out the street, then motioned Emily to follow him.

Locked doors were a rarity on Marseguro for the same reason the prison normally stood empty. They slipped silently through the building's front door into its pitch-black lobby. "We'll start at the top and work our way down," Domini said. Emily nodded and followed him up the stairs.

Despite their luck with the building's front door, the first apartment they tried *was* locked. They had tools for that, though, and within seconds Domini had the door open. Inside, a vidscreen on standby glowed faintly green in the corner, providing just enough light to make out a couch and a couple of chairs, pictures on the wall, an opening into the kitchen, and another opening that appeared to lead into a hallway. They slipped through that. A door to their right opened into the bathroom, a door to their left into a bedroom. They crept in, and found two landlings asleep in a double bed.

They carried two kinds of hyposprays: one just the vaccine, the other a vaccine and a hypnotic. "Let sleeping landlings lie," was the motto, and so they each took out the hypospray charged with both vaccine and hypnotic, placed them against the necks of the man and woman in the bed, and fired.

The sharp hiss and inevitable sting made the landlings stir, but then the hypnotic tucked them back into sleep. Domini and Emily slipped out and moved on to the next apartment.

They found no one awake in that first apartment building. Three of the apartments showed signs of occupation, but were empty. But in the fifth apartment they entered, a wide-awake man waited for them, armed with a baseball bat (Emily didn't see the appeal, but landlings had recently taken to the old sport in a big way). When he saw they were Selkies, he relaxed. "I thought you were Holy Warriors!" he said. When they'd explained what they were up to, he took the vaccine, accepted a supply of his own, and slipped out to see what he could do to help the cause.

As they worked their way through apartment building after apartment building, Emily saw several names she recognized on annunciator panels, but one in particular stood out, in one of the smallest and most run-down buildings: Chris Keating.

I wish I'd drowned him when I had the chance, Emily thought. *The bastard called them here.*

Well, if she ran across him, he'd sure as hell receive no vaccination from her, though she couldn't prevent someone else from doing the honors, someone who didn't know who he was or what he'd done.

Get this over with, and then we'll deal with Keating, if he's still alive.

The night wore on. They saw no Holy Warriors in the streets. At first, Emily wondered why they were so complacent, but then she thought of the ease with which they'd taken the planet and the complete lack of armed resistance. *Why shouldn't they be complacent? They think we're defenseless.*

They'll know better soon enough.

They began to encounter landlings who had already been vaccinated by other landlings. One, who gave his name as Drew Harper, offered to accompany them. With his help, they moved even faster, and as the sky began to gray toward dawn, they completed their sweep of their part of the city. All they had left was the prison. If it held any prisoners, there would surely be Holy Warriors guarding them, and so they had left it for last.

"I see two," Domini whispered to Emily as they crouched in an alley from which they could look across the paved courtyard surrounding the prison, a long, thick-walled building with small windows. Guards meant prisoners. Any Selkie locked up on land since the invasion would have died a horrible death from dehydration by now . . . Emily hoped to God *that* hadn't happened . . . so whoever was in there needed vaccinating.

Domini lowered the heatscanner through which he'd been observing the prison. Designed for use in the deep ocean and looking like a pair of odd, lensless binoculars, it could easily detect the thermal emissions of people through the prison's cold walls. "Three prisoners. We have to get in there."

Emily nodded. They had a plan, of course: a simple plan, because they'd had no time to practice a complex one and also because simple plans were usually the best—at least, so she'd always heard, and she fervently hoped it was true.

"Drew, you stay here," Domini said. "Keep watch. You see anyone coming, let out a shout and run like hell."

Drew nodded.

"Let's go," Domini said to Emily. They both stood, then stepped out of the shadows and strode toward the prison as though they belonged there. No one stopped them. Apparently, neither of the Holy Warriors in the guardroom had yet glanced out the window.

That might be good or bad. It depended on what happened next.

They walked around to the imposing front door, made

of native stonewood (an incredibly dense plant material that came by its name honestly), and positioned themselves side by side. Emily swallowed hard and hoped she'd be able to do what she was supposed to do next. She bent her right arm so that her right hand pointed toward the door. Beside her, Domini did the same.

And then Domini knocked.

At first, everything went perfectly. At least one of the Holy Warriors inside must have felt secure, because he pulled the door wide open. "What—" he began.

Emily heard a sharp "pfft" from her right as Domini fired the dart-gun strapped to his right forearm. A high-speed dart, designed to carry a scale-piercing punch through thirty meters of water, caught the helmetless guard in the throat and carried on through his spine and into and through the base of his skull. Blood, bone, and brains exploded from the back of the Holy Warrior's head, painting the low white ceiling of the guardroom a grisly, glistening red.

The corpse dropped. As it fell, Emily saw the second Holy Warrior, her target, farther inside the room. She fired, but the second Holy Warrior had had one second longer to react than his unfortunate companion—and had been alert enough to grab his weapon at the unexpected sound of a knock. He wasn't wearing his body armor, though, and Emily's dart tore through his chest, shattering his breastbone, piercing his heart, and slamming into the wall behind him. But he fired at the same instant, and the slug from his antipersonnel handgun ripped through Domini's belly and out his back, pulverizing his internal organs and smashing his spine.

Both men were dead before their bodies hit the ground, leaving Emily standing untouched, unharmed—and almost undone.

Her legs gave way and she fell to her knees on the pavement, then leaned over and retched, vomiting up the cold-pressed sea rations they had eaten when they first came ashore. She stayed there, bent over, her weight on the palms of her hands, her eyes closed, heaving until nothing remained in her guts to throw up, and then she stayed there longer, trying to catch her breath. Only the realization that daylight was breaking and more Holy Warriors could arrive at any moment drove her to her feet.

Domini's backpack, sticky with blood and bits of flesh, contained the remainder of their stock of vaccine. Emily pulled it off his body, taking a moment to close his wide eyes, glazing over now but still bearing a look of surprise, then staggered to her feet. She looked across the courtyard to where Drew still knelt, his eyes wide and white in the twilight, and waved to him. He hesitated—she couldn't blame him—but then got to his feet and dashed across the cobblestones. He didn't look at Domini's body. "We need to move fast," she told him. "There are cells down both sides of the interior hallway. You take the ones on the right; I'll take the ones on the left."

He nodded.

They went into the guardroom. Drew took one look and emptied his stomach as she had earlier. While he retched, she searched for a way to open the inner door, and found the keycard for it in plain sight on the blood-spattered desk the second Holy Warrior had been standing in front of when she shot him. The card, too, had blood on it, but the key slot accepted it, and the inner door, made of stonewood like the outer, swung open.

A second key slot caught her eye. She read the label on it, grinned, and shoved the key in.

Bright lights came on in the hallway and every cell door clanged loudly as it unlocked. Emily started down her side of the hall and found the occupant of the first cell, a fat man she didn't recognize, standing by his bed. "What's going on?" he demanded.

Emily swung open the door and entered the cell, digging in Domini's backpack for a fresh hypospray, fully charged and good for a dozen doses. "Call it a prison break," Emily said. "You're free to go, but you have to get this shot first."

The man started as she came in and he got a good

look at her. "You're a Selkie! I thought they'd killed you all." He gestured at the cell. "That's why I'm in here," he snarled. "I tried to save my business partner and his family—Selkies. The motherless bastards that attacked us had locked them and a dozen more Selkies in a cage—like animals!—but they left it unguarded for a few minutes and I managed to get the gate open. All the Selkies escaped into the bay. I don't know what happened to them after that. I hope they made it somewhere safe. But the Holy Warriors saw me and threw me in here to rot."

"There isn't anywhere safe for Selkies right now," Emily said. "But soon there won't be anywhere safe for the Earthlings. We've got a nasty surprise for them. I can't tell you what it is—" *not with Holy Warriors likely to capture you before you've gotten across the courtyard,* "—but to be safe, you need this." She indicated the hypospray.

"Whatever you do to them, serves them right," he said, and held out his arm.

Emily vaccinated him.

"Many thanks," he said, and ran—surprisingly quickly, for a fat man—out through the guardroom.

While she had been dealing with him, Drew had gone past her and entered the third cell on the right. She heard voices in there but raced past without looking in, concentrating on the cells on her side of the hall. Empty . . . empty . . . empty . . .

And then, in the last cell, sitting on his bed with his head in his hands, she found the landling whose life she had saved at Sawyer's Point . . . before she knew what his kind had done to hers.

She reached out, took hold of his cell door, and slammed it closed. It locked with a satisfying crash.

The landling looked up at her, and she saw the shock of recognition on his face, too. He got to his feet.

"Did you hear what I told the first prisoner?" Emily said.

The Earthling shook his head.

Emily grinned—or rather, showed her teeth. Her heart

raced, and she felt light-headed with rage. "Every non-Selkie human on this planet will die a horrible death tomorrow . . . every non-Selkie human who doesn't receive a dose of this, that is." She held up the hypospray. "We don't have guns on Marseguro, but we're not helpless primitives. You've slaughtered hundreds of us. Maybe thousands. But you're all going to pay."

"And we deserve it," the landling said dully. He sat down again. "Or at least *I* do. Do your worst."

His fatalism enraged her. She wanted him to beg for the vaccine, to plead, to cry, to experience just a little of the terror he and his kind had inflicted on her friends and family. "Don't you understand?" she yelled at him. "You're going to die. All of you! And I could save you—" Again she held up the hypospray. "But this time, I won't!" She thought of Dahlia, of the horrifying vid she had seen of the attack on Hansen's Harbor, of poor Domini's eviscerated body lying in a pool of blood on the pavement stones just outside the prison door. "Damn you, this time you're going to die, the way you should have died last time!"

The man in the cell lay down on his bunk and turned his back on her.

"Rot in hell!" she screamed at him, then turned and dashed out of the prison, through pools of blood beginning to turn sticky, weeping with rage and a grief she'd suppressed until then. Glistening red footprints marked her passage across the cobblestoned courtyard, as she ran to join her fellow Selkies and await the purifying plague.

A gunshot, the sound of locks unlocking, and bright lights switching on in the corridor brought Chris Keating out of a sound sleep. Heart pounding, he had just swung his legs over the edge when a landling he didn't know burst into his cell.

"I'm here to let you out," the stranger said. "But you have to have this first." He held up the hypospray.

"What?" Keating stared at it, brain still muzzy with sleep. "What's in it?"

"I don't know. Nobody's told me. I just know we all need it, all the landlings."

"You've had it?" The stranger nodded. "Who gave it to you?"

Someone raced down the hallway outside; Chris saw only a flash of black. "The Selkies. They're giving it to everyone."

Chris hesitated, but the open door beckoned and he finally held out his arm. The hypospray hissed, and the landling leaped up. "Nothing personal," he said, "but I'm getting out of here before any more Holy Warriors show up." He ran out without a second glance.

"Good plan," Chris muttered. He headed to the door, glanced right—

—and saw a Selkie in a black landsuit, a woman by the curves of her body, though the landsuit's hood hid her face, talking to Richard Hansen through the bars of his cell.

He's dead meat, Chris thought. *And I am, too, if she sees me.* He dodged back into his cell, and pressed his spine against the wall until, a moment later, he heard the Selkie run past. Then he looked out again. He hesitated, torn between his desire to run and his desire to know what the *hell* was going on. The latter finally won and he ran down the hallway to Hansen's still-locked door.

Hansen lay on his bunk, his back to the corridor. "Richard Hansen?" Chris said. "Are you—" *Dead,* he intended to say, but Hansen answered that question by rolling over and staring at him.

"Got your shot?" Hansen said.

"Yes," Chris said. "What's it for?"

Hansen didn't answer. "Better run, then," he said. "Holy Warriors can't be far off."

"I'll let you out . . ." Chris said, but then realized he had no way to do so.

"Don't bother," Hansen said. "This is where I belong." He suddenly looked so angry that Chris took a step back, even with the bars between them. "So do you," he snarled. "Get out of my sight."

Chris stared at him for a long moment. "You're crazy," he said. "Just like your grandfather." And then he dashed for the guardroom.

What he saw there brought him up short. He edged around the walls, trying to avoid the blood that covered, it seemed, everything, and trying not to look at the ruined bodies of the Holy Warriors who had been guarding him. Outside the prison, he found a Selkie almost cut in two. He ran past the bloody corpse, dashed between two buildings that hid him from the prison, then kept running, zigzagging at random through back streets and alleys until at last he stopped and leaned his back against a cold concrete wall, breathing hard, confident no one was following him.

The Selkies are up to something, he thought. *If I warn Ellers . . . maybe he'll finally trust me. And take me back to Earth.*

He rubbed his sore arm. *But* what *are they up to?* The shot had to be some kind of preventive medicine . . . or maybe a way to distinguish Marseguroites from Earthlings.

A biological weapon? He shook his head. Not the sort of thing you whip up overnight, complete with vaccination. He knew enough genetics to know that. It must be something else . . . something else you need an antidote for.

It came to him. *A chemical attack! It's the only thing they could have pulled together this quickly. They're giving an antidote to as many of the Marseguroite landlings as they can—then they'll try to poison as many Holy Warriors as possible.*

Well, we'll see about that. There had to be some time left before the attack. Once Ellers knew something was planned, he could order his men into pressure suits. And then, Chris thought savagely, the Selkies would discover that what had happened to them so far was nothing compared to the terrible price the Holy Warriors would exact for such defiance.

He turned the corner of the building to head to the Square—and stepped right in front of two Holy Warriors. Their guns swung up. "Halt!" one snapped.

Chris skidded to a stop on the dew-wet pavement. "I'm going to see—"

The second Holy Warrior suddenly swung his rifle to his shoulder. The guide laser flashed red across Chris' eyes, momentarily dazzling him, and he flung up a hand. "I know him!" the Holy Warrior cried. "I escorted him to prison two days ago. He's escaped!"

"Shoot him if he moves," the first Warrior ordered. He strode forward and seized Chris' arms, pinning them behind him. "How'd you get out?" he shouted, his mouth inches from Chris' left ear. Chris winced. "Who helped you?"

"Selkies," Chris gasped out, then grunted with pain as the Holy Warrior twisted his arm upward.

"Liar," the Warrior snarled. "The prison is two kilometers from the water."

"Selkies . . . can manage just fine . . . on land," Chris said. "Ow!"

"Sam," the Warrior said, "get the prison guardroom on the horn."

Sam shifted his gun to his right hand but didn't lower it entirely. He lifted his left arm and talked to the wrist. "Computer, comm route," he said. "Prison guardroom."

"Signal sent," a tinny voice answered. A pause. "No acknowledgment."

"They're dead," Chris said. "Both guards, and a Selkie. Send someone—"

"Better check it out," the first Holy Warrior said. "He's secure."

Sam nodded and trotted off.

"You've got to take me to the Grand Deacon!" Chris said. "The Selkies have a plan . . . they're going to attack!"

"Let them try," the Holy Warrior said. "Don't worry,

kid, the Grand Deacon is exactly who I'm taking you to. If you're telling the truth, he'll want to know. And if you aren't—" the Warrior barked a laugh. "He'll want to know that, too."

There's plenty of time, Chris told himself. *Plenty of time before they launch any attack. They only reached the prison twenty or thirty minutes ago. They wouldn't have cut it that close.*

But five minutes later, as the Holy Warrior frog-marched Chris into the Square, the ground beneath the toppled statue of Victor Hansen erupted.

The force of the blast knocked Chris and the Holy Warrior backward. Cobblestones smashed basketball-sized holes in the wall of the building behind them, and pebbles and dirt rained down. Chris found himself lying on top of the Holy Warrior, wriggling helplessly like an overturned turtle. Then the Holy Warrior pushed him hard in the back, hurling him into the air to crash down hard on his left side. For a moment, he couldn't think of anything but trying to recapture his knocked-out breath, but he could still see, and what he saw chilled him.

The Holy Warrior stood with his back to Chris, staring at a roaring geyser of white vapor shooting out of the crater in the Square left by the explosion. Overhead, a white cloud was already spreading and dispersing. This close to the source, Chris could feel the aerosol on his face as little pinpricks of ice, and when at last he managed to take a full breath, the stuff tickled his throat.

They did it, he thought. *The fishy bastards actually did it.*

He watched the Holy Warrior, expecting him to double over or collapse or at least start coughing, but instead the Warrior spun and yanked him to his feet so hard he thought his arm would come out of its socket. He yelped.

"I don't know what the *hell* that is," the Holy Warrior snarled in his face, "but I'll bet you do, and you're going to tell the Grand Deacon. Now!"

He half-dragged Chris across the Square to Government House, where a dozen more Holy Warriors stood looking at the thinning geyser of mist. As the Grand Deacon himself emerged, still pulling on his uniform jacket, the geyser's roar became a hiss and then stopped. The sudden silence seemed sinister.

"This one," Chris' escort growled, "showed up just before *that* happened." He pushed Chris forward, then unslung his rifle and kept it pointed at Chris' back as Chris stumbled to a halt directly in front of the Grand Deacon.

"You," the Grand Deacon said. His eyes narrowed. "You claimed you were the one who called us here. So why are Selkies breaking you out of prison?" He glanced over Chris' shoulder to the other Holy Warrior. "Your partner just called in. Calvert and Romanow are dead. So is a Selkie, wearing some kind of water-filled pressure suit. Hansen is still locked up. One prisoner unaccounted for."

"Jimmy Calvert was a friend of mine," the Holy Warrior behind Chris grated.

The Grand Deacon's gaze shifted back to Chris. "Calvert and Romanow were friends of a lot of these men," he said softly. "So you'd better give me a good reason why I shouldn't just turn you over to them."

"It's the Selkies!" Chris said. "They came into the prison, gave me a shot of some kind, told me to run. I came straight here. They're up to something."

The Grand Deacon looked at the geyser of white mist. "Tell me something I don't know."

"I think it's a chemical attack."

The Grand Deacon looked at him, and his eyes narrowed. "Chemical . . . or biological?"

"It *can't* be biological," Chris said. "Victor Hansen *hated* biological weapons, called them a 'subversion of the genesculpting art.'" The phrase came easily to Chris from long-ago history classes. As if making monstrous fishlike humans wasn't itself a subversion, a subversion of everything decent and good. "And they couldn't possibly have put together a biological weapon from scratch in the time you've been here. It's got to be chemical."

"If it is, since we're still breathing, it's not a very effective one," the Grand Deacon said. He pursed his lips. "Unless there's a time component." He looked around at the assembled Warriors. "Anyone feeling anything?"

"Bit of a scratchy throat, Grand Deacon," said a nearby man wearing only a towel around his middle.

"Me, too," said another Warrior, this one fully armored. "I think it's just an irritant, sir."

The Grand Deacon cleared his own throat. "Now that you mention it . . ." He turned to his aide. "Everyone's on high alert already, but I want you to double patrols. This stuff may not be killing us, but it might not be intended to: it could just be meant to make us feel ill, make it harder for us to counter some more conventional follow-up attack. Order everyone to either take a shower or—" He looked at the half-naked man in the ranks, "—finish the one they were in the middle of." Everyone laughed. "Followed by full chemical decon procedures, level one—eye irrigation, nasal irrigation, the works. And then everyone into full pressure suits until further notice." The laughs turned to groans. The Grand Deacon coughed. "Dismissed." The assembled men hurried back inside.

Ellers turned back to Chris and coughed again. "Damn irritating stuff, whatever it is," he growled. "I'll get the medtechs working on it, but if you're carrying the antidote in your blood, we'll need more lab power than we've got down here." The Grand Deacon's voice had a noticeable croak to it. He spoke to his wrist. "Computer, comm route. *BPS Sanctification*."

"*Sanctification* here," a tinny voice responded.

"I'm sending up a patient. A Marseguroite male, approximately twenty years old, standard. He was dosed with some kind of preventive drug. I want you to analyze his blood and tell me what it is—and make me some of it, if you can. We think it's designed to protect him from an aerosol chemical irritant." He paused. "But just in case . . . full biological quarantine procedures to be followed when the shuttle docks. Clear?"

"Roger."

The Grand Deacon nodded to the man who had escorted Chris to the Square. "You go up with him." He coughed again, and rubbed his nose with the back of his hand. Chris noticed a streak of red on it as he drew it away. So did the Grand Deacon. "*Damn* irritating," he grunted. He gestured at Chris. "If he causes any trouble, throw him out the air lock." He jabbed a finger at Chris. "Just remember, we can probably retrieve the antidote just fine from frozen bubbly blood." He went back into Government House.

"Just give me a reason," the guard warned. He grabbed Chris' arm and half-threw him across the Square toward the waiting cargo shuttle.

I'm going into space! Chris thought.

The pilot, a huge man, said, "Hello, Dodson," as he opened the crew hatch for them. He had a thick accent.

"Velikovsky," Dodson said. "Strap this one in good. I don't want him getting himself free."

"Will do," Velikovsky said. He grabbed Chris' arms and pulled him into the shuttle like a child lifting a marionette, shoved him into a contraption of metal straps and buckles attached to the wall, jammed a helmet on his head, and strapped the helmet down, too.

"What is this thing that has erupted in front of my shuttle and scratched my hull?" Velikovsky said as he took his own place in the pilot's seat and fastened his own straps. Dodson fastened himself into the rack opposite Chris. He had to shake off a fit of coughing before he could answer.

"Selkie chemical bomb," he said.

"Chemical?" Velikovsky squinted at him. "Not biological? Filthy genesculptors here."

"They don't have biological weapons," Chris dared to say again. "They don't have any weapons."

"Shut up," Dodson said, but then, "Kid's right. If they

had any interest in self-defense, they'd have had guns. My guess is they scraped together some industrial chemicals, sneaked some explosives in under the Square in a tunnel we didn't know about to disperse them. Doesn't seem to amount to much. About what you'd expect from subhumans with fish brains. But the Old Man has told the ship to take precautions, just the same. Full biological quarantine when we arrive." He grimaced. "Guess I won't get that comfy shipboard bed I'd been hoping for."

"Well, better safe than sorry, no?" Velikovsky said. He pulled on a flight helmet. "Ready to lift, Ground Control," he said.

Chris couldn't hear Ground Control's answer, but Velikovsky laughed. "You sound terrible, Ground Control. Plenty of sleep, plenty of vodka. Old Russian remedy. We're away."

The engines rumbled to life, and Chris suddenly felt much heavier than usual. *Good-bye Marseguro, and good riddance,* he exulted.

Whatever happened next, he knew he would never be back.

Richard Hansen had had little to say to the Selkie when she gleefully proclaimed his imminent death. He had little more to say to the Holy Warrior who arrived a half hour after she left and demanded to know what had happened. "You tell me," Richard said, not bothering to get up from the bed where he lay with his hands behind his head, staring at the ceiling. "I was locked in here the whole time."

"Who did it?" the Holy Warrior snapped.

"The only person I saw was a Selkie woman," Richard said. "I gathered she objected to the slaughter of her friends and family. I also gathered she'd freed the other prisoners."

"And why didn't she free you, clone?"

"It seems," Richard said in a flat voice, "that I am *persona non grata* to both sides of this conflict. An inhuman monster to both the religious fanatics I led here and the people whose genocide I facilitated. And so, here I rot." He said nothing about the woman's mention of a horrible death coming for all the Earthlings. It could have been hyperbole or an empty threat meant to terrorize him, but even if it were the truth, he wouldn't lift a finger to save the Holy Warriors whose barbarity he had been prepared to celebrate just two days earlier.

Nor would he lift a finger to save himself.

"We are all in God's hand, and that hand may close into a fist at any moment," Richard thought, remembering a quote from the Avatar's book. "Ain't it the truth," he muttered.

"What was that?" said the Holy Warrior.

"Nothing." Richard rolled over and sat up. "Are you going to let me out or shoot me? Doesn't really matter to me."

"Neither," the Holy Warrior growled. "The Grand Deacon put you here; he can let you out if he wants. There'll be new guards to relieve me soon enough. In the meantime, you can just sit there and think about whether there's anything else you should tell us. I've got to check in."

He went down the hall.

A few minutes later, the thundercrack of an explosion rattled the city. Despite his professed disinterest, Richard leaped to his feet. He waited to see what would happen next. When nothing did, he sat back down and waited some more.

Emily climbed to the rendezvous point on the ridge surrounding Hansen's Harbor. The other dozen Selkies who had gone into the city were all there, almost invisible in their black landsuits in the dark shadows beneath the overlapping canopies of giant bumbershoot trees. They stared at her as she stumbled into the glade. "Where's Domini?" said a young woman whose name Emily didn't know.

"Dead," Emily said, and then, to her embarrassment, she began to cry, great racking sobs that shook her whole body. She fell to her knees and then onto her side, where she curled into a near-fetal position and wept and wept . . . and wept.

No one moved to comfort her; no one had any comfort to give, and others who had known Domini better sat quietly sobbing also.

But Emily's tears weren't only for Domini. She cried for Dahlia, brutally slain by the killerbot; for the terrified families screaming and dying beneath the guns of the landing craft; for her father, missing and most likely dead, with whom her last conversation had been an argument; for John Duval, wounded and harried across the ocean and now possibly dead or crippled; and for her old life and old dreams of dance and music, now as crumpled, shattered, and charred as the buildings of Hansen's Harbor.

The sound of multiple explosions ended her tears. She raised her streaked face, then got to her feet and went to the edge of the grove. There the hillside fell away steeply, offering an unobstructed view of the entire town and the bay beyond.

From the center of Hansen's Harbor and half a dozen other places around the edge of it, geysers of white mist rose and spread.

"It's done," a woman said behind Emily. "God, I can't believe it."

"Those poor bastards," said someone else. "They don't know what's coming."

"Neither did we," Emily said, surprising herself with how harsh her voice sounded. "Let them die. To hell with them."

Her tears were over. She might cry again for her people, but she would not shed a tear for the Earthling butchers.

"Now what?" said the woman who had spoken first.

"Now we wait," said Fred Notting. "And watch."

For the rest of the day they did just that. Shortly after the germbombs detonated, a cargo shuttle lifted from the Square and rode the white flame of its rockets into the sky. "Going back to their ship," Notting said with quiet satisfaction. "And taking the plague with them."

That had been their biggest worry, that the ship would remain uninfected and might have powerful weapons with which to extract vengeance from orbit. But the shuttle had launched well after the germbomb detonation and had been sitting practically on top of it. It had to be thoroughly contaminated, outside and in, as were any Holy Warriors inside it. And the Marseguroite virus that formed the plague's backbone was smaller and tougher than any Earth virus. Emily's mother thought it would survive any ordinary decontamination procedures, and once on the ship, even if any human carriers of it were quarantined, would quickly spread through its symbiotic relationship to the Marseguroite bacteria that, being harmless, the Holy Warriors would have had no reason to quarantine against and which were likely, therefore, widespread throughout the vessel.

"If they take anything aboard the ship from the planet, no matter how thoroughly they think they've decontaminated it, they'll be infected," she'd said. "Unless they blow all the air out of the ship and suit up in pressure suits, it will find them."

Whatever they think *they're carrying to the ship,* Emily thought, *they're really carrying death.*

The idea of a ship full of dead Holy Warriors circling Marseguro forever almost made her smile.

Their landsuits kept their skins moist and provided them with water to drink, and the sea rations they'd brought with them, if uninspiring, were nourishing enough. They waited, and watched.

After the initial explosions, there was a flurry of activity for five or six hours. Ground transports rushed here and there, boats crisscrossed the bay, a few armored Holy Warriors dashed through open spaces in the city, and once an attack craft roared overhead, making them duck farther into the shadows of the bumbershoot trees.

As the sun passed the zenith and started easing toward the mountains, though, the amount of movement noticeably lessened, and by late afternoon, all vehicle traffic ceased. Emily studied the pier through binoculars. The Holy Warriors there had vanished. So had those who had been guarding the Square. She spotted a few foot patrols slinking through the shadowed streets, but they soon disappeared as well.

For the last couple of hours of daylight, nothing moved at all. The complete absence of Marseguroite landlings worried Emily. What if the vaccine hadn't worked?

"The Holy Warriors probably ordered everyone off the street," Notting said when she mentioned her concern. "They're just lying low."

Emily hoped he was right, because as the sun set behind the inland mountains, its final rays turning the sky, most appropriately, the color of blood, Hansen's Harbor looked like a ghost town.

"What's that?" a woman whispered, the desolation and silence having obviously affected her, too.

"What?" Notting said in a normal voice. He might as well have shouted, the word sounded so loud in the still evening air, and he repeated, "What?" in something closer to the whisper the woman had used.

"In the Square."

Emily raised her binoculars.

A single Holy Warrior had come into view. He staggered as he walked, like someone drunk. The setting sun had painted the scene orange, but the front of his armor seemed redder than it should have. *Blood*, Emily realized. *It's covered with blood.*

The Holy Warrior took one step, then another, then stopped. For a long moment he just stood there, wavering, then suddenly he doubled over. Dark red fluid spewed from his mouth, splattering the cobblestones with the force of a fire hose. He fell to his knees, mouth and eyes stretched impossibly wide, then tumbled forward to lie, facedown and unmoving, in the spreading scarlet pool.

Someone else who had binoculars stumbled away and threw up in the bushes surrounding the glade. Others closed their eyes; but Emily kept her glasses focused on the Holy Warrior, dead and prostrate in his own vomited blood, long after the others had turned away. *Payback,* she thought. *Payback at last.*

"We'll camp here overnight," Notting said. "At first light we'll survey the situation. If it's all clear . . ." He gave them a wan smile. "Then we have our planet back, ladies and gentlemen."

They cheered, then, and Emily cheered the loudest.

The flight into orbit was short and surprisingly rough, but Chris had a tough stomach—he'd never been in a boat, but he'd never thought he'd be seasick if he were—and when they arrived at *Sanctification,* just twenty minutes after launch, his heart pounded with excitement. *Once you're off a planet you're halfway to anywhere,* Chris remembered a teacher saying. *Well, that means I'm halfway to Earth.*

Dodson unhooked himself from his rack, then floated over to free Chris. He looked pale, and sweat beaded his forehead. "When I find the Selkie who cooked up this stuff, I will personally pull his guts out through his gills," Dodson said. "I feel like shit." With Chris half-freed, Dodson suddenly coughed and kept on coughing, so hard he ended up holding on to a metal handle on the bulkhead for support, his rifle clamped between his knees, covering his mouth with his left hand. Tiny crimson globules escaped from between his fingers and floated in the air between him and Chris, and when the spasm passed and he moved his hand to grip his rifle again, blood stained his lips and palm.

"You should see a doctor," Chris said.

"Shut up." Dodson straightened and finished unstrapping him.

The shuttle had been directed to a small zero-G landing bay, just big enough for one vehicle. Its outside doors remained open, leaving the bay in vacuum. Dodson pulled a pressure suit from a locker and shoved it at Chris. "Get in," he croaked.

Chris silently complied, though he found it awkward without gravity, and bounced off the walls a couple of times and once off of Dodson, who angrily shoved him away. When he was finally in, Dodson sealed the suit, then climbed into one himself, in half a dozen efficient motions, while Velikovsky held the rifle and watched Chris. Then Dodson took the rifle again and nodded to Velikovsky, who opened the inner hatch of the air lock. Dodson shoved Chris in, then slung his rifle over his shoulder and followed. Velikovsky sealed the two of them into the coffinlike space. The sound of air pumps quickly died away as they emptied the lock of atmosphere. At last, the outside door opened in eerie silence.

Dodson took hold of Chris' arm, bent his legs, and pushed off against the floor of the air lock. The two of them sailed across three meters of space, then collided with the padded walls, covered with silvery webbing. Dodson pulled them hand-over-hand toward an open hatch, Chris bobbing behind like a child's balloon.

The hatch proved to be an open air lock. Dodson clambered in, pulled Chris in behind him, then slapped a control. The outer door closed. The silence quickly gave way to the sound of hissing air, and at the same time, Chris felt his weight increasing: the "air lock" had to be an elevator, too, transitioning them from the microgravity of the ship's core to the spinning outer hull of the habitat ring.

A moment's heaviness, then they stopped. Dodson still gripped his arm. Their chamber suddenly flooded with a pearly white mist. "Decon," Dodson said, his voice crackling with startling volume in Chris' ear. "If your fishy friends did come up with a nasty little bug of some kind, this'll do for it."

"They're not my friends," Chris said.

"Shut up."

The mist cleared away. A brilliant purple light followed; Chris' pressure suit automatically darkened his visor almost instantly, but he still felt like his eyeballs had been scalded. And then, finally, the side of the chamber swung open, revealing a white, featureless corridor. At the far end, another door stood open. "Go down there, go into that room," Dodson said.

Chris hesitated. "What about you?"

"We get to go back to the planet so we don't contaminate anything," Dodson snarled. "Get going!" He gave Chris a sharp shove.

The last thing Chris heard from him over the suit radio was a long bout of hacking, gurgling coughs; then the elevator and he were gone.

A new voice spoke in his ear. "You can remove your suit helmet, Mr. Keating," it said. "Then please proceed to the quarantine chamber, where we will commence our tests."

Having nowhere else to go, Chris complied.

Chapter 14

FOR RICHARD HANSEN, the hours following the explosions in the Square and elsewhere passed not much differently from the rest of the time he had spent in the cell, with one exception: no meals.

He expected new guards to arrive and check in on their prisoner, and probably bring additional prisoners as the Holy Warriors rounded up people who were either involved in setting off the bombs or just unlucky enough to be in the wrong place at the wrong time. But after the Holy Warrior left, he saw no one. No guards, no Selkie women bent on rescue or revenge, no prisoners, Earthling or Marseguroite. No one at all.

They've left me here to rot, he thought. *Or starve to death.* At least he had water: the sink and shower continued to work.

The missed breakfast didn't matter much. By lunchtime, though, hunger clawed at his stomach, and by suppertime, those claws were long and sharp indeed. Something more had happened than just a few bombs being set off by Selkie resistance fighters.

He recalled the Selkie's parting words. *"You're going to die. All of you! And I could save you—but this time, I won't! Damn you, this time you're going to die, the way you should have died last time!"*

She'd held up something, he hadn't known what—at the time he'd thought it must be a weapon. But now, belatedly, it came to him: she'd been holding a hypo-spray.

An antidote? For a chemical weapon?

Or a vaccine?

Germ warfare?

If that were the case, the only thing keeping him alive might be his isolation in this prison cell, and a rescue might also be a death sentence.

Let me see if I have this straight, he told himself. *The clone of the creator of the Selkies sets a butchering army on them, is rescued by one of his original's creations, is condemned by the army's leader as being no better than one of those creations himself, is further condemned by the same Selkie who rescued him once, is saved from a plague by the prison meant to be his tomb, and will likely either die in that very prison anyway, or be released from it and* then *die.*

It might have made an interesting adventure vid. But to Richard it sounded more like just a screwed-up finish to a screwed-up life, and the piece of Victor Hansen squirming away in his brain didn't argue with that view.

All that remained now was to see which of the two possible endings occurred, and how painful it would be.

He went to bed hungry, and sleep took a long time to arrive; but "the body satisfies its own needs without regard to the spirit," as the Avatar had written, and eventually he fell into a restless sleep punctuated by vivid, ugly dreams.

He woke to hunger and silence.

No one had come, and as the day wore on and his hunger increased, he became convinced no one ever would.

The Selkies descended into the streets of Hansen's Harbor at first light and cautiously approached the nearest Holy Warrior outpost, a guard station on the main road from Hansen's Harbor inland. Fred Notting peered inside. He stared for a moment, then reeled out, retching, the sound loud in the otherwise utter stillness of the predawn light.

The others exchanged glances. No one moved except for Emily. *I need to see for myself what we've done,* she thought. *And it can't be any worse than what I saw at the prison.*

She was wrong.

She smelled the room before she entered it, a vile, nose-assaulting stench of mingled blood and urine and feces and incipient rot. The Holy Warriors manning the outpost had collapsed and died where they lay. Puddles of blood and piss, mingled with strange black flecks that looked like rice, surrounded the bodies. Faces stared at her, blood-filled eyes wide, mouths stretched so wide Emily thought the doomed men must have dislocated their jaws with the force of the final retching that had ripped apart their internal organs.

She swallowed, but she forced herself to look and to breathe the foul air. *This is what we did,* she thought. *They wanted us to die. But instead, we lived, and they died. It's the way of the sea. The way of all life.*

And very much, she thought with sudden viciousness, *the* human *way.*

She turned away at last. No one looked at her as she emerged. No one else went inside.

"Burn it," Notting grated.

As flames roared into the sky and black smoke poured up, the Selkies moved deeper into the town.

Everywhere the Holy Warriors had been, they had died, in scenes of mind-numbing horror. By the end of that long day, as the bodies burned, no one bothered to turn away anymore, and no one retched. As they found each body, they first stripped it of armor, armament, ammunition or communications equipment, which they set aside for later use: if the Holy Warriors reappeared, either from some unsuspected refuge on the planet or from orbit, they wouldn't have nearly as easy a time of it. Then they piled the bodies like bloody cordwood wherever they could find an open space, poured on alcohol and set them ablaze.

At first, only the Selkies who had been part of the Prophylactic Patrol carried out the grisly task, but soon the landlings they had vaccinated emerged from hiding to help as well. Together they cleansed and reclaimed the town.

A few landlings had not received the lifesaving shots. Those bodies were bathed and set aside for a proper burial at sea. *There will be recriminations and consequences,* Emily thought as she gazed at the line of sheet-wrapped figures. *How did we miss so many?*

And what had happened in the other towns? They still had no word.

The largest number of Holy Warrior corpses they found in Government House. As they moved from one blood-drenched room to another, Emily thought that the whole place might have to be demolished.

In what had once been the Chief Administrator's office, surrounded by vidscreens glowing the pale green of loss of signal, they found the man who must have been the commander, dead in his chair, head thrown back, red eyes staring at the ceiling, the front of his uniform stiff with dried blood.

A nameplate on his left breast pocket read ELLERS. "Take him out and burn him with the others," Notting said.

Emily stayed behind as the others hauled out the corpse. "Have we heard anything from Jumpoff Station?" she said. "Do they know how things went?"

Notting nodded. "I talked to them this morning. The subs should be here in a couple of hours and individuals coming by sputa by nightfall."

"Do they know . . ." Emily's voice faltered. "Do they know about . . . Domini?"

Notting nodded again. He put a hand on her arm. "Don't blame yourself. It could just as easily have been you—or both of you."

"I don't blame myself." Emily looked down the hallway, where "Ellers" was just being loaded onto the elevator. "I blame them." A thought occurred to her. "Have we checked the prison yet?"

Notting shook his head. "It didn't seem very—"

"Domini is probably still lying there," Emily said harshly. "And the two dead guards. And there's another body in one of the cells . . . some Earthling the Holy Warriors had thrown in prison for some reason." *Some Earthling I rescued when I should have executed him,* she thought. "I'll go."

Notting opened his mouth as if to protest, seemed to think better of it, and instead said only, "Take Farley with you."

Emily nodded and left, passing a cluster of landlings heading for the Chief Administrator's office . . . the Administrator himself among them, she saw. They were all deep in conversation, and didn't even acknowledge her as they went past.

Most of the landlings survived, she thought, moving aside to let them pass. *The Holy Warriors weren't out to kill* them. *But how many Selkies died?*

The thought held surprising bitterness, and she frowned, troubled. There had always been some tension between Selkies and landlings. But if the feelings she detected in herself had become more widespread, if the Selkies started thinking that the landlings had somehow escaped the brunt of the attack, or if the landlings were seen to be taking advantage of their new demographic strength, taking advantage, in other words, of the deaths of all those Selkies . . .

. . . and then, if the landlings who had lost friends and relatives in the germbomb attack blamed the Selkies . . .

She shook her head and moved on down the corridor to the elevator.

Recovery, for Marseguro, would involve a lot more than just fixing ruined buildings and burying the dead.

Her own internal recovery might be even more difficult, Emily acknowledged to herself as she and Farley, a much shorter and stouter Selkie woman a good ten years older, walked toward the prison. The person she had been just three days ago would not have been hoping to find the corpse of a man she'd once rescued—or any man—locked in the prison cell from which she could have freed him, slain by a horrible illness she could have prevented . . . but that was *exactly* what she hoped to find.

First, though . . . first, she would have to pass through that charnel house of a guardroom again.

She recognized the corner where she and Domini had paused before approaching the prison, and steeled herself. Farley must have heard her intake of breath, because she glanced up at her and said, "You can wait here if you want. I can deal with whatever's in there."

Emily shook her head. "I've already seen it once," she said. "And Domini was my partner. I want . . . I *have* to do this."

Farley nodded. "I understand."

Everything was as Emily had left it, but with the addition of a new body, that of another Holy Warrior, who had obviously died from the disease. Everything was also almost two days old. They couldn't do anything about the dried blood that seemed to be everywhere, or the smell, but they pulled the stiffened corpses from where they lay, put them together in the shade of the prison wall, and covered them with sheets taken from the cell closest to the guardroom, the one from which Emily had freed the fat man. They placed Domini's body separate from the others. The Holy Warriors would be burned; Domini would be returned to the sea.

Finally, Emily and Farley went down the long corridor to the furthermost cell.

By now, Emily knew what to expect: the stiffened body, the terror-stricken eyes, the gaping mouth, the stench of blood and vomit and shit. Even though the Earthling she'd inadvertently rescued hadn't been one of those who had killed Domini, he had been in the boat that had launched the killerbot that had slaughtered Dahlia. She wanted to see that he had suffered.

Bloodthirsty? She knew it, and didn't care.

She didn't get her wish. When they reached the door of the cell, the man inside it, alive and well, stood to greet them.

Richard Hansen heard the doors opening and closing at the far end of the corridor and knew someone had come at last. Despite his growing hunger, he didn't cry out. Instead, he listened, trying to determine who was in the prison. If they were Holy Warriors, they'd be looking for him soon. If they were Selkies . . . they'd probably kill him.

But the soft murmur of voices told him nothing. As those voices approached, he stood, holding onto the wall with one hand for support, his two-day fast having left him shaky.

The last person he expected to see was the same Selkie girl who had rescued him once, then on their second meeting refused to rescue him and promised him he was going to die.

Her mouth fell open when she saw him. For a moment, they stared at each other. Behind the girl, an older Selkie craned her neck, trying to see him over the much taller girl's shoulders.

He finally broke the silence. "You again," he croaked. "Come back to finish the job?"

"Why aren't you dead?" the girl said.

"Not the friendliest of greetings." Richard felt light-headed, and suspected he had nothing to lose by saying whatever he wanted. "If you want me dead that badly, you'll have to do it yourself."

The girl raised her arm as if to point at him, but the older woman pulled it down. "You can't shoot him in cold blood!"

"Why not?" The cold flatness of the girl's voice made Richard shiver. *Nobody that young should sound like that,* he thought. *There's something else I've accomplished. Good work, Hansen.*

"He could be useful. And if you're telling the truth about not vaccinating him . . ."

"I am," the girl said.

". . . then we need to study him. Find out why he's immune. If even a few Holy Warriors survived and are hiding somewhere with their weapons . . ."

The girl took a deep breath. "All right." She lowered her arm. "Come on, you," she said. "My mother should be here in an hour or so. I'm sure she'll be happy to dissect you."

The way she said it, Richard wasn't at all sure it was a metaphor.

With the bloodthirsty girl leading the way and the older woman keeping his arm pinned behind his back, Richard stumbled down the long hallway and through the guardroom. It looked like an abattoir, spattered with blood and . . . bits. More blood stained the cobblestones outside, and four corpses lay in the shadow of the prison, wrapped in sheets, one set apart from the others. Whether they were Holy Warriors, Selkie, or local non-mods, Richard couldn't tell, and he wasn't given an opportunity to look.

They left the prison courtyard behind and made their way through the streets of Hansen's Harbor. Richard saw no Holy Warriors, living or dead . . . until they reached the Square.

Richard gasped, and tried to stop walking; but the stocky woman wouldn't let him, forcing him to stumble forward.

In the center of Square, near the toppled statue of his "grandfather" and a huge crater where the fountain used to be, lay row upon row of bodies. Plastic or blankets wrapped them, but here and there an arm protruded, or a leg, almost always spattered with blood, and almost always wearing the telltale blue jumpsuit of the Holy Warriors. "How . . . ?" Richard gasped.

"Shut up." The woman behind him twisted his arm to emphasize her command.

Several people, Selkies and nonmods, stood around the entrance to Government House. As Richard and his escorts approached, two nonmods came out, dragging two more plastic-wrapped bodies. A third nonmod appeared. "Those are the last ones, Mr. Notting," he said to a Selkie wearing a black pressure suit garment like those worn by the two women with Richard.

"I wish we still had one of them," growled a nonmod next to Notting.

"Maybe we do," said the Selkie girl, and the woman holding Richard's arm released him and pushed him forward so hard he stumbled.

Notting frowned. "Emily? Who's this landling?"

Emily. So that's her name.

"He's not a landling, Fred. He's a Holy Warrior."

Notting's frown deepened. "He can't be."

"The first time I saw him he was on a Holy Warrior boat that had been tracking the killerbot that killed Dahlia Schaefer," Emily said.

"But he's alive," blurted out the man who had just said he wished he still had a Holy Warrior in precisely that condition. "If he's alive . . . there could be others."

"I doubt it," Richard said. They all stared at him, as if he were a dog that had suddenly stood up on its hind legs and started spouting Shakespeare.

Notting came closer. The stocky woman grabbed Richard's arm again and held it tight. "Why do you say that?" Notting growled. "Do you deny you're a Holy Warrior?"

"I'm a civilian," Richard said. "And the Holy Warriors would be the first to deny I could ever be one of them. They've decided I'm subhuman, like you."

"You're no Selkie," said the man behind Notting.

"No," Richard said. "I'm a clone." He hesitated. *Oh, to hell with it.* "A clone of Victor Hansen."

Astonished, dead silence for a long moment, then Notting barked a laugh. "You're joking."

"I'm not," Richard said. "I didn't know it myself until two days ago, but it's true."

"You expect us to believe that?" said Emily, behind him. He couldn't turn to look at her, not with the stocky woman's grasp having just tightened to something beyond merely viselike.

"Not really," Richard said. "But it's the truth. And as you've so astutely observed, I'm alive. Maybe that's why."

Notting's eyes narrowed. He looked closely at Richard. "There's certainly a resemblance," he said. "But why would a clone of Victor Hansen accompany the Holy Warriors sent to destroy Hansen's Selkies?"

Richard's arm and shoulder hurt, and when he glanced from Notting to the face of the man who had expressed a desire to have a live Holy Warrior in his hands and beyond to the glares of the other Selkies and nonmods, who had gathered since he'd arrived, he decided he'd been forthcoming enough. Twice in the past two days, he'd thought he was as good as dead. At one point he'd thought he'd even welcome his impending demise . . . but now he found he didn't particularly relish the idea of being torn to pieces by an enraged mob. *The body satisfies its own needs without regard to the spirit,* he thought again. *And staying alive is a pretty basic need.*

"I think I'd better tell my story to the authorities," he said. "If they still exist."

"Oh, they exist," Notting said.

"The Chief Administrator is in his office," offered the man behind Notting.

"This isn't a matter for the Administrator," Notting said. "I think Mr. Hansen . . . is that your name?"

Richard nodded. "Richard Hansen," he said.

"I think Mr. Hansen had better talk to the Council. I believe a quorum survives." He looked over Richard's shoulder. "Emily, will you and Farley escort him down to the pier?"

"Sure," Emily said. She stepped forward, back into Richard's sight. "But I think we should hand him over to my mother first, to figure out if he's telling the truth or not."

Notting nodded. "Good idea. All right, I'll leave him in your hands." He looked around at everyone else. "Let's get back to work."

The crowd broke apart. Emily set off in the direction of the pier, and Farley forced Richard after her.

"Who's your mother?" Richard said to Emily's stiff back. "How will she be able to prove I'm a clone?"

"My mother is Dr. Carla Christianson-Wood," Emily said without looking back. "She's the best geneticist on Marseguro. She knows the Selkie genome backward and forward . . . and she has full access to the Hansen archives." She glanced back at him for the first time, a fierce look on her face. "She's also the one who created the plague that just 'Purified' your precious Holy Warriors right off the face of the planet." She turned away. "She'll prove it . . . or disprove it."

Richard didn't reply, but he did wonder, as he stumbled through the rubble-strewn streets, whether he would be any better off in the hands of Emily's mother than he would have been in the hands of an enraged mob.

If she could unleash a weapon as terrible as the plague that had killed the Holy Warriors, he doubted he could throw himself on her mercy.

He doubted she had any.

The subs from Jumpoff Station hadn't yet arrived when Emily, Farley, and their unexpectedly living prisoner reached the shattered pier. Richard Hansen—if he really was who he said he was—found an undamaged bench to sit on and planted himself. Farley stoically took up a position behind him. But Emily couldn't stand still. She prowled the pier, glaring at the gaping holes in the bioplast planks, still reeking of burned seaweed. She'd stuck with the mission, helping locate the dead, going to the prison, escorting Hansen . . . but now she wanted—needed—to search for her father. She assumed he was dead, but she didn't *know*.

Like who knows how many other survivors? she thought. *We're all in the same hab. Nobody knows who's alive and who's dead, in Hansen's Harbor or anywhere else.*

Something caught her eye: a bulletin board where announcements concerning community activities had once been posted, near where the pier ran onto the shore. It had originally stood on two stout bioplast poles, and she'd passed it a hundred times. The poles were still there, but snapped off at the base. Someone, however, had propped the bulletin board back up again against a nearby bollard, and it appeared to have new notices on it. Emily strode over to it.

A gallery of faces stared up at her, each accompanied by a desperate note. "Has anyone seen . . . ?" "Any information regarding . . ." "Last seen wearing . . ." "Sweetheart, if you see this . . ."

Emily stared at the faces. Her eyes burned with tears, but the fury in her heart burned even hotter. She looked away, out over the greasy water of the bay. The bodies she'd seen floating in it in the vid her mother had shown her had been gathered up. If they hadn't been, she would have cheerfully added Richard Hansen to their number.

She resumed her pacing, but avoided the bulletin board.

As evening shadows crept across the bay and the sky once more turned the color of blood, the three big subs that had been moored at Jumpoff Station finally appeared, fully surfaced, Selkie crew members standing on their decks. The subs picked their painfully slow way through the flotsam and jetsam floating in the ship channel. Among other things, the blunt bows batted aside several quiescent killerbots, some smart landling having found the master deactivation code for the mechanical monsters and broadcast it from the Holy Warriors' own communications equipment at Government House.

Somewhere in the wakes of the big subs, Emily knew, another couple of dozen Selkies rode sputas or drove dolphin subs like the one she and Dahlia had taken to the Schaefer family habitat.

Aboard the subs, besides her mother, were three members of the nine-person Council. Two other members had been located, one in Firstdip and one in Outtamyway, and would be in Hansen's Harbor soon, if they weren't already. No one had heard from the remaining four Council members, all Selkies. Since all four were in Hansen's Harbor at the time of the assault, all four were presumed dead.

Like Father, Emily thought. *Well, just a few more minutes, and I can hand this murdering landling over to my mother and go look for him.*

Going to let the grown-ups take over? an inner voice snarled.

Yes, she answered herself. *But I'm going to make damn sure they hear what I think about whatever plans they make from here on out. I think I've earned that right.*

The subs maneuvered gingerly up to the undamaged portion of the pier, and crew members jumped onto the pier with lines. Several more minutes passed before the sub was snugly moored. Eggshells wouldn't have broken if they'd been used as fenders, but that kind of care took time, and even though Emily could see the skill of the sub skipper, she would have appreciated more haste and less grace.

Finally, the hatch opened.

Dr. Christianson-Wood appeared first, and to her astonishment and embarrassment, Emily burst into tears and ran for her mother's embrace.

"There, there," her mother whispered, stroking her back. "It's all right, Emily. It's all right."

"Daddy," Emily sobbed. "I haven't found Daddy."

Her mother nodded. Her own eyes were wet, Emily saw, and suddenly everything flipped and instead of wanting her mother's comfort, she wanted to comfort her mother. "But I'm not giving up," she said. "I'm going to swim down to the hab. It might be intact. He might still be hiding down there. Or somewhere else . . ." Her voice trailed off.

"Maybe, Emily," her mother said. "I hope so." Something in her voice made Emily step back and take a good look at her. Her eyes glistened, but her face didn't look like that of someone who was about to emotionally crumble. It looked hard, set in stone—and even older than Emily remembered it from just a few days ago. "But if he *was* killed, I think you can safely say I've had my revenge." And then she looked past Emily at Richard Hansen, and her face became even harder. "Who's that?" she said in a flat voice. "He's an Earthling, isn't he? Why isn't he dead?"

"That's why I've brought him here—so you can find out." Emily took a deep breath. "He says his name is Richard Hansen." At the last name, Dr. Christianson-Wood's eyes shifted sharply to her daughter. "And he's not just claiming to be a relative of Dr. Hansen. He says he's his clone."

"A clone of Victor Hansen!" Her mother's eyes widened. She strode over to the Earthling. "Stand up!"

Hansen stood.

"What makes you think you're a clone?"

"Believe me, it was as much of a shock to me as to you," Hansen said. "But that's what the Holy Warriors' geneticist told me. She also said that I had a genetic sequence in my junk DNA peculiar to the . . . Selkies. You." He looked at Emily. "That's why the hunterbot came after me. It detected my blood in the water and thought I was a Selkie."

"I should have let it have you," Emily said.

"I'm glad you didn't," Dr. Christianson-Wood said. Her face had lost some of its new harshness and taken on a little of the light Emily had sometimes seen in the past when her mother was engrossed in a scientific problem. "Let's get him to my lab and I'll . . ." her voice fell. She turned and looked out across the ruins of New Botany Bay. "I forgot," she said. "My lab is gone." She turned on Hansen so suddenly he flinched. "I'll have to make do with what's on the sub." She looked at Farley. "Take him aboard. Tell the skipper I want him locked up until I can get to him."

Farley nodded, and propelled Hansen toward the gangway.

Emily's mother turned back toward her. "You look terrible. When did you last sleep? Or eat?"

Emily shook her head irritably. "I don't remember. But I can sleep or eat later." She looked back at the bay. "I have . . . I need to go see the hab."

Dr. Christianson-Wood pressed her lips together, then nodded. "You're right. Go. Look. Tell me what you find. But then come back here. You can use my quarters—just ask; someone will point the way. Get out of that landsuit and take a good long swim—in clean water," she added, glancing at the bay, whose water looked absolutely black now that the sun had vanished behind the mountains. "The sub's ballast decks are filtered and open for Selkie use. Try those." She looked over her shoulder at the sub. "A Hansen clone . . ." she said, almost to herself. "If it's true . . ."

"How could it be?"

Her mother looked at her for a long moment. "I can't tell you," she said at last. "Not yet. Not until I've confirmed it." She sighed. "And I can't do that right now, because the Council is meeting up at Government House in an hour."

"Couldn't they do without . . . without you?" Emily said, yawning. *My mother suggests I must be exhausted and suddenly I feel exhausted,* she thought. *We should harness that mysterious Mom-power as a weapon. If we're ever attacked again, she could just tell the Holy Warriors to play nice, and they would.*

Dr. Christianson-Wood looked oddly uncomfortable. "Ah. Well, um . . . the truth is, Emily, I'm an, ah, ex-officio member of the Council. Have been for years."

Emily's yawn turned into a gape. "Huh?"

"Big secret, just like the work out at Jumpoff Station," her mother said. "You know the constitution allows the elected Councillors to appoint additional members to the Council as circumstances require."

"Uh . . ." Emily cast her mind back through dim remembrances of civics classes. Mostly she remembered the boy who had sat in front of her, whose looks and body had turned all the girls' heads, but who had also, alas, turned out to be gay. "If you say so."

"Trust me," her mother said. "It's in there. And I have been so appointed. So I really had better get uptown. You . . . do what you have to. If you find Daddy . . ."

"I'll come tell you," Emily said quietly. "Council meeting or no Council meeting."

Dr. Christianson-Wood nodded. "But if you don't, come back here, get on the sub. Rest. Swim. When you wake up, eat. And by then I'll be back and ready to tackle that . . . little problem you brought me."

Emily nodded. She started toward the edge of the pier, then stopped and turned back. "If you're a Councillor, Mom, then tell me. What happens next? After all this . . ." Emily's gesture took in the destruction surrounding them, and by extension all of the dead, Selkies and landlings and Holy Warriors alike. ". . . what happens? Where do we go from here?"

Her mother's face settled back into its new, harsher look. "Emily," she said, "I have no idea. None of us do." And with that, she turned her back on her daughter and strode inland.

Emily watched her go, left with that most unsettling of childhood feelings: the grown-ups were in charge . . .

. . . but they didn't know what to do.

Then she shook herself, mentally and physically. "Why am I still standing here?" she asked out loud. With relish, she stripped out of the landsuit, leaving it in a crumpled pile on the pier. Underneath, she had on a barely-there two-piece skinsuit of the kind Dahlia had always favored, the best choice for wearing under a landsuit. She bent down to the discarded landsuit and from one of its pockets took out the lightband she'd last used when she'd lured the killerbot into Sawyer's Point, and strapped it around her head. Then she jumped into the bay.

The water closed around her, but she held her breath instead of opening her gills, until she'd sunk far enough into the bay that she hoped she'd left the worst of the oil and other pollution fouling its surface above her. Even so, as the water streamed through her gills, it tasted . . . wrong. Metallic, and oily, and . . . foul.

I hope I'm not poisoning myself, she thought, then dove deeper.

Lights still glowed along the bottom, the self-powered globes that lighted the swimways. With their guidance, she got her bearings, and swam past habitat after habitat. Some of them looked undamaged, though cold and without power, which gave her hope; but then she passed more that had crumpled to the floor of the bay, or split from above like a rotten fruit, and she despaired.

When she turned down the swimway that led to their habitat, her hopes soared again: the first few habs looked undamaged. But then the far end of the swimway came into sight, and she backwatered sharply, horror stabbing her heart like a fish-gutting knife.

The end of their swimway had led to the below-water entrance of the largest of the amphibian towers, a tower her father had designed, and which had housed his offices.

The Holy Warriors' missiles had caused the tower to topple. Every habitat at the end of their swimway, their own included, lay buried under tons of twisted steel and shattered masonry. If Emily hadn't known exactly where to look, she wouldn't even have been able to say where the hab she had grown up in had been located.

"I left your father sleeping. I didn't even wake him," she remembered her mother saying. *"I didn't even say goodbye to him. . . ."*

There's still hope, she told herself frantically. *He might have woken up before the attack, swum out . . .*

. . . and swum to his office, in the tower now lying in ruins across their hab.

The fish-gutting knife ripped through her heart and her hope. Vision blurred by the tears flooding the space beneath her third eyelid, Emily jackknifed and drove hard for the surface, away from the worst horror of all the horrors the past three days had visited on her.

Chapter 15

FROM ONE PRISON TO another, Richard thought, surveying the bare and barely-big-enough-to-stretch-out-in cabin into which he'd been locked on board the Selkie sub. But at least he still lived, unlike any of the Holy Warriors on the surface.

Aboard *Sanctification,* though . . . that was an open question. Had anyone infected made it up to the ship? If they had, then presumably it was a ghost ship now, or soon would be. If they hadn't, then the Holy Warriors in orbit would be perfectly well aware of what had transpired down on the planet, and would even now be planning their revenge. *And next time,* Richard thought, *the Purification will be total.*

And a sub sitting in the open moored to the Hansen's Harbor pier would be a primary target, which meant any minute now his approximately coffin-sized new digs might be completely appropriate.

As the minutes and then hours dragged by without any attack from orbit, though, the alternative scenario—that everyone on board *Sanctification* had died of the plague—became more likely. He slept, and would have dearly loved to eat, but nobody provided him with any food. He did have water, fortunately—the tiny cabin contained a palm-sized sink—but his stomach, unfilled for days, was cramping by the time the door abruptly opened to reveal Emily's mother, Dr. Christianson-Wood.

Accompanying her was the largest Selkie man he'd yet

seen, his shaved head and naked upper body covered with intricate tattoos that slowly moved and changed color beneath his skin in a way that made Richard queasy. He tore his gaze away from the apparition and focused on Dr. Christianson-Wood, whom he strongly suspected held his life in her hands.

"I've come to test your claims," she said without preamble. "Follow me."

He stepped out into the narrow corridor, which the broad shoulders of the tattooed guard filled wall to wall. He followed Dr. Christianson-Wood and the guard followed him, along the corridor, down a companionway, then along another corridor to a door that opened into a relatively spacious chamber, a good four times the size of the one he'd just left. So much scientific equipment packed it, though, that it had very little free space. He just hoped the sharp shiny objects in the rack in the corner were surgical and not torture devices, although he'd always had a hard time telling the difference.

Dr. Christianson-Wood entered and motioned him to an examining table. "Sit down. Roll up your sleeve."

Richard complied. "If your blood tests require fasting, I'm more than prepared. In fact, if it requires fainting, I can probably manage that, too. Any chance of getting something to eat? Even a condemned man usually gets a last meal."

Dr. Christianson-Wood took a syringe from a drawer. "You haven't been condemned." But she opened another drawer and handed him a foil-wrapped bar.

Richard glanced at the tattooed giant in the hall as he tore it open. "But I've been convicted." He wolfed down the bar, which looked and tasted like he'd always imagined dried seaweed would look and taste.

He'd never tasted anything more wonderful.

Dr. Christianson-Wood held up the syringe. "You came with the Holy Warriors. You're an accessory, at least."

Richard finished the bar but said nothing more as she swabbed and stuck. He watched his blood, so dark red it verged on violet, bubble up into the syringe. She gave him a wad of fibrous material to hold in the crook of his elbow, then turned and busied herself with placing the syringe into a compartment of one of the more complicated-looking bits of equipment along the wall. "Will that device prove I'm telling the truth?"

"It will tell me if you're a clone of Victor Hansen," Dr. Christianson-Wood said. "And if you share the section of DNA that deactivates the plague virus."

"And if I don't?"

Dr. Christianson-Wood closed the compartment door. It sealed with a hiss, and a vidscreen lit up. Dr. Christianson-Wood pulled a keyboard from a slot on the front of the machine and typed for a few seconds. The machine beeped and began to hum quietly.

"How long?" Richard asked, when it became apparent Dr. Christianson-Wood wasn't going to answer his previous question.

"Five minutes," she said. "Be quiet."

Richard complied. The five minutes passed at a glacial pace. At last, the machine beeped again. Dr. Christianson-Wood examined the screen; the readouts on it made no sense to Richard. *What if I'm* not *a clone?* he wondered suddenly. *What if the Holy Warrior geneticist lied? What if the voices in my head are just my own conscience? Would it change anything?*

He shook his head. *No, it wouldn't.* He owed these people. Every death on this planet was in some way his responsibility. He had to try, however hopeless it might be, to somehow make amends.

What if the only way I can do that is to let them execute me?

Then that's what I'll do. He snorted softly. *Not that I'll exactly have a choice.*

Dr. Christianson-Wood turned to look at him, her expression unreadable. She stared for a long moment, then glanced into the corridor. "You can go, Peter."

"Are you sure?" the giant in the hallway rumbled.

"I'm sure. He's not going to do anything."

"If you say so, Dr. Christianson-Wood." Peter sounded doubtful, but Richard heard his footsteps moving away.

Then he heard the door close. He looked up. "Now what?"

"You're more than just a clone of Victor Hansen," Dr. Christianson-Wood said. "As I suspect you know. He also gave you . . . literally . . . a piece of his mind."

Richard's blood ran cold. "How do you—"

"I'm the leading geneticist on Marseguro. I'm an appointed member of the Planetary Council. I am also the current caretaker of the Victor Hansen archives, and one of the few people allowed to access any part of them I choose." She leaned back against the equipment cabinet, and folded her arms. "Dr. Hansen kept thorough notes. Among those he kept secured until his death—and the Council has kept secured since—are ones detailing his scheme to 'have his cake and eat it, too', as he put it.

"Before he left Earth, Victor Hansen made five clones of himself. He left the frozen embryos in the care of someone he considered trustworthy . . . his wife, Dianne. His ex-wife, really; she loved him, but nothing could convince her to leave Earth. She did agree to keep the clones, though, and to raise the first of them to adulthood, if she and they survived. The remaining clones would then be put into the hands of the first clone." Dr. Christianson-Wood leaned forward. "But these weren't ordinary clones. Dr. Hansen believed he had discovered a way of passing on, not just his genetic material, but also at least a portion of his memories and possibly even his personality. He believed he knew how to encode that information into a living brain. He built into his clones what he called a gene-bomb: a genetic package activated at a certain stage of development—he estimated it would 'go off' when the clone was around thirty—which would begin rewiring a portion of the clone's brain, encoding some of his memories and beliefs and . . . well, he didn't really know, because he did all this based on theory, without any experimental trials at all beyond mice and computer models." She paused, and looked away, at nothing in particular. "Dr. Hansen," she said after a moment, "did not lack for ego." Then she blinked and turned her attention back to Richard.

"Hansen did not believe the Body Purified would remain in power. He believed it would fade away. By which time, he believed, his clone would be grown, and would find, tucked away inside his head, the information he needed to find Marseguro, and the wisdom to decide whether or not it was time for Selkies and Earthlings to join together once more."

She stepped even closer. "And now here you are," she said. "The living image of a young Victor Hansen." And then, without warning, her hand lashed out, cracking across Richard's cheek like a whip, twisting his head half-around and making his ears ring. "Damn you! Damn you to hell! How could the clone of our creator help destroy us?"

Richard, hand on his burning cheek, turned his eyes back to her. He thought of all the reasons he'd had. He'd been doing God's will . . . well, God's will as proclaimed by the Avatar. He'd wanted to clear his family name. He'd wanted to advance his career. He'd . . .

All those reasons depended on thinking of the Selkies, as subhuman, evil, twisted creatures that God wanted destroyed.

But as a clone, the Body considered him just as subhuman, evil, and twisted as the Selkies.

And Emily had saved his life.

And . . .

He shook his head. "I don't have any reasons you'd understand or accept," he said. "I don't accept them myself anymore." He moved his hand from his stinging cheek to the back of his neck and rubbed hard. "And I don't even know if that's because of my own experiences or because Victor Hansen's ghost keeps whispering in my ear."

"Is that 'ghost' how you found us?" Dr. Christianson-Wood demanded.

Richard nodded. "Not directly. But I had a . . . what I thought was an intuition."

"Too bad it didn't take you over completely," the Selkie said bitterly. "But of course, it couldn't. Hansen himself figured it out, years later, when things had settled enough here on Marseguro for him to continue his research. His gene-bomb couldn't work: not the way he intended it. He suspected at best, his clones would have strange dreams, unexplained impulses, flashes of memory—which seems to be what happened to you. At worst, he suspected they would go stark, raving mad."

Richard nodded. "Father," he said.

"What?"

"My father—the man I thought was my father—he must have been a clone, too. He worked for the Body, until one day he went crazy. He killed himself." For the first time, though, Richard wondered if his father had actually intended to kill the Avatar, too, with that mad leap. He'd hit the pavement just a few meters in front of the motorcade. If he'd hit the Avatar's groundcar . . .

"The gene-bomb," Dr. Christianson-Wood said.

"Probably. I was thirteen. When I got older, the Body made sure I ended up working for Body Security. They gave me the job of finding out where my 'grandfather' had fled with his . . . creations."

"Which means they knew about the gene-bomb, too," Dr. Christianson-Wood said. "They used you. They've probably decanted the other clones, too. They've just been waiting for one of you to point the way to Marseguro." She shook her head. "Damn Hansen. Always so sure of himself. He was an idiot to leave those clones behind. In a way he betrayed us himself." She snorted. "Since you're his clone, in more than one way."

Richard nodded. "Looks like it." He met her eyes. "And being a clone . . . that's why I'm immune to the plague?"

"Yes, you murderous bastard," Dr. Christianson-Wood snarled. "All Selkies contain that same stretch of DNA because all of us are descended from Victor Hansen. He sculpted our race from his own genetic material—just like he sculpted you." She lunged forward, flaring her gills and eyes at the same instant, so that she became instantly, monstrously alien. He flinched; he couldn't help it. "Genetically, I'm your daughter. We're *all* your sons and daughters. And you helped to murder us! Hundreds of us!" Her voice dropped to a deadly, poisonous whisper. *"Including my husband!"*

"I know," he said. "I know. And . . . I'm sorry. So sorry." The inadequacy of the words choked him; he couldn't say anything more. Instead, he hung his head, unable to look at the face of his . . .

. . . daughter?

Two days ago, I didn't have any relatives. Now I have a whole planet full of them.

Not as full as it used to be, jabbed his conscience, or the ghost of Victor Hansen—he couldn't tell them apart, any more.

Dr. Christianson-Wood straightened, and finally broke the lengthening silence. "Well," she said. "We have one other thing in common besides our genetic heritage."

Richard looked up, puzzled. "What's that?"

"You're a mass murderer. And so am I."

"I didn't . . ." . . . *kill anyone,* he wanted to say, but the lie died on his lips. "I led the Holy Warriors here. You designed the plague that killed them. But you were just defending your world."

"And you were defending yours . . . or so you thought. Defending it from God's ongoing threat of vengeance if abominations like the Selkies were permitted to live." She made an impatient gesture. "There are always justifications. Some are better than others. I think mine is better than yours. But it doesn't change our guilt. We're killers, many times over.

"But here's the bottom line, Richard Hansen . . . and whatever of Victor Hansen is in there." She came close to him again, uncomfortably close. *Underwater adaptation,* he thought distantly. *You have to get closer to com-*

municate effectively. To a nonmod—a landling—it seemed like an invasion of personal space, a threat.

Her strange oversized eyes almost filled his vision. He wanted to look away, but wouldn't.

"What can we do to ensure neither of us has to kill again?"

The moment was deadly serious, the stakes couldn't have been higher, and they were, after all, discussing mass murder, but Richard couldn't resist.

"Take me to your leader?"

Richard had a hard time reading Selkie faces, but he was almost sure he saw a flicker of amusement cross Dr. Christianson-Wood's at that moment . . . and maybe, just maybe, her tone was slightly warmer when she said, "I think that can be arranged."

When Emily reached the pier, she went straight to the sub and demanded the captain put her in touch with her mother. He took one look at her face and didn't argue.

The link was audio-only. Emily could only imagine the expression on her mother's face as she told her what she had found in the bay. When Emily finished, there was a long silence.

"I . . . suspected as much," her mother said. "We'll . . . we'll keep looking, Emily. It's all we can do." Her voice strengthened. "Get some rest, sweetie. We'll talk soon."

The connection went dead. Emily turned to the tech at the communications console. "I need to make another call," she said. "To Jumpoff Station . . ."

This time, the link had video. Emily looked at Amy, who had stayed behind to help in the hospital, where wounded Selkies rescued from other deep-sea habitats were still being brought. "Emily!" Amy said. "Are you all right? Have you found Daddy?"

"I'm fine," Emily said. "And . . . no." She told Amy what she had told her mother. Amy's face crumpled, but she didn't cry . . . quite.

"Oh, Emily," she whispered. "What are we going to do?"

Suddenly I'm *the strong one?* Emily thought. *I'm the one putting out my hand to steady* her? *When did that happen?*

"What we have to, I guess," she said. "There's a lot for everyone to do right now." She hesitated. "How's John?"

Amy's face lit up again. "He's doing great!" she said. "He's awake, and the doctors think he'll make a full recovery—probably regain full mobility of his arms and upper body with enough therapy. We've been spending a lot of time together, talking, when I'm not on duty."

You've been . . . ? John Duval and my sister . . . ? She shook her head. The world really had turned upside down if Amy were interested in one of her "kid friends."

"I've got to get some sleep," Emily said. "If we find out anything more about Daddy . . ." her voice trailed off. "We'll talk again soon."

Amy nodded. "Good-bye, little sister. Take care of yourself."

"Good-bye, big sister." And although she could never remember having said it before, Emily added, "I love you," before breaking the connection.

The captain, a middle-aged Selkie with the unusual-for-Selkies affectation of a mustache, dyed red to match his hair, had been standing discreetly by during her conversation. Now he cleared his throat. "We've got quarters set aside for you . . ."

"I need to do one more thing first," Emily said.

Five minutes later, she walked the length of the pier again to the bulletin board. Kneeling, she thumb-tacked to it the photograph of her father the captain had retrieved for her from the sub's computers, which contained a backup copy of the planetary database, downloaded from the Jumpoff Station computers before the sub began its journey. The photo had been taken above-water, on the top floor of the building that had crushed their home as it fell. His huge green eyes sparkled in the sunlight, and behind him, Hansen's Harbor, undamaged, spread to the rim of the encircling ridge. He looked young, and confident, and . . . immortal.

On the white space below the image, she had written, "Has anyone seen this man, Peterson Wood? Please contact Dr. Carla Christianson-Wood or Emily Wood at Government House."

She stared at the photo for several minutes, her mind a jumble of memories and fears, longing and loss, all tinged with dark fury, then finally made her way back to the sub, her borrowed quarters, and, a long time later, sleep.

When she woke, she found her mother had come and gone while she slept . . . and taken Richard Hansen with her. Considering her unsettling feeling the night before that the "grown-ups" didn't know what they were doing, that should have reassured her—obviously, wheels were turning and plans were in motion—but now it just annoyed her. "Where did she go?" she demanded of the sub captain. "And why didn't she wake me?"

The skipper looked taken aback. "She went ashore, Miss Wood, that's all I know. And why would she tell *me* why she didn't wake you?"

Emily wanted to snap something at him about how captains were supposed know *everything* that happened on their vessels, but instead she turned on her heel and stormed off the sub. She didn't expect to be out of the water long enough this time to need a landsuit; instead she wore a plain white skinsuit left for her in her quarters, one that showed less skin than the one she'd been wearing the night before.

The devastation didn't look any better in the morning than it had at dusk, although most of the fires seemed to have finally burned themselves out and thus the air had cleared a little. Efforts at cleanup had begun here and there. The workers she could see, mostly landlings, with just a smattering of Selkies, seemed to be focusing on infrastructure basics like power and communications broadcast towers and water and gas lines. Others, wearing face masks, gloves and rubber overalls, were undertaking the grimmer task of searching the wreckage for bodies.

A big Selkie with morphing tattoos she remembered from Jumpoff Station . . . Peter, that was his name . . . stopped her at the shattered doorway to Government House. "Council is meeting, Miss Wood," he rumbled. "No one allowed in."

The rage that now seemed to be Emily's constant companion boiled up. "Try to stop me," she snarled, standing on tiptoe to deliver the message wide-eyes-to-wide-eyes, gill slits flaring, tingling as they dried in the morning air. "You'll have to knock me down and sit on me. And then you'll have to explain it to my mother. And when you let me up, I'll make damn sure you never father a child. Now get out of my way!"

Peter blanched, but held his ground. "I can't, Miss Wood," he said. "But," he added hastily as she opened her mouth again, "I'll escort you in. Then it will be up to the Council."

Emily closed her mouth and her gills and took a deep breath. "So escort!"

Peter turned to one side, and for the first time she saw the second guard, a landling, previously hidden by Peter's bulk. His wide grin vanished as Peter rounded on him. "Let anyone else in and I'll swim you to the bottom of the bay and leave you there!" Peter barked. Then he strode inside, Emily in his wake.

Most but not all of the blood had been cleaned from the walls of the broad hall that led from the entrance to the Council Chamber—really, despite its grand name, little more than a glorified conference room. No Holy Warriors had died in it, so at least its deep green carpet and round stonewood table were unstained. A cube of blank green vidscreens served as the table's centerpiece, and around it the surviving members of the Council, Emily's mother among them, sat in green fishleather chairs. Three chairs remained empty.

In one of the four blue-upholstered chairs normally

set aside for those having business with the Council sat Richard Hansen.

When Peter opened the door he paused as though about to announce her, but Emily brushed past him. "Why are you listening to this murdering bastard?" she said in a loud voice. "Why haven't you fed him to the nearsharks?"

Heads all around the table jerked to look at her. Only Richard Hansen and her mother seemed unsurprised and unperturbed. "Hello, dear," Dr. Christianson-Wood said. "I hope you slept well."

"Answer the question," Emily said. She pointed at Hansen. "Why is he here?"

A landling to the right of her mother rose to his feet. Thin to the point of emaciation, with a bald head and deep-set eyes, Ellison Jeter, Chair of the Council, had always looked rather like a walking skeleton. After the events of the past few days, he could have passed for the Grim Reaper himself. He pointed a bony finger at Emily. "Who let you in here?" he growled. "Peter . . . ?"

Emily heard the door closing behind her. Peter had obviously decided it would be prudent to return to his post.

"I let myself in," Emily said. "I saved this mudworm's life and I've regretted it ever since. I left him to rot in the prison where the Holy Warriors had put him. I found him alive and brought him here, and escorted him to my mother. I think I've earned a right to understand what you're doing with him. Why is he here? And why isn't he dead like all the rest of his murdering ilk?"

She stopped and waited. *I don't think I've ever used "ilk" in a sentence before,* a small part of her brain commented wryly.

Her mother's slightly amused expression hardened. "Don't be so quick to condemn people to death, Emily. Too many have died already."

Emily said nothing, unwilling to argue with her mother, God knew how she felt about the plague she had shepherded through her laboratory and finally unleashed

against the Holy Warriors. It must have gone against
everything she'd always professed to believe in. *It had to
be done, Mom,* Emily thought. *It had to be.*

But then Richard Hansen had the gall to say, "I
agree."

Emily's rage roared red-hot again. "*You* agree?" She
rounded the table at a run. Anton Scale stood up just in
time to grab her, or she would have flung herself at the
Earthling. She pulled against his iron grip. "You bastard!
After everything you . . . Dahlia and Domini and . . .
Daddy . . ." To her horror, she found herself weeping.
Scale released her arms and instead pulled her to him,
hugging her, comforting her like a little girl. *His beard
tickles,* she thought inanely. Then, *I wish I were still a
little girl. I want my daddy!* She wept harder.

"We've all lost friends and family, Emily," Scale said
quietly. "But we can't bring them back by killing one
more man. Especially *this* man."

Emily sniffed and swallowed and managed to bring her
lower lip under control. She pulled away from Scale and
looked up into his shadowed eyes. "It sounds like you
believe—"

"He *is* a clone of Victor Hansen, Emily," her mother
said from the other side of Scale, who glanced over his
shoulder at her, then released Emily and stepped to one
side. "He carries the DNA sequence that protected us
from the plague. That's why he's alive. He also carries a
small part of Victor Hansen's memories and personality.
And all of that means . . ." She spread her hands.
"He's family."

Hot tears flooded Emily's eyes. "He's not . . ."

"You saved my life once, Emily," Richard Hansen
said. She refused to look at him, but he kept talking. "I
can't bring back the people the Holy Warriors killed,
and I wish I'd never . . ." His voice trailed off. "Well, I
wish a lot of things. But I can help you now. That's why
I'm here.

"The Holy Warriors on the planet are dead. All of
them, we think. But there's a ship in orbit. We don't

know how many Holy Warriors are still alive up there."
He nodded toward Dr. Christianson-Wood. "Your
mother thinks her virus will have infected the ship even
if they used standard antibiological decontamination procedures on any shuttle that went up there, and quarantined anyone arriving from the planet's surface. Maybe
she's right, maybe not. But even if *they're* all dead,
sooner or later there will be another ship . . . and *that*
ship will carry many more Holy Warriors, and deadlier
weapons, and your plague won't stop it, because they'll
never set foot on the planet or breathe its air until every
Selkie above and below the water is dead . . . and likely
all the landlings, too.

"One way or another, this planet *will* be Purified."

Emily didn't want to believe him, or listen, but his
words made too much sense and echoed her own fears.
And from the somber faces of the Council and her
mother, it was obvious *they* believed him.

"So what can *you* do?" she demanded. "How are *you*
going to stop your all-powerful Holy Warriors?"

"I may be able to talk them out of attacking," Hansen said.

Emily stared at him. "Talk? That's all you have to
offer?"

"It's all I have right now." Hansen looked around the
table. "I have a . . . connection with the Archdeacon of
Body Security. Although I'm sure he knows I'm a clone,
it must be a closely guarded secret. Everyone else thinks
I'm . . . one of his favorites. I may be able to convince
any arriving force that everyone is dead from the plague,
Selkies and landlings alike, and I'm the only
survivor . . ." He paused, and sighed. "It's weak, I know.
But it's the best I can offer."

"We'll have to deliberate on this," Jeter said.

"I don't think we have a choice," Emily's mother said.

Emily wanted to protest, to say, "Of course there's a
choice!" but the words rang hollow in her own mind.
Hansen's scheme offered faint hope, but faint hope might
be the only hope they had.

"So we just wait for this new ship to arrive and attack?" said another Councillor, a Selkie woman with electric-blue hair and blue star tattoos around her eyes. For the life of her, Emily couldn't remember her name. *I never had to pay much attention to government before. It never seemed important who was in charge.*

Suddenly, it did.

"The first thing is to find out if *Sanctification* . . . the ship in orbit . . . has any surviving crew," said Hansen. "I need access to the Warriors' communications equipment."

"Don't trust him," Emily said. The words burst out of her. She believed in the threat, even believed Hansen might be their only hope, but giving him access to communications . . . "What if he orders them to attack?"

"We need to deliberate," Jeter said again.

"Do we have time?" said the blue-haired woman.

"We need to know *now*," Emily's mother said.

The other Councillors chimed in and the room erupted in pandemonium as they argued with each other. Emily's thought about the grown-ups not knowing what to do came back full force. The trouble was, she didn't know what to do, either.

Then all their arguing became moot. The door suddenly banged open, and the noise died as everyone turned to look at the newcomer, a young landling with a black eye and bandaged head. "We're getting a signal from orbit," he said breathlessly. "Somebody's alive up there."

Everyone turned to look at Richard Hansen, even Emily—though she promptly despised herself for the reflex.

"I guess I'd better talk to them," he said into the sudden silence.

The quarantine chamber Chris had been ordered into aboard *BPS Sanctification* had very little to recommend it over his former cell in the Hansen's Harbor Criminal Detention Center. Like his previous lodging, it contained a bed, a toilet, and a shower stall. It *did* boast the added luxury of a table and chair. A twenty-five-centimeter cube of pale green plastic centered on the table puzzled Chris until it suddenly dissolved into the 3-D image of a man in a white coat. "Mr. Keating," the man said. "Please sit on your bed."

"What . . . ?"

"Please cooperate, Mr. Keating."

Don't these people know I'm here to help them? Chris grumbled to himself, but he did as he was told.

Once he was seated, a door hissed open and a bot trundled in on six small black wheels. Cylindrical, it had eight spindly metal arms, all of which ended in something either sharp or pointed.

"Hold out your right arm, Mr. Keating," said the man in the holocube.

Chris did so. The bot extended one of its own needle-tipped arms and plunged the point of the needle into the crook of his elbow. He winced. It held the needle in place for ten seconds, then pulled it out. A second arm whipped around and neatly applied a small round bandage. Then the bot rolled out again.

"Rest, Mr. Keating," said the man in the holocube. "Once we are certain you are not carrying any unknown pathogens, we'll release you."

The cube turned opaque again.

After that, Chris heard nothing for several hours, although food and drink appeared shortly after the bot left. A previously invisible hatch above the table opened and two metal arms extended, holding a covered tray. They neatly deposited the tray on the table then withdrew again, the hatch closing, sealing, and vanishing behind them. Chris ate.

Shortly after that, a larger hatch opened, revealing a plain blue jumpsuit on a hanger, and a bag containing neatly folded underwear and socks, also blue. Chris took the hint, and took a shower.

Sometime after that, the lights dimmed, and he slept. And sometime after that, Chris woke and sat up on the bed as the door that had previously allowed the bot to enter slid open.

The lights brightened, and the doctor he had seen in the holocube staggered in. Blood dripped from his nose, spattering on the front of his already red-soaked white coat. He carried a hypodermic, and lunged at Chris with it. "You're . . . immune . . . your blood . . . serum . . ."

Chris leaped up on the bed. The needle plunged into the mattress. The doctor fell to his knees, his elbows on the bed. For a moment he looked up at Chris as though intending to offer a prayer to him; then his eyes widened, his mouth gaped open, and he vomited up black-flecked blood that exploded across the snow-white sheets and blanket, splattering the wall and covering Chris' feet.

The doctor, eyes wide but no longer seeing, slid sideways to the floor. The hypodermic remained upright in the mattress, quivering.

Chris looked from the corpse to the open door, then jumped from the bed and ran, leaving bloody footprints behind.

Many hours later, Chris sat in the main recreation room of *BPS Sanctification,* staring at the blue-white sphere of Marseguro on the wall-sized vidscreen. He liked the room not only for the view (piped in from a camera somewhere aft in the zero-G section because the three-rpm rotation of the crew cylinder would have made a live view both dizzying and annoying) but because no one had died there. Everywhere else in *Sanctification,* corpses floated or sprawled or sat at their posts in some horrible zombified mockery of life.

The cleanerbots had taken care of most of the spilled bodily fluids, except for the unfortunate few who had sealed themselves in pressure suits in a vain attempt to escape whatever was killing their fellows. The cleanerbots couldn't get inside the sealed suits, and Chris wasn't about to open them. The thought made him shudder.

Currently, the cleanerbots were working on taking away the corpses themselves, both suited and unsuited, to be dumped in the nanorecyclers, but they still had a long way to go.

Chris didn't understand it. The chemical bombs the Selkies had detonated below might have affected Dodson and Velikovsky, but how had they delivered the poison to the ship? The shuttle had been kept quarantined in vacuum.

It looked more like some kind of germ attack. But it *couldn't* be. Never mind the Victor Hansen-instilled horror of biological weapons. Never mind the fact the Selkies had had no time to concoct such a weapon. The Holy Warriors on *Sanctification* had taken all the necessary precautions against such an attack, and had *still* died.

Maybe it was a punishment from God. Not for attacking the Selkies—that was God's work if anything was, he had no doubt about it; if such abominations had been eliminated a century ago, God Itself would never have threatened to destroy the world—but for something else. Something they had done that had displeased God.

And then he had it. Like a light going on in his head. *Richard Hansen,* he thought. *Grandson of Victor Hansen. They brought him aboard* Sanctification—*and with him, they brought sin.*

Chris' eyes narrowed as he remembered Hansen heading out on the boat. What had he done out there? Had he helped the Selkies? And what had he done before he even got to the planet?

He could have poisoned them, Chris thought. *Poisoned the food and water on the ship. Something that acts slowly, or something that could be triggered to act by something on the—*

Oh . . . my . . . God.

He had it. He had it all figured out.

Richard Hansen had poisoned the whole shipload of Holy Warriors . . . but he'd been clever about it. He'd used a two-stage poison, one that built up harmlessly in the body until it was triggered by contact with the second part of the poison.

And then he'd sneaked away to the Selkies on the pretense of chasing John Duval, and told them how to cook up the second half. They'd planted it in aerosol bombs near the Holy Warrior positions on Marseguro. They'd dosed their own landlings—Chris rubbed the spot on his arm where he had been hyposprayed—to ensure they weren't affected, then set off their bombs.

Sometime during the trip here, Hansen must have also planted the second half of the poison in *Sanctification,* either timed to be released a certain interval after the ship arrived at Marseguro, or controlled by a signal he'd managed to send up from the surface. *Something like a rat poison,* Chris thought. *They bled to death in their own skins. Poor bastards.*

They weren't punished by God. They were murdered. Murdered by Richard Hansen and the Selkies.

He felt familiar, renewed fury at the monsters that infested his world and had ruined his life . . . and were *still* ruining it, even after he'd finally managed to get off the planet into space. Now he was stuck here, until . . .

He smiled as the thought completed itself.

Until the next shipload of Holy Warriors arrives.

When they do, they'll need information, he thought. *They'll need to know everything they can find out about what's happening on the planet.*

They'll need me.

But that meant he needed fresh information.

If his suspicions were correct—and he didn't doubt they were—Richard Hansen remained alive and well on the planet's surface, probably scheming to sabotage the follow-up attack that would surely come, maybe even scheming to make himself appear a hero of some sort who could return to Earth to fame and adulation . . . and poison the Body Purified as he had the Holy Warriors, spreading the toxin of his grandfather's abominable ideas about modifying God's Holy Human Genome.

Well, Chris could put a stop to that. And ensure that the next shipload of Holy Warriors did a *proper* job of Purifying Marseguro.

He headed for the rec room door. After his thorough exploration of *Sanctification*'s corridors during the last day, he knew exactly where to go.

Two minutes later, after tugging the pressure-suited body of the Holy Warrior who had been manning the post out of the way, Chris Keating activated the ship-to-planet communications system, and said into the microphone, "*BPS Sanctification* to Marseguro. Is anyone there?"

Chapter 16

THE COUNCIL ADJOURNED (at something approaching a run) to the lobby of Government House, where the Holy Warriors' communications station, the very place where Richard had first met Ellers and Chris Keating when he'd shuttled down to the surface, remained intact. Richard stood in front of one of the communications vidscreens and nodded to the tech, who did something at the main control panel.

The screen lit, and Richard found himself face-to-face with . . . Chris Keating.

They stared at each other.

"You bastard," Keating said. "I knew it."

"Everyone's been calling me a bastard recently," Richard said. *Technically, I suppose that's exactly what I am,* he thought, but didn't say out loud; Chris presumably didn't know he was a clone, and he wasn't about to tell him. "Is anyone else left alive up there?" He thought he already knew the answer: the Holy Warriors would hardly be allowing Chris Keating to access communications if any of them were alive to stop him.

Keating hesitated. "There have been some deaths," he said. "I'm not sure how many. Enough so I was able to escape and get to the communications station."

Escape? "You were a prisoner?"

"Of course!"

Off to the side, out of Keating's field of view, Emily shook her head. Richard didn't need her warning.

"There's no 'of course' about it. The last time I saw you, you were bragging about having activated the beacon that led the Holy Warriors here."

Keating's face smoothed. "I've changed," he said. "People do change." He smiled. "Isn't that what you've told your new 'friends' down below? Do they know that you were the one who heard the beacon and guided the Holy Warriors to Marseguro? Do they know the only reason you told them how to complete your poisoning of the Holy Warriors was so that you can return to Earth a hero when the reinforcements arrive?" Chris' smile grew wider. "Are you planning to poison the Selkies now, and claim the credit when the next ship arrives?"

Richard managed—just barely—to keep his face expressionless. *I poisoned . . . ?* He wondered what kind of bizarre theory Chris had assembled to explain events. Well, he wasn't about to set him straight.

"I don't think I'd call the people down here my 'friends,' " he said instead. "Though I hope I might be able to some day. As for the rest . . . they know the truth."

"I'll bet," Chris said. "So are you in charge now? The Great Savior from Earth?"

Richard looked at Jeter, whose skull-like face bore an expression as dark and threatening as a thundercloud. "No, I'm not," he said carefully. "I'm still a prisoner. Unlike you, I haven't managed a miraculous escape."

Jeter came to stand beside Richard. "Council Chair Jeter here, Mr. Keating. The Marseguroite Governing Council is in session and fully in control, though we've lost four of our members. Mr. Hansen replied to your communication on the assumption only a Holy Warrior would be talking to us from their orbiting vessel." Jeter's tone became icy. "Mr. Keating, if you are the one who activated the beacon at the Landing Site, you are directly responsible for the deaths of, at current count, two hundred and seventy-six nonmods and one thousand, four hundred and ninety-five Selkies. We expect those numbers to increase.

"I cannot speak for the Council, but I can speak for myself. I do not deny the possibility of someone changing. But it's going to take more than your say-so to convince us you deserve anything other than a traitor's execution."

"But . . . but Hansen led the Holy Warriors here!" Keating suddenly sounded like a petulant little boy. "You trust *him*? I'm one of you! *He's* from the Body Purified!"

"Who said we trust him?" Jeter said. "He has a long way to go to earn that, Mr. Keating. But that's neither here nor there. How can you prove you were taken to that ship as a prisoner and not a willing accomplice to genocide?"

Keating licked his lips. "I . . ." His voice trailed off and he bowed his head. For a moment he looked like he was praying, but when he raised his head again, fury twisted his mouth. "I can't," he snarled. "I can't, and I don't want to." He leaned into the camera so that his face filled the screen. "I was glad to see the Holy Warriors attack," he said, his voice fierce and hard. "I was glad to see the towers of Hansen's Stinking Harbor in flames. Selkies in cages? What a laugh. And when Emily set me free from the prison, you know where I went? Straight to the Grand Deacon. I tried to warn him. I told him something bad was coming. I didn't know about Hansen's poison, or they would have all been in pressure suits when you set off the trigger dose and you'd all be fish food.

"But I'll tell you this. When the next ship arrives from Earth, I'll be here to warn them. They won't listen to a word you say, Hansen. They'll listen to *me*. And they'll Purify that worthless pissball you call a planet like nothing has ever been Purified before. They'll Purify it to hell and gone. And then I'll go to Earth and my just reward and you, all of you, fishfaces and stinking fish-loving landlings, and especially you, Richard Hansen, can literally rot in hell . . . because hell is what Marseguro is going to become. Chris Keating out."

The screen went blank.

Hansen looked at Jeter. "So much for me talking the next Holy Warrior ship into leaving us alone," he said. "We need a Plan B."

None of the Councillors spoke, but Emily did. "I've got one." Everyone looked at her. "We've got the Holy Warriors' weapons," she said. "We fight."

None of the Councillors looked happy, Dr. Christianson-Wood least of all. But one by one, they nodded.

"It won't work," Richard said flatly. "Not if they know what to expect. If Chris Keating tells them what happened, they'll bombard the planet from orbit, not just send down an armed party. *Sanctification* could have done it. The only reason Ellers didn't order it was to avoid killing nonmods—the Body prefers to give them the chance to 'repent'—and because planets with breathable atmospheres are few and far between, and even one mostly covered with water might be worth colonizing. Next time, that won't be a consideration. They'll gladly write off the planet to kill everyone on it, modded or nonmodded."

"So what do *you* suggest, clone?" Emily snapped.

"Several things," Richard snapped back, her unwavering hostility finally getting to him. "We have to stop Chris Keating from talking . . . and then, when the next ship arrives, we have to keep the Holy Warriors guessing."

"How?" said Jeter.

"Stop surface reconstruction," Richard said. "Leave the wreckage where it is, and move everybody you possibly can into your emergency deep-water habitats. When the Holy Warriors' reinforcements arrive, we want them to see a planet all but devoid of human life—not just Holy Warriors, but nonmods and Selkies, too. Leave them wondering what happened. Then, when they land, either the virus will get them . . . or we will."

"That doesn't do any good if Chris Keating manages to warn them," Emily said.

"I have a solution to that, too," Richard said. "But I'll need unfettered access to this equipment." He indicated the Holy Warriors' communications station.

Jeter studied him for a moment, then nodded. "Done."

"I'm staying with him," Emily said instantly.

Jeter smiled. "I was about to ask you to," he said. "I'm making you Mr. Hansen's personal guard. I'm sure Mr. Hansen won't object, if he is indeed on our side now."

"I have no objection," Richard said. He eyed Emily. "Um . . . she doesn't have permission to shoot me, does she?"

"Only in the direst of circumstances," Jeter said. "Emily?"

Emily's face looked like a threatening sky about to be ripped apart by lightning and wind, but she pressed her lips together and held back the storm. "All right," she said. "I'll do it. At least it's something. But if the Holy Warriors come back, I want a weapon."

"You'll have one," Jeter said. "Councillors, I believe we still have things to discuss . . . ?"

The Councillors moved back down the hallway toward their meeting room. Dr. Christianson-Wood trailed the others, and gave a final, troubled look over her shoulder at her daughter and Richard before she disappeared from sight.

Emily folded her arms and glared at Richard. "Well?" she snarled. "Get to work."

Richard nodded. *I hope I know what I'm doing,* he thought, and turned his attention to the console.

After disconnecting, Chris sat in shuddering fury for a few seconds, then exploded out of the communications room, took the nearest elevator to the central shaft, and launched himself into zero-G. He needed to work off his rage before he could think straight, and half a dozen flying trips up and down the central shaft did the trick. By the time he had soared and grabbed and spun and leaped a few dozen times, sweat flew from him in glistening silver globules, and he could think again.

He transitioned back into gravity through one of the elevators. Once again in the rec room, he looked at the stabilized image of Marseguro in the giant vidwall, and indulged in a moment's vivid daydream of what the filthy planet would look like once the Holy Warriors sent reinforcements: dotted with mushroom clouds and glowing red craters where Hansen's Harbor and Firstdip and Outtamyway and all the other pustules that passed for towns now stood.

Richard Hansen would pay, just like the Selkies, just like the fish-lovers. When reinforcements arrived, it would be Chris Keating who finally got his due—and those who had taunted him, belittled him, stood in his way, killed his father and let his mother die, would get their just desserts.

He only had to wait.

He was sure it wouldn't be long.

He lay back in the relaxation chair and closed his eyes. Not long at all.

In his office in the basement of Body Security headquarters on Earth, Archdeacon Samuel Cheveldeoff frowned at a vidscreen. "Still nothing?"

"No, sir." The face of the communications tech visible on the screen gleamed with sweat, and he blinked a lot. Cheveldeoff liked the fact that his underlings feared him, except when it led them to alter their reports to say what they thought he wanted to hear rather than give him the facts. Cheveldeoff liked facts, even unpleasant ones. What he really hated was falsehoods.

"Could something catastrophic have happened to the ship?"

"Unlikely, sir," the tech said. "The null-brane carrier wave is intact, which means *Sanctification*'s communications system and Cornwall drive are also intact and operational. But she is not responding to our attempts to contact her and there has been no message from her now for four days."

Cheveldeoff grunted. The last message, brief and cryptic as an old-fashioned telegram due to the energy costs of transmitting information through branespace, had said merely, "NO RESISTANCE. PURIFICATION PROCEEDING." He'd already met with the Right Hand to plan their public announcement, how best to coordinate it with the announcement of the Avatar's death, and how best to use both to leverage more Council votes for his ascension.

But four days . . . standard operating procedure required a daily check-in. Energy costs or no energy costs, four days was too long. The ship might still be there, but something must have happened to the crew.

Cheveldeoff hadn't become Archdeacon of Body Security through indecisiveness. "Thank you," he told the tech, who looked visibly relieved. "Continue monitoring."

"Yes, si—"

He cut off the channel. "Computer," he said to his office system, "List Holy Warrior warships currently in orbit."

"*BPS Jihad,*" said the computer promptly. "*BPS Retribution. BPS Armageddon. BPS Angel of Death.*" The list stopped. Cheveldeoff drummed his fingers on the table. It wasn't much of a list; most ships were still committed to the blockade of New Mars and the pacification of Tuin. Of those just listed, *Jihad* and *Armageddon* were both in space dock and out of commission for at least six weeks. *Angel of Death* was a tiny scout craft, barely even armed. That left *Retribution.* She was no *Sanctification*—she lacked both an Orbital Bombardment System and the docking and launching facilities needed to carry *Sanctification*-style assault craft—but she could actually carry *more* Holy Warriors, albeit relatively lightly armed, and her four dedicated troop-insertion shuttles could deliver those Warriors in greater force to the ground than *Sanctification*'s could.

That should do, Cheveldeoff thought. *Ellers said there was no resistance, so it's unlikely they've been wiped out in a military attack of any kind. Something else must have happened to them.*

The timing couldn't be worse, though. Cheveldeoff took a deep breath, then put through an encrypted call to the Right Hand.

He appeared at once. "Rasmusson here."

Cheveldeoff filled him in. The Right Hand scowled. "This is serious, Sam. Nothing has changed on the Council. In fact, you may be another vote down. And I think we have a month, tops, before we have to announce the Avatar's death and convene the Council. If you can't deliver Hansen's Selkies . . ."

"I'll deliver them," Cheveldeoff said. "*BPS Retribution* is in orbit."

"You'll go yourself." It was a statement, not a question.

Cheveldeoff smiled grimly. "I might as well. If the mission fails, there's not much point in coming back, is there?"

Rasmusson didn't argue otherwise. "Then you've got another problem."

Cheveldeoff nodded. "Braun."

"You have to involve him. He's next in the chain of command."

"I know." He was also, like Ellers but even more so, Shridhar's man.

"Make sure the crew includes a complement of men loyal to yourself," Rasmusson said. "You have agents among Braun's staff and top-level commanders." Again, it wasn't a question.

Cheveldeoff nodded. "Of course. But you don't really think Braun would sabotage the mission, do you? Ellers didn't."

"I hope not," Rasmusson said. "But that doesn't mean he won't try to sabotage *you*. If he could complete the mission, but make it appear the success was in *spite* of your interference, rather than *due* to your involvement . . ."

Cheveldeoff snorted. "I'm an old hand at those kinds of games," he said. "Don't worry."

Rasmusson smiled, very slightly. "I'm not," he said pleasantly. "Whatever happens on Marseguro, Sam, I will still be Right Hand. I would prefer that you become the next Avatar . . . but I can work with Shridhar, if it comes to that."

Not if the secret recordings I've kept of our interactions find their way into Shridhar's hands, which they will if you somehow betray me, Cheveldeoff thought . . . but very carefully did not say. Making that move would not only end the game, it would overturn the board. All he said aloud was, "I understand."

"Good. Good luck." Rasmusson reached out, and the screen blanked.

Cheveldeoff turned to a different screen. "Computer, comm link to Grand Deacon Braun."

A man's lean, mustached face abruptly appeared in the vidscreen. "Yes, Archdeacon?"

"Prepare *BPS Retribution* for departure," Cheveldeoff ordered. "Full complement of Holy Warriors, weapons and ammo. You to command."

Grand Deacon Braun nodded. "We're checking up on *Sanctification*, I take it?"

"Yes. I'll provide operation details when I join you in orbit."

Braun's eyebrows lifted. "You're coming . . . sir?"

Cheveldeoff let his eyes narrow. "Do you have a problem with that, Grand Deacon?" He had the satisfaction of seeing the normally self-assured Holy Warrior blanch. *Shridhar's not Avatar yet,* he thought. *He can't protect you until he is.*

"No, sir."

"I'll be there within two hours. Cheveldeoff out."

He cut the connection, sat back in his chair and stared off into space in the general direction of the virtual copy of Rembrandt's *Night Watch,* currently hanging on the north wall of his office, which today appeared to be paneled in dark wood. *Something's wrong out there, I can feel it.* He smiled. *And I'll deal with it.*

Cheveldeoff had a supreme confidence in his ability to deal with anything that came his way. He hadn't failed yet. *Nor will I this time.*

He leaned forward and started making additional calls. Rasmusson was right: he needed as many people loyal to him as possible aboard *Retribution.* Braun might fear him here, but he might lose some of that fear once they were light-years beyond the supposed reach of Body Security.

If necessary, Cheveldeoff wanted to be able to make it clear to Braun that he would *never* be beyond reach of Body Security—no matter how far they went.

In the lobby of Government House, Emily watched Richard Hansen's fingers fly over the multiple keyboards of the Holy Warriors' communications control console. "We're in luck," he said after a few minutes. "Ellers never got around to canceling my security codes."

"Yeah, lucky," Emily said. "So why didn't he?"

"Why should he?" Hansen countered. "He had me tucked away in prison, and he had a planet to Purify. It probably never crossed his mind. And then he was dead." He punched a few final keys. "There."

"What have you done?"

"Listen." Hansen sat back. "Computer, confirm that all communications control functions have been transferred to this station and are under my voice command."

"Confirmed," the computer said.

"Computer, confirm my identity and security clearance."

"Richard Hansen, Adviser to Archdeacon Cheveldeoff, security clearance Alpha Three."

"Computer, lock control functions to my voice command."

"Controls locked to your voice command," the computer said. "Note that override is still possible by Alpha Two, Alpha One and Alpha Prime security ranks."

"Understood," Hansen said. "Computer, shut down all communications systems until further notice."

"Are you sure you want to shut down all communications systems?" the computer said.

Hansen grimaced. "I wish these things would just take your word for it," he said. "Computer, yes, I'm sure. And please provide detailed confirmation as you do so."

"Commencing shutdown," the computer said. "Satellite Alpha, switching to standby mode. Satellite Beta, switching to standby mode. Geosynchronous branespace booster, powering down . . ." The computer continued listing systems as it switched them off or put them on standby. When it said, "*BPS Sanctification* ship-to-ship communications functions disabled," Hansen gave Emily a thumbs-up and turned down the computer's audio volume, so that its continuing litany of disabled systems carried on at a whisper. "That's it," Hansen said. "Without security clearances Chris Keating doesn't have and can't get—since everyone with clearance higher than mine is dead—he won't be able to say boo to anyone."

"How did you know how to do that?" Emily said.

"It's my job . . . or was," Hansen said. "I analyzed communications, so my training included learning how to operate communications systems of all sorts."

"A communications analyst. And so you just happened to be the one who heard the *Rivers of Babylon* emergency beacon Keating activated."

Hansen shook his head. "I was actively looking for it. Cheveldeoff—the head of Body Security—had made that my primary mission. But I was looking in the wrong place. I wouldn't even have noticed the beacon if not for . . ." He tapped his head. "The gene-bomb my grandfath . . . grandclone . . . put in my head."

"I still can't believe I saved your life," Emily said bitterly.

"I'm glad you did," Hansen said. He pushed his chair away from the communications console and turned it to face her. "Not just because I'd rather be alive than dead—there were a few hours there when I'm not sure that was true—but so that I can help make amends."

Emily looked down at him. He looked back, his face deadly serious. She felt her fists clench. "Why should I believe you?" she said through a throat gripped so strongly by emotion she could barely squeeze out the words. "Chris Keating could be right. You could be orchestrating all of this so that when the next batch of Holy Warriors comes our way, you can betray us and be a hero back on Earth."

"Chris Keating also thinks I *poisoned* the Holy Warriors . . . and somehow got you to help me," Hansen said. "He's slipping into paranoia."

"Slipping? I'd say he plunged headlong into it some time ago."

"He had help." Hansen looked down. "The Body Purified is a powerful . . . organization. Its propaganda is extremely effective. I'd say Chris Keating was vulnerable to it and somehow got hold of it."

"Here on Marseguro?" Emily said incredulously. "How?"

"*The Wisdom of the Avatar of God* was readily available on Earth when your ancestors—and my clone—fled," Hansen said. "And not all of the normals . . . um, nonmods . . . on board the *Rivers of Babylon* were there by choice. Some of them were simply in the wrong place at the wrong time. It would have been astonishing, at that time in history, if some of them *hadn't* been part of—or at least sympathetic to—the Body Purified."

"Wouldn't we have known?" Emily said. "Or our ancestors?"

"Your ancestors were mostly children living in the water-filled holds of *Rivers of Babylon*," Hansen said.

"And any followers of the Avatar would have had to have been suicidal to let anyone know what they believed. My guess is they went underground. Maybe they even changed their minds. But not all of them. Not Keating's family, I'm guessing. And if they remained Believers, they would have kept their books . . . books which have swayed older and less vulnerable minds than that of Chris Keating."

"Yours, for instance?" Emily stepped closer to Hansen, so he had to tilt his head back to look up at her. "Why did *you* believe it? You thought you were Victor Hansen's grandson, for God's sake. Why did *you* fall for the Avatar's gospel of hate?"

"Because I wasn't suicidal, either," Hansen said. He kept his eyes on hers, even though it must have been uncomfortable. "My father . . . my predecessor clone . . ." his voice took on a bitter tone, "was marginalized all his life because he was perceived to be the son of Victor Hansen. He killed himself. I swore I would restore the family honor . . . and on Earth, the only route to success and respect is through the Body Purified. Those who do not accept the Avatar's 'gospel of hate,' as you put it, are beyond the pale: impoverished at the least, often imprisoned, sometimes executed.

"So I convinced myself I believed. I convinced myself that modded humans were the ultimate evil, the usurpation of God's creative powers that led the Creator to the brink of destroying the world. I had to convince myself I believed that, because otherwise my quest was entirely about my own selfishness, and I didn't want to believe I was that shallow a person."

He took a deep breath. "But here, when I finally saw the Selkies I thought I hated . . . I just saw people. Funny-looking people, by my standards, but people. A terrified little girl clinging to her mother for comfort in a cage . . . a young woman who saved my life after I had done everything I could to destroy her kind . . . Just . . . people. And then the ultimate blow to my professed belief, when I found out I was a clone myself, and hence in the eyes of the Avatar and the Body Purified as much a nonhuman abomination as the Selkies . . . worse, that in a very real sense I *am* Victor Hansen, the man I thought I hated . . .

"That's when I found out I didn't really believe anything I'd claimed I did. That's when I found out that everything I had done really *had* been based on nothing but my own selfishness and ambition." He blinked hard three times in quick succession. "Maybe it's my conscience. Maybe it's really Victor Hansen's conscience. I can't tell anymore, and it doesn't really matter. It's all me, now. However I've become what I've become, I'm not your enemy anymore. I'm your ally."

Emily looked into his narrow landling eyes, bright with unshed tears, and something inside her, some tight knot of rage, loosened just a little.

She hadn't forgiven him. She didn't know if she could.

But maybe . . . just maybe . . . she could trust him.

A little. For now.

"Okay," was all she said. "Where to next?"

"That's up to the Council." Hansen turned back to the console and boosted the computer's volume again. At some point it had quit talking. "But there's one more thing I want to do here." He cleared his throat. "Computer, repower Emergency Beacon Alpha-Two aboard *BPS Sanctification.*"

"Beacon repowered," the computer said.

"Computer, activate Emergency Beacon Alpha-Two, Code Black Three."

"Activated."

"What have you done?" Emily said, suspicion rushing back.

Hansen pushed back his chair and stood up. "When the next ship arrives, the only signal it will receive will be coming from that beacon. And that particular code means 'All dead here. Plague ship. Stay away.' " He shrugged. "And that's all I can do. Originally I thought maybe I could talk to any reinforcements myself, try to convince them to turn back, but I'd have to go through

Sanctification's systems, and there'd be no way to prevent Chris Keating from listening in—and maybe horning in—on the conversation."

"Will the beacon be enough to scare away another ship?"

"I doubt it. But it ought to keep their eyes off of *Sanctification* and on Marseguro, where we want it." He showed his teeth. "And Chris Keating can rot in orbit. He won't even have a clue what's going on." The bloodthirsty grin faded. "That's it. That's all the special expertise I can offer. Now . . . I'll do whatever is needed. I just want to help."

Emily's answering grin would have looked at home on a shark. "Then follow me." She headed toward the main entrance.

"Where are we going?" Hansen said, catching up.

"We're going to find some Holy Warrior weapons. And then you're going to teach me how to shoot them."

Chapter 17

THREE HOURS AFTER *BPS Retribution* entered the system *Sanctification* had been sent to Purify, Samuel Cheveldeoff stood on the bridge listening to the repeating voice loop that was the only communication signal they had so far detected. "This is *BPS Sanctification*. Code Black Three. This is *BPS Sanctification*. Code Black Three. This is *BPS Sanctification*. Code Black Three—"

Cheveldeoff motioned for the sound to be cut off, and the dispassionate male voice ended abruptly, replaced by the normal quiet hum of systems and murmur of voices from the crew manning the half-dozen bridge stations.

"Code Black Three?" he demanded of Grand Deacon Braun.

"It's a plague warning," Braun said. "Code Black means the crew is dead. Black Three means they're dead of an infectious disease."

Cheveldeoff nodded slowly. "And you're not picking up anything else?"

"Nothing," the Grand Deacon said. "*Sanctification*'s entire communications system—on board the ship, on the planet, the repeater satellites, even the branespace booster—they're all off-line or powered down. They could have been destroyed or deactivated through enemy activity, shut down deliberately by the crew—or they may have simply gone into standby because the computer didn't receive any human input for seventy-two hours. That would be consistent with a fast-acting plague."

Cheveldeoff stared at the holographic main tactical display, a spherical three-dimensional representation of the system from which the various bridge stations radiated out like spokes on a wheel. There wasn't much to look at: an icon representing the planet, an icon representing *Retribution,* an icon representing *Sanctification.* A green dotted line showed their projected course into orbit. A solid red line showed their route through the space they had already traversed.

"Aside from the emergency beacon, what do we know about *Sanctification*'s condition?"

"Long-range visuals show her intact," Braun said. "Spectrographic analysis reveals no atmosphere cloud around her, so we don't think she's been holed."

Cheveldeoff shook his head. "The beacon is telling the truth," he said. "They're all dead. I can feel it."

"You can't be certain, sir—" Braun began, but fell silent when Cheveldeoff turned his coldest stare on him.

"I'm certain. Forget the ship for now. If it's infected, it will take careful planning for us to visit it, and if it's empty, there's no point anyway, except to retrieve whatever records might be there. That's important, but not as important as finding out what's going on down on the surface. So get us into orbit, and let's get a good look. Prepare an armed reconnaissance party. Full pressure suits, and full decon procedures when they return to the ship. But don't launch them until I say so."

"Yes, sir," Braun said, and hurried off to give his orders. *So far, at least, he still defers to me,* Cheveldeoff thought. He'd been alert to any sign of betrayal since boarding *Retribution.* There'd been nothing. Some of the loyal operatives he'd managed to ensure were part of the ship's complement of ground troops reported grumbling about the mission among the rank and file, but Cheveldeoff would have been suspicious if there hadn't been grumbling at that level. Besides, the grumbling seemed evenly directed at him and Braun. However, he didn't have eyes or ears among

Braun's most senior command staff, though some of the lower-ranking officers were his, and that worried him. He'd made it clear he expected to be part of every meeting of the senior staff, and he thought he would have known if they were meeting without him, but clandestine discussions over the ship's secure internal communications were almost certainly taking place.

Well. All he could do was stay alert. He smiled. *Good practice for when I'm Avatar.*

He looked at the decreasing distance to the planet detailed in the tactical display, and wondered what they would find on the surface. Ellers' initial reports had made it clear there was no armed resistance. Everything had been on track, and then communications had simply stopped. If there had been a plague, had it been something the Selkies were immune to? Or had it taken moddies and nonmods alike? And where had it come from? If the planet hosted a native plague that killed humans, how had Victor Hansen ever settled it in the first place?

He frowned. Could the Selkies have unleashed a biological weapon? Victor Hansen, in the years before Salvation Day, had campaigned tirelessly against biological weapons, helping to craft a strong international treaty banning them and personally setting up the inspection agency that enforced that treaty. It seemed unlikely he would have allowed research into biological weapons to continue on the planet he took his pet moddies to, a planet where he presumably intended to set up some sort of perfect society.

But still . . . he dared not discount the possibility entirely.

He needed more information. He stared at the tactical display and silently urged the ship to go faster. But the laws of physics were, unlike humans, unaffected by even the coldest Cheveldeoff stare, and the ship continued its agonizingly slow approach.

"BPS Sanctification to approaching vessel," Chris Keating said hoarsely. He wore an earbud transceiver, and

he'd been saying the same thing over and over for hours, ever since the ship's computer had announced that another Holy Warrior vessel had entered the system. So far, he'd heard nothing in reply but static.

Richard Hansen, he thought. *Somehow, the bastard has jammed me.*

He'd had it all planned out, how he'd warn the Holy Warriors, tell them to attack the planet from orbit, tell them how Richard Hansen had betrayed them all. He'd visualized it in detail: they'd rescue him, take him back to Earth, fête him as a hero. . . .

But none of that could happen until he managed to speak to someone on the approaching ship.

Maybe when they're closer.

And so he continued to repeat, "*BPS Sanctification* to incoming vessel. Can you hear me? Please respond. *BPS Sanctification* to incoming vessel . . ."

For three weeks after his meeting with the Council, Richard threw himself into helping the surviving Selkies and landlings prepare for the inevitable follow-up attack. Emily became his almost-constant companion, leaving him each night only after locking him into the quarters he'd been given in one of the apartment buildings facing onto the Square. Sparsely furnished with a table and two chairs in the kitchen/dining area, a bed in the bedroom, and nothing else, the apartment beat a cell, he supposed, but not by much. It didn't even offer a view, since all its windows had been blown out, either by the explosion of the germbomb or the takeoffs and landings of the Holy Warrior shuttles. Rather than replace them, the work crews had simply boarded them over—acting on his own recommendations, he had to admit, since the only real repair work being done was to things out of sight, like sewers and water lines: everything else, as he had suggested, had been left in ruins to present to orbiting eyes as convincing a picture as possible of a dead or dying world.

He had found one other use for his expertise besides

passing on his meager knowledge, mostly picked up during his two weeks on board *Sanctification,* of the care and operation of Holy Warrior weapons: the repair and upgrading of planetary communications. He had even managed to construct, from equipment left behind by the Holy Warriors, a secure, untappable and undetectable network for the Marseguroites to use when the attack finally came. Other than that, he'd simply made himself available for any and all tasks. He'd donned the uncomfortable and remarkably smelly local equivalent of a rubber suit, made from the sap of the bumbershoot trees that grew on the hills around Hansen's Harbor, and dragged the rotting remains of Holy Warriors out of the holes they'd died in . . . and he'd helped grieving relatives pull the bodies of loved ones from the rubble of buildings the Holy Warriors had leveled.

He couldn't work in the water, so he and Emily had been ashore when workers found the body of her father in the ruins of her home. That had been the only time she had left him during the day, turning him over to the scowling oversight of Farley. He'd watched her walk slowly away with her mother, the two of them holding on to each other so closely he couldn't tell who was supporting whom, and his guilt, never far from the surface, rose up and squeezed his throat so tight it hurt.

When Emily came back the next day, she said nothing beyond the necessary minimum to him all morning, and he knew better than to say anything to her. They spent the morning on the firing range, where Emily had become a crack shot with a standard-issue Holy Warrior automatic rifle, and adequately accurate with both slug-throwing and laser sidearms.

An ammunition microfactory had been delivered to the planet's surface at some point, and its associated bots had filled an old concrete warehouse to the rafters with ammunition before running out of raw materials. Supplied with new feedstock by the Marseguroites, the factory had no difficulty keeping the warehouse full, so there were no restrictions on ammo use during training—

a good thing, considering the impressive rate at which Emily went through it that morning. Richard wondered just what faces she saw on the man-shaped targets she had chosen. He wouldn't have been surprised if one was his.

He didn't ask.

Three weeks after his first meeting with the Council, he met with its members again. The interior of Government House had been thoroughly cleaned and repaired by then, only a few discolored spots resisting the workers' scrubbing. Like everything else, though, it still looked completely ruined from the outside. The germ-bomb's explosion had sent half the facade sliding down onto the cobblestones in a pile of undifferentiated bricks, exposing the mundane gray cinder block underneath. Richard looked at the pile of rock with approval, then followed Emily into the still-wide-open main entrance— nodding to Peter as they passed—and down the long corridor to the Council Chamber.

Though it was only early afternoon, the Council had already been in session for hours, dealing with the thousand and one details of the contradictory tasks of both making the planet's cities and towns livable for landlings and Selkies and keeping them looking deserted. Many Selkies had moved out to the deep-sea habitats, Richard knew, but they were mostly children and the elderly and those needed to care for them and maintain the habitats. Able-bodied Selkies remained in Hansen's Harbor or the other towns, working hard on underwater repairs.

One isolated habitat far to the north of any others had been set aside for what they'd taken to calling the LDDF, for "Last Ditch Defense Force." If things went badly on land, the LDDF would attempt to mount a guerilla campaign. Richard privately thought that was a fool's hope—even the remotest habitats wouldn't remain secret for long once the Holy Warriors began seriously scouring the seas for them—but he supposed it was necessary for morale.

". . . last of the free-ranging hunterbots, we think,"

Councillor Petrie, the red-haired woman he hadn't had a name for the first time he'd been in this room, was saying as they entered. "A sputa patrol nailed it near Sawyer's Point. It may have been trying to rescue the one Emily trapped there; we've been picking up weak signals from it ourselves every now and then."

She sat down, and Jeter stood up. "Thank you, Linda," he said. "And perfect timing, Mr. Hansen."

I wish someone would call me by my first name, Richard thought. Out loud, he said, "I'm at your service."

Jeter nodded. "And have been for the past three weeks," he said. "We appreciate it. In fact, we've taken a vote . . ." he looked around the table, ". . . and we have decided unanimously that we will remove the restrictions we have placed on your freedom. You will no longer be locked in at night, and we will no longer require Miss Wood to guard you at all times."

Richard blinked, his own reaction surprising him: he felt both pleased and . . . sad. "Thank you," he said. "I promise I won't do anything to make you regret it." *Well, that sounded lame.*

He glanced at Emily, half-expecting her to object, but she didn't react. *She must have known. I wonder how she feels about it?*

He suddenly realized why he'd felt that tinge of sadness: Emily Wood was the closest thing he had to a friend on Marseguro.

Come to think of it, the Selkie girl who at one point would gladly have let him bleed out in a jail cell was probably the closest thing to a friend he had *ever* had.

Now that *was* sad.

"We believe we have completed the most crucial preparations you helped us identify," Jeter said. "Now, of course, we're wondering . . . just how long do we have to wait?"

"I wish I knew," Richard said. "Grand Deacon Ellers didn't tell me his check-in schedule. I suspect, however, that it was daily. If that's the case, then they've known for three weeks on Earth that something has gone wrong.

They will have sent messages of their own, which have gone unanswered. It will take time for them to decide on a course of action, and of course the transit time from Earth to here is about two weeks." He spread his hands. "I think the earliest they could arrive is next week. More likely the week after that. It all depends on—"

With a feeling of *déjà vu,* he saw the Council Chamber door thrown open, and the same tech who had burst into the room last time he'd been there burst in again. "We're receiving a signal!" he almost shouted.

"From *Sanctification*?" Jeter said.

"From the Holy Warrior sensor satellite Richard linked us to," the tech said, and hearing his first name, Richard thought, *Thank you.*

"And?" Jeter prompted.

"A second ship is approaching."

Richard's heart skipped a beat. "Or," he said carefully, "they could arrive today."

"Sound the alarm," Jeter told the tech.

Richard glanced at where Emily had stood a moment before, but she'd disappeared. He looked back at Jeter. "What do you want me to do?"

Jeter returned his gaze steadily. "I gave you your freedom, Mr. Hansen," he said. "That's up to you."

Richard stood very still for a moment. His original plan had been to try to talk the Holy Warriors out of attacking, but Chris Keating had fouled that up. He could flee to the underground shelters they'd constructed and wait out the coming events.

Or he could prove once and for all whose side he was on . . . and what he really believed.

He followed Emily.

Aboard *Retribution,* Cheveldeoff and Braun surveyed a vidwall in the main briefing room just off the bridge, watching the flow of data from the surveillance satellites they'd launched when they'd finally entered orbit. "Evidence of Purification is clear in all of the towns we've identified," Braun said. "The *Sanctification* contingent appears to have done an admirably thorough job of destroying major structures in and close to the water, while minimizing damage to land-based structures, in an effort to avoid unnecessary casualties among the normals.

"We've identified a few Holy Warrior-built control points and weapons emplacements," Braun went on, pointing them out with a laser pointer. The red dot flicked here and there too fast for Cheveldeoff to even register the structures indicated, but he didn't say anything. He didn't need the details, just the gist. "This indicates that Grand Deacon Ellers had taken over governance and was imposing order. Presumably that included a curfew, martial law, summary corporal and capital punishment—the usual measures."

"I'm familiar with the *modus operandi* of the Holy Warriors," Cheveldeoff said. "I wrote most of the manual. The question is, Grand Deacon Braun, are there any Holy Warriors on the planet now?"

Braun turned off his laser pointer with a click that fell just short, Cheveldeoff thought, of insubordination. "Not that we can detect, sir. Nor have we seen incontrovertible evidence of any other survivors. Certainly there is no evidence that any kind of large-scale human—or subhuman," he added hastily as Cheveldeoff cocked an eyebrow, "civilization continues to operate. There are some signs that rebuilding began, but then halted."

"Your conclusions?" Cheveldeoff said, although he'd already come to his own.

"A plague," Braun said. "As indicated by the Black Three code. A fast-acting plague that incapacitated and killed both Holy Warriors and planet-dwellers so quickly they could take no effective countermeasures."

"And where did this plague come from?"

"There's no way to be certain, sir," Braun said, "but—" he clicked on his pointer again and aimed it at a bombed-out building that looked no different to Cheveldeoff than any of the others, "—close analysis of this structure reveals it to be a biological laboratory. From the photographs, we've identified equipment identical to that used by the pre-Salvation genesculptors. Other equipment appears to be related to culturing microorganisms. Remembering that Victor Hansen created this society, it seems likely the Selkies and their normal collaborators were conducting gene modification experiments on local lifeforms. Conceivably, they accidentally created something deadly that the bombing of the laboratory released into the environment."

Cheveldeoff nodded thoughtfully. Braun's theory made sense, and the ruined lab, if not definitive, certainly bolstered its probability. The biological warfare scenario seemed less likely if the plague had killed most or all of the planet dwellers as well as the Holy Warriors.

Time to seek further evidence. "Very well, Grand Deacon," he said. "Send down your armed reconnaissance party."

Inside Government House, Emily stood by the Holy Warriors communications station with Richard Hansen, her mother, and the Council, watching the tactical display Hansen had somehow conjured on one of the vidscreens. The new ship had entered orbit more than three hours ago, and so far had utterly ignored its silently orbiting sister ship, *BPS Sanctification.* "Looks like they bought the Black Three warning," Hansen said. "But look." He pointed to half a dozen icons circling the planet in different orbits. "They're surveying. By now, every square centimeter of Hansen's Harbor and the other towns has been scanned, photographed, and analyzed a hundred different ways."

"They want to know if anyone is alive down here," Emily's mother said. "But can they tell that from orbit? Can they spot us in here?"

"Not from what I know of the technology," Hansen said. "And the habitats are deep enough they should be safe from orbital scans. Let them get down here in shuttles, though, and they'll soon track us down."

"They wouldn't live long enough," Emily said. "The plague . . ."

"Won't affect men in pressure suits," Hansen said. "Which they will almost certainly be wearing, if they believed the Black Three code."

"What do you think they'll do?" Dr. Christianson-Wood said.

"Probably send down an armed reconnaissance force," Hansen said. "I've worked with Cheveldeoff a long time. He wants firsthand accounts. He never believes intelligence that comes into his office until he's sent an agent to verify it personally. If he's true to form, there'll be a shuttle full of Holy Warriors heading our way very soon."

"We'll be ready for them," Jeter rumbled.

"As ready as we can be," Hansen said. He frowned. "I wonder . . . Computer, access *Sanctification* tactical computer."

Emily stiffened, hands gripping the automatic rifle she'd been practicing with for weeks, the rifle that no longer felt awkward in her hands but more like an extension of her own arms. "What are you doing?"

Hansen shot her a look. "Still don't trust me?" he said. "I'm not doing anything the new ship can detect. And if we're lucky . . . Yes!" He pointed. The icon representing the new ship in their own tactical display had suddenly sprouted a string of new numbers—and a name. Emily leaned in closer.

"*BPS Retribution*," she read.

Hansen whooped. "*Retribution*! That's a piece of luck."

"Why?" said Jeter, and Emily gladly let someone else play straight man for a while.

"*Retribution* is an old troop carrier," Hansen explained. "Lots of Holy Warriors on board—more than *Sanctification* had—but it's what it doesn't have that's important. It doesn't have assault craft—and it doesn't have an Orbital Bombardment System."

Emily felt a smile spread across her own face. The possibility more assault craft would swoop down on them again or, worse, the new ship would simply lob mass-slugs at them from space had worried all of them. If Hansen were right, then all they had to worry about was—

He stiffened. "Here they come."

Emily looked into the tactical display again. A small glowing speck had detached from *Retribution*'s icon. As she watched, the separation increased. It sprouted its own numbers and name: *BPS Fist of God.*

"When will we know where they're going to land?" Jeter asked.

"We won't," Hansen said. "They could change their destination right up until the last moment. But I think it's a safe bet they'll land in one of the towns. And knowing Cheveldeoff, I'd be willing to bet they'll land right here in Hansen's Harbor. In fact—" he pointed toward the door. "I'll be surprised if they land anywhere else but the Square. In about twenty minutes."

Emily hefted the rifle and checked the clip and chamber with smooth, practiced motions. Then she held the rifle at arm's length so she could inspect the dart-guns once again strapped to both wrists. Finally, she propped the rifle butt on her hip. "Well, we'd better prepare the welcome party, hadn't we?"

Cheveldeoff sat in the main briefing room of *Retribution* with Grand Deacon Braun, watching the video feeds streaming back from the descending shuttle. The twenty-four Holy Warriors on board *BPS Fist of God* could be accessed individually, but for now Braun had the feed coming from the shuttle's exterior cameras. The craft had just broken through a low bank of clouds hanging over Hansen's Harbor, giving them their first clear view of the town.

"Ellers clobbered it good," Braun said. "It looks worse up close than it did from orbit."

It did. Although there were signs some rubble had been cleared away, most of the debris lay untouched. Bricks and twisted steel and overturned, burned-out ground vehicles clogged the streets. Nothing moved except for stray bits of hardcopy skittering through the wreckage, pushed by a strong sea breeze.

Fist of God made one low pass over the town, then settled into the main square, where something had blasted a huge crater in the once-white cobblestones, near a toppled and scorched bronze sculpture. Cheveldeoff leaned forward as the cameras made a slow pan around the courtyard. All the buildings looked damaged: windows broken, roofs holed, facades fallen, pillars snapped off at the base. More paper swirled by as a dust devil howled across the square and disappeared into an alley. Otherwise, they might have been looking at a still photograph.

"Holy Warriors, check suit seals and sound off!" a voice crackled. Braun touched a control, and a new picture popped up in a separate window inside the main image. "Ground Commander Speitzl," read white letters across the bottom of the window, which showed the length of the troop hold inside the shuttle, full of Holy Warriors in full pressure suits, strapped into the two facing rows of seats, their weapons secured on the rack between them. "Ashcroft, tight!" "Umstattd, tight!" "Hughes, tight!" and so on through twenty-four names.

"Unship weapons," Speitzl said. Almost in unison, the two-dozen warriors reached out and pulled their rifles free of the rack. At the same instant, the straps holding them in their seats unsnapped and retracted.

"On your feet."

They stood. The seats disappeared, moving up into the ceiling.

"About face."

They turned sharply to face the now-bare outside walls.

"Go, go, go!"

The outer walls fell away, forming ramps down which the Holy Warriors charged, except for the four who stayed in the shuttle to provide covering fire from the raised turrets fore and aft.

Not that any was needed. The exterior view remained empty of life.

Cheveldeoff nodded. *As I expected.* "Tell Speitzl to secure the shuttle, then send out patrols to the Holy Warrior positions we identified. Starting with that big building facing the Square. They seem to have set up communications there." He stood up and turned toward the door. "I'll be in my quarters if anyone—"

Someone screamed. Cheveldeoff whirled back to face the vidscreen.

Down on the planet, all hell had broken loose.

From the darkness of the windowless, burned-out shell of a building that had once been the Office of Land Dweller Affairs, Richard watched the shuttle settle in the Square, its shrieking landing jets threatening his eardrums. Hot air drove a wall of dust and grit over the long-suffering fallen statue of Victor Hansen. Then the jets cut off, and the massive hydraulically cushioned landing struts groaned as the shuttle's full weight came to bear on them.

In the sudden silence, Richard could hear his ears ringing.

Sanctification hadn't carried this kind of shuttle, but he'd seen them in action often enough in various squelch-the-heresy and stamp-out-rebellion operations over the years. He'd told the others what to expect. For a few minutes, the shuttle just sat there, its name, *Fist of God,* gleaming on its flank in golden script. Then, with no warning at all, the sides dropped and twenty Holy Warriors swarmed out, ten to a side.

They hit the ground at a run, then dropped prone, weapons pointed out in a circle of potential death. Inside the shuttle, which Richard could now see right through, four additional Warriors crouched in turrets behind heavy machine guns that could deliver withering suppressing fire if required.

But just as Richard had suspected—or at least hoped— the Warriors weren't wearing their normal body armor.

Instead, they were in pressure suits. They obviously feared the plague more than any potential ambush. The pressure suits would keep out the killer virus Dr. Christianson-Wood had developed, but they wouldn't do a thing to stop bullets or lasers.

Emily crouched beside Richard. They didn't speak. They both knew what was supposed to happen next.

Richard would have waited a few minutes longer, in hope some of the Warriors would get to their feet and thus make better targets, but Fred Notting, who had been given overall command of the "welcoming committee," didn't have the same degree of patience.

"Go," said a voice in Richard's ear, in the Holy Warrior earbud transceiver he wore, tuned to the secure communication system he'd helped set up. And from all around the Square, the ambushers opened fire.

Richard had known exactly how many people the incoming shuttle held, and how many would come out of each side. They'd positioned their forces accordingly. In the few moments since the Holy Warriors had emerged, each one of the Marseguroite defenders had identified his or her target.

The most crucial were the four heavy gunners. They could only be hit from above, and so four snipers had been sent to four roofs around the Square, crouching out of sight in doorways as the shuttle descended.

When the command came, Richard was peering through his sight at the helmeted head of a man looking almost directly at his position. The reflective pressure suit faceplate kept him from seeing the man's face. He could almost pretend it wasn't a man at all . . . almost. Without giving himself time to think about it, he squeezed the trigger, firing a triplet of high-velocity armored bullets.

The smooth glass bubble didn't shatter. Three round holes appeared in front, a red-and-gray mist spurted from the back, and the pressure-suited figure slumped.

Richard swung to his secondary target—Emily's primary—but she'd taken care of it . . . *of him,* he corrected himself, unwilling to whitewash what they were doing. He'd never killed someone directly before, though he knew he had killed thousands indirectly. It had to be done. He believed that. But he would not lie to himself any longer about the consequences of his decisions and actions.

He lifted his head to survey the overall situation.

On his side of the shuttle, every Holy Warrior sprawled or slumped on the ground, dead or incapacitated, including the commander, crumpled against the side of the shuttle, a red smear marking where he had stood just seconds before. It looked like all the Holy Warriors on the far side of the shuttle were also *hors de combat* . . . but the snipers had gotten only three of the four machine gunners. Vengeful or panicked, it didn't really matter which, the surviving machine gunner was spraying the buildings on the far side of the Square, including Government House, with a murderous hail of bullets. As Richard watched, one of the surviving pillars holding up the Government House pediment split under the stream of fire and collapsed. A moment later the pediment crashed down on top of it, blocking the building's main entrance with rubble . . . and bringing down a large section of roof, along with the sniper who had been on it.

"We have to get him from this side!" Richard yelled, and scrambled up. Emily had already decided the same thing and led him by two steps as they burst into the open. Others from their side of the ambush followed, but Richard and Emily were the closest. They were halfway to *Fist of God* when its sides started to rise. A dead Holy Warrior, half on and half off the ramp, tumbled out like a rag doll. "The shuttle's lifting!" Richard shouted. "You take the gunner, I'll take the pilot." With the bulkhead almost a meter off the ground, he had no time for anything more. He jumped, cleared it, fell, rolled. He glanced left and saw Emily tumbling down the slope of the lifting bulkhead and the gunner in the turret turning toward her, but he had no time to watch what happened.

He turned right and crashed through the door into the shuttle cockpit. Behind him, he heard a burst of rifle fire.

The pressure-suited pilot barely had time to turn toward the door before Richard's rifle butt smashed his right shoulder. He yelled, the sound muffled by his helmet, and dropped the laser pistol he had in that hand. Richard kicked it away and the pilot lunged after it with his remaining hand. Richard's rifle butt came down on his outstretched left arm, and it snapped with an audible crack. The pilot collapsed, cradling his arm and moaning.

"Doors closed. Commencing automated takeoff in ten seconds," said the shuttle's computer. "Nine. Eight. Seven."

Richard's shipboard Holy-Warrior training had not included anything about flying a shuttle, but he knew how to read. A large red button clearly marked MAIN POWER EMERGENCY CUTOFF nicely put a stop to the countdown.

The pilot moaned again. With two useless arms, though, he didn't seem much of a threat. Richard ignored him and turned back toward the main compartment, remembering the shots he had heard. *Emily!*

"The shuttle's lifting!" Hansen shouted. "You take the gunner, I'll take the pilot."

Why not the other way around? Emily thought, but had no time to argue, not with the side bulkheads of *Fist of God* rising and the machine gunner demolishing everything on the far side of the Square and possibly slaughtering their compatriots at the same time. She angled left, and leaped.

She didn't quite make it. Her left foot caught the lip of the bulkhead. She fell headlong, and her rifle flew from her hand and skittered down the rapidly increasing slope. She slid down after it and ended in a crumpled heap at the bottom.

The bulkhead closed behind her and sealed. The machine gunner, his field of fire cut off, boiled out of his turret like a mad animal, unshipping his rifle and screaming something about God and vengeance. Emily twisted onto her back and lifted herself up as his barrel swung toward her—and shot him in the stomach with all four steel-tipped darts in her dart-guns.

The miniature harpoons ripped through his pressure suit as if it weren't there, tore apart his guts, and burst out the back, splattering bloody chunks of flesh across the ceiling. His rifle fired once, the bullets burying themselves in the bulkheads. His shout about God's vengeance turned into a high-pitched scream, then a gurgle fading to silence. With a final cough, the Holy Warrior pitched forward, his helmeted head slamming into the floor just inches from Emily's outstretched feet.

She heard the door to the cockpit opening behind her and lunged for her rifle. She grabbed it, twisted around again—

—and found Richard Hansen looking down at her, breathing hard. "Good work," he said.

She took a deep breath of her own. "The pilot?"

"Alive but incapacitated." Hansen held out a hand to her, and after a moment's hesitation, she took it and let him pull her to her feet. "We may need him."

"What, your limitless knowledge of things Holy Warriorish doesn't extend to flying shuttles?" she said, and to her own surprise, found herself grinning. *I'm teasing him,* she thought. *And* smiling *at him.* She felt sure she'd never done the former before and hadn't done the latter more than twice. *Well, I can't be suspicious forever. And after* that . . .

She remembered the barrel of the machine gunner's rifle swinging toward her, but she didn't glance back at his body. She'd thought she'd never tire of taking revenge on the Holy Warriors, but she'd seen—and shed—enough of their blood now to begin to realize her thirst for vengeance wasn't unquenchable after all.

I guess I'm not cut out to be a brutal killing machine.

Hansen—hell, she might as well go all the way and think of him as Richard—looked surprised at her smile, but then he matched her grin with one of his own. "I'm afraid not," he said. Then he grimaced and rubbed his knee. "I barely cleared that damn bulkhead. The Holy Warriors didn't teach me levitation, either, worse luck."

"It's probably in the advanced course," Emily said. "Along with walking on water and raising the dead."

Richard laughed. "Probably." Their eyes met, and Emily looked away, suddenly feeling oddly self-conscious. "So," she said, studying the blank bulkheads and the weapons rack down the center of the compartment, "how do we get out of here?"

"This way . . ." Richard hesitated. "I think." He led her tentatively toward the bow.

He's a landling, he is . . . or was . . . an enemy . . . and he's the clone of someone I could quite accurately describe as my Creator, Emily thought. *I can't start thinking about him in* those *terms.*

But remembering how good it had felt to laugh and smile with him, she wondered if she really had a choice.

"*Damn* them!" Cheveldeoff roared. He paced the briefing room, turning his head to keep his glare on the feeds from *Fist of God,* which showed the Selkies and their human accomplices dragging the bodies of the entire reconnaissance party away into the surrounding buildings. "And especially damn *him!*" He stopped and jabbed a finger at a figure that had just passed the camera, a much shorter Selkie female in black by his side. "Richard Hansen. A murderous traitor like his devil-spawned grandfather." Braun didn't know Hansen was a clone, and even in his rage, Cheveldeoff wouldn't give *that* bit of information away freely. "And I trusted him. Blood will tell, Braun. Blood will tell."

"Your orders, Archdeacon?" Braun said, his own face expressionless.

He's sensing an opportunity, Cheveldeoff thought, suddenly cautious. *A weakness. I ordered the shuttle down. He's not on my side. He wants me to fail, so he can step in and save the day.*

"I can send down another shuttle," Braun suggested.

"Two shuttles. We'd know what to expect this time. We could establish a beachhead."

"No." Cheveldeoff made a chopping motion with his hand. "You establish a beachhead when you want to invade and occupy. I don't want to invade and occupy. I want to destroy."

"We don't have any orbit-to-ground weapons," Braun said.

Cheveldeoff stopped his pacing, spun and snarled at the Grand Deacon, who paled even if he didn't—quite—flinch. "Don't tell me what I already know! I'm fully aware we don't have any orbit-to-ground weapons on *this* ship—but this isn't the only ship we have."

"What about the plague?" Braun said, and added, "sir," just in time to not sound insolent. "We'll have to manually bypass the security protocols to take over command of *Sanctification* from the computer. You can't do that work in space gloves. Someone will have to unsuit."

In those moments when duty required him to choose between two difficult possibilities, Cheveldeoff often felt an icy calm descend on him, a coldness that allowed him to make his choice on a completely rational basis, without regard for the moral niceties and ethical quibbles lesser authorities allowed to cloud their judgment. *That's why I'm Archdeacon,* he thought, relishing the feeling that gripped him now, as though he had plunged into a pool of cold, crystal-clear water. *That's why I'm going to be Avatar.*

"There may not *be* a plague, Grand Deacon," he said. "It may be as illusory as the utter desertion of the town below. But even if it exists, those who must unsuit must unsuit." His gaze bored into Braun's pale blue eyes. "But you will *not* permit anyone who unsuits to return to *Retribution* until we know for *certain* if this plague exists. Do I make myself clear?"

Braun's mouth tightened and his nostrils flared, but all he said—wisely—was, "Yes, sir."

"Board *Sanctification*. Activate the Orbital Bombardment System. And give *me* targeting and fire control. Do it."

Braun saluted and left the briefing room. Cheveldeoff looked back at the vidwall. Sometime in the past few minutes it had gone blank. Probably someone on the ground had suddenly realized that *Fist of God* had eyes and ears.

I don't have to see you to know you're there, you God-damned travesties of human beings, he thought. Then, out loud, he quoted the words of the first Avatar, "Vengeance belongs to God—and I am God's instrument."

He turned his back on the vidwall and strode out of the briefing room. *This planet* will *be Purified, O Wrathful One,* he vowed in silent prayer. *I swear it.*

Chapter 18

RICHARD SHOT A SIDEWAYS glance at Emily as they made their way past the shattered front of Government House, where medical personnel were carefully putting the badly injured-but-still-living sniper on a stretcher. With the front entrance blocked, they'd have to go in through the freight entrance at the back. Their route between Government House and Town Hall took them out of sight of everyone for a few seconds. Richard opened his mouth to say something, then closed it again.

She smiled, he thought. *She called me Richard instead of Hansen. She even joked with me.*

He felt like a young teenager. *Does she like me or doesn't she?*

She's a Selkie, he thought. *She lives most of her life underwater. Selkies even have sex underwater. I could drown!*

And besides that, she's more than 10 years younger. It'll never work out.

He intended the thought as a private joke—surely he didn't feel *that* way about her—but to his surprise, he realized he really did feel *that* way about her.

She attracted him . . . she attracted him a lot. And had for a long time. He just hadn't admitted it to himself.

She may like me, he thought. *It doesn't mean she wants to bear my children. She* can't *bear my children. Grandclone Victor made sure of that.*

Oy. Just drop it, Richard. This isn't the place, and it

certainly isn't the time. Be happy that at least she's un-likely to shoot you on the spot, and leave it at that.

But later, maybe, if they survived . . .

They emerged from darkness into light, literally if not, in Richard's case at least, metaphorically, jumped up onto the concrete loading dock, and made their way in through the storerooms and kitchens to the Council Chamber.

They found something of a celebration in progress, excited talk and laughter echoing down the hall so that they heard it before they saw it. *Time to be a wet blanket . . . or maybe, for the Selkies, a dry one,* Richard thought, as he and Emily entered to shouts of, "They're here!", applause, and claps on the back.

He put up his hands for quiet. Jeter saw him and helped him out by pounding his gavel. The room fell silent. Everyone looked at him.

Emily included.

He liked that.

He cleared his throat. "Sorry to be the bearer of bad news," he said, "but we haven't won yet."

"Let them come back," one of the Councillors called. "We'll be ready for them."

Richard shook his head. "They won't come back. Not the same way." *Not unless Cheveldeoff has turned into an idiot since I used to play chess with him.* "They're going to want to destroy us, and there's only one way they can do that." He pointed up. "From orbit."

"But you said they don't have any orbit-to-ground weapons on the . . . um, *Retribution*," Jeter said.

"They don't," Richard said. "But they know *Sanctification* does. And now that they know they need them, our plague beacon isn't going to stop them from boarding her."

Faces fell around the room. But Jeter kept looking at him steadily. "So you're going ahead with the second part of your plan?"

Richard nodded. "The job's only half-done."

Jeter shook his head. "You're going to get killed."

"Well . . . some would call that just desserts," Richard said. He very carefully did not look at Emily, but out of the corner of his eye he saw her drop her gaze, and it warmed him. *At least* she *doesn't feel that way anymore.*

Apparently Jeter didn't either. He frowned. "I'm tired of hearing that, Richard," he said, using his first name for the first time. "You've proven yourself over and over, especially just now, out on the Square. You don't have to die. We may be subhuman abominations, but we don't practice human sacrifice."

First name and *a joke,* Richard thought in wonder. *I might be accepted here some day after all.*

If I live long enough. Jeter was right: if he attempted what he had in mind, he probably wouldn't.

But there really wasn't any choice. If a shuttle hadn't already left *Retribution* for *Sanctification,* it would soon enough, and if Cheveldeoff got control of *Sanctification*'s Orbital Bombardment System, *none* of them would live much longer.

"I have to try," he said.

Emily's head suddenly came up. "Then I'm coming with you!"

He shook his head. "No. It's not an attack. Numbers don't matter. It will either work, or it won't."

"If numbers don't matter, then two are as good as one," she shot back. "And just maybe two is better. You'll need someone to watch your back."

"You've never been in zero-G," Richard said, and then stopped, surprised, as everyone in the room burst out laughing. "What?"

Emily flared her gill slits at him. For some reason it made him blush. "Selkie, remember?" she said. "I grew up in zero-G." She grinned. "Wanna bet I get around in it better than you?"

"Uh . . ." Knowing he'd already lost the argument, Richard gave in. "All right," he said. "You can come . . . um, I mean, I welcome the company."

She bowed her head a little. "Thank you so much," she said sardonically.

Jeter's own smile faded. "When?"

"I need to talk to the pilot." Richard hesitated. "He might need a little . . . persuasion . . . to tell me the truth."

"I can help there," Dr. Christianson-Wood said. Emily gave her a look halfway between startled and dismayed, and Dr. Christianson-Wood laughed. "I'm not talking about torture, Emily. Simple brain stimulation. He'll answer truthfully, and it won't hurt him at all."

"What about the plague?" Richard said.

"I'll give him the vaccine," Dr. Christianson-Wood said. "I'm not a monster." She blinked suddenly, and looked away. "Not entirely, at least."

Emily looked away, too, and Richard wondered if she were remembering that *she* had been perfectly willing to let *him* die in a cell without giving *him* the vaccine. *Well,* he thought, *if she's coming with me, I'd just as soon she was a* little *ruthless.* He looked at Emily's mother, who had engineered the disease that had brutally killed a shipload of Holy Warriors and not a few of her own fellow Marseguroites, and thought, *No worries there, if like mother, like daughter.*

He thought of what he'd done himself, on both sides of the conflict. *No worries here, either, I guess.*

He cleared his throat. "No time like the present," he said. "In fact, maybe no time at all."

"Let's go, then," Dr. Christianson-Wood said, and led the way.

The first that Chris Keating knew of the arrival of *Retribution*'s Holy Warriors aboard *BPS Sanctification* was the shrilling of an alarm that woke him from a deep sleep.

He sat upright on the couch in the rec room and stared around, trying to figure out the source of the high-pitched squeal. The ship's computer clarified things for him. "Unauthorized docking. Unauthorized docking. Unidentified shuttle craft in Bay One. Repeat, unidentified shuttle craft in Bay One."

Docking? Chris stumbled to his feet and half-ran, half-staggered to the vidscreen he had managed to slave to the main tactical display. He couldn't change the view from the last one the dying crew had used, however, since the computer only allowed him the absolute minimum control over any ship's systems—little more than "Lights on, lights off"—and all he could see was a blip representing the other Holy Warrior ship.

He rubbed his face vigorously with his right hand, trying to wake up. He'd spent hours, until he was hoarse, calling that ship. Eventually he'd crawled back here for a nap. How long ago had that been?

He didn't know. He'd long since lost track of time.

Had they heard him and finally decided to rescue him? Maybe they'd been replying all along, and for some reason he hadn't been able to hear them?

Or did they even know he was on board?

"I've got to get up there," he said aloud, then grimaced. *Talking to myself,* he thought. *That's a bad sign.*

Chris was good at zero-G maneuvering now, after weeks in orbit. Once he was out of the rotating habitat ring, he zipped down the central shaft and to the docking bay access tunnels in minutes. But he grabbed the maneuvering webbing and pulled up short of the hatch leading into the docking bay. *They've got to be nervous. And they may not know I'm here. No point in getting shot.*

All the way to the bay, he'd been accompanied by the computer's monotonous periodic warning of: "Unauthorized docking in Bay One. Unauthorized docking in Bay One." But suddenly it changed. "Security Alert. Security Alert. Unauthorized computer access. Unauthorized computer access. Unauthor—"

And then, silence.

Chris gripped the webbing even tighter, and waited.

Abruptly, the hatch slid open. A pressure-suited Holy Warrior popped out and convulsively grabbed the webbing himself as he caught sight of the young Marseguroite.

Chris tentatively raised one hand. "Uh, hi," he said.

"I'm Chris Keating. Welcome to *BPS Sanctification*." Then he couldn't help but break into a huge grin. "Boy, am I glad to see you!"

In *Retribution*'s briefing room, Cheveldeoff and Braun watched the feed from the *Sanctification* boarding party. Docking had proceeded without difficulty, although *Sanctification*'s main computer continued to squawk about it. They'd been worried about the ship's anti-boarding armament, but apparently the crew of *Sanctification* had had no concern about being attacked in space by the Selkies and had not armed it. The computer complained, but it didn't attack.

Watching through the shuttle's exterior cameras, Cheveldeoff saw the salvage crew emerge. Their first task would be to get out of the docking bay, which required manually severing the computer's control of the dock's hatches. As he watched, a Holy Warrior removed a plate from the floor and inserted something into the opening. *Sanctification*'s computer squawked something different, then fell silent.

"Got it," Cheveldeoff heard over the suit-to-suit channel. "The hatch is opening. I'll just go through and . . . Holy Wrath of God!"

"Computer, switch to helmet camera of man just transmitting," Cheveldeoff snapped.

The image flickered, and changed.

Cheveldeoff found himself looking at a young man—little more than a boy—with shaggy brown hair and a few wisps of chin hair that hardly qualified as a beard. Barefooted and bare-chested, he wore nothing but rumpled blue pajama bottoms, far too big for him, kept on only by a tight knot in the strings. "Uh, hi," he said, raising a hand. "I'm Chris Keating. Welcome to *BPS Sanctification*." He grinned, which made him look even younger. "Boy, am I glad to see you!"

"Who the hell is *he*?" Cheveldeoff demanded of Braun.

"I have no idea," Braun said. "He's obviously not a

Holy Warrior. And the only civilian on board *Sanctification* was Richard Hansen. He must be from the planet. But how he got there . . ."

"He's not a Selkie," Cheveldeoff said. "He's human." He frowned. "And he's obviously been unaffected by the plague . . . if there is one." He turned to Braun. "I want to question him. Get him into the shuttle."

Braun nodded, and gave the orders.

Chris wasn't exactly sure what he was expecting, but being grabbed like a piece of cargo and hauled across the docking bay and into the waiting shuttle certainly wasn't it. Nobody had said anything to him, although that might have been because they all insisted on keeping their pressure suits on and their helmets sealed. He could have told them they had nothing to worry about—that the *Sanctification* crew had been *poisoned* by Richard Hansen, not killed by anything infectious—but he hadn't had a chance yet.

Two Holy Warriors manhandled him into position in front of a comm terminal. A blank green vidscreen lit, revealing a square-jawed, bullet-headed man with a nose like a squashed grape and brown eyes that glittered like polished stone. "Who are you?" the man demanded without preamble, his voice a *basso profundo* rumble.

"I'm Chris Keating," Chris said. "Um . . . who are you?"

"Samuel Cheveldeoff," the man growled. "Archdeacon of Body Security. And that's the last question you get to ask until I'm done asking mine. What are you doing aboard *Sanctification*? What happened to the crew? And what happened on the planet?"

At last, Chris thought, and told Cheveldeoff everything he knew or guessed—how his family had remained faithful to the Body all these decades, how he had set off the emergency beacon in the hope it would finally bring richly deserved Purification to Marseguro, how thrilled he had been when the Warriors from *Sanctification* attacked, how he had met Richard Hansen . . . and how

Richard Hansen had betrayed the Holy Warriors, half-poisoning them on the ship, then finishing them off with the chemical bombs he had told the Selkies how to build. "He planned to present himself as a hero when you showed up," Chris said. "I'm surprised you haven't—"

"A chemical weapon killed them? Not a plague?" Cheveldeoff interrupted him.

Chris nodded. "It couldn't have been a plague. If there were any diseases like that on Marseguro all of us normal humans would have died a long time ago, wouldn't we?"

"The Selkies could have created it. A biological weapon."

"No!" Again, Chris shook his head. "Victor Hansen hated biological weapons. The Selkies wouldn't dare go against their Creator. And anyway, they didn't have time. I should know, I'm . . . I'm a geneticist." *Okay, I'm a laboratory technician,* he thought. *But they don't need to know that.* "It's impossible to create such a selective pathogen in two days. Absolutely impossible."

Cheveldeoff grunted, and looked over to his right, as though someone had said something. "What?" he said, not to Chris. "Damn. All right. I'm done here anyway." He turned back to Chris. "You'll forgive me if I don't take any chances. Stay on *Sanctification.* Help the crew there with anything you can. Once we're sure there's no infection, then . . . we'll see. If you're telling the truth, I'll personally make certain the Avatar knows you are a hero of . . . what did you call this planet?"

"Marseguro," Chris said. He felt himself grinning like an idiot, but he couldn't help it. "It means 'safe sea,' apparently."

"Marseguro." Cheveldeoff looked away again. "All right, I'm coming." The vidscreen blanked.

Still grinning, Chris turned to the Holy Warrior who had escorted him there. "You heard him," he said. "What can I do to help?"

The Warrior snorted. "Stay out of our way," he said, his voice issuing from an external speaker on his helmet. He grabbed Chris and hauled him out of the communications room with no more respect than he'd shown shoving him into it.

"Hey!" Chris protested, but the Warrior ignored him. So did the others, shoving him out of the way like a stray bit of floating debris when he tried to talk to them. Eventually, he settled for sulking in the background, following them as they moved through the ship, disabling and rerouting systems. They seemed in a hurry, and upset about something.

He wondered what it was.

Eventually the crew, now in the habitat ring, stood outside a hatch Chris had never been able to open, labeled ORBITAL BOMBARDMENT MAIN CONTROL. They had pulled up a large section of deck planking and were standing looking down into the cables snaking through the hole. To Chris' astonishment, one of them reached up and removed his helmet. As he did so, exterior speakers on the other's suits came to life. "Smell any germs, O'Sullivan?" someone cracked.

"It smells fine," O'Sullivan said. He sniffed. "Although I think the kid there needs a shower." He began undoing zippers and snaps on his now-deflated pressure suit and shimmied out of it. Underneath, he wore a blue jumpsuit with his name stitched across the left breast. Rank insignia Chris had no idea how to read marked both sleeves.

Chris ignored the gibe. "All of you could unsuit, you know," he said. "There's nothing to worry about. I mean, look at me. I've been living here for weeks, and I'm fine."

O'Sullivan glanced at him. "Gee, thanks, I feel much better now," he said. "Now shut up." In his sock-covered feet, he turned and descended into the opening in the floor. "All right," he said, looking up at his still-suited compatriots, "here goes nothing."

"Message from *Sanctification*," Braun said quietly to Cheveldeoff as they stood side by side on the bridge of *BPS Retribution*. "They're working on the final switchover. You should have control of *Sanctification*'s Orbital Bombardment System within a couple of hours."

Cheveldeoff glanced at the Grand Deacon. *He's still waiting,* he thought. *Waiting for me to screw up. Well, he'll have a long wait.* He turned his attention back to the main tactical display. In the middle of his interrogation of Chris Keating, he'd been informed that *Fist of God,* whose complement of Holy Warriors they had seen slaughtered, had just launched. Some time ago, it had vanished behind the planet. It should be coming up behind them, rising over the horizon as it ascended and accelerated to rendezvous with *Retribution.*

But who was on board?

There. "BPS *Fist of God* reacquired," said the computer. "Rendezvous in twenty-two minutes."

"Computer, open communication link to *Fist of God.*"

"Ready," said the computer.

"Occupants of BPS *Fist of God,* this is BPS *Retribution.* Identify yourselves." No response. He hadn't really expected one, but it never hurt to ask. "Occupants of shuttle *Fist of God,* respond." Still nothing. "Computer, end transmission." He turned to Braun. "We asked them," he said. "They didn't answer. The shuttle is on automatic approach, which means we get control of it for final docking." He smiled. "It might be contaminated, Grand Deacon. When we gain control, order it to open itself to space."

The Grand Deacon's smile was as predatory as Cheveldeoff's. His loyalty to the Archdeacon might be questionable, but not his desire for revenge on those who had killed his troops. "I can't think of a better way to rid a spacecraft of . . . contamination, sir. It will be my pleasure."

"See to it." Cheveldeoff turned back to the tactical display to watch.

Less than fifteen minutes later, *Fist of God* moved through the handoff point. Control passed from its computer to that of *Retribution.*

Two minutes after that, the shuttle fired retro rockets that brought it to a halt, relative to the ship.

And one minute after that, the sides opened.

Air exploded out, its moisture forming an expanding cloud of ice that swirled and glittered in the sunlight. Odds and ends of equipment spun and flashed in the cloud . . . but no bodies, pressure suited or otherwise.

Damn! "Braun?"

"Scanning," Braun said. "Stand by." A minute crawled past. "Empty," Braun said abruptly. "No one aboard. No one in the seats, no one in the cockpit, no one in the holds."

Cheveldeoff felt his fists clench and consciously relaxed them. "Then where the hell are they?"

Chapter 19

THROUGH THE FACEPLATE of his borrowed Holy Warrior pressure suit, *BPS Sanctification* loomed in front of Richard like a . . . *well, like an orbiting starship,* he thought, simile failing him.

They had bailed out of *Fist of God* while it was in Earth shadow from *Retribution,* carrying the POTs—Personal Orbital Transportation devices, the space equivalent of the Selkies' sputa. The wounded pilot had told them all about the POTs when properly brain-stimulated by Dr. Christianson-Wood. He'd also told them exactly how to program the automated return of the shuttle, what would likely happen to the shuttle when it reached *Retribution* ("They'll either open it to vacuum or blow it out of space"), how to use the *Fist of God*'s computer to calculate their best intercept course for *Sanctification,* what he'd had for dinner the night before, how he felt about his ex-wife, his deep longing to someday be a professional singer, and the nasty thing he'd done to his sister when he was twelve (and very nasty it had been, too).

Richard suspected he was still talking.

They'd left sometime during his account of getting beaten up in kindergarten and returned to *Fist of God.* They'd found the POTs right where the pilot had said they were, and the computer had been extremely helpful once presented with the security codes the pilot had handed over. It had programmed the POTs for them, told them when to enter the air lock, and expelled them at the proper time with careful bursts of gas. They'd watched the shuttle dwindle into a moving star while they coasted on their new trajectory.

Once both *Fist of God* and *Retribution* were below the horizon, the POTs came to life, driving them into a new orbit that now, two hours later, had brought them to a gentle rendezvous with *Sanctification*.

Emily, as she had smugly expected, had indeed had no difficulty at all getting used to zero-G. Richard's stomach felt unsettled, but not as badly as when he had first gone into space. Those weeks on *Sanctification* had eased his tendency to space sickness, it seemed.

If Richard turned his head, he could see Emily four meters to his left and slightly behind him. They hadn't spoken since they'd left the shuttle, not daring to break radio silence in case either *Retribution* or *Sanctification*—or both—were listening.

He looked back at *Sanctification* as a beep sounded in his helmet. "Programmed maneuvers completed," said a tinny version of the shuttle's computer voice. "Manual controls engaged."

The computer had done its part. Now it was up to them to make a safe landing.

Richard knew what to look for: four service air locks spaced equidistantly midway between the spinning habitat ring at the bow and the shuttle docking bays at the stern. But he couldn't spot them in the glare of the sun, and the ship was growing bigger with alarming speed.

Time to end radio silence.

"Computer," he said. "Activate suit-to-suit communication."

"Activated."

"Emily, are you there?"

"I'm here," the response came immediately. "What's next, Rocket Richard?"

Richard grimaced. Ever since she'd decided to use his first name instead of calling him Mr. Hansen, and in general become friendlier, she'd been experimenting with nicknames. "Richard is fine," he'd told her. "Just Richard."

Apparently, she'd decided to ignore his suggestion.

Oddly enough, despite his protests, he wasn't at all sure he really minded.

"We need to slow our approach. Two-second forward burst on my mark, count of three. Ready?"

"Roger."

"One . . . two . . . three . . . mark."

Two puffs of gas from each of the chairlike POTs, and the approach of the ship slowed markedly. But Richard still couldn't see any hatches.

"Computer," he said hopefully, "Magnify and enhance."

"The Mark 6 Space-Capable Pressure Suit does not have the inherent ability to modify visual input," the computer replied. "Please install a Mark 9 Enhanced Vision Helmet or a Neo-Zeiss Mark 67 Visual Enhancement Overlay Device."

Richard sighed. "Never mind."

"Are you looking for a hatch?" Emily said. "Because I can see two of them."

"You can?" Richard squinted. He still couldn't make out any details in the sun-drenched white surface.

"Nictitating membranes," Emily said. "Polarized, even, thanks to Dr. Hansen. They act like sunglasses. Reduce glare, enhance contrast. You should get some."

"Very funny. All right, you'd better take the lead, then." He nudged himself sideways, and eased slowly up on Emily's right side. "Computer, match our trajectories and velocities."

"Vector matching complete," the computer said after a brief puff of gas from Richard's POT.

"Computer, slave POT controls to Suit Two."

"Controls slaved."

"Okay, Emily, you've got the helm."

"Affirmative. Hold on."

To what? he wondered.

He needn't have worried. Emily maneuvered them in

with as much finesse as a veteran spacedock worker, until they floated stationary relative to the ship, close enough to reach out and grab the stanchions that surrounded all four sides of the two-meter-by-two-meter hatch.

"Now comes the fun part," Richard said. "We find out if my computer codes still work."

"They worked when you shut down communications," Emily said.

"Yes, but by now there must be Holy Warriors on board. And they're undoubtedly mucking around in the computer. There are no guarantees."

"*Now* you tell me," Emily muttered.

"Better late than never!" Richard poked a gloved finger at a glowing red button beside the hatch; a panel slid open, revealing an oversized keyboard. With one finger, he entered the twelve-character alphanumeric code he'd memorized back when he still thought the will of God—and his own career and ego—could be best served by sending a shipload of bloodthirsty killers to ravage a peaceful planet.

He had changed, but the code hadn't: the hatch opened.

They clearly couldn't both fit in the lock with their POTs. Richard only hesitated a second. "Dump the POTs," he said. "We probably won't need them again, and if we do, the ship must have some."

It made perfect sense, but Richard still felt a brief surge of worry as he unbuckled from his POT and gave it a gentle shove. It drifted slowly away, out of reach within seconds. *No going back now,* Richard thought, and then had to laugh at his groundlubber brain, which insisted on thinking he could simply retrace his steps to the shuttle. The shuttle was either destroyed or on board *Retribution* by now. There hadn't been any going back since the moment they'd squirted into space. There was no "back" to go back *to.*

He turned to Emily, who had likewise dispatched her POT, and swept his arm toward the air lock. "After you, miss."

Emily made as much of a bow as she could in a pressure suit, and pulled herself into the lock.

Sanctification swept through the terminator. The air lock's interior changed in an instant from a forbidding black hole in a glaring wall of metal to a welcoming, well-lit cubbyhole in a forbidding sea of blackness.

Taking that as an omen, Richard followed Emily inside.

As she waited with Richard for the air lock to cycle and let them through into *Sanctification,* Emily slipped her laser pistol from its holder. The thing could only manage a few shots before it needed recharging, but as Richard had had to remind her—underwater wasn't *quite* the same as zero-G, and shooting guns underwater just didn't come up on Marseguro—mass-throwing projectile weapons and microgravity didn't go together well, thanks to Newton's Third Law.

Richard pulled out his own laser pistol. Together they watched the light over the inside door. At last it turned green. The door opened, and . . .

. . . nothing. Just an empty spherical chamber maybe six meters in diameter, with hatches across from the air lock and above, below, and to either side. Silvery webbing covered the bulkheads, as though a giant Earth spider had been hard at work.

Richard holstered his pistol, reached up, and took off his helmet. Emily did the same.

"They're not waiting for us," he said. "That's something. And if they're working on the Orbital Bombardment System, they're clear up in the habitat ring. On the down side, that's where we have to go, too."

"Well, if we have to fight, I'm not doing it wearing this," Emily said. She began undoing the straps and zippers that held the pressure suit in place. "I can barely move."

Richard hesitated. "We might need them," he began, then stopped and laughed. "And if we do, there are plenty on board. You're right." He began struggling out of his own suit.

Underneath the pressure suit, Emily wore her black, water-filled landsuit . . . in a way, just a different kind of pressure suit, something to protect her from a not-entirely-friendly environment. She flexed her neck, encased in a watery collar. Her gills were cramping from being cooped up for so long. The collar kept them moist, but the suit's water supply held little oxygen, so she couldn't really use them. What she wouldn't give for half an hour in the open sea. . . .

Richard, now wearing a blue jumpsuit and soft white leathery slippers—"standard Holy Warrior microgravity ship wear," he'd explained when he'd taken it from the shuttle's storage locker and put it on, down on Marseguro—pulled his laser pistol from the floating, crumpled form of the pressure suit. Emily grabbed hers, too, but she also took a moment to check her wrist dart-guns. They'd saved her life twice now. She'd become attached to them.

"Ready?" Richard said.

She nodded.

"This way." He pushed off from the wall and sailed across, landing on the webbing on the far side of the chamber and grabbing on. Emily followed him. Using the webbing, they worked their way to the hatch opposite the air lock. It opened at the touch of a button on a panel beside it, and they slipped through.

A square cross-section corridor ran away from the hatch, more hatches opening periodically from each of its four sides. "Straight ahead," Richard said. "The far end of this corridor should open into the central access shaft, the zero-G highway that runs fore to aft. That'll take us to the habitat ring, where the bridge is."

"Wouldn't it make more sense to have the bridge on the nose of the ship?" Emily said. "So you could just look out and see where you're going?"

"You can't fly something the size of *Sanctification* by

the seat of your pants," Richard said. "You don't need to see where you're going. So you might as well put the bridge in gravity and make it easier for the crew to function. Besides, one reason for the central shaft is to allow shuttles or lifecraft to fly through the ship to get out if the docking bays are damaged. The nose of the ship is just one big hatch. Come on."

She expected him to launch himself down the corridor like a missile, but instead he grabbed hold of the webbing and began pulling himself along it. Emily followed.

All the hatches were closed. Emily wondered what had happened to the dead Warriors she knew must inhabit the ship. *It's like those old Earth stories about ghost ships.* She'd never been superstitious, but she still had to repress a shiver.

She spotted the opening at the end of the corridor that presumably led into the central shaft. "The end is in sight!"

"Not to me," Richard grumbled. "But it's about time. My arms are wearing out."

"Why not just push off?" Emily said. "From here you could probably shoot through the opening without touching anything—"

"And zip right across the central shaft, smash into the far wall and break my neck," Richard said. "I prefer slow and steady." The opening, dim and blue, loomed ahead. "The ship's still running day/night cycles for the crew, looks like," Richard said as he pulled himself the last couple of meters. "Just our luck to hit a night cycle . . . oof!"

As he emerged from the corridor, something traveling fast toward the stern collided with him, and he disappeared.

It happened so quickly Emily didn't have a clue what the fast-moving object had been. She gripped her laser pistol and launched herself through the opening.

Too fast! She lost her grip on the webbing and fell into the central shaft, drifting across its thirty-meter diameter unable to do anything but wriggle. But by jackknifing, she at least managed to turn herself around to see what had happened to Richard.

He drifted in the shaft, struggling with another figure, a half-naked barefoot landling youth—

Chris Keating.

As she watched, Richard shoved hard, and Chris sailed into the shaft wall with an audible thud and grunt. Richard accelerated in the opposite direction, more or less toward Emily.

Chris grabbed the webbing and clung like a wallcrawler, staring up at them. Emily raised her pistol, ready to fire—

—and Chris scuttled away, still heading toward the stern.

He'd never said a word.

"Where's he going?" Emily said. He'd already gotten too far away to waste a precious laser shot on. As she watched, he swung through an opening and disappeared.

"Could be anywhere," Richard said. Something in his voice made her look more closely at him. He had drifted within a couple of meters of her but would soon pass her—tossing Chris away from him had given him a lot more impetus than her leap into the shaft had given her. He held his left arm cradled against his body, and his laser pistol had disappeared. "I think my arm is broken," he gasped. "Keating hit me like a ton of bricks."

Emily looked around. "We're almost across the shaft. Will you be able to grab the webbing?"

"I'll have to, won't . . . unnh." He'd hit the wall. He groaned, but grabbed a silvery rope with his right hand and held on.

Emily reached the wall herself a minute later. She spidered her way down to him. "Let me see your arm."

"It's all right," he said. "I'll . . ."

"It's *not* all right, Dicky," Emily snapped, knowing the nickname would annoy him and hoping it would also refocus his mind.

"Don't call me—" He stopped and said, "You're right. But what can you do with a broken arm?"

"I can't set it, but I can wrap it up." She looked around. "If I can find something to wrap it up with."

"There's nothing in the shaft."

"I can look in some of the compartments—"

Richard shook his head. "No. There's no time. I don't know where Keating is headed, but we have to figure he'll tell the Holy Warriors we're here. And we can't fight them all. Our only hope is to carry out our original plan. We have to get to the bridge."

"But your arm . . ."

"It's not going to kill me. It just hurts. I'll live. Let's go." And he started to crawl forward, one-armed. He moved at about the same pace as a squeegeefish scraping muck off the bottom of a rock pool, and Emily only followed for a few seconds before saying, "Stop."

"We can't—"

"I said stop, all right?" She made her way in front and stuck her bare foot in his face. She wriggled her webbed toes at him. "Grab hold."

He didn't argue, for once, just grabbed hold of her ankle.

"No tickling," she said. "Especially not the webbing. Or I'm likely to kick your teeth in. Purely by accident, of course."

Richard managed a wan smile. "No tickling. I promise."

She tucked the laser into a pocket of the landsuit, took hold of the maneuvering webbing, and began pulling them hand over hand toward the bow, the habitat ring— and the bridge.

Chris hurried toward the docking bays, a sharp pain in his side from the collision with . . . Richard Hansen. He couldn't believe it. Hansen himself, the Machiavellian mass-murdering monster, returning to the scene of his crime . . . with Emily Wood, the sea-bitch herself.

He needed to warn the Holy Warriors . . . but he couldn't get back to the habitat ring without going through the central shaft, and Hansen and Wood were there, and armed—he'd seen a laser pistol in Wood's hand.

And besides, if he went back, he'd lose his only chance to do what he had to do if he wanted to be sure of getting off this hulk.

The Warriors are soldiers, he thought. *They can handle one normal and one moddie. There's no way Hansen and Wood can do anything to stop them before they have the Orbital Bombardment System up and running. And when they do—boom. No more Hansen's Harbor, or Firstdip, or any other settlements. No more Selkies. No more Marseguro.*

No more landlings, but he could live with that. *Toadying fishfuckers, the lot of them.*

He rubbed his aching right side. A cracked rib, almost certainly. But he must have hurt Hansen, too. Something had snapped when they'd collided.

The Holy Warriors can take care of themselves. It's about time I took care of me.

He kept heading aft.

"Status," Cheveldeoff snapped, for the fifth time that hour.

"Nothing has changed." Braun didn't quite manage to keep the impatience out of his voice. "*Sanctification*'s central computer is a higher order AI than *Retribution*'s. There are difficulties in convincing it to allow us to hand over control to what it sees as a less-capable system, even though we have hardwired a shunt past the—"

"I don't want the technical details, Grand Deacon," Cheveldeoff said, with more than a hint of dry ice in his tone. "I want an estimated time of completion."

"Half an hour, minimum. Sir."

Cheveldeoff glared at the tactical display. "And how long until the next opportunity for maximum-velocity, maximum-mass bombardment of Hansen's Harbor?"

"Forty-seven minutes. After that, there are lesser-velocity launch windows, of course, but the maximum-damage launch window won't open again for one full orbit—a little under two hours."

Cheveldeoff turned the full power of his coldest stare on Braun. "I can wait if I have to, Grand Deacon. But I don't want to."

The Grand Deacon's lips thinned. "Understood."

"Good." Cheveldeoff stared at the tactical display again. He'd been waiting for the other shoe from *Fist of God* to drop. So far they hadn't picked up anything . . . but *Retribution*'s sensor suite wasn't even close to state of the art. The ship hadn't been left in Earth orbit during major operations on New Mars just because the Archdeacon of Naval Operations didn't like its name, after all.

Still, they couldn't have missed a second shuttle launch. Cheveldeoff had begun to allow himself to believe Braun's comforting theory that the shuttle had been preprogrammed to return to the ship automatically by an overcautious—and now presumably thoroughly dead—pilot, and its launch had taken the Marseguroites as much by surprise as it had the Holy Warriors.

He'd left *Fist of God* drifting outside the ship. Nothing from the ground would be allowed aboard *Retribution* until he was certain they weren't dealing with either a natural or Selkie-made plague.

He resisted the urge to ask Braun for the status of the salvage party again. He would wait. But if he didn't have orbital bombardment control within forty-seven . . . make that forty-five . . . minutes . . .

Well, Cheveldeoff's spies informed him that Braun's loyalty to Shridhar wasn't as solid as all that. When the mission succeeded, Cheveldeoff suspected Braun, recognizing Shridhar's bid for the Avatarship was doomed, would start sucking up to the Archdeacon in earnest. Cheveldeoff also suspected Braun was smart enough to realize that if he did anything to obstruct Cheveldeoff's efforts, and the mission succeeded anyway, he'd soon find himself running anti-Islamic revival operations in Saudi Arabia.

Cheveldeoff had long worked by the theory that the best way to ensure obedience was to punish someone. Anyone. The Marseguroites' punishment was sure. The Grand Deacon's still hung in the balance.

As for Richard Hansen . . . Cheveldeoff only regretted that if Richard Hansen were in Hansen's Harbor when the mass hurled from orbit arrived, he'd never see it coming.

Chapter 20

RICHARD CRADLED HIS left arm and held on to Emily's webbed foot. Keeping his arm motionless kept the pain bearable enough that he only gasped once. But any movement caused bone ends to rub against each other and agony to skewer his arm like a red-hot poker. The second time it happened, he squeezed his eyes closed. *How in hell am I going to do what I need to do with one good arm?*

Emily slowed. "Now what?" she said.

Richard opened his eyes and blinked away tears. On the other side of a webbing-free, meter-wide strip of bare silvery metal, the central shaft continued—except the webbing on the other side of the strip rolled past at about the speed a man could run, as the entire shaft rotated at three revolutions per minute.

Eight small cubical elevator heads protruded from the rotating shaft, four equidistant around the shaft about twenty meters from where they waited, and four more forty meters beyond that. Brightly lit, they were all Richard could see in the dim blue light . . . but they were the last thing he wanted to use. Anyone monitoring ship's systems would immediately detect an elevator being put into operation, and either shut it down or have a welcoming committee waiting for it when it reached the outer deck.

Somewhere out there, though, there were also hatches, each of which opened onto a shaft called, for reasons lost to history, a Jefferies tube. The tubes provided access to various systems for repair and maintenance. Each had a ladder in it that allowed the person doing that repair and maintenance to climb from the outer deck to the central shaft and back again. And one—the one Richard wanted—led to the corridor just outside the bridge.

"We're looking for hatches," he said. "They're painted yellow . . . no webbing on them. But I can't see them in this light. Can you?"

Silence for a moment as Emily set her oversized eyes to the task. "I think so," she said finally. "Half a dozen of them, at least. Which one do we want?"

"Farthest. Closest to the bow." Richard closed his eyes as a wave of pain and nausea swept over him. He swallowed hard four or five times. He would *not* throw up. He would *not* . . .

As seemed to happen every time he issued that command to himself, he promptly disobeyed it.

At least the air circulation system took the globules of liquid and floating undigested bits of the military rations he'd eaten back on the shuttle toward the stern. *Maybe they'll hit Chris Keating,* Richard thought.

Emily waited stoically until he'd quit heaving and coughing. He spat a couple of times, and wished he had water to rinse his mouth. "Let's go," he said, taking hold of Emily's foot again. "The usual method is to . . . unnh."

Not bothering to wait to hear what the usual method was, Emily had simply launched herself . . . and him . . . onto the rotating webbing. She grabbed hold. The jerk as they were swept "up" made him gasp.

"Sorry, Ricky," she said.

"Just get us to the hatch."

Even this close to the center the spin imparted weight, enough so that instead of bobbing along like a cork behind Emily, Richard found himself being dragged across the webbing like a balloon without quite enough helium in it. He turned onto his right side to save his broken arm as best he could. As a result, he had a perfect view of the lone pressure-suited Holy Warrior emerging from one of the elevators.

The Holy Warrior's half-silvered helmet hid his face, but Richard didn't have to wonder long if he'd been seen: the Warrior instantly launched himself toward them.

"Look out!" Richard yelled at Emily.

The shout was too late to do her any good, but she must have seen something out of the corner of her eye, and Victor Hansen had given the Selkies unbelievable reflexes by nonmoddie standards. So fast he hardly saw the motion, she turned, drew, and fired.

He couldn't see the beam in the clear air, but sparks, bright as stars in the dim light, burst from the neck of the Warrior's pressure suit. For a moment, Richard thought the suit had stopped the laser, but then the oncoming body separated into two parts. The still-helmeted head drifted up and away from them, while the now-headless body continued forward in a slow, stately, end-over-end spin, spewing shimmering scarlet globules.

The body bounced off the webbing and over Richard's head. He ducked. Blood spattered the webbing around him. One crimson globe hit him on the cheek, clinging and half-blinding him; he frantically wiped at his face with his good hand.

Selkie faces were always pale, but Emily's looked paler than usual. "Too close! Did he call for help?"

"No way of knowing. Let's get to that hatch." He grabbed Emily's heel again, and she resumed the scramble.

By the time they reached the hatch, the Warrior's body and head and most of his blood were drifting back down the shaft in the air circulation currents. Richard was surprised he could still see them; then he realized what must be happening.

The night cycle had ended. "Dawn" was breaking.

The hatch opened readily to Richard's security codes, and bright light strips came on in the Jefferies tube. He couldn't see the bottom—not surprising since he calculated the tube was roughly the height of a twenty-story building.

Emily looked down, then at Richard. "Are you sure you can do this?"

"I don't have much choice, do I?"

"We could take the elevator."

He shook his head. "Too dangerous."

"They may not even know we're here," Emily argued.

The webbing to their right suddenly came apart in a puff of acrid smoke, its severed ends glowing red for a moment. Richard dove headfirst into the shaft, grabbed hold of the ladder with his right hand, and swung around, crashing into it so hard his ears rang. Emily jumped in behind him and clung to the ladder just below the raised hatch.

A glowing red line streaked across the inside of the hatch and vanished, leaving behind a long black mark. Emily slapped at the controls. The hatch slammed shut and sealed with a hiss.

Through the red roaring haze in his head, Richard heard a faraway voice say, "They know."

It took him a minute to realize the voice had been his own.

"Intruders in *BPS Sanctification*," Braun suddenly announced to Cheveldeoff on the bridge of *Retribution*, just five minutes away from the end of the estimated half hour until handover of the Orbital Bombardment System.

"Intruders? *How?*"

"They must have used POTs," Braun said. "Probably launched themselves from *Fist of God* out of our sensor range, then just coasted to a rendezvous with *Sanctification*."

"And why didn't we see them?"

"Our sensor suite is old and overextended."

Is it? Cheveldeoff thought. *Or are you being very care-*

*ful to only do what I specifically order you to, and since
I didn't tell you to look for coasting pressure suits, you
didn't instruct your men to look for them, either . . . so
that if these "intruders" succeed in screwing up the mission, the fault will be entirely mine?*

Deal with the immediate problem first. "How many?"

"We have visual confirmation of two, a normal male
and a female Selkie. There could be others we haven't
seen."

I'll bet I know who the male is. Cheveldeoff's mind
flashed back to the sight of Hansen and a Selkie girl
walking away from the shuttle after the ambush of the
reconnaissance party. "Where are they?"

"They're in a Jefferies tube . . . not sure where it goes
yet. We're checking ship schematics . . . got it." A pause.
"It leads to just outside the bridge."

"Then I suggest you get some of your people to just
outside the bridge, Grand Deacon."

Braun's brows knit. "That order has already been
given, Archdeacon."

"Good to know you aren't entirely incompetent,"
Cheveldeoff snarled. "Here are *my* orders: kill them, and
get me control of the Orbital Bombardment System
within the next twenty minutes."

The Grand Deacon didn't move. "Those orders," he
said carefully, "have *also* already been given. Sir."

Oh-ho, thought Cheveldeoff. *Time to show some teeth.*
"A word in private, Grand Deacon?"

Braun nodded. Cheveldeoff led him into the briefing
room. The door closed automatically behind them, and
Cheveldeoff whirled and put his face just inches from
Braun's. "Grand Deacon," he said, soft as a breeze but
with the focused intensity of a blowtorch, "let's be perfectly clear. I know, and you know I know, that you
favor Shridhar in the upcoming vote to select the next
Avatar. I don't know your reasons; I don't care. What I
do care about is this mission. You may think, Grand
Deacon, that by sabotaging this mission you are only

sabotaging me, and ensuring that your favored candidate wins the post of Avatar. Perhaps he has offered you my job if you succeed in causing this mission to fail.

"But know this, Grand Deacon. No matter who eventually becomes Avatar, when we return to Earth, I will still be head of Body Security for several weeks or months to come. And during that time, I will have little compunction about using all of the considerable powers I will still enjoy making your life, and the lives of all those dear to you, hell. Of course I cannot, in my official capacity, order anyone's death or torture, but I cannot vouch for some of my more overenthusiastic followers, who might take it upon themselves to punish those who have openly declared their enmity toward me . . . something I am beginning to suspect you may be on the verge of doing yourself."

Cheveldeoff moved even closer to Braun, who kept his eyes rigidly focused on the wall behind Cheveldeoff's head. He dropped his voice to the barest whisper. "Do I make myself clear, Grand Deacon?"

Braun pulled his gaze down as though from a great height, and looked into Cheveldeoff's eyes, his face pale but utterly stoic. "Perfectly, sir," he said. "Now if you'll excuse me . . ." He turned and went back out through the briefing room door onto the bridge.

And Cheveldeoff felt an unaccustomed pang of uncertainty. In his experience, no one remained as calm as Braun just had in the face of such threats from the Archdeacon of Body Security.

What's he up to? he wondered. *And why haven't my spies found it out?*

Unsettled, he returned to the bridge.

Emily didn't like the way Richard looked. Of course, the overbright, over-blue lighting of the Jefferies tube didn't do his complexion any favors, but she didn't think his paleness was entirely a result of the lighting, and it certainly hadn't caused the sheen of sweat on his face. "Can you move?" she said.

"I'll have to, won't I?"

"I could carry you—"

He shook his head. "No. You need your gun hand free."

She couldn't argue with that.

"Let me by," he said, and she squeezed to one side so that he could heave himself up the ladder to just under the hatch and punch buttons on its keypad. "I've keyed in a manual combination. I doubt they have complete control of the computer, so they shouldn't be able to bypass it easily. They won't come after us this way."

"But they'll be waiting for us down below?"

"If they can get there fast enough. But unless they're already there, they've got to follow a roundabout route— that part of the habitat ring is practically a maze, and the layout of the rooms and corridors is somewhat mutable; it's a security feature. We, on the other hand, are taking a straight line. So let's move."

Emily took the hint and began to descend.

Their weight increased as they went down deck by deck, and with it, the number of moans and grunts coming from Richard. But he didn't complain or ask for help, and as they came closer to the bottom of the shaft, Emily focused her attention downward, straining her eyes for any glimpse of movement, afraid the first—and last—she would know of the arrival of the Holy Warriors below her would be the flash of a laser.

But there was the bottom hatch, still closed. Emily stopped. "It should open automatically," Richard panted above her. "They're locked against entry to keep unauthorized people out of the tubes, but there's no default need to lock them against people inside them."

Emily nodded. "If they're waiting on the other side, we won't have much of a chance, will we?"

"If we don't try this, Marseguro doesn't have any chance at all," Richard said. "A half-ton rod of ceramic-tungsten alloy impacting at eleven kilometers per second makes a hell of a hole."

Emily felt a flash of her old anger at him. *None of this would be happening if not for you!*

But that wasn't really fair . . . not anymore. Chris Keating was the real culprit . . . and above all, the Avatar of the Body Purified, whose bloody-handed predecessor had driven them to Marseguro in the first place and whose so-called "wisdom" had turned Keating against his own people.

Hell, maybe *she* was even partly to blame for having jumped Chris on the pier that day with John Duval and her Selkie friends.

Lots of blame to go around. Lots of actions by lots of people, leading to lots of consequences, good and bad. Her anger at Richard faded. *At least he's tried to make up for what he did. Whether it's because of Victor Hansen's gene-bomb or his own conscience, he's changed.*

She grinned. *So have I,* she thought, and jumped off the ladder.

The hatch opened underneath her and she dropped heavily into the corridor below, crouched, laser out, ready to cut in half anything that moved.

But nothing did.

"All clear," she shouted up to Richard.

He dropped down a moment later, hit the deck with a groan and fell to his knees. He remained there for a moment, leaning on his one good arm, then sighed and straightened. She held out her free hand and helped him to his feet.

"Thanks," he said. He looked around. "We can't have very long. This way." He led the way down the corridor to the right.

After a few meters, he stopped in front of a heavy black pressure door with the crossed-sword-and-starship emblem of the Holy Warriors embossed on it in red. "Computer," Richard said, facing it. "Biometric scan, please."

"Scan complete," the computer said. "Greetings, Richard Hansen."

"Computer, open bridge door."

The door didn't budge. "Input verbal security codes."

Richard reeled off a string of numbers and letters. Emily held her breath.

"Codes accepted," the computer said. "Standing down bridge security. Laser turrets deactivated. Sonic stunners deactivated. Please wait for pressurization."

"Laser turrets? Sonic stunners? Pressurization?" Emily said.

"Security features," Richard said. "If the bridge is abandoned by the crew, the computer takes steps to ensure that no one without authorization can gain control of the ship."

"How long will it take to pressurize?"

"Just a minute or two—"

From down the hall came the clatter of footsteps.

Emily spun and dropped to one knee. The first Holy Warrior to round the corner screamed and fell back out of sight as her beam slashed across his leg.

"I don't know if we have a minute or two," Emily said.

"They can't come around that corner without you nailing them," Richard said.

"Is there any way for them to circle around and hit us from two directions at once?"

Richard hesitated. "Yes. But it will take them—"

"—a minute or two," Emily said. "Great."

She caught a hint of movement and fired. The beam harmlessly scored the wall . . . and an indicator on top of the pistol flashed yellow. *Charge warning,* Emily thought. *This just gets better and better. You'd think the Holy Warriors would make sure their laser pistols were fully charged before hanging them in a shuttle for anyone to use . . .*

. . . and just how many shots do you get after the charge warning appears, anyway?

She found out two shots later, when she pressed the trigger and nothing happened. Since both shots had missed, the odds remained unchanged . . . as did the bridge door, still stubbornly closed.

"Computer," shouted Richard, "How much long—look out!"

Emily had glanced at him just for a second. Now she jerked her head around again to face the corner. Only her Selkie reflexes saved her life. She saw the emerging Holy Warrior as if he were moving in slow motion, saw his laser pistol coming up, and threw herself forward, firing her right-hand dart gun as she fell. The darts slammed the Holy Warrior back against the wall. He slid down, leaving a trail of blood, and slumped to the ground.

Some sixth sense—or more likely Selkie hearing—warned her to twist around the other way. A Holy Warrior had just started to come around the corner in that direction; he leaped back as she turned, and the darts fired from her left wrist shattered harmlessly against the wall.

Out of darts, out of time, she thought . . .

The bridge door opened.

. . . but not out of luck.

Richard darted in. Emily followed. A searing pain lashed through her right calf as she jumped, and she screamed and crumpled to the ground just inside the bridge.

"Computer! Secure bridge!" Richard shouted, and the door slammed shut behind them.

Emily felt a surge of fear. "It will blow the atmosphere!"

"Not with authorized people in the room. Different procedure." Richard knelt beside her. "Are you all right?"

"My leg . . ." Emily stretched it out in front of her. The pain made her gasp.

A laser had sliced a six-centimeter gash in her calf muscle, passing right through. Since the laser had cauterized the wound at the same instant it made it, she hadn't bled much, but nothing she'd ever felt had hurt worse. A puddle of water had formed under her calf from the hole in the landsuit, but its self-sealing skin stopped the leak before more than a couple of hundred milliliters escaped.

"I'll live," Emily said weakly. "Can't fight, though. No ammo." She felt light-headed; shock. "Might pass out . . ."

"End game," Richard said. "Either I can make this tub do what I want it to, and we win, or I can't, and we lose."

"Warning," said the computer suddenly. "Unauthorized access of Orbital Bombardment System. Unauthorized access of Orbital Bombardment System. Unauthorized remote control initiated. Unauthorized remote control initiated." A pause, then, "Launch detected. Five-hundred-kilogram mass."

Richard swore. Emily felt her heart skip a beat, then another, then settle into a strange, syncopated rhythm. The room whirled.

"Too . . . late . . ." she whispered, and fell into darkness.

"Who authorized that mass launch?" shouted Cheveldeoff on the bridge of *Retribution*. "Because I sure as hell didn't!" He clenched his fists. *Is Braun slipping into outright mutiny?* He looked around the bridge. The Holy Warrior manning the communications console returned his gaze steadily. *One of mine,* Cheveldeoff thought. *But he's the only one in here who is.*

Braun said nothing, listening to a voice in his ear. "A glitch," he said after a moment. "During the switchover."

"Show me where it hit!"

The tactical display changed to a three-dimensional image of Marseguro. A spot of light blossomed in the middle of the ocean, ten thousand kilometers from the continent, almost halfway around the planet.

"Wasted!" Cheveldeoff snarled. "And the angle was all wrong. It burned off most of its speed and a good chunk of its mass in the atmosphere. It won't even raise a ripple in Hansen's Harbor."

Braun spoke quietly to his earbud transceiver; listened, then said, "Roger that," and looked at Cheveldeoff. "Fifteen minutes to reload. You'll still get your shot this pass."

No mutiny yet, then. "I'd better. What about Hansen and that moddie bitch? Dead?"

Braun shook his head. "Not yet. They killed two Holy Warriors and made it onto the bridge. They're both wounded, though. They may not be able to—"

"They're on the bridge!" Cheveldeoff roared. "Damn you, Braun—"

"They can't do anything there," Braun said. "Hansen is an intelligence analyst, not a spaceship pilot."

"*Sanctification* is moving, sir," a Holy Warrior shouted—not Cheveldeoff's man.

"They can't do anything, can they?" Cheveldeoff spun to face the crewman. "Moving where?"

"Unknown, sir." A pause. "She's slowing." Another pause. "I think she's changing orbits, sir."

"Restore tactical display!"

The globe vanished, replaced with the display he'd been watching for hours.

"Detailed view!"

Numbers and projected trajectories flashed into view. Cheveldeoff took one look. "She's not *changing* orbits, you idiot, she's *de-orbiting*. He's scuttling her." He looked at the numbers again, and his lips pulled back from his teeth in what might have been mistaken for a grin. "But he can't scuttle her fast enough. Computer! Confirm control of *Sanctification* Orbital Bombardment System has passed to this vessel."

"Confirmed," said the computer.

"Computer, program *Sanctification* Orbital Bombardment System as follows: target, Hansen's Harbor. Mass: largest available. Velocity: maximum possible." He leaned forward. "Put it in the middle of that precious Square of theirs."

"System programmed," the computer said. "Please confirm auto-launch."

"Computer, confirm auto-launch."

"Auto-launch in six minutes . . . mark."

Cheveldeoff straightened and took a deep breath. "Grand Deacon," he said, without looking around.

"Yes, sir," said Braun.

"Call your people back." He paused. "Except for the one that took off his suit. He stays."

Braun sucked in a sharp breath. "You're leaving him to die?"

"He could be infected. If he returns to the ship, we may all die."

"That Keating kid said . . ."

"Grand Deacon," said Cheveldeoff. With the hammer about to fall on Hansen's Harbor, he no longer felt any uncertainty at all, and he turned and gave Braun the hardest of his extensive repertoire of hard stares. "*Don't* argue with me."

Braun's mouth worked, but all he said was, "Yes, sir." He moved away, talking into his transceiver, and left the bridge.

Cheveldeoff watched the tactical display. "Checkmate, Mr. Hansen," he said softly. "Checkmate."

Chapter 21

IT TOOK RICHARD ONLY two minutes to discover that his plan to disable the Orbital Bombardment System from the bridge would not work.

He'd suspected as much when he'd told Emily that the Holy Warriors had hardwired a shunt around *Sanctification*'s security systems. He'd worried they had cut the ship's computer out of the control loop entirely . . . and the ship's computer had just confirmed he'd been right to worry.

Their best hope had been to get to *Sanctification* before the Holy Warriors even boarded it. Failing that, they'd had to get to the bridge before the Warriors gained control of the OBS. Having failed *that,* he seemed to be out of options.

He glanced at Emily. She lay unconscious, face pale, on the steel plates of the bridge floor, a pink pool of mingled blood and water beneath her wounded leg. He wanted to go to her, do something for her, but there was no time.

How little time was brought home an instant later. The ship jerked, just a little, and the computer said, "Unauthorized launch from Orbital Bombardment System."

Richard felt cold. "Computer, show me where it hits."

Screens lit. He watched the slug slash a claw mark of white fire through the atmosphere. It impacted in a snowball of vaporized water in the deep ocean a long, long way from Hansen's Harbor, and he relaxed . . . a little. *What was that?* he wondered. *Warning shot?*

Nonsense. Cheveldeoff didn't give warnings. It must have been a glitch. When Cheveldeoff acted, he wouldn't miss.

"Computer," Richard said, "how long until ship is in position for a maximum-velocity, maximum-damage mass launch aimed at Hansen's Harbor?"

"Thirteen minutes, forty-six seconds," the computer said.

That's it, Richard thought. *That's how much time I've got.*

He stood on the bridge, his broken arm cradled against his side, each beat of his pounding heart driving another hot steel spike of pain into it. *So it comes down to this. My whole life, leading to this moment.*

He had dreamed, once, of rising high in the hierarchy of the Body Purified, of making the name Hansen respected instead of vilified. Less than half a year ago? It seemed an eternity.

He had learned a lot since then, about himself, and about other things.

He had learned he would never rise in the Body Purified. By the teachings he had accepted all his life, or at least given lip service to, he wasn't even fully human: he was a clone, an abomination, a subhuman monster with no right and no place in the assembly of God.

Chris Keating thought Richard had engineered everything that had happened to gain prestige and power back on Earth. But even if he had carried out the bizarre scheme Chris had concocted in his Avatar-addled brain, even if he had carried out such a scheme and it had *worked,* he could never have prestige and power because of who—what—he was.

He glanced at Emily. But he had learned something else. He'd learned that the abominations and subhuman monsters he had come to help destroy were, like himself, neither: they were just people, maybe people who looked different and even thought different, but people. Good people, bad people, indifferent people.

Monsters and abominations acted according to their character, like wild animals. The Avatar had proclaimed that moddies must be destroyed because their very existence offended God Itself: they were imperfect copies of God's perfect creation, corruptions of God's Holy Human Genome.

But unlike animals, people—even different-looking people—could *choose* their course of action. They could choose to do evil . . . or choose to do good. They could kill, or heal. Hinder, or help. Stand by and do nothing . . . or take a chance, and act.

Richard had chosen a course of action on Earth. He had chosen to fight back against what he saw as the unjust treatment of his father and himself, to take a chance and attempt to prove his worth to the Body Purified with a great deed, like a prince in some old fairy tale. He had chosen to set the Holy Warriors on the path to Marseguro.

But discovering the monsters of Marseguro were no more monstrous than himself, that they were simply a different kind of people, had left him with another choice: to help them, or let the Holy Warriors keep hurting them.

Thinking back, he thought he might have made his choice without realizing it when he saw the little Selkie girl in the cage with her mother at the Hansen's Harbor pier. Or maybe he had made it when Emily had helped him escape the hunterbot. Or perhaps he had made it when he suddenly found himself on the other side of the equation, when Grand Deacon Ellers had ordered him locked up, not because he had done anything against the Holy Warriors, but simply because he was a clone.

Maybe it had taken all of those things together to turn him around.

Or maybe none of them had turned him around; maybe the part of his brain rewired by Victor Hansen had turned him around, in which case, maybe his decision hadn't been his decision at all, but an echo of the decision his "grandfather" had made half a century ago when he decided to create a new race of humans.

No, he thought. *I don't buy that. So what if he rewired a portion of my brain? We rewire our brains all the time, through what we think and feel and experience. I am what I am. My mind is my mind. However I reached my decision, it is my decision.*

That it had been the right decision, he had no doubt, and though it had led irrevocably to this point, he wouldn't have changed it even if he could.

He looked at Emily again. She had made her own irrevocable decision when she chose to accompany him into space. If she had chosen otherwise, he had to admit, he would already have been dead several times over. She'd helped him get this far. Now it was up to him to make good use of what she had won for him.

His feeling toward her remained tender . . . but confused. He suspected—hoped—she had similar feelings toward him.

He hoped they would still get the chance to discover where those feelings might lead.

He suspected they would not.

He spoke at last, surprising himself with the steadiness of his voice. "Computer. Confirm I am the only surviving member of the registered crew of *BPS Sanctification.*"

"Confirmed," said the computer. "All other crew members are deceased."

"Computer, transfer full command of this vessel to me, as ranking member of the crew."

"Security clearance required."

Again Richard reeled off the string of numbers and letters he had memorized during the trip to Marseguro.

"Clearance sufficient," the computer said. "Mr. Hansen, the ship is yours." The traditional phrase sounded odd coming from a talking machine.

"Computer," said Richard, "Course change. De-orbit ship for impact in the ocean, minimum distance from land two hundred kilometers." That should be far enough away to prevent radioactive or chemical contamination, and near enough that the Marseguroites could salvage valuable resources from the wreck.

"Cannot comply," said the computer.

Richard felt cold. *No!* He couldn't have come this far, made the final decision, only to be forced to ride out the destruction of the entire population of Marseguro while watching helplessly from the bridge of the very ship carrying out that destruction. "Computer, explain!"

"Stated course is tantamount to self-destruction," the computer said calmly. "Self-destruct commands can only be issued by officers of Grand Deacon rank or higher."

Damn! Richard thought quickly. "Computer," he said. "Program quickest and most effective course to halt use of Orbital Bombardment System."

"Done," said the computer.

"Computer, execute new course."

"Course executed," said the computer.

Richard didn't bother asking what the new course *was*. It didn't matter. "Computer, will new course prevent operation of Orbital Bombardment System before ship reaches coordinates for maximum-damage launch against Hansen's Harbor?"

"Negative."

Richard closed his eyes. "Computer," he said. "Is there a weapons locker on the bridge?"

"Affirmative."

"Computer, open bridge weapons locker."

A panel slid open in the wall beside the bridge door. Richard darted to the newly opened compartment and peered inside. Laser pistols, laser rifles, slug throwers, automatic rifles, a sniper rifle—an impressive arsenal, but not what Richard . . . there! A rack of grenades.

"Computer, explain operation of grenades found in bridge weapons locker."

"Press red button to arm. Press green button before throwing. Use LED panel and associated buttons to set delay between pressing of green button and detonation, range zero to six hundred seconds."

He didn't have time for that. "Computer, what is the default delay on these grenades?"

"Three seconds."

Good enough. The grenades hung on an equipment belt, but he couldn't possibly strap it on with only one good arm. Instead, he slung it over his neck and chest like a bandolier.

Then his eye caught on something else: a pouch with a red circle on it, the Body's symbol for a first-aid kit. With his good hand, he opened it and found what he'd hoped: a hypospray full of general-purpose analgesic. Without hesitation he pressed it against the side of his neck. It felt like he'd sprayed needles of ice into his skin, but almost instantly the agony in his arm lessened. He unzipped the top of his jumpsuit and stuck his broken arm inside it, Napoleon-like. *Best I can do. Now . . .*

"Computer, locate Holy Warriors."

"All surviving Holy Warriors except one are returning to their shuttle."

"Computer, where is the one Holy Warrior who is not returning to the shuttle?"

"Outside Orbital Bombardment System control room," the computer said.

Might have guessed. "Computer, open bridge door."

The door opened. Richard gave Emily one last regretful glance, then darted out into the hallway and ran toward the OBS control room.

Emily's eyes fluttered open. Her heart had steadied, but she gasped as the pain in her leg registered. She didn't pass out again, though. She lifted herself on her elbows.

Richard had vanished. The bridge door stood open. Next to it, so did the door of a locker full of weapons. Inside the locker she could see an empty rack.

"Computer," Emily shouted, not even sure the ship would acknowledge her, "Where is Richard Hansen?"

It must have been programmed to answer nonsensitive requests for information from anyone, because it promptly responded, "Richard Hansen is approaching the Orbital Bombardment System control room."

"Computer, show me a map."

The main screen lit with a schematic of the habitat ring. A green line traced a path from the bridge through a half-dozen hatches and corridors to a room labeled "OBS Control." A red dot labeled "Acting Captain Richard Hansen" (*Acting Captain?*) was approaching the room.

Another red dot, labeled "Unknown Holy Warrior" waited for him.

Emily struggled to her feet, yelping involuntarily as she put weight on her leg. She limped to the weapons cabinet, grabbed a laser pistol to shoot and an automatic rifle to use for a crutch, then set off at a reasonably rapid hobble after Richard Hansen.

Saving his life has gotten to be a habit. I don't see any reason to break it now.

As he approached the OBS control room, Richard slowed, even though his internal clock screamed at him to hurry. With one corner to go, he got down awkwardly on his knees, then his belly, and wormed his way to where he could peer around it.

A Holy Warrior crouched in an opening in the deck plates just in front of the OBS control room door, his rifle resting on the deck, his head barely showing—which put him at eye-level with Richard. Their eyes met. For an instant they stared at each other, then Richard realized what was about to happen and scooted backward.

Bullets spattered against the far side of the corridor and ricocheted off the floor right where his head had been a second before.

In the echoing silence after the burst of rifle fire, Richard heard the Holy Warrior cough.

He's not wearing his pressure suit. The plague's got him.

Maybe that would make it easier to do what he had to do. Richard reached for one of the grenades he'd brought with him . . .

"Let's try something else first," said a voice.

Richard's heart thumped hard. "Good thing I didn't already have one in my hand," he said, turning his head to look at Emily. She leaned against the wall, a rifle in her left hand serving as an impromptu crutch, a laser pistol in her right. "Are you trying to scare me to death?"

"Sorry," Emily said. "You're just lucky I'm not a Holy Warrior."

"Unfortunately, he *is*." Richard nodded toward the corner. "The last one left on board, or will be soon. And he's settled in right where we need to get to if we're going to keep Cheveldeoff from turning Hansen's Harbor into a glowing crater sometime in the next five or six minutes. If that isn't a time for grenades, I don't know what is. One to take care of the Holy Warrior, another one in that hole he's standing in to break the shunt they must have hardwired in to take *Sanctification*'s computer out of the control loop."

"That's your plan? Throw a grenade into the hole and hope for the best?"

"It's all the plan I've got time for," Richard said. "And it's *your* bloody city I'm trying to save."

"We need an expert to return control to *Sanctification*," Emily said. "He's our expert. He must be the one who wired it. Why else would he be out of his pressure suit?"

"Why should he help us?"

"He's *out of his pressure suit*," Emily repeated. "He's infected."

"All the more reason for him to fight to the death. I say we take him up on it. We'll just be putting him out of his misery." Richard stopped. He couldn't believe he was talking about murdering a human being in such cold terms, but the ethical calculus seemed clear, though brutal.

"Give me two minutes," Emily said. "If I can't persuade him to help us, then it's bombs away."

We may not have two minutes, Richard thought, but

Emily had a point—a strong point. Just throwing a grenade into the works might or might not break the shunt. And if it didn't, there would be no second chance.

And there was one other thing, a small thing, maybe, but it tipped the balance.

He was sick of killing.

"Go ahead," he said. "Two minutes."

Emily had come down to the OBS control room expecting to help Richard kill the Holy Warrior and retake control of the weapons threatening Hansen's Harbor . . . and, after that, she was certain, every other town and identifiable habitat on the planet until her people and the landlings who had helped them were wiped from the face of the universe.

She understood the stakes. But when she realized only one unsuited-and-therefore-infected Holy Warrior held down the fort, she also realized there might be a better way than brute force to solve the problem.

Now that Richard had agreed, she had to deliver.

She limped to the corner. "Holy Warrior," she shouted. "Can you hear me?"

A long silence, then, "I can hear you." The man's voice sounded ragged and hoarse, and he coughed again after speaking.

"What's your name?"

"O'Sullivan. What's it to you?"

"My name is Emily." No answer. "How are you feeling?"

A ragged laugh. "Like hell. Looks like this really is a plague ship, after all. You'll be sick soon enough."

"No, I won't. I'm immune." Emily paused. "And I have a vaccine."

Another long silence, but even across several meters, Emily could hear the Holy Warrior's strained breathing, the struggle to draw air through swollen bronchial tubes into lungs already beginning to fill with fluid. "You're lying," he said finally. "There isn't any vaccine. If you're immune, it's because you're a moddie."

Emily glanced at Richard, who nodded.

"She's not lying," he shouted. "Holy Warrior, this is Richard Hansen speaking. You know who I am."

"You're a bloody traitor," the Holy Warrior snarled. "I know that much."

"But I'm not a moddie. I'm a normal—" he shot a look at Emily, as though to apologize, "—human being, like you. And I'm not sick, even though I've been breathing the infected air of this ship as long as you have. That's because I've had the vaccine."

Which isn't strictly true, of course, Emily thought, *but . . .*

"Doesn't change the fact you're a traitor," the Holy Warrior mumbled.

"Did you *plan* to stay behind here, O'Sullivan?" Emily shouted. "When they told you to take off your suit, did they tell you you'd be stuck here?"

"Just until quarantine was over," O'Sullivan said. "Unless I got sick." He coughed again. "And I got sick." He frowned. "After the others left. They don't know. I've got to tell—"

"Cheveldeoff gave orders to leave you here to die," Richard shouted. "You could have been quarantined in the shuttle. You could have been put into isolation and treated. But this way Cheveldeoff could use you, use you to ensure we didn't manage to disconnect the command shunt you've installed. I know Cheveldeoff. I worked with him. He's good at using people, O'Sullivan."

"So I die," O'Sullivan said. "At least I die with honor, serving the Body Purified."

"You die a mass murderer, O'Sullivan," Richard said. His eyes blazed, and he seemed to have forgotten talking to the Holy Warrior was Emily's idea. Emily gladly let him take over. Richard understood the Holy Warriors and the Body Purified in a way she doubted she ever could. "Cheveldeoff is going to hit Hansen's Harbor with a maximum-impact OBS strike in the next couple of minutes if we don't stop it. Thousands will die."

"Moddies and their sympathizers," O'Sullivan said.

"Women and children. Young men. Girls. Old men. Grandmothers. Babies. Toddlers. Schoolchildren," Richard said. "Struck down from heaven, just like Earth would have been if not for the Miracle. But that was God's judgment. This is man's. This is Cheveldeoff's—and yours, because you can put a stop to it.

"It's God's right to destroy us like an artist erasing a mistake. But It doesn't need men for that. It doesn't need fallible men like you, or evil men like Cheveldeoff, or . . . whatever kind of man I am. The God who sent Its Hammer against the World, and chose at the last minute to push it aside, does not need human hands to carry out Its punishments.

"So if you choose to let those people on Marseguro live, O'Sullivan—and if you choose to live yourself—you aren't acting against God. You're just acting against Cheveldeoff.

"You know the stories about him, what he's capable of. Is acting against him really such a bad thing? Especially when it means you get to live yourself?"

Silence. Emily gripped her rifle, and saw Richard's hand close over the grenade again. *No time,* she thought. "On my mark," Richard whispered. "Five . . . four . . . three . . ."

An inarticulate cry came from around the corner, then a hammering sound, tearing sounds, and finally a flash of light. Emily exchanged a look with Richard, then both of them peered around the corner.

White smoke hung under the ceiling, hazing the blue-white lights. O'Sullivan, coughing, blood dripping from his nose, tossed his rifle across the floor at them and crawled out onto the decking. "Cheveldeoff can go to hell, if the Devil will have him," he said. "And if God wants to kill you all, let It do it Itself." He wiped his nose with his sleeve, looked at the blood on it and said, "What was that about a vaccine?"

They'd decided back on Marseguro that Emily should bring several doses of vaccine just in case they found nonmods still alive on *Sanctification.* Emily unzipped a pocket on her landsuit and pulled out a hypospray. "Right here, O'Sullivan," she said. "Right here."

"Good for you, O'Sullivan," Richard said. He'd managed to leverage himself off the floor with his one good arm and stood leaning against the bulkhead, face pale.

O'Sullivan looked at him, then spat blood on the floor at his feet. "You're still a bloody traitor."

"I can live with that," Richard said. A deep, throbbing gong sound suddenly reverberated through the ship. Richard's eyes widened. "Uh-oh," he said. "I think I'd better get back to the bridge."

He turned and disappeared back down the corridor toward the bridge, leaving his belt of grenades behind.

"Now what?" Emily called after him, but got no answer.

O'Sullivan rubbed the place on her arm where she had sprayed him with the vaccine. "Atmosphere warning," he said. "We're falling out of orbit." He snorted. "Looks like your vaccine may have been wasted, moddie."

"The name's Emily," she snapped.

O'Sullivan opened his mouth to say something else, then closed it and looked down at the deck plates. "Emily," he said. "Um . . . thank you. I've seen how the *Sanctification* crew died. I . . . wouldn't want to go like that. I'd rather die burning up in the atmosphere."

"I'd rather not die at all," Emily said. She put out an arm. "Let's get to the bridge. Maybe we can help."

O'Sullivan hesitated, then took her arm. "All right," he said. "Guess I've made my bed. Might as well lie in it."

"That's the spirit," Emily said dryly. "Come on."

Calm and certain, Cheveldeoff watched the tactical display as the minutes ticked down to the moment when *Retribution*'s computer would issue the order that would send half a ton of ceramic-tungsten alloy slamming into the heart of Hansen's Harbor at forty thousand kilometers an hour. The shuttle carrying the salvage party had cleared *Sanctification* and would be docking with

Retribution—in an unpressurized hold, with the crew destined for indefinite quarantine—within an hour. *Sanctification* continued to lose altitude, but *Retribution*'s computer assured him that the course change would be insufficient to prevent a devastating attack. With Hansen's Harbor and its stock of weapons and ammunition taken from *Sanctification*'s dead Holy Warriors vaporized, Cheveldeoff's remaining troops could quickly reduce the smaller population centers and underwater habitats, even if *Sanctification* burned up in the atmosphere and prevented any further use of the OBS.

The time to launch slipped to under a minute . . . under thirty seconds . . . twenty . . . ten . . . five, four, three, two, one . . .

Nothing happened.

Cheveldeoff felt as though a trapdoor had opened under his feet.

Nothing happened!

"Launch command issued," the computer said without prompting. "No response from *Sanctification*. Orbital Bombardment System not under this computer's control. Probable cause: hardware failure of shunt mechanism."

"Computer, reissue command!"

"Command reissued." A pause. "No response. Analysis unchanged."

Cheveldeoff's hands clenched into fists. "Grand Deacon!" Braun stood on the opposite side of the tactical display from him, consciously or unconsciously keeping the maximum distance between them. "I heard," he said.

"Well, *do* something about it!"

Braun hadn't let a readable expression cross his face in his conversations with Cheveldeoff since their confrontation in the briefing room, but Cheveldeoff could well imagine the glee boiling merrily beneath that bland exterior. *The bastard loves to see me fail. Well, he won't be laughing soon.* Cheveldeoff scratched the right side of his nose. The Holy Warrior at the communications console casually got to his feet and moved one console over, bending over it. He pulled out a keyboard and began to type.

"I'm open to suggestions . . . sir," Braun said.

"Are you?" Cheveldeoff resisted the urge to "suggest" that Braun do something anatomically improbable with a laser pistol. "What I *suggest*, Grand Deacon, is that you prepare to execute our main invasion plan."

Braun's eyes narrowed. "Sir?"

"You heard me. Their only weapons are in Hansen's Harbor. We'll land inland, and take the smaller centers first. Then we'll strangle Hansen's Harbor at our leisure."

"Fighting in pressure suits, sir? The plague . . ."

"You will fight naked if I order you to, Grand Deacon," Cheveldeoff snarled. "This planet *will* be Purified. You *will* make that happen. Do I make myself clear?"

A long moment of silence as the Grand Deacon stared at him, his face unreadable. Then, "Yes, sir," Braun said. "I will call a briefing of the subcommanders for one hour from now."

"Good idea," Cheveldeoff said icily. "Just do your job, Grand Deacon. That's all I ask." *Because it sure as hell won't be your job for long.*

The Grand Deacon inclined his head slightly, then spun on his heel and left the bridge.

Cheveldeoff turned back to the tactical display. He glanced at his agent, who had returned to his usual post. Cheveldeoff smiled. He had his own briefing to conduct before the subcommanders met: every man on the ship he knew to be loyal to him had been warned to expect orders within the next hour.

But vital as those orders were, giving them could wait. "Computer, visual of *Sanctification*." The ship appeared, wrapped in an orange borealis as she encountered the outermost wisps of atmosphere. "Still there, Mr. Hansen?" Cheveldeoff growled under his breath. "At least I'll have the pleasure of watching you burn."

He crossed his arms and waited for the end.

Chapter 22

RICHARD KNEW IT MUST be his imagination, but he couldn't help feeling the temperature inside *Sanctification* had already gone up a couple of degrees by the time he reached the bridge. "Computer," he shouted as he entered, "situation report."

"*Sanctification* has entered atmosphere," the computer said. Its usual lack of inflection, no doubt meant to reassure, infuriated in these circumstances.

"Why?"

No answer.

I didn't say "Mother, may I," Richard thought. *Calm down and concentrate.* "Computer, why has *Sanctification* entered atmosphere?"

"*Sanctification* is following the orders of Acting Captain Richard Hansen."

Following orders . . . ? I didn't . . .

Or did I?

"Computer, restate last order."

"Execute quickest and most effective course to halt use of Orbital Bombardment System."

"Computer, does this course take us into the atmosphere?"

"Affirmative."

But . . .

"Computer, you previously indicated you could not self-destruct on my order!" Behind him, Emily entered the bridge, leaning on the arm of the still-very-sick-looking Holy Warrior, although his nosebleed seemed to have stopped.

"Affirmative."

"Then why . . ." *That won't work.* "Computer, explain why you are driving *Sanctification* into the atmosphere if you cannot self-destruct."

"Non sequitur," the computer said. "Prohibition against self-destruction does not prevent entry into atmosphere."

I'm wasting time. "Computer, change course. Lift out of atmosphere."

"Unable to comply."

"Computer . . . !"

Clarity came from an unexpected source.

"It's the emergency landing protocol," croaked the Holy Warrior.

Richard stared at him. "The what?"

"Emergency landing protocol. These ships have an automated landing system. They're too expensive to just throw away—that's why they won't self-destruct. But as a last resort a captain can order them to land themselves."

"Without a spaceport?" Richard said. "Without a landing cradle?"

"I told you, it's a last resort," the Holy Warrior said. "The landing site has to be carefully chosen. If it's not within a very few degrees of perfectly level, or if it's too rough, the struts will collapse and the ship will roll. And possibly blow up," he added helpfully.

"Computer!" Richard called. "Are you executing the emergency landing protocol?"

"Affirmative."

"Computer, can you abort it?"

"Negative," said the computer. "Once initiated, emergency landing protocol passes out of control of the computer."

"That's in case the central computer has been 'killed' along with most of the crew," said the Holy Warrior, who was beginning to get on Richard's nerves.

"You seem to know a lot about it," Richard growled at him. "Got any sage advice for the Acting Captain?"

"Sure." O'Sullivan coughed, then grinned. "Hold on. The emergency landing protocol doesn't really take into account the possibility that there might be anyone aboard left alive. Things could get a little rough."

"Hold on," O'Sullivan had said, and Emily did her best, strapping herself into one of the empty crew chairs that ringed the cylindrical "tank" of the tactical display. "Things could get a little rough," he'd added.

That proved to be a miracle of understatement. They'd barely strapped themselves in before they found that out.

"Rotation ending . . . now," the computer announced.

Emily's body pressed painfully into the straps that held her into the crew chair as the rotating section of the hull—moving at about 100 kilometers per hour where they were—braked hard into motionlessness relative to the rest of the hull. Richard groaned as the straps cut into his broken arm, and O'Sullivan started coughing again.

But the rough part had just begun.

The ship shuddered and bucked, throwing them up and sideways, crushing them under multiple Gs, hanging them upside down in their straps as the floor suddenly became the ceiling. The temperature climbed and kept on climbing, overwhelming the cooling mechanisms of Emily's landsuit, strained by the loss of water when the laser cut her leg, until she felt she might be boiled alive like a crustacean in a pot. She risked a broken neck by shooting a look at her companions. Both had their eyes closed. Fresh blood streaked O'Sullivan's face—his nosebleed had started up again. Richard's head rolled loosely from side to side. Sweat glistened on his white face and plastered his hair to his forehead.

The buffeting went on and on, accompanied by a deafening roar, like the wind of the worst storm Emily had ever experienced multiplied a hundredfold.

A particularly hard jolt broke loose an equipment cabinet. It careened across the floor, smashing into other cabinets. A sudden drop hurled it into the air; it crashed down with killing force just centimeters from Richard's head.

Richard didn't flinch.

Emily closed her eyes and wished she were unconscious, too.

The roaring changed pitch, lessened . . . then redoubled with a new bass note she hadn't heard before . . . and then . . .

. . . stopped.

So did the buffeting.

The ship creaked and groaned. The floor began to slant. The wayward cabinet slid another meter and fetched up against the base of the tactical display. Emily waited for the ship to roll, as O'Sullivan had warned it might . . .

. . . but the slanting stopped, the creaking and groaning diminished to just an occasional pop—and then the floor moved again, leveling out.

"Emergency Landing Protocol completed," said the computer. "Ship condition: good. Relaunch capability: intact. Minor interior damage. Bridge and other gimbaled rooms reoriented to local gravity. Detailed report available upon request. Awaiting further orders."

Emily felt like an enthusiastic sadist had beaten every square centimeter of her body with a grappling hook, but she forced herself to unbuckle and swing her legs over the side. To her left, O'Sullivan groaned, but she ignored him, instead pulling herself upright and then lurching, almost falling, against Richard's chair. "Richard," she croaked, then summoned up more breath and more energy and said, "Richard!"

His eyes fluttered, opened, closed . . . then opened again, and this time focused. "Emily?" He blinked. "Wait. We're . . . we made it?"

"Down in one piece," she said. "I don't know where . . . but if it's solid ground, we can't be too far from Hansen's Harbor."

"Help me . . . help me sit up." Emily unbuckled him and pulled him to a sitting position. He slumped for a moment, eyes closed, then opened them and said, "Computer. How far are we from Hansen's Harbor?"

"Sixty-nine kilometers," said the computer.

"Computer, external cameras."

The tactical display tank flickered, then displayed a view of the surrounding area. Richard blinked. "What's that cylinder thing . . . ?"

Emily looked and laughed. "I should have guessed," she said. "Sixty-nine kilometers . . . we're in Landing Valley." She pointed. "That's all that's left of the *Rivers of Babylon.* And that low building next to it is the Landing Valley Museum."

"We've set down by the *Rivers of Babylon*?" Richard laughed. The laugh turned into a wincing cough, then he managed to compose himself. "The best landing site then and now." He frowned. "But sixty-nine kilometers? Computer! Activate radio communications." He looked around. "Activate manual controls at bridge communications station."

"Ready," said the computer.

Richard, broken arm still slung inside his jumpsuit, hobbled over to one of the bridge stations and began awkwardly typing with his remaining hand. "I'm connecting to the secure comm network I set up for the Council," he explained as he did so. "At least, I hope I am . . . yes!" He cleared his throat, then pressed a button. "This is Richard Hansen aboard *BPS Sanctification,*" he said clearly. "Emily is here, too, and . . ." he glanced at O'Sullivan, who had managed to get himself into a sitting position, ". . . a guest. Chris Keating may be on board somewhere, too."

Chris! Emily had forgotten about him. *If he didn't strap himself in when the atmosphere warning started to sound, he's probably just a pulp at the back of the central shaft.* She couldn't work up much sympathy at the thought.

Richard was still talking. ". . . need armed reinforcements here ASAP. Also any qualified air pilots you can scrape together. I doubt Cheveldeoff expected us to make it down in one piece, but it won't take him long to come after us now we're here. And if he gets here first . . ."

Emily glanced at the still-open weapons cabinet by the door. *The whole ship is crammed with weapons,* she realized. *If Cheveldeoff gets them—especially those assault craft, if they're still intact—it's game over, despite everything.*

But if our people get here first . . .

She grinned. Then the Holy Warriors would be marching into the teeth of people armed, armored, and unencumbered by pressure suits—and with a lot of incentive to win.

She thought of Cheveldeoff targeting Hansen's Harbor, of the havoc wrought there by *Sanctification*'s own Holy Warriors, and her grin turned into something much fiercer and much less amused.

A *lot* of incentive.

"No, sir, I don't know how a desk clerk like Richard Hansen managed to activate *Sanctification*'s Emergency Landing Protocol," Grand Deacon Braun said. "Perhaps he had help from the Holy Warrior you insisted I exile there."

Cheveldeoff, Braun, and the subcommanders of the Holy Warriors aboard *Retribution* stood around the oval table in the main briefing room. There were chairs, but Cheveldeoff had not asked anyone to sit down. The vidwall showed a still satellite photo of *Sanctification,* in one piece, on the ground in an inland valley near what appeared to be a single hull section from an antique starship—presumably *Rivers of Babylon.*

"Are you telling me the loyalty of your men is in question?" he said softly. "Because that loyalty is your ultimate responsibility, Grand Deacon. If you cannot vouch for it—"

"Loyalty is a two-way street, sir," Braun said. "I betrayed my loyalty to my men when I ordered that Corporal O'Sullivan be left behind with no evidence he was, in fact, infected with anything at all. I can hardly fault him for doing whatever he had to to survive."

Cheveldeoff stood very still. He had never heard the Grand Deacon skate so close to outright insubordination—hell, outright *mutiny* . . . and he had no illusions about his own hold over the subcommanders gathered in the room with them. He had given his orders to his loyalists throughout the ship. They were in position to seize all the key stations . . . but they would only do so on his order, and he had to get out of this room alive and able to communicate to give that order.

"I don't suppose we'll ever know the truth," Cheveldeoff said finally. "And whether you believe it or not, Grand Deacon, I regret the necessity of leaving Corporal O'Sullivan on board *Sanctification* as much as you.

"Let us set aside *how* Richard Hansen did it, and move on to what *we* are going to do to complete our mission. I take it your plans have changed with the successful landing of *Sanctification*."

Braun stood very still himself for a moment. Cheveldeoff could almost see him weighing the pros and cons of continuing down the path of mutiny against those of drawing in his horns and concentrating on the Purification of Marseguro. Success, after all, would wipe away all other concerns once they got home . . . or so he must have decided, because in the end he simply nodded and said, "They have. If the locals gain control of the armament on *Sanctification* before we do, especially the airpower shuttles, our position will become . . ."

The door slid open, and a Holy Warrior came in, dragging—

Cheveldeoff stared. The Holy Warrior was dragging a boy wearing tattered pajama bottoms and nothing else, a boy with a few wispy whiskers on his chin and a mat of tangled brown hair.

"Chris Keating?" Cheveldeoff said.

The Holy Warrior looked startled and relaxed his grip.

"We found him in the hallway outside," he said. "I don't know where—"

Keating pulled himself free and straightened up. "Mr. Cheveldeoff," he said, and strode forward, holding out his hand.

Cheveldeoff was so bemused he took it for a moment before snatching it back. "How the hell did you get on board?" he bellowed.

"Stowed away," said Chris. "Spare pressure suit, empty equipment locker. Good thing, too. I hear *Sanctification* made it down intact." He grinned. "Which is more than I would have if they had gotten me down there with it. But you're in luck. Here I am, and I can tell you what's what and who's who down there. To properly Purify that cesspool of a planet, Mr. Cheveldeoff, sir, you need me." His grin faded. "I don't think you've fully appreciated that. I don't think anyone has."

"Lock him up," Cheveldeoff growled, "Full quarantine." He looked around the room. "Proceed with your plans, Grand Deacon."

"The plague, sir?" Braun said.

Cheveldeoff wanted desperately to wash his hand, but he very carefully folded it behind his back with its mate instead. "What plague, Grand Deacon? Chris Keating himself told us it was a chemical attack that killed *Sanctification*'s crew, not anything biological. If that were not true, he would hardly have risked us all by coming here, would he?" Considering the little creep had just shaken his hand, he dearly hoped his logic held water.

"No, sir," said Braun.

"Carry on, then," said Cheveldeoff. "I'll be in my quarters. Report when you're ready to launch." He went out. *Braun backed down again. Maybe I'm overly concerned.*

Well, he'd keep his loyalists in position, just in case.

As he walked toward his quarters, Cheveldeoff cleared his throat, trying to get rid of an annoying tickle that had just started.

Too much talking, he thought. *I'd better rest my voice for a while.*

One small part of his brain, however, gathered a seed of panic to itself, planted it, and waited for it to grow.

The reinforcements from Hansen's Harbor arrived two hours after the message went out from the grounded *Sanctification.* By that time, Richard had a pretty good idea of the extent of damage to the ship, thanks partly to the computer but especially thanks to O'Sullivan, whose knowledge of the Holy Warrior vessel seemed encyclopedic, far exceeding what Richard had picked up in the few days he had spent on board. O'Sullivan obviously felt much better since receiving the vaccination. In fact, he'd become positively garrulous, showing them around the ship as if he owned it.

Parts of it, of course, they couldn't even get to. The bridge and other vital control rooms maintained proper orientation when the ship landed, but less important rooms were supposed to be secured for landing. With the crew dead, they hadn't been. The violent descent and just the fact half the rooms were sideways and a quarter completely upside down had played havoc with everything not nailed down.

Weapons and ammunition, however, were all properly stored and readily accessible. And the all-important air-attack shuttles had ridden out the descent in fine style, their gimbaled landing pads keeping them upright and ready for launch at a moment's notice. Richard suspected that just such a launch would be called for the minute they had pilots who could fly them . . . if anyone could. Until someone more qualified got a look at their controls, that was anybody's guess.

One room they found contained a docbot that made quick work of setting his arm and cleaning and sealing Emily's leg wound and pumping them both full of fast-heal—although it would also have pumped her full of drugs she didn't need that might have killed her if they hadn't been monitoring it closely: apparently her perfectly normal Selkie vital signs indicated to the docbot deathly illness.

Throughout the two hours, Richard wouldn't have

been surprised to see shuttles from *Retribution* dropping out of the sky. He didn't relax after the reinforcements from Hansen's Harbor showed up; they remained vulnerable until the weapons from *Sanctification* had been dispersed and the assault craft were either under Marseguroite control or disabled.

Eventually, he had to sleep, first giving strict orders (not that he had any particular right to issue orders, but somehow people kept doing what he said) to wake him if the Holy Warriors showed up or if they received any communication.

He slept well and long , . . too long. He checked and double-checked the time, then hurried into his clothes and out of the captain's cabin he had appropriated for his nap, out the nearest access hatch and down the ladder extruding from it to the ground.

"Why didn't you wake me?" he demanded of Council Chair Jeter, who had shown up with the first batch of reinforcements and stood watching crates being loaded onto a groundcar in the early morning light.

Jeter raised an eyebrow. "You said to wake you if something happened. Nothing happened."

That brought him up short. "Nothing?"

"Nothing untoward. It took all night, but we've dispersed almost all the weapons and ammunition. The pilots are still puzzling over some of the controls for the assault craft, but they're confident they can get them in the air if they have to, even if they can't use the weapons systems. But so far, we haven't heard or seen anything of the Holy Warriors." Jeter pointed to the First Landing storage cave in the steep red hillside a hundred meters away, where they'd set up headquarters. "Emily is in there with her mother. Dr. Christianson-Wood said she'd like to talk to you when you woke up."

"Uh . . . okay." Bemused, Richard trudged across the blackened near-grass covering the valley floor.

No sign of the Holy Warriors after more than twelve hours? Cheveldeoff couldn't have been fool enough to let a plague-infested shuttle on board his ship . . . could he?

The storage cave had been the colonists' first shelter. The Selkies had relied on the water tanks on the ship for their comfort and survival, while the landlings had lived in the cave. Very little natural rock remained exposed. Corridors and rooms had been carved out and lined with fast-setting-but-damn-ugly gray concrete. It felt exactly like what it was, a bunker providing shelter from a possibly hostile world.

Richard found Emily and her mother in the only room in the complex with a window, a small round portal camouflaged from the outside by an overhanging rock. Through a screen of near-grass stems, it provided an adequate if slightly obscured view of *Sanctification* and the people bustling around it.

Dr. Christianson-Wood, wearing a plain white landsuit, stood looking out that window as he entered. The rooms had long ago been stripped of their original furnishings, but someone had moved in a folding table and chairs, and judging by the empty food and drink containers piled in an old cargo crate in one corner, people had been taking their breaks here. Emily sat at the table, wearing an electric-blue landsuit with green lightning bolts slashing down the sides. He'd gotten so used to seeing her in black that the bright colors startled him.

"You wanted to see me, Dr. Christianson-Wood?" Richard said. "Hi, Emily. Get some sleep?"

"Not as much as you," she said. "But some." She nodded at her mother. "We've been talking, mostly."

Dr. Christianson-Wood turned from the window and faced him. "We've been talking about what we should do next," she said quietly. "Because we can't stay here."

Richard opened his mouth; closed it again. He'd been so focused on the here and now that he hadn't looked any further down the road. But of course she was right. Even if the Holy Warriors aboard *Retribution* decided not to attack—and now that the Marseguroites had the weapons and assault craft from *Sanctification,* it would be suicide—they'd only bought a temporary reprieve. Cheveldeoff would head back to Earth, and return with however many ships he needed to purify Marseguro—purify it right down to bare and glowing bedrock.

He won't bother with Holy Warriors next time. It will be orbital bombardment from the beginning, and likely with nuclear weapons. "You're thinking of evacuating on *Sanctification*?" he said quietly.

"That's what I'm thinking." Dr. Christianson-Wood shook her head. "But it won't carry the entire population. Not even close. And anyone who is left behind . . ."

"Hidden habitats," Richard said. "New ones, stealthed so they can't be detected from orbit. Move the population into the deep oceans. Send out *Sanctification* for help."

"Who will help us?" Dr. Christianson-Wood said. Her gill slits flared, pink, gaping mouths on her neck, and her oversized eyes opened wide. "Who will help us against the Body Purified? Against Earth?" She glared at him, then relaxed. "No one, that's who. Fifty Earth years ago, at least, even the colonies that opposed the Body Purified barely tolerated moddies. Has that changed?"

Richard had to shake his head. "No."

"Then all we can do is hide." She sighed. "I did the best I could, with my nasty little plague. But in the end . . ." Her shoulders slumped. "I killed all those people . . . became a mass murderer . . . for nothing."

"*Not* for nothing," Emily snapped. "We've been over this. For *survival.*"

"But we still may not survive," Dr. Christianson-Wood said. "Certainly many of us won't."

"But many will," Richard said. He understood Dr. Christianson-Wood's pain because it matched his own, the pain locked down deep where he'd also tried to bury the unassuageable guilt of the agony he had brought to this planet and its people. "Many will survive on *Sanctification*. The ship recognizes me as Acting Captain, and O'Sullivan has the technical know-how we need. She came down in good shape. We can get her back into space. And she can carry hundreds, even if she can't carry everyone. The Selkies will survive. I'll see to it.

They're . . ." His voice trailed off. He'd just realized that he was echoing, almost word for word, what Victor Hansen had said before the *Rivers of Babylon* headed into space from Luna fifty Earth and forty Marseguro years before, ultimately ending up in the broad, flat valley bottom right outside the window. *Well, why not? I am Victor Hansen, or at least part of me is.*

"We'll have to decide who gets to go, and who stays," Dr. Christianson-Wood said. "It won't be easy."

"No, it won't," Richard said.

"It may be easier than you think," Emily said. She stood up. "I won't go, for example."

Both Richard and Dr. Christianson-Wood jerked their heads toward her. "Yes, you will," said Dr. Christianson-Wood.

You tell her! Richard thought.

"No, I won't." Emily came over to her mother. "You asked me, back before this all started, what I was going to do with my life. You didn't want me wasting it on something frivolous when so much work remained building Marseguro, expanding our presence here. Well, in the past few weeks I've learned you . . . and Daddy . . . were right. I've fought . . . I've *killed* . . . so Marseguro will survive, Mother. I'm not going to run out on her now."

"But if you're on *Sanctification,* we can find a new planet. A new world to build," Richard said. "For the Selkies . . ." *And I don't want to leave you behind!* But he couldn't say that.

Not yet.

Especially not with her mother standing right there.

"This planet is my home," Emily said. "I won't let it be destroyed without a fight. We have the shuttles. We have the know-how to make planet-to-orbit missiles, smart bullets, dumb dust, even missile interceptors."

"But you may not have time to—"

"But we may," Emily said. "You didn't think we even had time to take the weapons off of *Sanctification.* But where are the Holy Warriors?"

As if on cue, a young man burst into the room. "Transmission coming in," he gasped. "For you, Mr. Hansen."

Richard glanced from Dr. Christianson-Wood to Emily. "I guess we're about to find out." He turned to the young man. "I'm right behind you," he said, and followed him out of the cave.

Chapter 23

*L*OCKED UP AGAIN, Chris Keating thought gloomily, sitting in the brig of *Retribution*. On the plus side, at least they'd given him proper clothes—a blue Holy Warrior jumpsuit and shoes. Until they had, he'd begun to think he'd never be warm again. The pressure suit he'd donned in the shuttle locker must have had heaters on it, but he hadn't known how to raise them from what must have been a minimal default setting, and he'd felt like a walking iceberg by the time the shuttle had docked with *Retribution*.

He'd almost hidden in the locker without the suit. If he had, he would have been dead the instant they'd left *Sanctification*, because shortly after launch they'd blown out the atmosphere. He'd expected them to repressurize at some point, but they never did. And when he finally dared to exit the locker and peer out of the shuttle after they reached *Retribution*, he'd found it locked down in an unpressurized bay, Marseguro swimming in space outside the open hatch.

What had happened to the crew, he had no idea. He'd found an air lock, cycled through, and stripped off his pressure suit without seeing anyone.

Retribution felt much smaller than *Sanctification*, but had a similar layout. Chris had avoided the open central shaft and made his way toward the bow through secondary passageways. He'd been nabbed, not trying to get into the briefing room as the guard seemed to think, but trying to get to the bridge. It didn't matter; his real goal was Cheveldeoff, and lo and behold, he'd finally met the Archdeacon face-to-face, shaken his hand, offered his help . . .

. . . and had been cooling his heels in here ever since.

A sound brought him upright, an unmistakable sound with no place on a spaceship:

Gunfire.

More shots, and the distant thump of an explosion. Running footsteps outside the door, passing without slowing. Vibrations. More noises. A hint of shouting voices . . .

What's going on?

A particularly loud bang rang his cell like a gong. The normal lighting flickered, went out, and gave way to the sickly green glow of emergency lights . . . and his door unlocked itself and slid open.

Chris peered out. The brig cells all opened into a central area with a circular desk at which the guard on duty passed his time. But no one sat there now. All the other cells stood open and empty.

Another rattle of rifle fire.

Feeling more naked than he had when he'd been running around in nothing but pajama bottoms, Chris crept out into the open and headed for the sound of fighting.

The first burst of gunfire brought Cheveldeoff to his feet behind the desk in his quarters, laser pistol in his hand. He held his breath, and listened.

More shots. A few shouts.

"Computer, status report," he said.

"You are not authorized to issue commands to this unit," said the computer.

What?

He slapped at the comm button on his desk. "Bridge, this is Cheveldeoff. What's going on?"

No answer.

Cheveldeoff coughed. The damn tickle had turned into a scratch and now a raging sore throat. He felt something trickle from one nostril, and brushed at his nose with the back of his free hand.

It came away red.

What the hell . . . ?

The part of his mind nurturing the seed of panic let it bloom. *Plague! Keating lied. He's a carrier!*

I have to get to the sick bay . . .

Gripping the pistol, he opened the door to his quarters . . .

. . . to find the Holy Warrior he'd last seen manning the communications console on the bridge—Greist, that was his name—just reaching out to open the door from the other side.

Two other Holy Warriors Cheveldeoff recognized as part of the loyal contingent that he'd managed to get assigned to the mission stood behind Greist. "Braun twigged," Greist said without preamble. "There are running battles all over the ship for all the key positions we'd lined up. We're holding engineering and the shuttle bays, but Braun still has the bridge. We've been working on the crew since we launched, but Braun still has the edge in manpower." He coughed. "What's left of it. People are getting sick, sir, all over the ship."

"Damn," Cheveldeoff said. His throat felt like sandpaper, and he wheezed when he drew a breath. "Keating brought it on board. Whatever killed *Sanctification*'s crew and the Warriors on the ground. We've got to get to sick bay. There must be something they can do."

Greist shook his head. A tiny ruby drop flew from one of his nostrils and landed on Cheveldeoff's cheek; he wiped it away. "Braun's men hold sick bay."

"Then I've got to talk to Braun," Cheveldeoff said. "We need a comm channel to the bridge. He's killed my computer privileges, but he has to be getting reports from key stations."

"The brig is closest," one of the Holy Warriors said. "There should be a comm station there with manual controls."

Cheveldeoff nodded, his throat so raw the motion felt

like he'd swallowed glass. He wiped more blood from his nose. "Let's go," he said. "I don't think any of us have much time."

The brig stood open. All the cells were empty. "Didn't we put Keating down here?" Cheveldeoff said.

"Looks like something blew the security circuits," Greist said. "Keating must have run for it." He sat down at the desk. "Comm channels work." He looked up. "I can put you through to the bridge."

"Do it." Cheveldeoff cleared his throat, but it didn't really help; it still felt like ground glass and sandpaper.

"Bridge," a voice said tersely—Braun's voice.

"Braun, it's Cheveldeoff."

Silence for a moment. "Your plan has failed, Cheveldeoff. I knew you intended to take the ship. I moved first. You've only got a couple of key stations. You can't get any more. Tell your men to stand down."

I don't have time for this, Cheveldeoff thought. The panic had bloomed and spread and now threatened to choke off all reason. "How many of your men are sick?" he snapped.

Another pause. "I don't know what you mean."

"Braun, Keating lied. There's no poison. It's a plague, and he brought it on board this ship when he stowed away on the shuttle. It's the same plague that killed *Sanctification*'s men. It will kill all of us if we don't . . ."

"If this is some kind of ploy . . ."

"How many of your men are sick?" Cheveldeoff demanded again.

A very long pause, this time. "A lot," Braun said finally.

"You."

Pause. "Yes."

"Braun, I surrender," Cheveldeoff said, ignoring the sudden, startled stares from Greist and his men. "Give me computer control, and I'll put an end to the fighting. If any of us are going to survive, we need access to—"

"Shit!" Greist swore.

Gunfire. Cheveldeoff ducked behind the desk, but not

before a spray of blood and bits of bone and meat spattered his upper body. Which of his men it had come from, he had no idea.

All three, he discovered when he raised his head. Greist and both of the others lay dead, slumped against the console. The back side of it had been as shattered by gunfire as their bodies. Wires sparked and smoked. An alarm suddenly shrilled.

"Braun?" Cheveldeoff said. He coughed. "Braun!"

No answer.

"Braun, we have to—"

The door into the corridor slammed shut. The doors into each of the cells followed an instant later.

"Security breach detected," said the computer. "Brig is locked down."

"Computer!" Cheveldeoff yelled. "Open brig doors."

"You are not authorized to control this system."

"Dammit, computer—" a fit of coughing choked off his voice. He covered his mouth with his right hand.

"You are not authorized to control this system."

Cheveldeoff pulled his hand away, The blood staining it hadn't come from his slaughtered men.

He couldn't stop coughing. His chest felt on fire. He couldn't catch his breath. And every cough sprayed scarlet across the floor.

His gut twisted, then burned, then spasmed with a pain so sharp he might have been stabbed. He doubled over, retching now mingling with the coughing. So much blood . . . he didn't even know he *had* that much blood.

Then: pain. Pain such as he'd never known, pain such as he'd never imagined, though he'd imagined a lot of pain in his life, mostly inflicted on others.

He screamed, then, or tried to, but he had little voice left, and the scream died in the final twisting, retching spasm that tore through his guts. His insides seemed to be trying to hurl themselves from his mouth. He had no choice but to stretch his jaw, as wide as he could . . .

As black-flecked blood spewed across the cold metal floor of the brig, Cheveldeoff's last dim thought was how ugly it looked, and how glad he was someone was dimming the lights.

By the time Chris Keating found the first body, he hadn't heard any shooting for at least ten minutes.

He stared down at the dead Holy Warrior, who stared back. A laser beam had taken off the top of his head. His unmarked face bore a mildly surprised look.

Why are they fighting amongst themselves? Chris wondered. He felt angry. *Why aren't they busy Purifying Marseguro? What's* wrong *with them?*

"It's not fair," he muttered. Everything he did went wrong. He'd called in the Holy Warriors, only to be locked up. He'd gone to warn them about the Selkies' plans to poison them, but he'd been too late. He'd made it to *Sanctification* only to watch everyone die. He'd failed to warn Cheveldeoff in time when he entered the system . . . and when he did talk to Cheveldeoff, the Archdeacon had ordered him kept on board *Sanctification*. He'd managed to get to *Retribution* and, most generously, he thought, considering how he'd been treated, had once more offered his help—only to be locked up *again*. And now the Holy Warriors, the soldiers of the Avatar, were killing each other instead of slaughtering Selkies.

It's a test, he told himself. *The Avatar spoke of God testing us, but not to destruction . . . unless we* fail *the tests.* Then *comes destruction.*

He didn't feel he had failed any of the tests he'd faced, but maybe Cheveldeoff was failing *his*. Maybe the Holy Warriors were failing *theirs*.

He turned his back on the dead Warrior and pushed farther into the ship.

"Halt!" shouted a hoarse voice from behind him before he'd gone another hundred meters. He put up his hands and turned slowly to face the Holy Warrior who, armed with a slug thrower, stood behind him. "State your loyalty," the Warrior croaked.

"I'm loyal to the Avatar," Chris said, wondering if that

answer would get his head blown off. But the Warrior just grunted.

"Aren't we all," he said. "Don't be smart. You know what I mean."

"No, I don't."

The Warrior came cautiously nearer. He looked pale, and sweat beaded his forehead, glittering as he passed under one of the cold green emergency light strips in the ceiling. "You're not a Holy Warrior! You're that kid that came over from *Sanctification.* You're supposed to be in the brig."

"The power went out. The cells opened," Chris said. "You couldn't expect me to just sit there."

"I suppose not." The Holy Warrior cleared his throat, swallowed, and grimaced as though he'd tasted something bad. "You'd better come see Grand Deacon Braun. *Cheveldeoff* ordered you locked up. His orders aren't operative anymore. The Grand Deacon may have other plans."

Chris cautiously lowered his hands. The Warrior didn't object, just motioned down the corridor with the slug thrower. Chris walked in the direction he'd already been headed. "Where *is* Cheveldeoff?"

"Locked up in his quarters, last I heard. Sick." The Warrior coughed. "We're all sick."

Oh, no, Chris thought. *No, Hansen couldn't have . . .*

But Hansen had been on *Sanctification.* They'd literally run into each other. And he'd been coming from the direction of the shuttle.

He put something on the shuttle, and they brought it aboard with them. He's poisoned them. Just like the others. Damn him!

He didn't say anything to the Holy Warrior. But he'd tell the Grand Deacon. If they knew it was poison, not an illness, they might be able to find an antidote.

"When are you planning to attack?" he asked the Warrior.

The Warrior laughed, coughed, laughed again. "Attack?" He hawked and spat, the sputum glistening bright red where it landed on the floor by Chris' advancing foot. "We're not attacking."

Chris' feet stuttered. "You're not?"

"Keep moving," the Warrior said, and gave him a shove that sent him into a staggering run for a couple of meters. "No, we're not. We've already broken orbit, course loaded and locked.

"We're heading to Earth, boy. And then we'll come back with a proper fleet and Purify that worthless ball of water back there till there aren't three microbes left alive.

"Here we are."

The Warrior ushered Chris into a briefing room, the same one where he'd shaken hands with Cheveldeoff.

Braun sat behind the table. He looked worse than the Holy Warrior who had escorted Chris. Wads of tissue at his right hand were stained red, and his eyes were devilish, black pupils floating in a sea of red. "Get out," he told the Warrior when he saw Chris. The Warrior sketched a salute and left.

"Hansen got the poison on board, didn't he?" Chris said. "You've got to get me to sick bay. I was given an antidote. Maybe they can . . ."

"It's not poison, you miserable little shit," Braun said, almost conversationally. "It's a plague, bioengineered by Hansen's God-damned Selkies, and, yes, you will get yourself to sick bay, because if any of us are going to live, we're going to need whatever antibodies you have swimming in your skinny little veins."

He struggled to his feet . . . then his bloodshot eyes rolled up into his head, he made a gagging sound, and he dropped like a felled tree. Chris heard his body thrashing around on the ground behind the table, heard horrible gurgling and retching sounds, and slowly backed away until he'd pressed himself tight into a corner. "Not again," he whimpered. "Not again not again not again . . . please, God . . ."

But for whatever reason, God Itself did not seem to be answering the prayers of Chris Keating, or any of the other frantic but increasingly fewer prayers issued from *BPS Retribution* that day.

And so, a few hours later, once more alone on a ship full of bloody corpses, Chris Keating made his way to the communications room.

"I think it's recorded," the tech who had come to fetch Richard from the cave said breathlessly as they climbed up the ladder into the strangely canted corridors of *Sanctification*. The communications room was gimbaled, but it was also currently on top of the ring, and getting to it required something approaching mountain-climbing skills. Richard looked at what he had once thought were decorative niches in the walls and now realized were handholds, looked at his arm, still in a sling—just climbing up the ladder had been hard enough—and said dryly, "Surely there's an easier way."

Emily, who had limped her way to the ship, said through gritted teeth, "I'm sure there must be."

The tech looked from one to the other, and comprehension dawned on his face. "Oh! Um . . ."

"I'm sure it can't be too difficult to route it to the portable comm station you set up outside, can it?" Dr. Christianson-Wood said.

The tech's face cleared. "Oh, of course. I should have thought of that. I'll have it in a minute."

He scrambled like a monkey up the handholds to the communications room. Dr. Christianson-Wood sighed and shook her head, and led the one-armed Richard and her limping daughter back down the ladder and over to one of the tents the Hansen's Harbor contingent had put up. A small console of black metal had been set on a folding bioplast table. A moment later the tech reappeared and touched a control, and an all-too-familiar voice filled the tent.

". . . Chris Keating calling Richard Hansen and anyone else listening in the Marseguro system," the voice said. "Congratulations, Hansen, your poison has done its work. They're all dead. How does it feel to be a mass murderer?"

Richard exchanged glances with Emily and Dr. Christianson-Wood, and saw in Dr. Christianson-Wood's eyes a dawning horror that puzzled him until he heard Chris confirm what she must have already guessed.

"But don't get too cocky, you son of a bitch. *Retribution* is already en route to Earth, course locked in, computer in command. I'm just along for the ride, but once we reach Earth and I tell my story, there's going to be a whole fucking Holy Warrior battle fleet heading your way to scrub that slimepit of a diseased planet down to magma.

"Enjoy your last few weeks, you and your Selkie whore and all the rest of the monsters and monsterfuckers on that God-forsaken ball of mud. The Avatar is coming, and God's vengeance will not be denied a third time."

A click.

"This is Chris Keating calling Richard Hansen and anyone else listening in the Marseguro system . . ."

"Kill it," Richard said, and the tech touched the controls again, silencing Keating in mid-rant.

"How did he get on board *Retribution*?" Dr. Christianson-Wood whispered, face stricken. "*How could they have let him on board?* They must have known what happened to *Sanctification*."

"I think he sneaked on board," Richard said. "He was heading toward the shuttle bay when we . . ." he flexed his arm, ". . . met."

"He's a carrier," Dr. Christianson-Wood said. "God Almighty, he's a carrier of the plague I made. The plague that killed every Holy Warrior. He's a carrier . . . and he's going to Earth."

"They'll quarantine him . . . ?" Emily said, but she said it as a question.

"Will they?" Dr. Christianson-Wood sank into a chair and covered her face with her hands. "*Will they? And* even if they do, can they stop it? *Sanctification* must have quarantined the shuttle that took Chris up in the first place, and every last one of them died.

"God, what have we done? What have *I* done?"

Her daughter put her hands on her shoulders, but had no comfort to give.

Half a Marseguroite year later, Richard Hansen stood once again on the bridge of what had once been called the *BPS Sanctification*, and now bore the name *MSS Victor Hansen.* A miniature statue of his . . . original . . . graced the alcove that had been a weapons locker, and a full complement of both Selkies and nonmods—the term "landling" no longer being acceptable in polite company—crewed the consoles surrounding the tactical display.

A screen by his currently unoccupied captain's chair lit with Emily Wood's face, the central pool of an underwater habitat in the background. "Getting close to launch," she said.

"Very," said Richard. "How's the new deep-water Selkie village coming?"

"On schedule, for a wonder," Emily said. She glanced behind her. "I guess we learned some things building the first two. If the Holy Warriors show up, we've at least got a chance of surviving whatever they can throw at us. And if they don't show up . . . well, it's about time we settled more of this planet, anyway." She grinned. "Funny thing, there don't seem to be any Consolidationists left anymore."

Richard just nodded. After half a year—more than half a year, in Earth terms—he didn't believe the Holy Warriors were still a threat. Even with Cheveldeoff dead—*especially* with Cheveldeoff dead—vengeance would have been the primary aim of the Avatar once he found out what had happened on Marseguro. The fact that a Holy Warrior fleet had not yet appeared in the system had to mean that things on Earth were bad . . . very bad.

"How's your mother?" Richard asked. "I haven't spoken to her for . . ."

"The same." Emily shook her head. "Half the time she thinks Dad's still alive and the attack never happened, some of the time she's almost catatonic, and sometimes . . . sometimes she just sits and rocks and weeps. Amy has been wonderful about looking after Mom. And John has been wonderful about looking after Amy." Her face hardened. "The Body Purified took my family and my friends and tried to take my world, Richard. Don't ask me to approve of what you're trying to do."

"I won't," Richard said. "But the Council agreed with me."

"I know." Emily blinked and managed a small smile. "Look, I didn't call to argue all that out again. Just . . . don't let the Body get you, too."

Richard smiled back. "I won't."

Something splashed into the water behind Emily, raising a small tsunami. She looked over her shoulder. "What the—no, no, no, that should go into the main—" She glanced back. "Got to go. Be safe. Come back. Love you."

The screen blanked.

Richard found himself grinning, and couldn't stop. But then, he didn't want to.

He raised his head, checked the time. "Computer, status report."

"All systems operating within normal parameters," the computer said. "Ready to launch on command."

Richard looked around at the crew, who looked back with blue eyes and brown eyes and green eyes, small and large, with and without nictitating membranes. Some had gills, some didn't, but they were all human.

And so were the people of Earth.

The holds were filled with water for the Selkies—and the microfactories necessary to create the hypervaccine for Dr. Christianson-Wood's plague. The course was laid in and locked.

They weren't fleeing Marseguro, and they weren't heading out to find a new home. They were going back to their old one, to see if they could save its people—some of them, at least—from a threat as deadly as the incoming asteroid that had led to the rise of the Body Purified. That one might have been sent by God, but this one had definitely been sent by man. And even if it had been, in some way, justified, it had never been intended to slaughter the innocent.

The Body believed God had miraculously rescued Earth from Its own threatened vengeance last time. This time, the very people hounded and murdered by the Body to appease God would provide the rescue.

Richard suspected the Avatar, if he still lived, would soon face a serious theological crisis.

He glanced at the statue of the original owner of his personal genome, and wondered what he would have thought of it all. Then he snorted.

Richard Hansen knew exactly what Victor Hansen would have thought of it all . . . and had already thought it.

He turned, surveyed the crew, and nodded to them. "Computer, launch," he said.

On a mission of mercy, *MSS Victor Hansen* headed for Earth.